W9-CCY-092

SCHAUMBURG TOWNSHIP DISTRICT LIBRARY

3 1257 01940 3673

WITHDRAWN

Schaumburg Township District Library
130 South Roselle Road
Schaumburg, Illinois 60193

GAYLORD

In
OFFICE HOURS

ALSO BY LUCY KELLAWAY

The Real Office

With "Martin Lukes": *Who Moved My BlackBerry?*

Sense and Nonsense in the Office

In OFFICE HOURS

Lucy Kellaway

WITHDRAWN

GRAND CENTRAL
PUBLISHING

NEW YORK   BOSTON

Schaumburg Township District Library
130 South Roselle Road
Schaumburg, IL 60193

F
KELLAWAY, L

3 1257 01940 3673

This book is a work of fiction. Names, characters, places, and incidents are the product of the author's imagination or are used fictitiously. Any resemblance to actual events, locales, or persons, living or dead, is coincidental.

Copyright © 2011 by Lucy Kellaway
All rights reserved. Except as permitted under the U.S. Copyright Act of 1976, no part of this publication may be reproduced, distributed, or transmitted in any form or by any means, or stored in a database or retrieval system, without the prior written permission of the publisher.

"It's No Use Raising a Shout" by W. H. Auden. Copyright © W. H. Auden, used with permission of The Wylie Agency.

Grand Central Publishing
Hachette Book Group
237 Park Avenue
New York, NY 10017

www.HachetteBookGroup.com

Printed in the United States of America

First Edition: February 2011
10 9 8 7 6 5 4 3 2 1

Grand Central Publishing is a division of Hachette Book Group, Inc.
The Grand Central Publishing name and logo is a trademark of Hachette Book Group, Inc.

The publisher is not responsible for websites (or their content) that are not owned by the publisher.

Library of Congress Cataloging-in-Publication Data

Kellaway, Lucy.
    In office hours / Lucy Kellaway.
        p. cm.
    ISBN 978-0-446-56569-1
    1. Sex in the workplace—Fiction.   2. Office politics—Fiction.   3. London (England)—Fiction.   I. Title.
    PR6111.E49I5 2010
    823'.92—dc22

                                                                        2010016493

For David

Stella

Two words: four letters, then eight. The shape of them was so familiar and yet shocking to see now, after all this time.

Stella had just got back to the office after lunch and there his name was, sitting in her in-box next to an e-mail containing the minutes of yesterday's board meeting. The subject line read: "hi."

She knew what she must do. She had rehearsed it often enough with Dr. Munro and with any friends who were still willing to listen. With an unsteady hand she picked up the mouse, highlighted his name, and clicked delete.

"Are you sure you want to delete this message?" the computer asked.

But that was the problem: No, she wasn't sure.

The therapist had explained that there was nothing inherently upsetting about either him or his actions. The trouble was Stella's thoughts, which in turn caused her emotional responses. The answer, the woman had said, was to learn to control her thoughts, and then her emotions would fall into line.

As a concept, Stella had found this seductive. But in practical terms it was useless. Stella, so good at controlling most aspects of her life, had had no success in controlling her thoughts—or those that had anything to do with him. And it was also nonsense to say that his actions had been neutral—except perhaps in some far-fetched, philosophical sense.

In fact, they had been devastating: five lives damaged, one of them, it seemed to her in her more hysterical moments, beyond any chance of repair. In the end, she had canceled her therapy sessions and gone to Selfridges and squandered the £210 that she would have spent on fifty minutes of Dr. Munro's time on face cream instead—which hadn't made her feel any better, either. Worse, as she kept studying her reflection to see if it was having an effect on the deep lines between her eyebrows and the loose skin around her jaw.

Two years ago, when Stella had first met him, she had given little thought to her appearance. She had felt younger than forty-four, particularly because she was tall and slim clothes hung well on her. She wore almost no makeup, though she'd started having blond highlights threaded through her hair to hide the gray. But now, if she looked in the mirror and let her eyes go dead and her face relax, an old woman's face stared back at her.

Stella looked at the computer screen, which was still demanding a reply to its question. It had helpfully highlighted the button Yes, as if knowing that this was the path of sanity and righteousness. She moved the mouse and clicked No instead. She stared at his name. It was extraordinary, she thought, to hear from him today of all days. Just yesterday she had been on Primrose Hill with Clemmie, who was taking a break from GCSE revisions from exams. The two of them had got coffee from the Italian deli and were sitting drinking it in the winter sunshine on a bench. A small, fat man with a Great Dane on a lead walked in front of them, and Clemmie had said, "Opposites attract," and Stella had laughed, thinking it the first normal, friendly thing her daughter had said in a very long time.

Stella had turned her head to watch the big dog and its tiny owner pass, then had thought she'd seen him sitting at the next bench along. He wasn't sullen and cowering, as he had been when he came into her office and stood there wordlessly as she had packed her things. Instead, she could tell from the back of his fair head and from the lazy way he was sticking his legs out that he was at ease. He had his arm around someone young and blond with skinny jeans tucked into high-heeled boots. On the pretext of putting her cup in the bin, Stella had got up and walked toward him, and at just that moment, he'd turned toward her. It wasn't him.

"You know," she had said to Emily on the phone that evening, "I think I am really over it. I thought I saw him yesterday with someone young and pretty on a park bench. And I felt curious, and, yes, I suppose if I'm honest, I was a bit...*disturbed*. But I wasn't destroyed. I wasn't even churned up. Even when I was certain it was him, I thought, It's okay, I've moved on."

There had been a brief silence at the other end of the line.

"Well," her friend had said, "maybe you have, maybe you haven't."

Why were one's closest friends, the people who had witnessed all one's ups and downs, so superior? Maybe it was simply that for four decades, Stella's friends had witnessed one huge "up" after another and so were relishing this catastrophic down for its novelty value.

But what was even worse than her friend's superiority was the fact that she was right. Stella's dry mouth and thudding heart did not belong to a woman who had moved on. She got up and closed her office door. She didn't want to do this under the appraising eye of her PA.

She took the mouse, moved it to the message, and clicked on it to open.

"Dearest S," it began.

From long practice, she could gauge the state of his feelings toward her from the first couple of words of his messages. Once, long ago, during an interminable conference call, she had written a list of them in order of affection:

my own dearest, funniest, cleverest, sexiest F (this had happened
    only once, in the very early days)
dearest f
dearest ferret
my S

dearest S
f—
s—
hi
hallo
Dear Stella

"Hallo" she disliked doubly, first for its lack of affection and then for its wretched spelling. But "Dear Stella" was the worst, as it was coldest. That was how the final and most awful message of them all had begun, its correct capitals underlining the correctness of the sentiment it contained.

But now here he was, e-mailing her after a long, arid year, and now she was his dearest again. She returned to the message.

it's been a long time. I've no idea how you are, or if you want to hear from me at all anymore. I don't even know where you are working now, but I've just googled you and I'm sending this to what seems is your new work e-mail. I hope it reaches you. I often think of you, ferreting things out. Do you still do that? I bet you do.

I've got something to ask you, and something to tell you. So I wondered…will you have lunch with me one day next week? we could meet at the bleeding heart for old times' sake or anywhere else would be fine too.

cheers x

First she read it quickly. And then slowly, looking at every word. The bit about the ferret was a giveaway. Referring to that was tantamount to saying that he hadn't moved on at all either. Stella hit reply and typed:

Dearest—

Yes to lunch. Yes to the Bleeding Heart. Thursday? One?

Much love,

Stella.

PS Yes, I still ferret things out. Of course. xx

Was it too keen? She reread his message. It was definitely warm, and he did say that he still thought about her, but he didn't say in what way. She read it again. Maybe it wasn't that warm. At least not effusive. "Cheers" was a pretty distant ending, as well as being an ugly one. Respond, don't react, Dr. Munro had said. It had been one of her more helpful instructions.

Dear—

Lunch would be nice. Have an AFJ board meeting in Rome Monday to Wed, so could do Thursday or Friday?

xS

But did he really want or need to know about her schedule? He used to resent her packed diary, so perhaps it was best not to mention it now. She tried again.

How nice to hear from you. Lunch would be lovely. Thursday or Friday good for me. Let me know, Stella

She pressed send.

Bella

Bella stared at her BlackBerry in disbelief. How odd to get a message from him today of all days.

She hadn't thought of him in a long time. Or at least she might have thought of him a little bit, sometimes, but not in a bad or heavy way. But then, just yesterday, she had been packing things into boxes, finally moving on and out of her flat off the Holloway Road, and she had come across the Van Morrison CD he had given her just before it had begun. And that had got her thinking about it again.

He'd come into the office that morning—almost two years ago now—and produced the CD from his briefcase and said, "Please tell me what you think of this." The tone of his voice was just the same, just as authoritative, as when he said, "Please reschedule my four o'clock meeting." She had looked at the CD in confusion, and he had said, "It's not for anything, except to listen to, I daresay you know the track called 'Brown Eyed Girl.' It's one I especially like. I know you think that I can't see what is under my nose. But it has not escaped my notice that you have brown eyes."

None of his other presents had survived—when she had got back to her flat on the day after their last, awful lunch, she had rounded up all of them, put them into a Tesco carrier bag, and taken them to the Marie Curie shop on Highbury Corner.

The next Saturday, when she had changed her mind and gone back to retrieve the gold earrings and the pearl necklace that were far too grown up for her ever to wear, it was too late. They were sold.

Last night, she had put "Brown Eyed Girl" on the CD player.

Do you remember when we used to sing,
Nah nah na . . .

Millie had objected: "Who's this old man?"

And Bella had said: "This song reminds me of a friend I used to have."

Millie blanked this, grabbed the remote, put on "Love Machine" by Girls Aloud, and started to strut her skinny nine-year-old body around the removal boxes.

Bella looked again at the message. He'd sent it on the old company address, so he must still work for Atlantic Energy. The subject line said simply: "Hello."

Dear Bella.

I expect you will be surprised to get this message, unprompted.
But I have something to ask of you, which, on balance, I think
might be better not committed to e-mail. Would you allow me to
buy you a drink next week? I am not sure what time you currently
finish work or, indeed, where you work. However, if it were
convenient, might you be able to meet me at Green's champagne
bar next Thursday at 7 pm?

Love—

She read it, frowning. She'd half forgotten his turn of phrase: polite
and precise; even his love letters (of which there had not been many)
could not quite shake off the tone of the business memo. Bella felt a flash
of the old resentment, hit reply, and typed quickly:

Hi—thanks for your message. Hope you don't mind if I say no to
a drink—I just don't think there's much point in meeting up. Hope
all is well with you. Bella.

She read it over and thought it sounded mean. Maybe the favor was
something simple. And would it really be so horrible seeing him after all
this time? The memory of that last day, when he had escorted her to the
lift, looked at her as if they were perfect strangers, had stopped hurting.
She had not seen him at all for a year, not counting that time, a couple of
months after she'd left AE, when she had seen him on the Piccadilly line
with his two boys, both of whom were clutching large *Spamalot* programs.
She was sure he had seen her. But he had made no move toward her and
she'd made none toward him. She had gone home and wept.

But now his words didn't tug at her at all. The miracle of indifference,
which she had prayed for, had crept up on her unawares, and now she
really was unmoved by his message. And so maybe it would be fine to
meet up. Only not for a drink—lunch would be safer.

Perhaps something nice would come out of it, she thought. It would do her good to be able to say: Look at me now. I'm so over you. I've got a proper job—I'm an account manager now, and I love it, and I'm making better money. And I've even started seeing someone nice, who really wants me in his life properly, which—let's face it—was more than you ever did. Bella deleted what she had written and started again.

Hi—yes, it would be great to meet up but drink is difficult for me as I'm always dashing home to be with Millie (so no change, there!). could do a quick lunch. am working as an assistant client manager at Lambert Finch (ad agency) so all is well with me.

maybe you could pop into my office in Charlotte St., and we can go around the corner and grab a sandwich?

bella x

She looked over what she had written. That was better. She pressed send.

Part One

TEMPTATION

Stella

Stella's story—a story she told and retold to herself in the hope that she might come to understand what had happened to her and why she had behaved as she had—started two years earlier, on the day that Julia Swanson resigned.

That morning, Stella had got in to the office early. She was writing a presentation for the board, and unless she stole a march on the day she would get caught up in endless meetings and nothing would get done.

She walked across the marble floor toward the glass barriers and reached into her handbag for her wallet, which contained her security pass. She put her bag on the receptionist's desk—manned at this early hour by a uniformed night security guard—and started to rummage through its contents. Nothing.

In her head, she retraced her movements from the night before. She had left the office early for a lecture on the newly attractive economics of nuclear power and then had gone on to a dinner party with Charles's old boss from his days at Granada. She had paid for the cab on the way home—Charles, as ever, having no money with him—so she must have had her wallet then. Which meant that with any luck, it was now sitting on the table in the hall.

She asked the guard for a temporary pass, and he opened the visitors book. "Name?"

"Stella Bradberry."

"How are you spelling that?"

"I am spelling it," she said crisply, "B-r-a-d-b-e-r-r-y."

Slowly he wrote it down, omitting the second r. "Department?"

"Economics."

"Who's your line manager?"

Stella sighed. Why, she thought, do I have to give my line manager's name in order to get into an office where I have worked for the last twenty-two years?

"Stephen Hinton," she said. The name of the CEO seemed to mean nothing to him, and he wrote it down indifferently.

Under "Time in" he entered 7:12, looking up to check the clock, which was a giant elliptical Atlantic Energy logo set into the wall over the lifts. He handed her an oblong of plastic on a string to wear around her neck.

She smiled at him and felt a little jab of discomfort when he didn't smile back. Charles used to laugh at the way Stella always needed everyone to love her, even people she didn't especially like herself. As she got older, she was getting a bit better: She could tolerate not being loved by security guards, but only just.

She pushed through the glass barrier and pressed "Home" on her mobile. "Darling. Are you still in bed?...No, I've just got in...Can you check and see if I left my wallet by the front door?...Oh, thank God... I'll get Nathalie to send a bike later..."

Stella took the lift to the thirteenth floor and went along the corridor past the aggressive works of modern art that Stephen Hinton was so proud of. She eyed the latest arrival: an oversize blue canvas with some hessian fabric stuck to it. She looked at the name of the picture. *Tower of Nothing*, it was entitled.

Her office was on the wrong side of the building, looking north over the building sites of the City of London, and was slightly smaller than her status merited. Some of her male colleagues made a fuss about this sort of thing, but she quite liked the way that her office was smaller and her pay lower than her worth to the company. It made her feel off the hook in a way that she knew was illogical, but she didn't care. Stella had made no attempt to make her room homely—others had filled their offices with photos of their families, but she considered that sentimental. She had only one picture—of herself with Nelson Mandela taken when she visited Atlantic Energy's South African subsidiary six or seven years ago.

She turned on her computer and waited while it clicked and whirred and played the triumphant four-note symphony that welcomed her to Windows. She opened up her e-mail and scanned down the ninety-four messages that had arrived since last night. At the bottom, with a red exclamation mark beside it, was an e-mail from Julia Swanson.

Must talk. Tried to catch you yesterday but you were in meetings all day. Wanted you to know that I'm seeing Stephen this morning to hand in my notice. Eeek. Lunch?

Jules x

Stella wasn't surprised it had come to this. Julia had been unprofessional and unwise, and now she was paying for it. Yet the news made Stella feel unsettled. She didn't really like Julia, but neither did she want her to go, as without her there would be no other women in senior management to gossip with.

She typed:

God are you sure? That is terrible news (for me)...I'll miss you...
Yes to lunch, though am v busy doing board presentation so will
have to be quick. 12:45? xS.

Bella

For Bella it began that same day, the day that Julia quit. She was half an hour late getting into the office—which wasn't like her. But that morning everything had gone wrong. Millie had refused to put on her school sweatshirt, and Bella had ended up screaming at her. Millie had started to cry, and Bella had said that if she didn't stop, she couldn't go to the party at the weekend. Millie had recovered by the time they got to school, helped by a strawberry Chewit, but Bella hadn't: These pointless scenes left her feeling distressed and almost envious of her contemporaries who were spending their twenties getting drunk and behaving exactly as they pleased.

Then there were delays on the Piccadilly line—someone was having an even worse morning than she was and had decided to fling themselves under a train. Stuck under a man's armpit on a stationary tube, Bella opened *Metro* and read her horoscope: "Your career is progressing well and it seems that your plans cannot fail. Do not get carried away with your ambition. All work and no play will get you down so also take some time out for you." What crap, she thought. Progressing well? I don't think so.

She changed at King's Cross onto the Northern line and then ran the short distance from Moorgate tube to Atlantic Tower, fearing her boss's wrath. She never knew where she was with Julia. One minute she would behave as if her PA were her best friend, the next she would be shouting at her over some minor transgression.

Bella went up in the lift, and at the third floor Stephen Hinton got in. The CEO fixed his eyes on the security pass that Bella had hung around her neck, making her feel that he was staring at her breasts.

"Good morning, Bella," he said, reading her name off the pass.

"Hi," she replied, and then neither of them said anything and looked at their shoes. What are you meant to say to the CEO? She wasn't sure, but she hated silences, so she said: "There was a person under the train this morning at Caledonian Road."

He stared and then guffawed, which didn't strike Bella as the right way to respond at all.

She got out at the thirteenth floor and went along the corridor past the new work of art, which was a bit of old rag stuck to a canvas. She'd heard that the company had paid $140,000 of shareholders' money for that, which was pathetic.

The plate of blueberries that catering delivered every morning was still waiting outside Julia's office, which must mean that Julia was late, too. Bella picked up the shrink-wrapped plate, pushed open the glass door with her foot, and was surprised to see Julia's coat left carelessly on her chair. Bella picked it up, admiring its swirly Paul Smith lining. She took off her own H&M duffle coat and slipped on the other coat. It was both too long and too tight; Julia almost never ate and so, despite being six inches taller than her PA, was considerably thinner. Bella envied her both the coat and the figure. Hastily she took it off, hung it up, and started going through her boss's e-mails. At the top was a message from Stella Bradberry, saying, "I'll miss you." What was that about? And why had Julia fixed a lunch with Stella when she was meant to be taking out the new oil correspondent from the *Financial Times*?

She looked up to see Julia approaching. She was immaculately made up as ever, though Bella noticed a tightness about her, an intensity that she had seen only once before, and then by mistake.

"Sorry I was late," Bella started to say, but Julia batted it away.

"I wanted you to be the first to know: I've just resigned."

"Oh!"

Bella knew this was an inadequate response but didn't know what else to say. What she was thinking was: I would have quit in your shoes. Though she never would have been in Julia's shoes, as she would have had more sense. But she couldn't say anything because she had never worked out if Julia knew that she, Bella, knew all about it. Sometimes she thought Julia must know—as it would be stupid to expect her not to have read the e-mails. Though not as stupid as writing them on the office e-mail system in the first place. Julia's approach to privacy would have made Bella laugh if it hadn't been so tragic. She had simply transferred all her messages to and from him into a folder marked "misc," which was available on the desktop for anyone who wanted to look.

"What are you going to do?" Bella asked at last.

"I've been headhunted. I'm going to join Wiley and Marston as a senior political lobbyist."

Bella wasn't quite sure what this was. "Congratulations," she said. "When are you actually going?"

"They've asked me to leave today, so I'll be on three months' gardening leave at home."

Bella thought this unfair. If you quit on a salary of £140,000, they pay you to stay at home for three months. But if she were to quit on her salary of £29,000, she'd have to work out every last minute of her four weeks' notice period.

Stella

Stella looked at the sentence she had just written:

"We support urgent but informed action to stabilize greenhouse gas (GHG) concentrations by achieving sustainable long-term emission reductions at the lowest possible cost."

She was wondering whether to redraft it to make it snappier when Julia put her head around the door. "Ready?" she said.

Stella got up from her desk and told Nathalie, who sat in a glass antechamber to her office, that she'd be back in an hour.

They walked around the corner to Le Pain Quotidien, a bakery shop with scrubbed wood tables pretending to be in rural France, and Stella ordered a tricolor salad. Julia said she'd have the same, though she told the waiter that she didn't want dressing or pine nuts and only one slice of mozzarella.

"So," said Stella once the waiter had taken their orders. "How did Stephen take it?"

"I've never seen him so upset," Julia said. "It was just *extraordinary*. He put his head in his hands and for a second he didn't say anything. Then he said I was the best head of press we've ever had and he offered me a pay rise *and* a promotion."

"So weren't you tempted to take it?"

"Well," said Julia, "it's not entirely about the money. It's more about me, and where I see myself ten years from now. You know what really scares me? It's being bored. Doesn't that thought worry you?"

Stella started to say that she wasn't bored, but Julia went on:

"You and I are totally different. You've morphed into an Atlantic Energy person—it's in your blood in a way it never was in mine. And I'm a risk junkie, while you always play it safe."

It was a funny thing about people who left, Stella thought. They always tried to make you feel bad for staying.

"Maybe you're right," she replied evenly. "I suppose I stay because I like it. Mostly."

"Yes, but don't you worry that one day you'll wake up and you'll be fifty-five, forced into early retirement, and it'll be too late to do anything else? So better to leave now in your early forties—or your mid-forties or whatever—before it's too late."

Stella received Julia's reminder that she was three years older in silence. At least I have kept my professional dignity, she thought, which is more than you have.

Stella's mobile rang.

"Darling...Yes, I know, it's in my diary...Yes, that's wonderful, well done. I'm looking forward to hearing about it...Of course I mean it. I'm just with someone...That's ridiculous. Stop it..." She frowned and hung up.

"Sorry about that. It was Clemmie—she's flapping about her parents' evening tonight."

"No, *I'm* sorry," said Julia. "It's tactless of me to be so happy."

Stella was finding the conversation surreal. There was no mention of that cab ride two weeks ago when Julia had, suddenly and inexplicably, wept and told Stella the story of how she had been having an affair with

James Staunton and had destroyed her life and career in one stroke. Stella had tried to be sympathetic, but really she had been amazed and ever so slightly shocked. How did they find the time? And how had she, Stella, completely failed to notice that two close colleagues were sneaking off for steamy encounters in Julia's flat? She had also failed to understand what they saw in each other. James was neither handsome nor charismatic and so surely not Julia's thing. Instead, he was clever and straight and decent (at least she had thought he was decent until now) and so would surely be able to see Julia for the shallow person she was.

"Well," Stella said, "I'm really glad it's all worked out so well for you, and that a situation that could have been so awful has been fine."

Julia ignored this and started to talk about the PR firm and how its political lobbyists were shaping government policy behind the scenes and how one of them used to work at Buckingham Palace...

As they ordered coffee, Stella asked: "Did you tell James you are going?"

Julia looked suddenly stricken. "No. I don't owe him any openness. He wasn't open with me."

Bella

All day she had been helping Julia clear her office. All sorts of random things accumulate in five years. Among the books and photo frames and pens, Bella found a pale blue lace bra, which Julia calmly took from her and put into her handbag. She kept a large number of shoes in her bottom drawer—four pairs of trainers and an almost new pair of green Kurt Geiger wedges that Bella had seen her wearing only once.

"These are cool," said Bella, even though she thought them horrible.

"What size are you? They are much more you than me—have them if they fit."

"No, I couldn't," Bella protested.

"Take them," Julia insisted. "If it hadn't been such a mad rush today,

I would have really liked to get you a proper present and something for Molly."

Bella corrected her in her head: Millie.

"Is there an easy way of deleting all my e-mails in one go?" her boss went on. "I suppose I should leave a clean sweep."

"Shall I do it for you?"

"No! It's fine, if you can just remind me..."

Bella knew the content of the messages that Julia didn't want her to see well enough anyway. In particular the last and most lethal addition to the collection, sent exactly two weeks ago. This, Bella knew almost by heart.

> Dear Julia,
>
> I don't really think I expressed myself well at lunch. I felt tongue-tied and taken aback by your emotional response. What I was trying to say was that we must stop this. The chief reason you know already: I can't go on doing this to my wife. But also I have felt that we seem to have reached a natural end: the initial lighthearted entanglement between us has latterly become more complex and less enjoyable. Obviously I still value you highly, and I hope we can go on having a good professional relationship and that in time we can be friends.
>
> James.

Bella felt sick every time she thought of this. The guy was a complete tosser. *Initial lighthearted entanglement*—what a pompous prat! And how clever of him to have suddenly discovered that he was married. It made her feel slightly better about Xan, who might be a junkie and a thief but at least was emotionally honest.

The day Julia had got the message, Bella had watched her read it, stand up and go to the loo, and come back holding herself frighteningly straight. She had not said one word about it.

Bella read the e-mail that Julia had drafted:

Today is my last day at Atlantic Energy. The last five years have
been some of the most stimulating of my life, but it is now time to
move on to even greater challenges.

Above all what I will miss is the quality of the people: you are not
only professional and talented but so many of you have become such
good friends. I will miss every one of you. Please keep in touch—

Bella looked at it and thought: Whatever. And then she forwarded it,
as instructed, to all seventeen thousand employees worldwide.

"I don't suppose," Bella asked, "that you have any idea who is going
to take over from you?"

Julia shrugged. "I don't. But there's no reason why you need to stay
in the press office. I'll put in a good word with HR and tell them to find
you someone really fun to work with."

Since she'd joined Atlantic Energy four years ago, Bella had had three
bosses. First was George Matthews in Chemicals, who was okay in a dull
kind of way. Then Giles Conville, who was nicer but such a control freak
that he never gave her anything to do for fear that she might screw it
up. And finally, Julia. It was the first time she'd had a woman boss, and
on balance she didn't like it. There was something confusing about the
mateyness. Julia wanted to be liked but wasn't really all that likable.

Bella called a taxi for her and helped carry everything down in the
lift. There was a yellow plastic crate with PROPERTY OF ATLANTIC ENERGY
written on its side, a black bin liner, and a Jo Malone carrier bag. These
seemed sad remnants of five years' work.

To her surprise, and not altogether to her pleasure, Julia put her thin
arms around Bella and gave her a hug.

"We *must* have a girls' lunch as soon as I'm settled. I'll call you. You've
been a fantastic help to me, Bella. I'm going to miss you."

Bella had watched this woman lie and cheat. She had lied for her. She had never been thanked. But now, seeing her fighting to keep her dignity, she suddenly felt that maybe she would miss her after all.

Stella

"Russell is trying to find you," said Nathalie as Stella returned to her office after a weekly planning meeting.

He seemed to have been trying very hard indeed: There were two e-mails waiting for her, a voice mail, and a Post-it note on her computer screen. This was the key skill of being in Human Resources, she thought: perseverance. She clicked on his first e-mail.

Hi Stella.

Can I beg a favor? Julia was due to give a keynote at the trainees' induction workshop tomorrow. Obviously I'm mindful of the diversity agenda, and so I'm looking to find another woman to do it instead. I know it's incredibly short notice, but it would be really helpful if you could step up to the plate just this once?

All best, Russell

She sighed and opened the next one.

Hi Stella

Don't know if you've had a chance to consider my earlier e-mail. I know it would mean a lot to the trainees to listen to such an inspirational figure as your good self. I also wanted to ask if you could take the fast-track trainee assigned to Julia? You are already due to get Beate Schlegel, but if you could also take Rhys Williams? Rhys isn't an economist, but on our competency tests

he scores very highly on leadership potential. I'm sure he'll be able
to add value in the economics team with you as a mentor.

Russell

Why did Russell have to talk like this? Stella wondered. And why
were senior women expected to not only do their jobs, but be representatives of their sex as well as glorified school prefects?

She resolved to say no. This was one of the few things that Stella was
excessively bad at; she frequently found herself doing things just because
she could not bring herself to refuse. She realized it was ridiculous and
also understood and despised the reason for it: She feared causing dis-
pleasure. Resolutely she replied:

Russell— Would love to help. Unfortunately have to leave office
promptly that evening—it's my daughter's parents' evening—so
I'm afraid it's not going to work out.

However, I'm happy to take on an extra trainee. As you correctly
point out, there is never any shortage of work in economics.

Stella

As it happened, the parents' evening had been the previous night.
Stella and Charles had sat side by side in the wood-paneled assembly
hall and heard from one teacher after another that their daughter—who
only that morning had twice told her mother to fuck off—was a delight,
industrious, cooperative, creative. Only Clemmie's form teacher had said
she was looking a bit thin and asked if everything was all right. Stella
had assured her Clemmie was fine. At least fine at eating. And as for
thin, Stella had been thinner than that at fourteen, and Charles had
also been a wisp when she had first met him. Not that one would know
that now. There had been a substantial thickening around the middle.

Her e-mail started flashing. Russell again.

Hi thanks for reverting so promptly. The agenda tomorrow is something of a movable feast, so if you could give your speech to kick the session off in the morning? It would only take ten minutes. If you can make time for this it really will help us in our mission to deliver a world-class, diverse workforce.

All best, Russell

Shit, damn, bugger, she thought, and e-mailed back:

OK, can do 10 mins at 9:40

Bella

Bella was enjoying having no boss. No one seemed to want to tell her whom she was going to work for, so she remained at her old desk in the press office, fielding a few calls and not doing terribly much.

When the phone went, she said: "I'm afraid Julia Swanson has left the company. Can I put you through to Ben Thomas, her deputy?"

She liked Ben and hoped they'd give the job to him. "Are you going to go for it?" she'd asked when he popped his head around her door.

"Don't know. I talked to Russell about it this morning, but he fobbed me off with something about a reorganization."

"Great," said Bella. "They can reorganize the whole place and no one ever thinks of telling me anything."

"I tell you everything. At least, I would if I knew anything."

There was something sweet about Ben. He used to be a journalist himself, and the scruffy boyish air hadn't left him, though after years of expense account lunches he had grown somewhat stout. He also had crooked teeth and breathed noisily.

"Do you want a drink tonight?" he asked suddenly.

In low moments, Bella had sometimes wondered if she could bring herself to go out with Ben. It was nearly three years since she had had a boyfriend of any sort, and Ben was keen and kind and even quite funny. But she always decided that he was simply too ugly—she did not mind that much about looks, but there was a threshold below which she would not fall.

"Sorry, Ben. I have to get back to my daughter."

He looked crestfallen. "Another time?"

"Yes, that'd be lovely."

A call came through from a journalist wanting to know why Atlantic Energy was raising petrol prices at the same time as declaring exceptional profits. Bella knew the answer to this herself, having heard Julia go through it often enough. But she put the call through to Ben and she was left on her own.

Stella

Stella had opened the e-mail that had just arrived from the CEO.

have you got a moment?

Stephen's e-mails were never one word longer than strictly necessary, and the summons never gave any clue as to what he wanted to see her about. Stella wondered briefly whether it was ominous but decided it wasn't. When Stephen had bad news to impart, he got his PA to ring and make an appointment. She e-mailed back:

Sure—on my way up now. Stella

The CEO's office was two floors above her own and occupied the corner of the tower with a view down toward the gray dome of St. Paul's. There was a large Persian carpet on the floor, and on the bookshelves, next to Sun Tzu's *The Art of War*, was a leather-bound copy of *Paradise Lost*. Stephen Hinton wanted people to know that not only was he CEO of one of the biggest oil companies in the world, he was also a man of culture. Perhaps he wouldn't make quite such a big deal of it, Stella sometimes thought, if he wasn't the son of an electrician from Hull. She had nothing against electricians from Hull. In fact, she admired their hard work. Stella, as the daughter of a distinguished professor of philosophy at Oxford University, had always felt relatively uncultured, and her way of dealing with it was to keep quiet. Stephen always looked undersized in his huge office, and today he was waiting for her, pacing up and down like a small, hairy animal in a cage.

"Thanks for coming up," he said, reaching out a hand and touching her upper arm with it.

She didn't like being touched by people at work, but her smile didn't falter.

"I've got a people issue that I'd like your take on," he went on. "Now that Julia Swanson has quit, I've got to decide what to do about Press Relations. We need a hard hitter there. Did you see that crap in the *Daily Mail* this morning saying that we should be paying a windfall energy tax?"

Stephen spat out the words scornfully, and Stella, who had not seen the article, nodded knowledgeably.

"We need someone who will knock some sense into these stupid hacks. So I was thinking about giving the department to James Staunton. It makes sense to bring media under the umbrella of External Relations. James is highly capable, but I worry about his leadership style. Question: Is he a great listener? You and he go back a long way, and so I wondered what your take was...?"

Stella and James had joined AE as trainees at the same time, and he had always measured his progress against hers. In the early years he had done better, but more recently, especially since Stephen had become CEO and made her head of Economics, Strategy, and Planning, Stella had overtaken him. Although she didn't set store by such things, she wasn't anxious to see his empire expand. Neither did she think it fair: He'd had an affair with Julia, which he'd ended. Julia was made to walk the plank; and for him to benefit from her departure did not seem right.

"It's complicated," Stella said slowly.

"I know," he said. "But I rely on you, Stella. You're one of the few people in this organization that I can trust to tell me the truth."

"Well," she ventured, "obviously James is very...competent. I mean, he was great in seeing off the Monopolies Commission on petrol prices. I know he would *in theory* be capable of handling media. *However*...I think there are issues around depth versus breadth. He already has a huge department—and so adding press might mean stretching him rather too thin—"

"Say no more, Stella," Stephen interrupted. "As ever, you are right on the money. James is the man for the job. Thank you."

And then he said: "Where are you on the sustainability presentation for this month's board?"

Stella said she would let him see a draft soon and walked back to her desk, feeling annoyed. For all his claims to be a great listener, Stephen never heard a word you said.

Bella

The day was passing inordinately slowly, and Bella was revising her opinion about it being nice not having a boss. The clock said 4:32—she was tempted to leave now and pick up Millie early, but she didn't dare. Idly, she clicked on the Gap website and saw in the sale some navy hoodies with white stars on them that she knew Millie would love. Bella wondered if they were worth it at £8.99. Maybe if she waited, they'd be reduced some more.

"I can see someone's busy."

She turned around to see Jackie Lewis, the CEO's PA, approaching and smiling in a way that pretended to be friendly but wasn't particularly.

It was annoying to be caught out like this. Relations between her and Jackie were not straightforward. Jackie considered herself superior to Bella, but Bella felt better educated and brighter and didn't really want to join Jackie and the other assistants at lunch to discuss their latest diets. Jackie took Bella's standoffishness as a sign that Bella thought herself above administrative work and so always liked to point out all the little ways in which Bella was falling short.

"What do you think of the reorganization?" Jackie asked.

"What reorganization?"

"Hasn't anyone said anything to you?" A look of mock surprise crossed her face. "I've just done a memo from Stephen to the whole company about changes affecting the press office, and I thought everyone here knew."

Bella's e-mail flashed. She clicked off the Gap fleeces and opened the new message.

Following the departure of Julia Swanson to a new challenge, Press Relations will be integrated with the existing External Relations Department going forward and will be overseen by James Staunton in addition to his existing responsibilities. All other positions will remain unchanged. This move is aligned with our strategy of streamlining our support operations to provide critical added value at the point of delivery.

Fantastic, Bella thought. Find out by e-mail that your job has gone, only no one bothered to tell you.

"So what happens to me?" she asked.

Jackie shrugged. "Don't worry," she said, "I'm sure it will all work out for the best. You could go back to Chemicals—the pace is a bit slower there, and that might suit you better with your family responsibilities. Would you like me to put in a word?"

"No. It's fine. Really."

The clock said ten to five. As a small act of protest at having now lost not only her boss, but also her job and having to suffer the patronage of Jackie, she decided to go home nine minutes early. Just as she was getting her coat, the phone went.

"Hi, Bella, how are you?"

It was Julia, suddenly sounding different. How odd, Bella thought, that the very minute someone stops being your boss, everything changes. Stripped of office, Julia sounded smaller and quieter and almost apologetic in asking her to forward some e-mail addresses.

And then, after she had asked how Molly was and failed to listen to the answer, Julia asked: "So what's the gossip? Who's taking on the poisoned chalice of my job?"

Bella considered saying that she didn't know, but what was the point? "It's James," she said.

There was a pause on the other end. "Really? Is he moving sideways into my job?" There was a note of hope in her voice.

"Um...I think he might be taking on your job in addition to his own," Bella said tentatively.

"You're not going to work for him, are you," Julia said quickly.

"I don't think so. He hasn't asked me. I imagine that he'll keep his current assistant. So I don't know what I'm supposed to be doing. Which makes a change."

Stella

Stella stood before thirty-five management trainees in the refurbished cinema in the basement of the building. They looked impossibly young and serious and had their notebooks out, ready to take notes.

Last night, she had taken her laptop to bed with her and had meant to plan what she was going to say, but Charles, who had got back slightly drunk from the private screening of a documentary about Afghanistan, seemed to think they might have sex. Stella performed a swift mental calculation. Which would be quicker: to submit at once, in which case she could get back to the presentation within five minutes, or to say no and have him vaguely clawing at her for the next fifteen minutes? She had hitched up her nightdress and rolled toward him.

Afterward, she hadn't returned to the presentation as planned, because Charles had insisted that she turn out the light, as he was tired and had a production meeting the next day.

The fact that Stella had meetings all day, every day, didn't seem to count. But she was tired, too, and couldn't be bothered to argue. She would wing it in the morning.

Stephen was just finishing his welcome address. He was brilliant at this sort of thing. What he was saying was nonsense, of course, but the way he said it made one inclined to believe him.

"Diverse people, common goals—that sums up Atlantic Energy. All over the world we look for people who share our ambition to be competitive, successful, and a force for good. The way we work is guided by our values—integrity, creativity, dignity, partnership, transparency, and sustainability. This is the organization you are joining, and we are proud to have you on board. I wanted to say two more things. Welcome. And congratulations. You have joined the most dynamic oil company in the world." He finished, collected his papers, and swooped out, raising an eyebrow at Stella.

Russell stood up and said, "Thank you, Stephen, for that. Truly inspirational, as ever. It now gives me great pleasure to introduce you to our next speaker, Stella Bradberry. Stella joined us as a management trainee, in—hope I'm not betraying any trade secrets—1986. At this moment in time, I think it's fair to say that Stella is the most senior woman in the company. Not only does she head up Economics, Strategy, and Planning, she has driven the diversity initiative, she has been one of the key players supporting our work/life balance program. That's it. You don't want to hear me droning on. Stella, over to you."

Stella got up. "Thanks, Russell. Do you mind if I disagree with almost every word you've just said?"

There was some embarrassed laughter.

"Alas, the only thing I agree with is that I joined in 1986, but I'm not wild about being reminded of that. I feel old enough already. As for me being the most successful woman in the company, I really don't like this idea at all. I don't measure myself against other women, though I don't really think I measure myself against other men either. I just try to do my job well. I don't always manage . . . but that's the general idea.

"I think I'm meant to tell you that this is a great place to work. But

I'm not going to. I think I'm meant to say that this company values diversity. But that's all bullshit."

The trainees shifted uncomfortably, and Russell gave a pained smile.

"The fact that, as Russell has so kindly pointed out," she continued, "I have been here for a long time says something about how much I like it. Twenty-two years ago, I was the only woman on this course. Now there are twelve of you. But that in itself means nothing. I'm not passionate about diversity but about hiring really good people and creating an environment in which they can do what they're great at. Look, I don't want to give you a lecture. I want to say that I hope you thrive here. And you will thrive if you work hard and use your brains, and every time there is something you don't know, you find the answer by asking someone. So let's start as we mean to go on. Over to you. Ask me whatever you like—anything at all—and I'll do my best to answer..."

The trainees said nothing, and Stella looked around the room, smiling expectantly. She hated these moments. The speech had not been quite right: It was too brusque and too strident. She really should have given it some proper thought last night.

Russell broke the silence. "Well, Stella, thank you, that was incredibly...stimulating. Um...short but sweet. Let me put a question that I'm sure will be top of mind for everyone. How do you yourself manage to juggle your work and home life, keeping so many balls in the air?"

"With difficulty. I've got no ball sense whatsoever."

There was a polite murmur of laughter.

"No, in fact, I manage entirely thanks to others. I'm really lucky to have a supportive husband, and a nanny, and a cleaning lady. And I think my kids appreciate the fact that I'm doing something stimulating—even if they don't always appreciate it when I go home in a towering rage and scream at everyone. Atlantic Energy expects you to work hard, but we don't expect you to mortgage your souls."

A girl at the front in a black trouser suit put up her hand. "What would you say were the three key characteristics that summed up your personal brand?"

This girl looked straight out of business school: She had the telltale desire to order everything into groups of three.

"I'm not a great believer in personal brands or in values. I suppose I could say: Work hard, play hard, have fun—but I don't want to insult your intelligence with that. If you put a gun to my head and made me name three, I'd say: Be brave. Be inventive. Try to do the right thing."

The girl nodded, apparently satisfied with these platitudes.

Then a red-haired man at the back said, "Do the right thing? What is the right thing? Have you ever done the wrong thing?"

Stella looked at him. He was tipping his chair backward and put the question in a way that struck her as slightly impudent. It was okay for her to break the rules. She had earned that right over two decades. It was less okay for him.

"There are three questions there, and the middle one is too philosophical," she replied. "We are an active organization, not a reflective one. What I am saying is that over time you get a better feeling for what the right thing is. And have I done the wrong thing? Yes, often, but usually because I didn't know it was wrong until it was too late."

He fixed his light blue eyes on her and gave a smirk.

Bella

"Hi, Bella, it's Russell. We need to talk later today re your new position. But for the minute can I cadge a favor? Can you help out with the graduate trainee induction day this morning—it's going on in the Cormorant Cinema Suite. I need you to check the trainees off against the managers they are assigned to and look after them at lunchtime."

Bella slipped in at the back of the cinema, where Stella Bradberry was on the stage talking about work/life balance and nannies and supportive husbands. It was all very well, Bella thought. Try having work/life balance when you are a single mother and when your child is collected from school every day by an obese child minder who demands extra money if you are five minutes late picking her up.

Though maybe Stella wasn't too bad, Bella thought. At least she talked like a human being. As she watched, she could see why Julia had been so jealous of her. There was a naturalness about her, attractive in a blue-stockingy, not-trying-too-hard way. Bella wondered how old she was. If she had been a trainee twenty-two years ago—when Bella was barely at primary school—that must make her about forty-four or forty-five now, though she looked much younger.

Stella was talking about how everyone at AE was encouraged to do what they were good at. This, Bella knew from experience, was a lie. No one had ever taken the remotest interest in finding out what she was good at. She stopped listening and instead imagined that she was Trinny or Susannah and was giving Stella a makeover. For a start, she would tell her to throw away the gray trouser suit and flat pumps. The suit fitted her well but wasn't very feminine. Bella would have put her in killer heels with a small platform at the front, which would make her half a head taller than the CEO. And then a simple black dress that was stretchy and showed how slim she was. Or maybe not black; Stella's skin was too pale for that. Red might be nicer—she'd seen a Kate Moss dress in a magazine that would be just right. The plain gold chain necklace Stella was wearing was boring. A silver Tiffany pendant would be more striking.

A trainee was asking a question in an aggressive fashion. Bella looked at the name on his badge—which said "Rhys Williams"—and saw that he was due to have been Julia's trainee. Now someone else would have to take him instead.

The session came to an end, and it was Bella's job to take the trainees down to the canteen. Most of them squeezed into one lift together, and Bella found herself rammed up against Rhys. The whole lift fell quiet.

"Where are you from in Wales?" she asked him to break the silence.

He muttered the name of a town that she didn't catch.

"I went to uni in Wales," Bella volunteered. "In Bangor."

No one said anything to this, so she added, "But I left after the first year."

Conversation over lunch was desultory. The trainees discussed the morning with one another; Bella's views were not invited. One of the girls said, "I thought Stella Bradberry was impressive, and nice. Incredibly down-to-earth."

"I thought she was patronizing, and she clearly thinks the sun shines out of her arse," said Rhys.

He looked at Bella and almost smiled. If you forget the hair, she thought, he's quite sexy in an ugly sort of way.

Later that day, Bella was summoned to see Russell's number two. The head of HR didn't deal with assistants directly and had delegated the task to his deputy, Suzi Best, who explained to Bella about the reorganization.

"James Staunton already has a PA, but we're looking to recruit an additional assistant to work alongside Anthea Stephens, deputizing for her and working as a team to deliver world-class support," she said.

It sounded like a bra, Bella thought.

Suzi then assured her that the position would be advertised internally in line with company diversity policy. However, as Bella already had experience of the "press office function" and therefore possessed some of the "key competencies," her application would be fast-tracked.

Bella wanted to say that she was being asked to apply for a job that was junior to the one she currently occupied and so no, she wasn't interested. Instead she said, "Thank you."

Bella stood on the threshold of James's office and knocked gently on the doorjamb. He was speaking on the phone but waved her in. He went on talking and turned away from her toward the window, giving her a view of a bald spot made all the more noticeable by the darkness of his hair. Other balding men cut their hair close, but his was long, accentuating the pink of his scalp. Her mum had always said that you can tell more about people by looking at them from behind. And from behind he looked like a balding man of average height in a blue shirt with a largish bottom. How could Julia have found this man attractive? she wondered.

"We'll have to see what the Saudis do," he was saying. "I've got a meeting with Michel next week. Will update after that."

Bella wondered if she should sit on one of his dark red leather sofas but decided to stay standing. Because James was senior to Julia, he had two sofas and a chair; she had had just one sofa. He also had a glass sideboard on which were displayed some photos. There was a picture of a pretty woman in a vest top and sun hat squinting at the camera and laughing. Then another picture of three young boys in school sweatshirts with one of those special school photo backgrounds with a yellow-and-green marbled effect that made Bella think of vomit. The youngest seemed to be about the same age as Millie.

He put down the phone and looked at her quizzically. "Did you want something...?"

"HR said you wanted to interview me at three thirty?"

James sighed. "I can interview you if you like, but I don't think it's a great use of either of our time. I know you're good at dealing with the administrative side of the press office, so it makes sense for you to go on doing that. I don't understand why some idiot in HR wants me to waste time interviewing candidates when I've told them that you will be perfectly adequate for the job."

And that was it. It seemed she was both hired and dismissed. "Should I talk to Anthea?" she asked.

He nodded vaguely and went back to his computer.

Why was he like this? Bella wondered. Maybe he knew that she knew about his affair with Julia and was embarrassed. But in that case, why did he want her to work for him? Or maybe he was just emotionally retarded. She was used to this, having worked for George Stephens, who had been much happier communing with plastics than with her. The other possibility was that James Staunton was a perfectly nice and balanced man who was simply having a bad day and was being unusually graceless. She doubted it, somehow.

Stella

Stella was on a conference call. Sixteen senior AE managers from all around the world were discussing Russian oil production. Or at least the Russian manager was discussing it, and fifteen others at different desks in different time zones were barely attending. There were some problems, he was saying, with the Russian authorities, who were making further difficulties over damage to local wildlife.

Her mobile started to vibrate, and she pressed mute on the conference phone and took the call. It was Charles.

"NBC are interested in buying it. Their head honcho has completely bought into the concept that this is not merely a class portrait of Britain, but touches universal themes of dispossession in an era of postglobalization..."

Charles never started conversations by saying hello; he just launched straight in. She used to find this sweet when they were students together at Oxford. She had loved his single-mindedness about his work and had been in awe of his talent. When his film about prostitutes in Northern Ireland won a BAFTA, making him—at just twenty-six—the youngest winner ever, she had been almost as pleased as he was. But the trophy, which spent ten years on the sitting room mantelpiece, was then moved to Charles's study and then disappeared altogether. Just the other day, Stella had found it in the back of their wardrobe. These days, Charles hated it when people went on about his past triumphs, as it was a reminder that there had been no more recent ones. But now, suddenly, here was that same obsessive enthusiasm, only this time he was just a deputy producer on a project that wasn't really his. The talk this time, because some of it was fantasy, made her sad. Still, a Charles who was up and enthused was a lot better than a Charles who was down—as he had been so much in the last year or so.

"Darling," she said, "that's really wonderful. But can we talk about it tonight—I'm on the other line?"

"Sure," he said, and hung up.

Stella clicked back into the conference call.

"What's your take on that, Stella?" Stephen was asking.

"Well," Stella bluffed, "I think it's complicated…"

"Yes," said Stephen. "I think Stella is quite right."

Bella

"I don't have any problems with him at all," Anthea was saying.

She was sitting at her desk, spooning yogurt into her mouth, her lipstick leaving a shimmering peach smear on the white plastic spoon.

"Obviously I've been working with him for quite a few years, and it took him a while to get the way I work, but I keep him on quite a short lead. I arrange his diary, do all his meetings and his correspondence."

Bella's mobile bleeped. There was a text from Xan.

```
Want to see M. can I come over tonight? X
```

Bella glanced at the text and deleted it. There was no way he was coming, not after what happened last time. She looked back at Anthea.

"Obviously he's got a brain the size of a planet, and the key thing to know is that he doesn't suffer fools. I always say that he's married to his work. And adores his kids."

But not his wife, Bella thought.

"It's going to be ever so helpful having you here," Anthea went on. "Give me someone to natter to in quiet moments—not that there are any quiet moments. I'm owed so many holiday days. Last year I was ten days short…"

Bella could see some of the press calls stacking up, so she took one of them.

It was the *Daily Mail* with a query about the CEO's pay. Why had he been awarded a bonus of £1.6 million and deferred pension contributions of £6.4 million, when all the company profits were at the expense of the motorist? Why indeed, she thought.

"I'll have to get one of the press officers to call you back on that. Let me take your number."

She wrote down the number, still thinking about Xan's text. He didn't have a right to see his daughter. He had to earn that right by behaving as a responsible father should. She replied:

Sorry. Not after last time.

Within two seconds, the text came back.

Last time was different. You didn't let me explain. She is my daughter and I love her, and I love you, too.

Bella sighed. That wasn't going to tempt her.

No. Tonight no good anyway.

Anthea looked on disapprovingly. "You're popular," she said.

"It's just arrangements with the child minder," Bella said.

Anthea pursed her lips. She had no children, whether by design or not Bella had no idea. The phone bleeped again.

You'll regret this. My lawyer says it's illegal.

She turned off the phone. He couldn't frighten her with tales of lawyers. She was sure he was bluffing—he didn't have any money for lawyers, and any spare cash he had went straight up his nose or into his veins, or however he was taking his drugs these days.

James put his head around the door. "What is this meeting in my diary? I have no idea who these people are. Call them and say I can't see them."

Bella wanted to say that she had no idea either, as she had been working for him for only an hour, and that she hadn't made the appointment, and it would be really nice if he called her by her name or made an effort to be even slightly amiable.

"Sure," she said, and smiled.

Stella

Russell bustled into Stella's office, followed by the two young trainees who had been assigned to her for the next four months. One was the tall, thin woman who had shown such a keen interest in Stella's personal brand values.

"This," said Russell, "is Beate Schlegel."

Beate shook Stella's hand coolly.

"Beate will be able to hit the ground running, as she has a master's in economics from Harvard. And this," Russell went on, "is Rhys Williams."

He gestured toward the redhead who had been so irritating the previous day. Rhys gave Stella a familiar nod. His eyes were light and clear, and he had long eyelashes that you had to look carefully to see because they were reddish blond, like his hair. The effect was slightly disconcerting. In between his eyebrow and his ear, he had a strawberry birthmark the size of a two-pence piece. He was wearing a navy suit with too wide a pinstripe and slip-on shoes.

"If you'll excuse me," said Russell, "I have people waiting for me upstairs."

He handed Stella the two CVs, said, "Cheers, all the best," to the trainees, and hurried off.

Stella glanced at the CVs. As well as her economics degrees, Beate had an MBA from Harvard and spoke five languages fluently. She was twenty-four. Rhys, she saw, had a first in English from Jesus College, Oxford, appeared to have done no further degrees, and was twenty-seven. He had spent five years since he graduated working for a property company in Wales.

Stella asked Beate where she grew up, and she said she was born in Germany to a diplomat family and had lived as a child in Berlin, London, New York, and Islamabad. Rhys appeared not to be listening to this list of cities but was prowling around Stella's office. He picked up the picture of her with Nelson Mandela, examined it closely, and put it down without comment. Stella cleared her throat to express disapproval, but he didn't respond.

Nathalie put her head around the door. "I've got Goldman Sachs on the line. They want to know if you and Charles are going to Covent Garden on tenth October."

"Accept for me, but call Charles and check if he can make it."

She could feel Rhys's eyes on her and had the uncomfortable sensation that she had had in the staff cinema the day before.

"And Nathalie, can you run off two copies of the current draft of my presentation with all the statistical appendices?"

Turning to Beate and Rhys, she went on: "I am going to throw you both in at the deep end and have you help me with a presentation I am doing for the board next week on sustainability. I want you to do a fact check. Fresh eyes can spot all sorts of things. Nathalie, can you make sure they have somewhere to sit and know where everything is?"

She watched them follow Nathalie out, walking about six feet apart. They didn't much like each other, that was clear.

Bella

Bella sat at her new desk, feeling dismal. Last night, she had gone to pick up Millie from the child minder to find that Xan had got there before her. The child minder hadn't let him in and had—as she'd been instructed—threatened to call the police if he didn't leave. Eventually, he'd given up and gone. The child minder said that Xan was looking "a bit twitchy," which almost certainly meant he was using again. As Bella had walked Millie home, her daughter had said, "Dad came to the door today, and June said he couldn't come in, and Dad shouted through the door that she was a fat, fucking bitch."

Millie reported this with apparent glee. She did not ask, as she never did, why she could not see her father or why he behaved like this. She had gone skipping ahead, and if she felt distress at what had happened that day, she gave no sign of it. Bella sometimes worried that Millie was repressing her feelings; she seemed far too self-contained for a child of seven. Mostly, though, Bella admired her little daughter and marveled at her strength and resilience.

The phone went, and Bella answered. "James Staunton's office," she said.

"Hello, Anthea," said the voice on the other end.

"It's not Anthea, it's Bella Chambers," said Bella, vaguely offended that her North London voice should be taken for the refined estuary spoken by Anthea.

"Oh," said the voice. "It's Hillary Staunton, James's wife. Is he there?"

"No," said Bella, and as this didn't seem to be quite good enough, she added: "I'm afraid he's not."

"Well, where is he?" She spoke in a plaintive way, as if it were Bella's fault that her husband wasn't at his desk awaiting her call.

"I don't know...I think he's in a meeting. Shall I ask him to phone you when he returns?"

"No, it's okay. I'll text him."

Bella thought she was quite good at getting the measure of people from their voices on the phone, but this time she wasn't sure. Cool and posh. Not very friendly. Shy? She put down the phone.

"That was James's wife," she said to Anthea. "What's she like?"

Anthea pursed her lips and rolled her eyes. "Hillary can be...funny, especially at first."

"She looks really pretty in the photo in his room," said Bella.

"That was taken *years* ago," said Anthea.

Stella

Stella turned up to work feeling worn. On days like this, her office was a refuge from the clamor of home. That morning, Clementine had got up late and was in a rage about her hair—which was wrong in some unspecified way. She'd refused to eat any breakfast, and when Stella had pressed a mango smoothie on her, she'd looked at her mother with the coldest contempt. When she'd asked about the poetry competition, Clemmie had said she was a selfish bitch who was only pretending to be interested.

Finn had sat through this scene impervious, eating his fourth helping of Cheerios. He'd then announced that he'd left his swimming kit on the bus and would get a detention by turning up without it. He hadn't seemed particularly bothered at the idea. Stella believed in empowering her children. Let them get detentions. They would learn in time. Unfortunately, Finn didn't seem to be learning, and Stella often worried that she was too lax and should be monitoring him more closely.

Once in the office, Stella usually managed to stop fretting about her children. Though now, thanks to Russell, she had two older charges, who were turning out to be like the children she had at home—only they didn't swear at her.

Beate had crunched through every number in the presentation and at ten p.m. the previous night had sent a detailed e-mail outlining two errors in the presentation. She was hovering, waiting for praise—and for more work.

Rhys was also lurking outside her office, with no sign of having done any work at all.

"Have you gone through the numbers?" Stella asked.

"Sure," he said. "But it seems to me that the data isn't really the issue."

"I wasn't asking you to comment on the suitability of the presentation," Stella said sharply. "I was asking you to check the numbers."

He gave a sullen shrug. The only difference between him and my son, she thought, was that Finn was charming and this guy was not.

Later that day, she sent Russell an e-mail:

Russell,

Rhys Williams is not pulling his weight and has an adolescent approach to work. I don't have time to train him up, and would be grateful if you'd take him off my hands. Why did we hire him?

Stella

To which she got the following reply:

Hi Stella

With all due respect, he has only been with you for a short time. I was hoping that you would mentor him. You might be interested to know that his scores on all the psychometric tests were higher than any of the other trainees.

All best,

Russell.

Later that afternoon, Stella was working at her desk with the door closed; this was not in line with the AE open door policy, but she found that otherwise it was impossible to get any work done. She was interrupted by a loud bang on the glass door and looked up to see Rhys standing on the outside. He swaggered in and threw himself onto her leather chair. He sat with legs slightly apart and drummed his fingers on the table. She looked at his nails, bitten to the quick.

"Thanks for coming to see me," Stella said. "Normally we would have this meeting once you had been on the job for a couple of weeks. But I thought it would be helpful to have a conversation now."

Rhys nodded.

"We are meant to agree on four objectives that you are going to achieve before Christmas," Stella went on. "But in your case, I don't know if there is any point in doing that."

"Why not?" He looked surprised.

"Because," she said, "you aren't trying. I am told that you have talent, and I'm sure you have, but to be perfectly frank, I haven't seen much evidence of that—"

Her mobile went. Charles.

"Hi...No, not a good moment...Yes, in my address book. See you tonight. Bye."

"Sorry," she said.

He raised his eyebrows slightly.

"I've lost my thread...Now—what was I saying? Yes, that this is a merito-cratic company. Everyone is talented, or they wouldn't have got through the selection process. But those who succeed get there through hard work."

"And by being well connected?" He gave her an impudent smile. His teeth were strong and white, but one in front was chipped, giving him a rakish air.

"If you would like to know," Stella said icily, "I slogged my guts out when I was your age, and went on slogging when my children were babies. However, I feel no particular need to prove myself to you."

There was a silence, which she did not help him fill. Then he said: "You accuse me of not trying, but you haven't given me anything decent to do. You asked me to check some numbers, and I did. I'm not a statistician, but they seemed okay to me. Or at least they seemed as okay as their assumptions, which were that people feel rational about sustainability issues, which clearly they don't. Have you seen today's *Sun*?"

"No. Surprisingly, I don't read the *Sun*. I don't find there's much in it that helps me with my job. And I don't really think it's relevant to this conversation."

He ignored the unpleasant tone in her voice, took a thumbed copy of the paper out of the folder he was carrying, and turned to page three. The topless model had large green breasts. GORGEOUS GREEN GODDESS, it said.

"For Christ's sake," said Stella. She gave him a distant, regal look that she knew was frightening.

"What I suggest you do," she said, making her vowels at their most open, "is that you complete this form. Fill in the objectives. Send it to Russell and ask him for another placement. I will be happy to explain to him why your placement with me in Economics is not working out."

She stood up, which Rhys eventually grasped was his signal to leave.

Before the presentation, Stella went to the ladies' loo. She lowered herself onto the seat and closed her eyes, trying to memorize the first few lines of her speech. What had seemed like a great way to start the previous night now struck her as both fatuous and dangerous.

From the neighboring cubicle came a voice talking on the phone.

"You can't see her. I'll go back to court to get another injunction...I'm sorry, you can't talk to me like that...I'm not listening to this...Fuck off."

There was a sniff and the sound of the toilet flushing. The door opened and out came Julia's old secretary, who looked embarrassed on seeing Stella but then gave a bright smile.

Stella, pretending not to have overheard, said hello, and the two stood side by side, washing their hands in silence.

Stella looked at the young woman's tight black trousers and clinging sweater and thought she didn't really look much older than Clementine. She was very pretty, like a miniature doll with rosy cheeks and dark curls. Despite an anguished expression on her face, she had what Jane Austen called bloom.

Stella, by contrast, did not have bloom. The sharp overhead light was making the roots show in her hair, and she thought she looked tired and wan. Mostly she didn't really care, but today was a day when it would have been nice to look good. She smudged some blue onto her eyelids and some gloss onto her lips, wishing her mother had balanced her lectures to her daughter on free will versus determinism with some tips on how to apply makeup.

At four p.m., the board members were sleepy. The room was hot, and discussion of the budget had been long and tedious. The chairman smiled at Stella and got up when she came into the room.

"I think you all know Stella Bradberry," he said.

Stella looked around the table at the eighteen-strong board. Six executive directors and twelve non-executives, plus James, who was sitting in. Of the non-execs, all were male except for Dame Judith Babcock, with whom Stella had shared a platform the previous year at the Women of Achievement awards.

"Good afternoon," she said.

She could feel a pulse in her throat and that giddy, light-headed feeling, as if she were outside her own body, observing. Her voice sounded thin and high.

"I wanted to start by showing you something that doesn't normally make its way into the boardroom. This is just a guess, but I'm judging that most of you aren't devotees of page three of the *Sun*."

There was a surprised titter.

"I thought as much. In fact I'm not myself, but this is rather special."

Another titter. Stephen, who had run through the presentation with her before she had decided to rework the beginning, was looking alarmed. Stella clicked the mouse of her laptop, and a large picture of a naked woman was projected onto the wall, displaying her huge, apple green breasts.

Sir John Englefield, the chairman, gave an amazed guffaw. What am I doing, thought Stella. This is going horribly wrong.

"There is an economic point here," she plowed on. "You can't put a value on this. This newspaper is read by seven million people. Green is an issue for them. They aren't interested in the economics. This is something that they take on trust. If we don't embrace it wholeheartedly, our consumers and all our stakeholders will turn on us."

They were all listening, ready now for the meat of the presentation, which Stella had rehearsed in the bathroom the previous night and again that morning. As she talked, she stopped being nervous and started to perform. For the next twenty minutes, she elegantly described the economics of sustainability, concentrating on the economics of fuel made from algae, which, she argued, was economically viable not just at today's oil price of

$150, but at any price above $40. It was a hugely exciting opportunity that could transform the company's fortunes in as little as five years.

"That was fascinating, Stella, thank you for your time. Let's take a nature break and resume in five minutes."

Stella got up to leave, and the directors nodded their congratulations. As she walked back toward the lift, she turned on her mobile and saw a text from her daughter.

```
I won!!!! Have been put in for National
poetry reading prize!! Luv ya C xxx
```

And then one from Charles.

```
Where's your address book??
```

She called him and explained where the address book was. "I've just come from the board meeting."

"Oh yes, how was it?"

"Triumph."

"Good," he said absently.

Stella would have liked more enthusiasm from her husband, but after years of getting little, her expectations were low, so she rarely felt put out by his lack of interest in her work.

"See you later," she said.

"We start filming on a council estate near Swansea tomorrow, and so I'm going to go down tonight…"

"You didn't tell me," she said. "When are you back?"

Bella

Bella was trying to change James's travel arrangements. The previous day, she had booked the flights for his trip to the United States, only to be told that she would have to change them because of a family emergency. James returned from the board meeting, walked straight past Bella's desk and into his office without looking at her.

"Can you get Stella for me?"

Bella disliked it when her bosses couldn't pick up the phone themselves, but she said nothing and dialed the number. Stella answered, and Bella put the call through to James. Through the open door she could hear his voice, deep and serious.

"Do you mind if I'm completely straight with you?"

As opposed to what, Bella wondered. Completely crooked?

"You put me in an impossible situation just then," he went on. "If, in the future, you plan to discuss the media impact of any initiatives, it would be really helpful if you gave me a heads-up beforehand...I can only repeat...Yes, but media is my responsibility. And frankly, I don't think that green breasts are relevant to this complex issue."

He slammed the phone down and emerged from his office. "I don't suppose you've had a chance to change those flights," he said.

"Yes," she said, "I have. It's all fine—if you fly out from Stansted. And then you can still make all your meetings and get back by Thursday night."

"Oh," he said. "Good. Thank you."

For the first time since Bella had been working for him, he looked at her properly and smiled. He had nice teeth, she noticed.

Going down in the lift, Bella bumped into Rhys. He was looking glum, she thought, and minus the cocky manner, he seemed really rather attractive. His red hair was tousled. He had a sort of naughty schoolboy look that appealed to her. And his eyes were an extraordinarily light blue.

"Hi. How's it working out in Economics?"

He shrugged and gave a sarcastic smile. "I probably won't be working there for much longer. Stella Bradberry seems not to appreciate my talents."

And then Bella said: "Well, she's not exactly flavor of the month with my boss, either. He's just had a massive blowup with her over the phone— something to do with green tits."

Bella knew she should not have said this. One of the things that had made each one of her different bosses value her was that she kept her mouth shut. She could have done Julia a great deal of harm had she chosen to talk. But today she was feeling awful, and she was vaguely attracted to this guy, so she didn't see why she shouldn't engage in some mutual moaning.

"What?" His pale eyes widened. "Green tits?"

Bella found this comic. Mention breasts to men, she thought, even ones who have first-class degrees from Oxford, and you have their full attention. He did fancy her, clearly.

"How about a drink?" he asked.

"When?"

"Like, now?"

"I can't," she said with regret. "I have to get home." She didn't want to mention Millie, not at this stage.

"What about tomorrow?"

Stella

Stella had an eight a.m. breakfast on the fourteenth floor with three economists from an energy think tank who were trying to get AE to sponsor a research project. She liked this role and was good at listening and asking the right questions, but today her mind wasn't quite on it.

Stella's BlackBerry was winking its red light at her. Surreptitiously, she touched the mouse ball and glanced at the new message. It was from Rhys Williams.

```
i gather green tits proved useful
```

Whether it was the word *tits* or whether it was his discovery that she had stolen his idea, the message made her blush. How had he found out what had happened in the board meeting? she wondered. He could not have spoken to Stephen or to James. And what should she do now? To have banished him for being a lazy idiot, but then to lift his idea without giving him any credit, and then to be found out—it didn't look good. Bad, in fact.

Stella tried to compose her face as if she were taking in every word of the economists' presentation. The red light blinked again. Nathalie.

```
Hi. Mrs. Stephenson—Oscar's mother?—wants
you to call re Finn. Not urgent. N
```

Then why, she thought, ring me at work with it? There was something about all the other mothers at Finn's school with their perfect blond high-lights and the way that they did their children's projects for them that was aggravating. Last time Stella had tried to help with a project on the economy of Canada, she had flown into such a rage over Finn's messy handwriting and mislabeled pie charts that she had seized the sheets and ripped them in two. Finn had stomped off; Stella had ended up doing the whole thing herself and had been somewhat put out when the teacher had queried her account of the trade figures and not given her a commendation.

Stella dragged her attention back to the economists and asked a per-tinent question about the difficulty of data collection.

Bella

Today, Bella said to herself as she got onto her bike to go to work, I am going to be positive. Cycling saved £1.50 on the bus, and pedaling made her happy. Even weaving through the heavy lorries and buses on Hol-loway Road and Upper Street was oddly enjoyable: She arrived in the office feeling victorious.

Bella didn't cycle every day because sometimes she heeded her mother's warning: that Millie needed her alive. This was true; yet the way her mother said it was unpleasantly pointed, rubbing in the fact that Millie had only one functioning parent and that no one apart from Millie would mind much if Bella was flattened by a cement mixer. Bella was well aware of both facts, yet on mornings like this, she didn't mind. She had been greatly cheered up by her meeting in the lift with Rhys the previous night, and on the phone to her sister she had admitted that she had given up looking for the right man; instead she was simply trying to avoid another disastrously wrong man. She had a list of six criteria, and they went like this:

No drug addicts
No alcoholics
No depressives
No bipolar
No unemployed
No employees of Atlantic Energy

Rhys appeared to meet all these criteria except for the last. Go for it, her sister had advised her. She didn't say it with much conviction, but that was only because she was longing to get the subject back to herself.

The phone was ringing as she reached her desk. It was Anthea.

"Hello. Have you just got in? I just tried a few minutes ago, but there was no answer."

Bella looked at the clock, which said 9:03. "Oh? I've been here for a bit," she lied.

"Can you please tell himself that the headache I had yesterday has developed into a migraine, so I'm in bed feeling poorly."

The only time Bella had had a migraine, she'd spent the day not making cheerful phone calls, but being sick into a bowl in a darkened room. "Oh dear," she said, "poor you."

James's door was open, and he was hunched over his computer. This time he looked up at the sound of Bella's voice.

"Anthea called in to say she's got a migraine," she said.

"Ah. She suffers a lot."

He caught her eye, as if there were a shared joke between them. His eyes twinkled at her, and Bella felt herself blushing.

"Thanks for rearranging the tickets yesterday," he said.

"It's nothing."

"And can you call the *Times* journalist I'm having lunch with today and say I'd like to meet at twelve thirty instead of one."

"He won't like that," Bella said. "I've dealt with him before. He's a really difficult one."

James suddenly banged his hand down on the desk. "I don't give a shit who he is or what he is like. My time is much more precious than his."

What was the matter with him? Bella wondered as she picked up the phone to make the call. One moment he was in his own world. The next moment he was giving her complicit glances, and the next, shouting. Bella hoped he wasn't going to do much more of that. She hated being shouted at.

Just as she was thinking this, he came out of his room and stood by her desk. "Sorry. I shouldn't have raised my voice. I wasn't cross with you. Things are a little…trying…at the moment. I simply need an earlier lunch today, as I'm taking my wife to a hospital appointment." He looked awkward.

"Don't worry," said Bella.

It was a funny thing, she thought, that when someone gets angry but then says sorry nicely, you can end up liking them more than if they hadn't lost it in the first place. She wondered whether she should say she hoped there was nothing serious wrong with his wife but then thought, No, best not.

James was still hovering around her desk looking distracted, so she asked: "Is there anything you'd like me to do?"

And he said that for his press trip next week, he would like her to prepare a short briefing note on the journalists who were attending. Bella liked doing this sort of thing, as it made her use her brain and allowed her to exercise her natural curiosity about people.

For each of the journalists, she found a brief CV and attached their last few articles in which AE had been mentioned. On some of them she wrote a few notes of her own. Who had an ax to grind, who was a troublemaker, who was solid, and so on. About the *Times* journalist she wrote: "Quite flaky. Julia had a run-in with him over his coverage of our last results announcement." But then she decided to leave Julia out of it. James hadn't mentioned her name once—though, now she came to think of it, he hadn't mentioned anyone's name. So maybe he didn't do names. Or conversation of any sort, come to that.

Bella turned to her e-mail, and there was a message from Rhys. The subject line said: "lunch today?" She opened up the message but the rest of it was blank—which didn't strike her as being sufficiently enthusiastic. Still, she messaged back: "Yes. See you in lobby at 1?"

She printed out her briefing notes and took them to James, but he had already gone out to lunch.

Stella

What was she going to do about Rhys? Stella wondered. E-mail would be best, she thought. She sent this:

Rhys—I meant to contact you last night after the board meeting to thank you for a useful input to the presentation. It lightened up some otherwise rather difficult material.

Stella

It was a bit stiff, but then she meant to be stiff. Within a minute he had e-mailed back:

Does this mean that I get to stay in your department?

Stella sighed and did what she did with tiresome messages: She ignored it and hoped it would go away.

Her phone rang. "Stella Bradberry," she said in her briskest, most professional voice.

"Hi, Stella, it's Nancy Stephenson."

Nancy was a pushy American mother of a boy in Finn's class whom her son tolerated rather than liked.

"I really hope you don't mind me butting in at work. I know you must be really busy. I don't know *how* you manage it. I saw an article about you in the Sunday *Times* about senior women in business—I was *so* impressed."

"Thank you," said Stella. "Those pieces are stupid, they don't mean anything."

"Oh, but they *do*!...Look, why I'm calling—and I don't know if your assistant mentioned this, but I also called yesterday? It's about Finn. When he was having a playdate here on Monday, I got the guys to do some work on their French for the test today—"

What French test? thought Stella.

"—and I couldn't help noticing that Finn had his face really close to the page, which I thought might explain why his reading and writing are...?"

Are what? thought Stella. Useless by comparison to your son's?

"So I just thought—and I hope you don't mind me calling—but I just thought that if someone noticed something that was wrong with Oscar, well, I'd really appreciate them getting in touch right away. I guess what I'm leading up to here is that I just wondered if you might think of getting his eyes tested?"

Stella took a breath. "Thank you. It's really nice of you to bother to call. But really you shouldn't worry. I've had them tested, and they're normal. But thanks so much for the call. And it would be really nice to get Oscar over to our place soon—it's wonderful that they seem to get on so well."

She put down the phone. "Stupid, annoying, interfering cow," she said.

Next door, Nathalie looked up and gave a knowing smile.

James put his head round Stella's door.

"Hi. You aren't by any chance free for a quick lunch today, are you? I've had a cancellation."

Why did men always have to make such a show of a full diary? Stella wondered. Why couldn't he allow her to think that maybe he had nothing booked? Her diary was blank for lunch; indeed, she tried to keep it that way where possible, but it was uphill work. That day, she had been considering going to the gym for the first time in three weeks. Though the thought of struggling in and out of her clothes and spending half an hour on the cross-trainer was so unappealing that she was not altogether disappointed when something else came up.

"Okay, but can we do one thirty, as I've got to give one of my recalcitrant trainees a swift kick first?"

Stella was curious about James. He was such a dark horse. She wondered what had really happened with Julia and resolved to try to get it out of him over lunch.

At ten to one, Rhys knocked on her office door. She beckoned him in and glanced purposefully at her watch to make the point that he was five minutes late and to invite him to apologize. He didn't; instead he sat down in his casual, sprawly way.

Stella started without preamble. "As I said in my e-mail, I was grateful to you for unwittingly offering inspiration for the start of my presentation. However, I was...Look, can I be honest with you? There are a lot of people who want to be trainees here. Of the twenty-five we take every year, ten won't make it through to the end of the year. It is really tough, and you need to play the game. Sending me snarky texts is not playing the game."

"Yeah," he said. "I know. Sorry. I've been a prat."

Suddenly he looked crumpled, like a small boy. Ten minutes ago, she would have bet money that he was incapable of apologizing, but here he was saying sorry with all the outward signs of sincerity.

"So how did it go?" he asked.

"How did what go?"

"Your presentation."

"It went very well," she said. "The board has approved the entire budget, and we have an additional hundred million dollars to put into the research project, making fuel from algae."

"And did they like the tits?" he asked.

"I'm not sure if they liked them. But they did appreciate the point I was making."

"That's good," he said. "I was impressed you did that."

Was he trying to suck up to her? she wondered. "Well, yes. There was a minute when I thought it was going to backfire. Dame Judith Babcock looked even more hatchet-faced than she usually does."

"Dame Judith? I didn't know she was on the board. She's a joke."

This wasn't what Stella had planned at all. It was meant to be a bollocking, not an opportunity for the two of them to denigrate members of the board.

"Look," Stella said firmly. "We are skirting around the issue here. The issue is this. I have room for one trainee on my team. I have two—and so far it seems to me that one does all the work and the other is sloppy and arrogant and his sole contribution is a green page three girl. Let me ask you this: In my position, which would you choose?"

"What if the lazy bastard promised to pull his finger out going forward?"

Stella winced at the phrase *going forward* and thought how peculiar his speech was. He had a strong Welsh accent, and his vocabulary was part English graduate and part jock. On top was a thin layer of corporate jargon.

"Okay," she said. "I'm shelving the decision for now and am giving you one more chance."

"Thank you," he said, looking at his watch and standing. "I've got a lunch, so I'd better go."

Stella sighed. He still didn't get it. It was for her to call an end to the meeting, not him.

Bella

"Where shall we go? You know the places around here better than I do," said Rhys.

Bella hesitated. Was he going to pay for her? she wondered. In her experience, the fact that a man might earn three times as much as you didn't mean that he would necessarily pay.

"Shall we just get a sandwich at Pret?" she suggested.

He ignored this. "What about that place?"

He pointed toward a glass-and-steel restaurant opposite Atlantic Tower called Roast. It looked expensive, but Bella decided it would be best not to make a fuss.

They pushed through the doors, and there at a table in front of them sat James and Stella. She was leaning across the table toward him, and he was smiling.

"Help," said Bella. "It's my boss and your boss. Shall we leave before they see us?"

"No, this place looks cool. And she's practically my ex-boss now. I *think*."

The waiter led them right past James and Stella, making it necessary to say hello before settling at a table just out of earshot.

Fabulous, thought Bella. We're somewhere that I can't afford, and I'm right under my boss's nose, and this guy who I told my sister definitely fancies me isn't sending out any interested vibes at all. She looked at the menu.

"I'm not very hungry," she said. "I think I'll just have the soup." The soup was the cheapest dish on the menu and was £8.90.

He looked a bit surprised, but he didn't protest and ordered a large, well-done steak and chips.

"So are you enjoying working here?" she asked.

"Are *you* enjoying working here?" He batted the question back in a way that was more clumsy than flirtatious.

"Well," she said, "I've been at AE for four years, which is quite a bit compared to your four minutes. What can I say? It's fine. It just about pays the mortgage."

He nodded, as if quite satisfied by the answer. He didn't ask what she was doing working as a PA. In a way this suited her, as she didn't want to mention Millie or Xan. But still, she didn't like men who showed no curiosity about her life. It was not a good sign.

He looked over her shoulder at James and Stella. "She's a tough bitch, isn't she," he said.

Bella recoiled at the harshness of the word. "No, I don't think she is. I don't really know her personally, but other people seem to like her. She apparently lives in this incredible house in Primrose Hill. Julia—she was my old boss—told me about it. Her husband is quite a famous documentary maker, I think, and they give these glamorous parties. The prime minister and his wife went to the last one, I think."

"What's he like?"

"I haven't really decided yet. I haven't been working for him very long. He's obviously superbright, but it's weird putting someone in charge of External Relations who isn't any good at communicating—but I suppose he can turn it on when he has to."

"I didn't mean your boss. I meant *her* husband."

"Stella's husband? I don't know. I've never met him. Why would I have? I'm not exactly going to get asked to their parties, am I?"

Bella sipped her soup and moved the conversation on. "You didn't answer my question," she said. "Do you like it here so far?"

"It's a bit of a letdown," he said. "You get told that being a fast-track management trainee at AE is a massive big deal, and then you arrive and are given nothing interesting to do and everyone's on your case. You're expected to be grateful just to work here—basically to sign up to something that means you work twelve-hour days. And most of the other trainees are right plonkers."

Bella said she thought that on the whole, people were surprisingly pleasant.

"Yeah, well, it's different for you. You've probably got a trust fund."

"A *what?*"

She didn't know whether to be flattered that he thought she was in that bracket or furious that he had taken in so little about her. "How many trust fund babes do you know who are executive assistants in oil companies?"

He smiled, and she felt a bit less resentful.

"Yeah, well, I just thought, with your middle-class accent. You don't really seem like a typical assistant."

And she almost said: And you don't seem like a typical fast-track trainee with your thick Welsh accent and dodgy taste in shoes.

As if knowing what she was thinking, he said: "I've made a deal with myself. I'm going to make it in this company. The other trainees are geeks, and they've always had what they wanted handed to them on a plate. I haven't. I've had to fight for it."

I've done a bit of fighting, too, thought Bella, but she didn't say it. Not because she thought he would stop liking her if he found out that she was raising a daughter on her own, hindered by a junkie ex-boyfriend, but because it was quite clear that he didn't really like her anyway. And she didn't much like him.

The bill came, and she moved to get her wallet.

"Don't worry," he said, to her relief, "I'll get this. Sorry I wasn't better company. I had an odd morning. Let's do it again."

Maybe he wasn't so bad after all. A bit brash and self-pitying. But still, there was something about him.

"Yes, let's," she said.

Stella

"So where do you want to go?"

"I'm in a hurry," said James, "so let's go to Roast."

Stella didn't much like Roast, but at least it was nearby. Her discussion with Rhys had left her in high spirits for reasons that she could not quite fathom.

The main problem with Roast, from Stella's point of view, was that almost everything on the menu was an enormous piece of meat. "I think I'll just have soup," she said after scanning the menu.

"Is that all?"

"Charles is away, and I try to give myself a complete holiday from meat, in fact from food altogether."

This sounded stupid, but she couldn't be bothered to explain that her husband's obsessive carnivorous spirit wore her down. He had started doing all the cooking at home at weekends when the children were small. But since she had been working more and more and he had been working less and less, he cooked on weekdays, too. Sometimes she thought these meals were a punishment. Whenever she told him she had had a business lunch and wouldn't be hungry, she would come home in the evening to find pork with prunes, dauphinoise potatoes, and ratatouille, sometimes with crème brûlée for pudding.

We need to eat as a family, he would insist.

James was pouring sparkling water, and he lifted his glass toward her. "Congratulations. Your board presentation yesterday was...extraordinary."

His compliment struck Stella as slightly ironic.

"I also just wanted to clear up any misunderstanding over my phone call last night."

"Oh, don't worry," she said, "it was nothing."

"It wasn't nothing," he said, holding up his hand in a let-me-finish sort of way. "Frankly I had no business lashing out at you. I'd had quite a difficult day. Obviously it's no excuse, but..."

Today was turning out to be a peculiar day, Stella thought, with not one but two men apologizing to her in the space of an hour.

Over James's shoulder she saw the door opening, and Rhys came sauntering in with Julia's old assistant behind him. What were they doing here? she wondered. And why were they having lunch together? Assistants and fast-track trainees didn't usually socialize. Probably he fancied her, which would not be in the least surprising. Bella was looking lovely, Stella thought, with her dark hair scrunched up into a knot with curly tendrils escaping round her face.

The two walked past their table.

"Hello again," Stella said. She was mainly addressing Rhys, but he didn't meet her eye. Bella smiled and said hello. James said nothing.

When they had found a table, Stella said: "That was the trainee I was telling you about. Very odd boy. I don't think he'll last here more than six months. And that's Julia's old PA."

She looked at James closely as she said Julia's name. She thought she saw a flicker, but when he replied it wasn't about Julia at all.

"She's my PA now. I took her on with Julia's job. She's a bright girl—I have a feeling she's going to go far."

"And gorgeous," said Stella.

James didn't comment on this, so Stella asked: "So what's it like now running the press office well as the whole of ER?"

"You know," said James, "I really want to do media differently. I think for too long we've been focused on spin. We have tried to tailor our announcements to the media according to what we think will be well received. I am trying to persuade Stephen to adopt an approach that will build trust. At the moment trust is zero—they think we are evil—greedy, plundering the planet, filling our boots. If we let them see us as we really are, their opinion of us can't be worse than it is now."

Stella looked at his hands with their clean fingernails and his wrists with dark hair sprouting out from under his cuff. She looked at the gold band of his wedding ring. How did he manage to seduce Julia? she wondered. Perhaps, she thought, watching his hands stroke the side of the water glass, he was terribly good in bed. People said plain men had to try harder.

"That's brave," said Stella. "Though I think you may be right. Honesty is generally the best policy."

And then she said: "One could never accuse Julia—for all her brilliance and flair—for wanting to play things straight."

Stella waited to see if he would take up this invitation to denigrate his former lover and was both impressed and disappointed when he turned it down.

"Julia did an excellent job, but it's time for a change."

"Yes," said Stella, trying again. "I really miss her, even though she was maddening and terribly indiscreet. I would never trust her with a secret—she couldn't even keep her own." She looked at him pointedly.

"I don't know what she has told you," he said, sighing. "But whatever it is, I'm not going to try to defend myself. I behaved very, very badly. It was a...brief chapter in my life about which I feel nothing but shame."

His face had changed. The look of competence and control had gone, and he looked vulnerable.

"I'm so sorry," said Stella, suddenly feeling guilty. "I didn't mean to pry. It's none of my business."

"No," James agreed. "But could I ask one thing? Whatever it is that you know, to keep it to yourself. I'm not worried about sordid details damaging me—it's Hillary I'm worried about—she hasn't been well recently."

You might have thought about her earlier, Stella thought. But seeing his cowed expression, she said: "I've known for a few weeks and have told no one, and I'm not going to start telling them now."

"Thank you," he said.

James called for the bill, which he paid, folding the receipt carefully into his wallet.

Bella

Bella had had an aimless weekend. Gone nowhere, done nothing. The highlight had been doing times tables with Millie, something for which her daughter seemed to have great aptitude. While her classmates were still on two times two, Millie could tell you that seven times eight was fifty-six. To Bella, who was hopeless at math, this was a miracle and a sign of Millie's separateness from her.

On Saturday night, Millie had slept over with a school friend and Bella had gone on a blind date with the cousin of a college friend to the Ice Bar in Camden. He'd said he was a successful painter, and Bella had had visions of Damien Hirst, but he turned out to paint houses and didn't even seem to be doing that at the moment. He announced that he was broke and made Bella buy the drinks. At the end of the evening, he had tried to snog her and she had been too tired and depressed to push him away.

Bella was pleased when Monday came around. She put on a red skirt and high-heeled boots and blow-dried her hair carefully with the thought of Rhys in her mind. She got into the office ten minutes before nine to find Anthea already there and taking a couple of paracetamol rather more ostentatiously than was strictly necessary.

"I'm still feeling terrible. My better half said I was mad to come in, and maybe he's right. But I'm not one to lie around at home. I'm someone who needs to be busy all the time, and I was stressing about what was happening here. If I'm away for more than a couple of days, things here get out of control and it takes me ages to sort them out."

"It was all quite easy last week," said Bella. "There was very little to do. I did a briefing paper for James on the hacks he's taking on the oil field trip."

Anthea pursed her lips. "Well…Obviously I don't want you to take this the wrong way, but when you've been a PA as long as I have, you'll know that it's getting the basics right that they thank you for. The add-ons are the cherry on the cake. But if you aren't doing the basics—they are the meat and veg…"

All this talk of food seemed to be making Anthea feel hungry. She reached into the drawer of her desk and got out a biscuit. "Why don't you take one of these to himself? He's rather partial."

Bella felt disinclined to disturb her boss with a caramel HobNob, but neither did she want to upset Anthea. So she got up and put her head around his door.

"Do you want a cup of tea and one of Anthea's biscuits?"

James looked up, frowned, but on seeing Bella standing there, he smiled. "Thanks. I've had three cups of coffee and God knows how many biscuits in the heads of department meeting."

He looked down at his stomach and gave it a pat. Bella glanced at it, too, round like a dome through his expensive blue cotton shirt.

"While you're here, Bella," he said, "you were right about that *Times* journalist. Look what he wrote. I spent the entire lunch last Thursday explaining our strategy, and he has written some crap about us using our windfall profits to reward ourselves and screw the motorist. It's pathetic, lazy, inaccurate drivel! I'm just composing an e-mail to his editor now ... come and read what I've written ..."

Bella walked around his desk and stood behind him so that she could read the message over his shoulder and noticed a pleasant scent of soap.

"'I am disappointed that a newspaper like yours has no regard for the facts of the matter,'" she read.

"You've been in this department longer than I, what do you think?"

Bella could hardly believe that he was asking for an opinion, but he seemed to be waiting, so she began:

"I don't know much about it, but it seems that journalists are arrogant and quite thin-skinned. So if you complain and make them look stupid, then they will screw you next time. So I think that unless they've really got the facts wrong, it's better not to say anything?"

He had pulled his chair back from his desk and was looking at her appraisingly as she spoke. Bella started to blush again. She put down the HobNob and retreated to her anteroom, where Anthea, who had just come in, had overheard the last couple of remarks, which appeared not to have pleased her.

"You were in there a long time," she said disapprovingly.

Stella

That morning, Stella was to speak on a platform with the former chancellor of the exchequer, Nigel Lawson, who had recently written a book debunking climate change.

When the invitation had arrived last May, she had wanted to say no; it was too daunting. She hated public speaking, and this was to an audience of almost a thousand. But Stella despised her own weakness and forced herself to do whatever she found most demanding. And when it came to managing her own diary, she was more inclined to accept difficult or unpleasant things in the distant future, as she always assumed that if they were a long way off, the day would somehow be less likely ever to arrive.

But the months had passed, in the way they tend to, and there was no getting out of it. Stella had spent most of the weekend writing and rewriting the speech and reading it out loud in the kitchen the previous night to Charles, who pronounced it excellent but undermined his verdict by yawning his way through the performance.

The previous day, Stella had asked Rhys to prepare some PowerPoint slides. They had had an altercation over the color of some of the graphs: Rhys had chosen yellow, which Stella said would not show up. He had protested that they would be fine and had refused to change them. She had told him that detail mattered, and he had replied by getting a facsimile of the U.S. Declaration of Independence and pinning it up to the board in his cubicle.

"Look at this," he had said when she'd walked by. "There were two typos in this, but it didn't stop it from being the most important document in history."

"That's hardly the point," Stella had said.

"But as it happens," he'd said, "I did change the graphs to green. And I read through your speech again. It's brilliant."

Stella usually found direct compliments embarrassing. Yet there was something about the way that Rhys offered his praise—almost grudgingly, as if an afterthought—that pleased her. Stella had found herself saying that if he'd like to, he could come and listen to her deliver it.

He had said that yes, he would like that very much.

Bella

Bella sat at her desk, opening James's post.

Most of it was junk; hardly anything interesting came through the post anymore, which she regretted, as she liked the feeling of the silver paper knife in her hand and the satisfying noise it made when cutting the paper.

She picked up a cream manila envelope and sliced it open. Inside were four pieces of paper stapled together. At the top it said "The Priory, Roehampton," and underneath, INVOICE.

Patient name: Mrs. Hillary Staunton. The bill was interminable, every item listed separately, with a running total at the bottom of each page. The grand total on the final one was £14,120. Bella looked at this, marveled at the amount, and then looked back at the envelope, which was marked PRIVATE AND CONFIDENTIAL.

"Anthea," she said, "have I just opened something I shouldn't have?"

"Give it to me. He trusts me to do all his private stuff. When Hillary has been not very *well*"—she wriggled her second and third fingers to indicate quotation marks and made a double clicking sound with her tongue—"I've done all sorts for him. Even interviewed for a nanny once."

This discussion was halted by the arrival of James himself.

"Bella," he said, "have you got a second?"

She followed him into his office, and he closed the door behind her.

"Thanks for your advice this morning," he said. "I didn't send the e-mail. You saved me from looking an arse."

Again Bella felt herself blushing and so shook her hair over her face, hoping he might not see.

"And one more thing," he said.

"Yes?"

For a second he looked confused, as if he had been going to say something but changed his mind. "Can you check where we are on this year's training budget, and do some research into suitable team-building courses for the whole department? Stella is taking her team to bond over a Shakespearean play." He rolled his eyes. "To bond, or not to bond, that is the question," he said.

Bella laughed, even though it wasn't especially funny. And he laughed, too, whether at his own joke or at the sudden lightness of mood. His laugh was deep and rumbling, Bella thought. She liked the sound of it.

There was a bewildering choice of team-building courses, and most of them struck Bella as being very silly indeed. She rejected all the outdoor ones, as James did not look the type to enjoy scrambling through freezing mud. She rejected circus skills and African drumming and was about to give up when she came upon one where you learned to cook in a hotel restaurant. "By preparing food as a team, barriers are broken down and bonds forged," it said on the website. Bella, who had watched a lot of shouting in kitchens in the Gordon Ramsay program on TV, thought this unlikely but nevertheless liked the sound of it.

"Does James enjoy cooking?" she asked Anthea.

"What a funny question. He certainly enjoys eating. But I doubt if he has the need to do any cooking, as Mrs. S is a wonderful cook—or so I've heard."

Bella was prevented from asking any further questions, as her mobile was ringing. It was the school secretary at Hathaway Primary, saying that Millie had fallen over in the playground and bumped her head.

Bella could hear Millie's voice in the background, saying, "Is my mum going to come and get me?"

"She doesn't sound badly hurt," said Bella.

"It's school policy," the secretary said firmly. "If they bang their heads, they must be taken home. I'll keep her in the office till you come."

Bella rang her mother, but her mother said it wasn't a good moment. Bella explained that Millie had fallen and asked if she could pick her up. "I'm working on something important for a new boss and I'd really like to finish it."

"Well, that's a turnabout," said her mother.

In the past, when Bella had moaned about how boring the work was, her mother had said she was lucky to have it. But the news her daughter was now enjoying work didn't please her, either.

"You know what?" said Bella. "Forget it. I'll go and get her."

Bella got her coat, and as she was hurrying for the tube, she sent James a text:

```
V sorry but I had to leave early as my
daughter has banged her head. Have found
fab course based on cooking. To be or not
to be...a chef. Bella
```

Up from the tube at Caledonian Road, Bella heard her mobile bleeping. She gazed at the name "James" in the in-box and thought how much she liked seeing it there. She opened the message, which said:

```
I trust your daughter will make a swift
recovery.
```

She looked at this and felt slightly foolish. It was formal and correct and made hers seem too casual.

At the school, Millie was sitting and reading a Jacqueline Wilson book about a girl who gets beaten up by her stepfather. She greeted her mother cheerfully and skipped through the school gates.

"Can I have an ice cream?" she asked.

Stella

Rhys pushed into the cab first and sat on the folding seat. Stella positioned herself on the bench diagonally opposite him, as far away as the enclosed space of the taxi would permit. She was aware of his body, the solidity of his thighs under the tight material of his trousers, and could smell his aftershave. The smell was musty and not unpleasant, reminded her of the Lynx that Finn sprinkled over himself so liberally that when she sat down to breakfast with him in the morning, she felt she was swallowing it with her coffee.

The taxi was edging slowly along the Embankment, and Stella kept looking at her watch. She hated being late, and the double anxiety of lateness and public speaking was making her sweat into her new silk blouse.

She leaned forward and slid open the window hatch to talk to the driver. "I'm in a hurry. Would it be quicker to go down the Strand?"

His heavy shoulders gave a shrug. "Both are bad, it's up to you."

They drove along for a bit in silence, Stella looking over the speech and trying to memorize the first few paragraphs.

"Are you shitting bricks?" Rhys suddenly asked.

The babyishness of the phrase, and the sheer cheek of it, made Stella feel unexpectedly better.

"I always shit bricks—as you so elegantly put it—before talking in public, which is pathetic, as I've been doing it for twenty years. But then when I'm actually doing it, and if it's going okay, I love it."

He listened and nodded. "I'm a total show-off," he said. "But I also hate talking in public. I heard my voice and I sound retarded—like Dafydd on *Little Britain*."

Stella hadn't watched *Little Britain* so didn't know what he was talking about, but she laughed nevertheless. The taxi turned in to Park Lane and drew up outside the Hilton. A young woman with an organizer's badge was waiting for her.

"Am I late?" Stella asked.

"No," she said. "You're just on time."

In the cab on the way back to the office, Stella was feeling dismal.

She had misjudged her audience, who were generalists rather than economists. There had been a fat man in the front row who had yawned and fiddled with his BlackBerry throughout, and she felt she had delivered her speech into a wall of blankness and boredom.

"You were great," Rhys said to her.

"I wasn't," said Stella. "I was awful, but at least it's over."

"No, really," he said. "You are a brilliant speaker."

Stella, who hated doing things badly, found his words consoling. "Thanks," she said. "I'm not, but it's nice of you to say so."

She opened her briefcase and got out the proofs of that month's energy market update, which she was meant to have corrected the previous day. Not to be outdone, Rhys rummaged around in his bag and fished out a Twix.

"I'm starving," he said, putting one of the bars into his mouth, and with half of it rudely sticking out, he offered her the other bar.

"Thanks," she said, taking the chocolate. Once it was in her hand, she couldn't understand what had made her accept it. She hated Twix and hadn't eaten cheap chocolate for years. She bit into it and winced. The caramel clung to a part of her tooth where the gum had receded and gave an unpleasant twang.

"Did you learn anything from Lawson's talk?" she asked.

Rhys shrugged and said: "The funniest bit was when he started waffling on about how Saudi oil reserves were infinite, you gave him such a patronizing look, and calmly pulled out all these numbers that totally floored him."

Stella laughed. "Nonsense," she said. "People like that are never floored. They believe they are divinely right."

Then Rhys said, "Do you mind if I ask you something?"

"I don't know if I mind until you tell me what it is."

"It's my girlfriend's birthday tomorrow, and I need to get her something. I'm crap at presents. Have you got any ideas?"

Stella found that she did mind this question, or rather that the word *girlfriend* gave her a little jolt. She was shocked at her own response. Here was a young, not unattractive man. Of course he had a girlfriend. Why wouldn't he, and what difference could it possibly make to her?

"I've no idea," she said. "It depends what she's like."

"Well, she likes all the normal things. Clothes, music. She's at film school. She wants to be a director."

"Really," said Stella. "How funny. My husband is a director of documentaries."

"Yes," he said, "I know. I told her that you were married to him, and she had heard of a famous documentary he made in the 1960s about hookers."

"It was the 1980s," she said, bristling at the implication that she was married to an old man. She did not wish to discuss Charles with him and so said, "So what were you thinking about buying?"

"Last year, I got her a traffic light. I bought it from the council and wired it up for her. We had a joke about whether our relationship was on or off—whether the light was red or green. But I don't think she really liked it. I think she must have got rid of it, as it doesn't seem to be in her flat anymore."

Stella laughed and said that she thought the traffic light sounded delightful. But mainly she thought that a man who went to such trouble to find a gift for a girlfriend that was a metaphor based on a private joke must have been deeply in love. This year, she noted, he had left it to the very last minute before buying her anything at all.

The taxi pulled up outside their office. Stella paid and took a receipt, and they both walked through the revolving glass doors, which rotated slowly in order to prevent heat loss, and into the marble reception. As they got out at the thirteenth floor, James was waiting to go down.

"Where have you been?" he asked. "Haven't you seen my e-mails?"

Stella realized that she had not looked at her BlackBerry for two hours. "What's happened?"

"Russia," he said.

Bella

James emerged from his office, marched past Bella, and said to Anthea: "Any idea if anyone in the department speaks Russian? I need to get something translated from the Russian newswires."

"I do," Bella said.

Anthea stared, and James raised his eyebrows.

"I studied it at university," she said.

"You never said you had a degree in Russian."

It showed how carefully he had looked at her file. Her languages had been one of the things that had helped her to get this job, though in all of her four years no one had ever asked her to use them.

"Come," he said.

So she went back into his room, and on his screen were items taken from the Russian newspaper *Vedomosti*. Bella sat at his desk and started to translate slowly.

"It says: 'On Monday, the Federal'...something or other, natural resources agency?" James nodded, and Bella went on: "'demanded that building of two pipeline sections by Atlantic Energy be stopped immediately because of the failure of the operator to follow Russian environmental law.' Does that make sense?"

"Perfect sense," he said. "What else?"

"It says that 'in a television interview, Valery Golubev from Gazprom said the CEO of Atlantic Energy was behaving like Goebbels in the spreading of propaganda.'"

"Lying bastard," said James. "Go on, Bella—you're a star." He moved around behind his chair, where she was perched, and leaned over her as she went on:

"'The field contains oil reserves of one hundred and fifty million tons and gas reserves of five hundred billion cubic meters and—'"

"Thank you," he said, interrupting her. "That's enough for now—I'd better go, or I'll be late for the press briefing."

Bella felt dashed. She would have liked to go on translating for him forever—doing something that he could not do and being admired for it.

She got up to leave, and he said, "I could print some more of this out and you can come with me in the cab and translate as we go. Would you mind?"

In the cab, James was talking on his mobile to Stephen.

"Have you seen what is coming out of the Gazprom press conference in Moscow?...The new chief has accused you of behaving like Goebbels—"

James held the phone slightly away from his ear to protect it from the stream of abuse that was pouring out. "I know," he said, "I know...Yes; quite inexcusable. But we are bound to get questions on this. I assume you want me to play it down?"

While James talked, Bella imagined what it might be like to put her head against the shoulder of his gray cashmere coat and thought it would be very nice indeed. He was not handsome, certainly. But there was a solidity to him, a powerfulness, that she didn't find unattractive.

At the press briefing, he sat on a raised platform and Bella took a seat in the back row, behind thirty journalists. She watched him calmly tell them that the Russians had revoked the license on spurious environmental grounds. He explained that the central problem was that the noise of building the new platform was interfering with the hearing of whales. Then one of the journalists asked:

"What is the company's response to the Russian allegation that Stephen Hinton is like Goebbels?"

James nodded solemnly and said: "On the specifics of that allegation, we do not deem it worthy of a reply. However, on the broader question: This is not about schoolboy taunts. This is about getting our licenses back into play, proving that our environmental record is second to none, and getting on with the discussions of the sale of our stake on a fair basis."

When they got back into a cab, Bella wanted to tell him that if anyone ever accused her of being a Nazi, she'd want him on her side defending her. But she decided it would be presumptuous, so she said nothing.

He took his BlackBerry from his pocket, checked his messages, and put it back. The taxi moved forward slowly. As he didn't say anything, Bella said:

"You know that course you asked me about? I know it sounds a bit trivial given all that's going on, but I've found something that sounds more fun—and more useful—than doing Shakespeare, or whatever. It's going to a hotel kitchen and cooking—"

"*Cooking?*"

He frowned at her over the top of his reading glasses, and Bella, fearing his disapproval, started to gabble.

"It's all about working in teams under stressful conditions in a kitchen. I mean, I know it sounds stupid in a way, because I don't really see how cutting up leeks or whatever is going to help all that much, but everyone ends up eating the food they've made and getting quite drunk. So maybe that's how they bond—"

James let out a loud laugh. "I can't boil an egg," he said. "It's shaming, but it's true. I used to be able to, but my wife deskilled me years ago."

So Anthea had been right on this point, but Bella felt her spirits fall a little in a way she didn't understand. Why would she mind if he talked about his wife? She knew he had one, and what did she suppose they ate, baked beans?

The taxi crawled up Northumberland Avenue and into Trafalgar Square, and Bella looked out of the window and saw a couple pressed together in a passionate embrace. James seemed to have observed this, too, but he said nothing. The lights changed, and the taxi moved on.

"Have you spent much time in Russia?" he asked.

Bella explained that for the second year at university she had been sent there, but soon after she'd arrived she'd found she was pregnant and come home and that after Millie had been born, she hadn't finished her degree.

"Is your husband a linguist?"

Bella wanted to laugh. Was this how he saw her? As a woman not ambitious enough to have finished her degree and to have settled into a little secretarial work to ease the boredom while her linguist husband used his languages to greater effect?

And then she thought of Xan and his knowledge of Russia. This amounted to a vodka-drinking spree when he had gone out to see her after she had phoned from Veronezh to tell him that she was pregnant. That evening had ended with him lying on the lino of the student hostel, being sick through his nostrils, and her crying and telling him to get out of her life.

"No," she said. "No, he isn't. I'm not married." And then, to forestall any further questions about a partner, she said: "I'm a single mother."

"I see," he said, and got out his BlackBerry.

The rest of the journey passed in silence.

Stella

Stella was going to Moscow. There wasn't much point in this, as it wasn't a project that she was involved in and there were already twelve people from AE going—three engineers and six geologists and the head of legal counsel as well as James and Stephen. In addition, there was a professor of marine biology from the London School of Economics, three environmental consultants, four civil servants, three corporate lawyers, and two translators.

Stephen had insisted that Stella fly out with him, as he had something he wished to discuss with her on the flight. Then he would have his meetings with the Gazprom chief as well as with representatives from the environmental agency the following day, and Stella and James would fly back with him afterward. The others would get an internal flight to Siberia to look at the platforms and assess the evidence of environmental damage.

Stella sat in a wide first-class seat next to the CEO, while the other members of the party made their way down the aisle to business class beyond. This arrangement suited no one. Stella did not want to be sitting next to her boss for the whole four-hour flight, as it meant she could neither sleep nor read a novel. The other members of the party took this as a sign of favoritism and felt aggrieved.

"Fancy seeing you here," said the senior engineer, leering at her. "Stephen has kept the eye candy all for himself."

Stella looked at him coldly; she was used to such taunts from engineers, and they no longer upset her. Stephen pulled a pile of papers from his briefcase and started to flip through them. He scanned the environmental summary that James had prepared for him, then shifted in his seat so that he had turned his body toward hers. Stella looked at his narrow hips and gold belt buckle and shuddered.

"Stella," he said, "I've got a proposal to make to you. I'm really excited about it, and I hope you will be, too."

Stella smiled anxiously, knowing that his profession of excitement was not necessarily a promising sign.

"I am proposing to make some changes to my top team," he went on. "Our business is getting ever more complicated, globally and strategically. What we excel at is the functional side of the business. We have the best engineers, geologists—even economists." He smiled at her, revealing a set of perfect white fronts fitted on a recent visit to the United States.

"You are too kind," Stella said.

"What we need are visionary leaders within the business whose task it is to break down those silos and ensure that we have joined up thinking at all levels. As CEO, this is my role, but I can't do it single-handedly. So what I propose is to create a new position that I hope you will fill. Your title would be chief of staff, and you would head up my private office. You would be deputized for me in all strategic matters, back me up, and advise me."

He looked at her with an energy and intensity that Stella did not find altogether pleasant. She felt, as she had felt on all previous occasions in her life when she had been offered a promotion or a challenge, a small stab of panic.

When Stella finally got to her hotel room that night, she was exhausted. Dinner had gone on interminably, and she had sat between a pair of thick-necked Russian oil magnates, one of whom ignored her completely in favor of the impossibly beautiful teenage model on his other side, who seemed not to object to having her breasts fondled by a sausage-fingered man.

James had showed no interest in the Russian model who had been placed next to him, and every time Stella looked up at him, he was looking down at the BlackBerry in his lap. Stephen, on the other hand, was evidently delighted by the six-foot blond nineteen-year-old who was caressing his thigh under the table, though he was pretending to be unmoved.

Once alone in her ludicrously opulent room, Stella arranged herself among the silk cushions on the bed and opened her laptop to do her e-mail. There was a long, funny message from Clemmie telling her about her day at school, signed off with "Loveyaloads xxx." Stella had been brought up in a household where no one would have dreamed of telling any other member that they loved them; such things were taken for granted. Even though she knew her daughter had picked up the habit of emotional incontinence from trashy TV shows, she nevertheless was pleased and amused by the warmth of the sign-off. She also thought, not for the first time, that it was easier to communicate with one's teenage daughter by e-mail than face-to-face.

She looked farther down the list, and there were two messages from Rhys. Stella clicked on the first one.

Hi,

Hope KGB haven't got you. Beware honey traps and Russian gigolos. Nothing happening here. V dull without you. I'd like you to know that I've spent a vast amount of time today collating data for your paper on our internal cost of capital, so have been very well behaved.

Only thing to report is that have noticed Beate sniffs all the time. Have decided she has a coke habit.

Cheers, Rhys

And then another one sent about ten minutes later:

Hi Stella

am concerned that previous message may have sounded a tad unprofessional. Sorry. R

Stella read them again and smiled. It was unprofessional, but also funny. Still, she wasn't going to reply. She brushed her teeth and got into the big bed, whose oyster satin sheets felt unpleasantly slippery against her brushed cotton pajamas. She slithered around and could not sleep, the dumpling and vodka mingling uneasily in her stomach. The conversation on the plane was troubling her, and she was also worried that the permission slip for Finn's skiing trip had to be handed in the next morning. So she turned on the lamp by her bed and sat up.

It would only be ten at home, so she called and Charles answered.

"How's Russia?" he said.

"Russia's fine, but I'm worried about Finn's permission slip. I think it's in the kitchen—can you make sure it's signed tomorrow?"

"Okay," he said. "When are you back?"

"Probably in time for supper tomorrow. I've been offered a new job."

"Oh? I'm watching the football with Finn."

"Tell him to go to bed. And give him a kiss from me."

She put down the phone, slid into the bed again, and turned off the light but found herself even more awake than before.

Maybe she would type a quick reply to Rhys, just to reassure him. So she sat up against the cushions and turned on her laptop again, but the computer would not let her log on to her AE e-mail. Undeterred, she opened up her Hotmail account instead and typed:

Dear Rhys

Thank you for your warnings. There have been no suspicious young men, though just had extraordinary dinner with Russians. Gorgeous women on tap for Stephen and James, though both doing their best to show no interest. I had to talk to bruiser from Gazprom and had too much caviar and feel sick.

You might also like the detail that before dinner we met in Stephen's room for a briefing and such is atmosphere of trust that we wrote things to each other on whiteboards, fearing that the room was tapped. I daresay there were cameras in there too, but in that case Russians will have got an eyeful of twelve dithering Brits with no decent game plan. Sat next to Stephen on plane on way out, and he has plan for me to leave economics and work directly with him. Please keep that under your hat, as not at all sure what I'll do.

And no, I don't think Beate has a coke habit.

Stella

She read through what she had written and sent it, feeling uncomfortable about just how much she had enjoyed writing it. She had also told Rhys much more about the trip than she had told Charles; but then Charles hadn't asked, or if he had asked, hadn't really wanted to know. Outside she could hear the funny whine of Russian sirens. She hadn't slept for thirty-six hours but felt wide awake, and the inside of her head felt dry. She flicked through the telly channels and watched Gordon Brown on CNN explaining why he wasn't going to call for an election after all.

Her BlackBerry winked its red light at her. There was a message from Charles:

Can't find the form—where did you say it
was? xC

And one from Rhys:

Hi Stella

V excited to get your message. Was fearing
that unprofessional behavior might have sent
you straight to Russell to make further
complaints re unsatisfactory trainee. Well
it's a rough life...caviar, prostitutes...my
heart goes out to you all. New job sounds
v exciting...I'm now sitting in a bar in
Covent Garden waiting for my girlfriend.

```
In the end got her new ipod for her b'day,
which she claimed to be delighted with.
```

```
What time is it there?
```

```
R
```

Stella sat up in bed to study this. The cocky confidence that once enraged her now delighted her. She smiled down at the little screen and read the message again. Then she messaged back:

```
Will tell you about job when I'm back. Enjoy
drink. It's late here, so must sleep.
```

And instantly the reply came:

```
Night night.
```

Bella

Bella was sifting through the messages in James's in-box. Nearly two hundred had arrived since yesterday, mostly things that he had been pointlessly copied on. But then she came on a message with a red exclamation mark by it sent by Russell with the subject line "Headcount." Bella opened this and read:

James—I have been tasked by Michael Evans to conduct a head-count audit throughout the ER function looking to find synergies resulting from the merger with Press Relations. It appears that you have two executive assistants, which is no longer in accordance with the operating plan. Can you revert to me on this asap?

Best, Russell

Bella read it twice.

"Have you seen the e-mail from HR about head count?" she asked Anthea.

Anthea nodded. "It's classic," she said. "He has never seen fit to follow the rule book, and in my experience of this company, if you don't do it by the book, it bites you on the ankle in the end."

The books and ankles created a surreal picture in Bella's mind, which distracted her from a more troubling idea: Anthea was pleased by the memo and wanted Bella gone.

The phone went, and Anthea got there first. "James Home," it said on the display.

"James Staunton's office," she said. "Oh, hello, Hillary...Well, no, I haven't spoken to him this morning, but I'm expecting him to call in any moment now...If his mobile is off, then I imagine he's in meetings...Is all well?...Ah, I see. Oh dear...Well, I will tell him when he calls."

Anthea put down the phone. "That was Mrs. J," she said. "Completely hysterical. She's gone and lost some tickets to their son's play tonight."

The phone started to ring again, and this time Bella answered. It was James.

"Have you spoken to your wife?" she asked.

"Not recently," he said.

"Well, she just rang to say she's lost the tickets to your son's concert tonight. I think she's rather upset—"

"Oh God," he said, his voice sounding heavy. "I've got the tickets. They are in the top of my desk. Bella, can you help her? She is a little... fragile...at the moment. Can you bike them to her, or maybe, if you've got time, take them yourself?"

Bella went into his office and opened the top drawer. It was almost empty: a packet of Nurofen, and a neat line of pens, and the tickets in precisely the place he'd said they would be. Bella closed the drawer, but then—without any clear idea of what she was doing—found herself opening the next one down. There was a file labeled EXPENSES, and below that another marked RECEIPTS—PERSONAL. She opened the folder and saw one was for lunch at the National Portrait Gallery restaurant, dated three months earlier.

This rang a bell. She knew from her reading of Julia's e-mails that he had taken her there. She looked at all the other receipts, and all were for lunch or dinner, six in all and over a period of four months. Was that all it had been?

"Having a snoop?"

Bella wheeled around to see Anthea standing at the door. She shoved the folder back into the drawer and picked up the tickets.

"No," she said. "I'm just getting the tickets. He wants me to take them over to their house in Wimbledon."

"Why not bike them?"

"He asked me to do it. He says she's fragile."

Anthea stared at her disapprovingly but said nothing.

Bella got out of the cab outside number 16 Willowdale Crescent. There were stucco pillars on either side of the front door, and through the large bay window on the ground floor she could see a handsome rocking horse.

Bella rang the china bell, which made an old-fashioned ring deep inside the house. After a while, she heard slow footsteps crossing the hall. A woman with a slightly puffy face, almost unrecognizable as the smiling one in the picture, opened the door and looked at Bella in surprise, as if she had forgotten that she was coming.

"I'm Bella," said Bella. "And I've brought the tickets."

"Ah yes," said Hillary. "Thanks for coming all this way." She took the tickets and then hesitated. "Would you like a cup of tea?"

She didn't look cold, or mad, or a handful, as Anthea had warned she would be. Instead she looked vague and detached and oddly diffident for the mistress of such a large and beautiful house.

Bella badly wanted to go in and look around. She was curious about where people lived and thought the fridge and the bathroom cabinet usually held as many clues to what someone was like as their faces did.

But standing on her boss's doorstep, she had a strong sense of being somewhere she did not belong.

"I'd better get back to the office. But could I just have a glass of water?"

Hillary opened the door and led Bella over the pale wooden floor and into the kitchen. There was every outward sign of the cooking that James had talked about. There were mixers and a pasta machine and a granite island with saucepans hanging from an old wooden clothes dryer. But there was no smell of food or evidence of any meals ever having been made, and all the implements looked new. Bella thought of her own Ikea kitchen, the whole bought for 360 quid, including the sink.

Hillary produced a heavy glass tumbler and poured some Badoit into it.

"Lovely kitchen," Bella said.

Hillary smiled weakly.

"You've got some amazing gadgets. I wouldn't have the first idea what to do with most of them. I'm really hopeless at cooking. The only thing I can make is pasta, and even then all I do is boil it and then empty some sauce on the top. Do you do masses of cooking?"

Hillary gave this question a lot of thought, as if struggling to remember the answer, and then said, "Yes, I suppose I do."

"The reason I asked," said Bella, "is that James has asked me to research team-building courses, and I've found one where they will go and cook together to get to know each other, or bond..."

James's name hung in the air between them. It sounded wrong on Bella's lips spoken so casually, here in his house.

Bella took a sip of water, and Hillary said: "So he has two secretaries now."

Bella cringed at the word *secretary* but didn't correct her. "Yes," she agreed, though she didn't say that perhaps not for much longer.

"I imagine he's delighted with the arrangement," Hillary remarked.

Was she bitter? Or possibly amused in a patronizing way? And why did she have to imagine what he felt? Didn't they talk?

Bella put down the glass and said she had better get going. Hillary showed her to the door, and Bella stood outside in the street and looked around her. Hillary hadn't offered to get her a taxi; she didn't know which way the tube was, and the neighborhood was so quiet that there was no one around to ask.

Stella

On the flight back from Russia, Stella asked James what she should do about the new job. She was well aware that James would be jealous but had worked out a long time ago that the best way to take the sting out of the competition was to act as if James were unquestionably the senior partner. As long as she deferred to him, he was more than civilized and lavished his wisdom upon her.

So Stella explained about the job, and James's face darkened for a second, but then, just as she had expected, he recovered himself and assumed the air of a wise doctor prescribing medicine to a sick patient. Lucidly, he laid out the pros and the cons. The pros he dispensed with quickly.

"You'd see more of the CEO, if that's what you want. I also assume that this would mean more money and arguably might look good on your CV."

But then he settled into the cons, of which he found a larger number. He said it didn't sound like a well-defined role. He pointed out that Stella was a gifted economist and that her intellect might not be satisfied in a more administrative job.

"It would also make your position in the company more vulnerable," he said. "If you are someone who Stephen has expressly promoted, if he falls, then you will fall with him."

The more Stella listened to this negative case, the more positive about the job she became.

When she got home that night, she asked Charles what she should do. He was standing over the chopping board, beating ginger and coriander into a pulp for a marinade, and Stella explained the pros and cons of the job to his hunched back.

"You must do whatever you want to do," he said, bashing a clove of garlic with the back of a knife.

And she replied that she didn't know what she wanted—that was the trouble. He then quoted a university tutor who had said that the harder a decision was to make, the less it mattered which way you decided.

In twenty years of marriage, he must have said this to her at least a hundred times, and each time she had disagreed. It might be true logically, but in her experience if a decision was hard to make, that was because it was terribly important to get the outcome right.

Stella got to work before eight a.m. the next morning to find that Rhys was in already. The cleaner was just finishing, lugging the vacuum out of Stella's office.

"Hello," said Stella. "How are you? How is your daughter getting along?" On another early morning, this woman had told Stella that she had a daughter who was the same age as Finn and who was doing exceptionally well at school.

"She's working so hard."

"Wonderful," said Stella, looking toward Rhys. He had taken off his jacket, and his shirt, which was white with a thin gray stripe, had been carefully ironed. Had he ironed it himself? Stella found herself wondering.

As soon as the cleaner had gone, Rhys got up and wandered over. "Hello," he said.

"What are you doing in this early?" Stella asked. The question came out sounding rather more accusatory than she had intended.

"Loads of work," he said.

"I'm going downstairs to get a coffee. Do you want anything?"

"I'll come with you."

In the canteen, they queued at the coffee machine, and then instead of taking their cardboard cups back upstairs, they hesitated by the sofas in what the facilities manager laughably called the "chill-out zone."

Rhys sat on the edge of the sofa, and Stella sat next to him, feeling self-conscious and wishing that there were a table between them.

"So what's up with this job," he said.

She repeated what Stephen had told her and explained that it would mean being closer to the decision-making heart of the company.

"It sounds great," Rhys said, looking at her with an earnestness that she had not seen before.

"I'm not sure if I want it," she said.

"But why not?" he demanded. "It's a massive promotion..."

Stella wasn't sure what she was doing sitting on this sofa and allowing a trainee to interrogate her like this. It was none of his business whether she took the job or not. But at the same time, she could not help being flattered that he was taking such a keen interest in her career. Unlike James or even Charles, Rhys appeared genuinely to want to see her promoted.

"I mean," Rhys was saying, "it's a lot more power. And I assume it'd be a lot more money...?"

"You may be right," Stella said doubtfully. In fact, she had not even thought to ask Stephen whether it would be more money or not.

"Doesn't that matter to you?"

"No, it doesn't. I don't think I'm really interested in power or money. I used to be, but now I think I've got enough of both."

He looked at her, his eyes narrowing. "So what *are* you interested in?"

"I'm not sure. I suppose I've never asked myself such a blunt question. But I guess I'm interested in having some control over my life, and in never being bored and—I suppose most of all—being thought to be good at what I'm doing. Does that sound priggish?"

"Yes," he said. "Disgustingly." He laughed, and so did she. Then he added: "I also don't believe it."

Stella stopped laughing. Was he claiming to know her better than she knew herself? "You may not believe it," she said, a new coolness in her voice, "but it happens to be the case."

"Sorry," he said. "It is just really weird to me. I've always wanted to be incredibly successful and to make a lot of money. When I was a kid I used to sell crisps at a hundred percent markup in the playground, and at Oxford I used to sell my essays to posh thickos who couldn't write their own. I suppose I just about understand that you aren't interested in money. I mean, if you've always had it, then maybe you take it for granted..."

Stella winced at the chippy edge to his voice.

"But I don't believe that you're not ambitious," he went on.

"Really," Stella protested, "I don't think I am. Well, I must be a bit, or I wouldn't be where I am. But when new things are offered to me, I never really want to take them. It's not that I feel I should be with my children more—though that does come into it. It's more to do with fear. I'm really terrified of things that I think I won't be able to do."

"You're *frightened*," he repeated, looking at her incredulously.

Stella felt she had gone too far. She didn't want him to see her weakness, so she asked: "What about you? What do you really want?"

"After I left Oxford, I didn't apply to any of the jobs that my friends applied to, which was partly because none of the jobs appealed to me, but also because my mum was ill and I needed to be in Wales to be close to her. I got involved in this property business run by a friend of my cousin's, and we made shedloads renovating warehouses in Cardiff and Swansea, and at one point, we were both worth about five million pounds on paper. We were going to cash in, but then Northern Rock happened and we lost everything and the company went bust. It was a crap time, and now I'm playing safe and doing the company man bit for a while."

Stella bristled at the idea that he was playing safe at AE, that it was the place to be when one's grander ambitions had failed.

"I must go and do some work," she said suddenly, standing. "There's a mountain of e-mails waiting for me. What I was going to say was would you like to come to supper with us next week? I was planning to ask Beate, too. Do bring your girlfriend—Rosie? I know that Charles would love to discuss film school with her."

"Rosa," he said. "And yes, thanks, that'd be great."

Bella

Bella had been looking forward to James's return from Russia, and that morning she had got dressed in a new pair of black trousers and a pink shirt and applied two coats of mascara. When she got into the office, she found her boss bent over his e-mails, moving his lower jaw from side to side in the way he did when he was concentrating. He did not look up at her arrival.

Presently, she heard a crash. James had slammed his fist down on his desk. "Bloody hell! Do you know anything about this?"

He got up from his desk and came to face her accusingly. "This is insane. I'm told that I'm not allowed two PAs. And at the same time as Stephen is beefing up his department, taking on any number of bag carriers. I'm expected to perform the jobs that used to be done by two people...and then I'm told I can't have one more sodding person to help with the admin."

Bella said nothing, as he didn't seem to be talking to her.

"I'm sorry," he said an hour or so later. "That was a mad rant. And I meant to say thank you very much indeed for taking the tickets to my wife. I know she greatly appreciated it. In fact, she was much taken with you."

Bella thought this unlikely and said, "Well, I thought she seemed lovely." Which wasn't true either.

"In any case," she continued, "I'm completely cool with anger. My ex-partner used to lose it all the time and throw furniture around."

James laughed uneasily, not sure if she was joking. But Bella hadn't been joking; in fact, she had been putting a positive gloss on it. During one of his rages, Xan had punched a hole in the wall and come at Bella with a chair over his head and would have smashed it down on her if his mobile hadn't gone, distracting him for just long enough to allow her to get out of the way.

James went on: "I try to refrain from throwing furniture about. Still, I do find it aggravating to have arbitrary rules imposed on me by imbeciles, though what really made me angry about the edict is that for the first time in ages I have someone really intelligent working for me."

He looked at her briefly and then looked away. Bella didn't know what to say. She picked up her iPod to hide her confusion and carefully started winding the headphones around the body of it, waiting for him to go. But he didn't go. He went on standing there.

"What do you listen to on that?" he asked.

She pushed the gadget toward him, and he scrolled down through the names. "Who are these people? Franz Ferdinand? Kings of Leon? Who is Leon?"

Bella laughed. "I've no idea, but they're good. Want to listen?"

She offered him her headphones, which he held to his ears without putting them in, as if doing so would be too intimate a gesture. She clicked play, and he heard the last thing she had been listening to. Through the crackle of the earphones, Bella could hear Franz Ferdinand singing about leather hips and sticky hair.

Bella turned it off hastily. "What sort of music do you like?" she asked.

"Mostly classical, but I'm fond of some pop songs that were written before you were born. Van Morrison, Dylan, the Police—"

At this moment Anthea got back from her lunch break, and as she came in, James put down the iPod, moved away from Bella's desk, and said in a quite different tone of voice: "Can you move this afternoon's departmental meeting back by half an hour to three thirty?"

Stella

Stella really didn't have time for lunch with her friend Emily. The head of the chemicals business was up in arms over a paper she had written arguing that AE's investments in chemicals should be evaluated using a higher internal cost of capital due to their more risky nature. Stella needed to take some time to calm him down. There were also meetings taking up most of the afternoon, in between which she was expected to find time to complete the cumbersome annual appraisal forms for each of the thirty-two members of her team.

In addition, Stella felt she ought to go to the gym. She hadn't been for a long time, and that morning as she'd got dressed, she'd noticed how her bottom was collapsing and how the flesh on her upper arms was hanging slackly. She used not to think that she'd mind about this sort of thing, but now she found she did.

Stella couldn't cancel Emily—again—as it would mean having to put up with her being childish and huffy and could well take several months of humoring to bring her round again.

Stella got into a taxi to take her to the Holborn branch of Pizza Express, chosen for being halfway between them. To have made Emily travel to Moorgate would have meant acknowledging that Stella's time was the more valuable of the two, and that would never have done.

As they faced each other over their pizzas, they moved briskly through the usual agenda of children, houses, mutual friends, and work. Stella told Emily about her new job, which she was now feeling inclined to accept. Emily pulled a face.

"Bad idea," she said. "Last time we sat here, I listened to you saying how you were really stressed with how much you had on. I know you're only happy when you push yourself to the limits—and that's brilliant—but there are costs, you know. It's not that you ought to see more of your kids—I'm not into guilt trips at all. But as your oldest friend, I sometimes worry that you never make time for *you*."

Stella was used to her friend's advice and had taken a positive decision a long time ago not to let it annoy her. Emily had taken voluntary redundancy six months earlier from the bank where she had worked, more out of boredom and a desire to increase the value of her divorce settlement than out of any wish to spend more time with her children. Her desire for her friend to lead a slower life was nakedly self-interested.

"Well," Stella said lightly, "there's no need to be concerned. I'm fine. How are things with you? Any glimmers on the love front?"

"You won't believe this," Emily said, "but I've been doing Internet dating. At first, I went on Match.com, but the best bet was a computer scientist from Rutland who said he was 'under five feet ten' but turned out to be five five. But now I've been on an affairs website, and I'm dating married men, who are infinitely more eligible."

"*Really*," said Stella. "Is that wise?"

"I knew you'd disapprove."

"I don't disapprove," Stella lied. "I just can't see it ending terribly well for anyone."

"Ending? There hasn't even been a beginning yet. It's just that there are millions of men on the site who aren't failures or sados. They don't want to leave their wives, but they want a bit of excitement. I'm meeting someone tomorrow night who's a hedge fund manager. I looked him up on Google, and he's loaded. Unfortunately I also saw his picture on Google images and he's got enormous jowls and his teeth look a bit suspect."

Stella laughed.

"I don't know if I really want to have an affair with him," Emily went on, "but it's been nice e-mailing him. Just having someone to think about makes life so much less humdrum. I've reached the conclusion that, in the end, it's not really about sex, is it? It's about fantasy, about having somewhere to go in your head."

"Yes," said Stella. "I know what you mean."

She must have said it with more feeling than she intended, as Emily replied: "Do you?"

"No," said Stella. And then she said, "Yes. I mean, not really. Sort of."

Emily gave her friend a look of amused indulgence. "What the hell, Stel?"

And then Stella found herself telling her childhood friend something that she hadn't planned to say, something that until that moment she hadn't even admitted to herself. "Okay, I do have a fantasy. But it is tiny, and really silly. It's someone at work. We send each other e-mails."

"What sort of e-mails?" Emily asked.

"Oh," said Stella, "nothing special. You know: things about work and what we are doing, and our attitude to our careers—that sort of thing."

"Sounds a pretty dull fantasy," said Emily.

Stella should perhaps have left it there. But once she had broached the subject of Rhys, she found that she wanted—needed—to tell Emily all about him.

"In fact the e-mails are a bit more than that. Yesterday I counted and he sent me eighteen, and since I went to Russia last month he and I have got into the habit of sending the messages on Hotmail rather than on the AE system, as my PA sees my messages and would think it was odd. It *is* odd, I suppose, but it's innocent odd. Most of the messages are jokes—he's really funny. He also keeps on popping into my office for a chat. And in the mornings we both get in early and have coffee together."

"Jesus," said Emily. "That doesn't sound innocent to me. Where does Charles fit into any of this?"

"Don't be stupid, Em. I'm not saying that there is anything going on. It's just a distraction from the tedium of the office. It's a harmless flirtation. That's all."

Emily seemed mollified by this and said: "Well, in that case, you're lucky. I remember when I had a crush on the senior vice president in office. When we were working on the same deals and going off for flirty drinks—they were some of the happiest times I've ever had at work."

"But then you married him," Stella said. "And that—I think we have to agree—was less happy."

Emily gave a grim laugh.

"But in any case," Stella went on, "this is different. I'm not going to have an affair with him, let alone marry him. But even so, the sad truth is that I know I should put a stop to it. It's really distracting, and doesn't feel terribly professional, as I'm his boss and he's quite a bit younger—"

"You're his *boss*? Oh dear. And how much younger is he?"

Emily looked disapproving again, and Stella started to regret having said anything at all. "Quite a lot," she said vaguely.

"How much," insisted Emily.

"Do you really want to know?"

"Yes, I do, and I can't see why you are being so coy about it."

"He's twenty-seven."

"*Twenty-seven?* Jesus, Stella. Well, you're safe, then. It's not exactly as if he's going to fancy you, is he?"

Stella was wounded, as indeed she was meant to be. No meeting between the two old friends was complete without a few minor injuries inflicted on each other. Stella pointing out that Emily's choice of husband was less than ideal. Emily suggesting that Stella was too driven.

But whereas the earlier stabs left no mark, the wound from this latest injury went deeper. And the reason it hurt, Stella knew perfectly well, was that it was true. She fished in her bag for her wallet to perform the neat splitting of the bill and, looking down, saw her hands looking old and gnarled. On her third knuckle was a small brown mark. Is that a mole, or could it be a liver spot? she wondered.

Bella

"Where's James?"

"The CEO was standing looking down at Bella crossly, as if her boss's failure to be seated behind his desk were somehow her fault.

"He's got a breakfast meeting with analysts from Merrill and Citi, and then will be back here for a meeting with the trainees at ten thirty. Would you like me to tell him to call you as soon as he's back?"

"Please," he said abruptly, and turned tail.

When James reappeared, he was looking cross.

"The CEO wants to see you," Anthea said.

"What about?"

"He didn't say," she said.

James disappeared down the corridor and returned ten minutes later, looking even more bad-tempered than before.

"It's some bloody crackpot scheme to have our share price and the oil price displayed in real time in reception on an old oil barrel. I can't think of anything more stupid, but he's wedded to the idea. Would you mind looking into it, Bella?"

He returned to his office, leaving Bella in silent contemplation of how on earth she was meant to go about getting a barrel into reception.

The office she shared with Anthea was positioned just outside a meeting room, and that morning she was distracted from her worries about the barrel by watching the trainees arrive for their ten thirty meeting with James. At ten twenty-nine, she saw Rhys walk past, put his nose through the door of the meeting room, see it empty, about-turn, and go into the men's toilets. After a while, two others approached the room and then retreated to the corridor. At exactly ten thirty, Beate went straight in and sat down. The other trainees started to circle, and by ten thirty-four enough of them seemed to be outside the door together, and they all went in at once. A few seconds later, Rhys sauntered in looking casual, followed by James himself, clutching the printouts that she had just photocopied for him.

Bella watched this charade with amusement. It was a game that she often observed her bosses playing, the aim being never to be kept waiting by anyone of your own rank or below. To see the trainees already at it impressed her. They learn quickly, she thought, and Rhys, by arriving later than his peers but just before his superior, was showing the greatest leadership potential of the bunch.

That day, Bella had arranged to have lunch with Karen, her oldest friend. They had taken to seeing each other every month or two, which was nice; or rather it should have been nice, but in fact these meetings often left Bella feeling low afterward for reasons she could never quite put her finger on.

Karen and Bella had been best friends in school. They had been the pretty ones and the clever ones, and their friendship had been cemented by a fierce competitiveness. Until they were about sixteen, Bella had had the upper hand. But by the time they were starting A levels, Karen had pulled ahead and went on pulling ahead. She had got into Bristol, and Bella had gone to Bangor. Karen had gone out with a succession of glamorous men, and Bella had gone out with Xan. One path had led ever upward toward a traineeship at the BBC, the other had dipped and fallen into nappies and the absorption and tedium of raising a child on your own.

As soon as Bella saw her friend swinging into Wagamama, she noticed she was shining. There could be only one reason for looking like that: Karen was in love.

There is, Bella realized, something horrible about seeing your girl-friends in love. It is a bereavement of sorts; they are floating off on a boat of happiness, you are standing with both feet on the hard shingle of the shore. They wave happily at you, not really caring whether you wave back or not.

Breathlessly, Karen told Bella about her new boyfriend, who was a music producer and totally fit and funny and a really nice guy and really into her. He'd arranged for her to have backstage passes at all the festivals that summer, and she was going to Glastonbury and Latitude and Sziget.

Karen continued in this vein for some time, with Bella smiling and nodding and saying, "Sounds great," and, "Lucky you!" in all the right places. Eventually, when she'd said all she had to say, Karen asked: "How's Millie?"

"Fine," said Bella. "She's brave and lovely despite Xan's heroic efforts to fuck her up. She's doing really well at school—"

"That's great," said Karen without conviction. And then she asked: "How's your love life?"

"Zero," said Bella.

"Can't be zero. You aren't trying."

"I *am* trying," said Bella. "It's just really hard. I never meet anyone since all I do is work and look after Millie."

"That's *awful*," said Karen. "I really need to rack my brains for some-one I can fix you up with."

Bella did not enjoy being cast in the role of someone incapable of finding a boyfriend, and to silence her friend she said: "There's a guy I vaguely like at work."

"I knew there must be *someone*," said Karen. "Is he gorgeous?"

"Um," said Bella. "Not really, no. He's quite a lot older."

"Older guys can be sexy," Karen said. "Remember that Irish script-writer I went out with—he was *thirty-five*. He was sex on legs."

Bella hadn't remembered, as there had been so many of Karen's boy-friends. She nodded, keeping to herself the fact that James was ten years older still. "Mine isn't sexy at all. At least not in an obvious way. I'm not sure if I fancy him—sometimes I think I do, and sometimes I'm not so sure. It's more that he is really clever and there is something powerful about him..."

The conversation was making Bella feel peculiar. Saying something had changed it. Until then, James had been a shadow in her mind, but telling Karen about it was making the shadow seem real.

"That sounds cool," Karen said encouragingly. "So what's the prob-lem?"

"Um," said Bella, "he's my boss. And he's also married."

"What? Are you joking? I never would have thought you'd do the naff female cliché of PA shagging her boss. Unless you are doing it ironically, in a postfeminist sort of way?"

"This isn't about irony or feminism," Bella said crossly. "It isn't about anything. I'm not shagging him. All I'm saying is that I'm just saying I quite like him—or I like him more than I expected to."

"You've always been a crap picker. But with Xan, at least he was gor-geous. This man isn't sexy, and as he's your boss and married, if you do anything with him, you'd be putting your job on the line."

"You're not listening," said Bella, who was much regretting having said anything. "I'm not going to have an affair with him, for lots of reasons. It's just a fantasy that makes the days drag a bit less. He's not perfect, but then who is? Honestly, Karen, I can't explain it. It is about how he makes me feel."

"What is it, a sort of father thing? That you can rely on him the way that you couldn't on your own father? Your father had a thing for younger women, too, didn't he?"

Bella didn't want to hear Karen attacking her father. She was quite happy to attack him herself, but that was her right as his daughter. "Not being reliable wasn't the problem with Dad, as you well know. The attraction of James is, I think, how he looks at me. When I'm with him, I'm not a PA with big tits. He makes me feel like I'm the person that I'd like to be, rather than the person I am. Do you know what I mean?"

Karen frowned, indicating that she did not know what her friend meant at all.

"When I'm with him—when he's really talking to me—I'm clever. He makes me feel that I've got something to offer, as if I've got promise. He also laughs at my jokes—it's lovely having the power to make someone laugh. He's not particularly funny himself—in fact, he's quite serious. But he seems to think I'm funny."

"Hmm. Well, it sounds pretty dodgy as far as I can see," said Karen. "I hope you know what you're doing."

"I've already told you. I'm not doing anything."

Stella

Rhys arrived on the doorstep on the stroke of seven thirty. Stella was upstairs getting out of her work suit and into jeans. She had been trying on various tops, but all of them looked wrong. At the moment the doorbell went, she was getting out of an orange satin blouse, and even though it looked even less right than the others she had tried, there was no time to change it.

Clemmie opened the door and then, seeing her mother appear at the top of the stairs, looked her up and down and said disparagingly: "Very rock chick."

"You see what I have to put up with at home," Stella said to Rhys, who laughed uneasily.

Clemmie scowled. Rhys stood in the middle of the sitting room, looking around at the high ceiling and ornate overmantel mirror as if he were being shown it by an estate agent. Stella poured him some wine, which he took, and then he sat on the very edge of the deep cream sofa, his usual ease quite gone.

"Rosa should be here soon," he said, and at that moment there was a knock at the door.

But it wasn't Rosa, it was Beate and her management consultant boyfriend, Friedrich. Stella accepted the large bunch of pink-and-white flowers that Beate was bearing and showed them into the sitting room. Rhys got up and the four of them stood, marooned on the kilim rug, while Stella talked, rather too loudly and too fast, about Charles's passion for cooking, about the house, about the time she invited the Abu Dhabi deputy oil minister over. She could not remember ever feeling quite so awkward in her own house.

Rhys's girlfriend was the last to arrive. She was not at all as Stella had expected. She must have been nearly six feet, a good inch taller than Rhys, and with a mad tangle of black hair.

"Fab house," she said, coming in and kissing Stella on both cheeks with the easy physical intimacy of her generation. She blew Rhys a kiss, and he smiled and waved from the other side of the room but did not move from his spot.

Rosa's arrival allowed Stella to slip away into the kitchen, where Charles was removing some guinea fowl from the oven. "Go and talk to everyone," she hissed. "They see me all day—they're fed up with me. I'll bring the food in."

But Charles didn't like his wife interfering with his food, as he thought—with some justification—that she would spoil it. "Why did you ask them if you don't want to talk to them?" he asked.

"I don't know," she said. "I suppose I was trying to be friendly. It seemed like a good idea at the time."

At dinner, Rosa sat next to Charles and turned her wide, smiling face toward him as he held forth about filming in Wales. Stella always enjoyed hearing Charles talking to others—he was still so good at being charming when he put his mind to it. At the other end of the table, Rhys was chatting to the children. He had been asking Clemmie which clubs she went to, and even though at fourteen she was too young to go to any, she was enjoying being knowledgeable about which ones were cool.

Stella herself was left in the middle of the table to make conversation with Beate and Friedrich. She asked him about his work and listened to a deadpan discourse on the pro bono work he was doing for charities in the United States. He said that it was terribly unfair that consultants got a bad name when they were so interested in making a difference. Tiring of this, Stella asked them about their long-distance relationship and how they liked working three thousand miles away from each other. She told them that she and Charles had lived apart when he was filming in the United States when she was pregnant with Clemmie and how it had been one of the most successful times in their marriage.

Just as she was saying this, the conversation around the table died and Stella was aware of both her husband and Rhys looking at her.

"What are you saying about our successful marriage?" Charles asked.

"That it worked best when we didn't see each other," Stella replied.

He laughed and looked at her fondly and then turned back to Rosa. Stella was aware of Rhys's appraising glance.

"The place where we've been filming is the ugliest place on earth—but we've got great shots of grimy shops all boarded up. Even the pubs were mainly empty. We've captured a cinematic beauty in the bleakness."

Rhys had run out of anything further to say to Clemmie and so asked Charles where they were filming.

"In the armpit of the earth—a small place called Merthyr Tydfil."

There was a pause.

"I grew up there," Rhys said.

"Really," said Charles.

He didn't seem at all embarrassed. And Rhys didn't seem terribly put out, either: In fact, he agreed what a dump it was. Stella seemed to be the only person finding the conversation awkward, and she winced as Rhys wrote down his mother's phone number on a piece of paper, saying that he was sure she would love to be in the documentary, as she was always longing to get onto reality TV shows.

Beate, meanwhile, was asking Rosa why she wanted to go to film school, as if it were quite beyond her why anyone would want to do such a thing. Rosa smiled wanly and said that she always followed her heart; the nine-to-five had no appeal. Beate, failing to see that she had been slighted, asked a follow-up question about the employment prospects on graduation from film school.

Rosa had had enough and moved around to where Rhys was sitting and put her hand on his shoulder. "We've got to go now," she said.

Stella found she did not enjoy the sight of Rosa's possessive touch and got up to find their coats and show them to the door.

"Thanks *so* much for a great evening. Really enjoyed it. Amazing food," said Rosa, kissing her again on both cheeks.

"Thanks," Rhys said gruffly.

He was holding back, wondering whether to kiss her, and Stella was wondering the same thing. She had decided not, just as Rhys had reached the opposite decision and moved toward her. In her embarrassment, she moved her head the wrong way and he landed a kiss by the corner of her mouth.

"He's an odd guy, isn't he," Charles said as the two of them got into bed. "A bit ingratiating and chippy. Gorgeous girlfriend, though." He turned out the light and went straight to sleep.

Stella lay by his side, wide awake and running through the evening again in her mind. She could not dislodge the sensation of Rhys's lips, warm and smooth, touching her face.

Bella

Through the glass wall, Bella could see Anthea settling herself on James's sofa, legs crossed neatly, looking garish in a turquoise wraparound dress. This was her annual performance review, and she was holding forth and James was nodding and laughing.

Surely, Bella thought, he could not possibly be finding all that moronic drivel about sandwiches and stationery interesting, let alone amusing.

After about half an hour, Anthea emerged with the sort of straight face that meant things had gone entirely to her liking. "You can go through to the boardroom, Sir James will see you now," she said.

Bella smiled thinly at the imitation of the PA on *The Apprentice*. "Right," she said.

"Sit down, Bella," said James. "I don't like playing games, so I am going to tell you this straight. I'm afraid you can't go on being my PA. The bean counters say I'm only allowed one, and that one has to be Anthea."

"Yes," said Bella. "I know."

She looked at his face, which seemed perfectly normal. In fact, he was smiling at her in a way that she had thought was just for her. But now she saw what a pathetic, deluded fool she'd been. There was not a trace of regret in his voice. If anything, he seemed pleased, almost excited. I thought you minded about me, she thought. I told Karen that you made me feel wonderful. Scrap that: You make me feel worthless—and miserable.

"I'm afraid that we still need to go through the charade of this report, or else I'll have to endure the wrath of HR."

He smiled at his own pleasantry. Bella looked at his nice white teeth and did not smile back. She was putting all her energy into not looking upset.

"First, we need to write down your three objectives for the current year."

"Well," she said, "to have kept this job would have been nice."

"Yes, obviously. But I don't think we can write that. What else?"

"Do you really want to know my objectives?"

He ignored the bitterness in her tone and simply nodded.

"My objective is to bring up my daughter," Bella said slowly, as if talking to someone very stupid. "And to pay my rent. The rest I'm not that bothered about. I'd rather do something not entirely brainless, and I'd rather work with people who treat me with respect. But at the minute I guess I'd just settle for a job."

James looked at her in a way that Bella could not read: It might have been embarrassment or it might have been sympathy. "How old is your daughter?" he asked in a softer tone of voice.

"She's seven," said Bella.

"Is she? Well, I don't want you to worry about your daughter. You have no need. You are bright and I will make sure that something good is found for you that uses your skills."

"Thank you," Bella said flatly.

"In fact, I have a little plan," James went on. "I'm not meant to tell you this now, as Finance hasn't signed off on it. I've greatly enjoyed having you on the team, and I don't want to let you go. You've got terrific promise, much more than I think you are aware of yourself. I can see you doing all sorts of things at AE one day, but for now I'm planning to keep you in this department as a junior researcher."

"Oh," Bella said uncertainly. The rush of pleasure she felt was instantly swamped by anxiety. He does want me, she thought exultantly. But then she thought: I won't be able to do the job; it'll be too hard and I'll fall flat on my face. And what about the hours? She couldn't possibly work the sorts of hours she saw Rhys working—he boasted to her that he was now getting in at seven thirty most mornings. In fact, it wasn't going to work at all.

"I need to think about it," she said.

James, who had got up and moved toward his computer, said nothing. Then he said: "Fuck!"

Bella stared at him. She knew his precise use of language sometimes gave way to bouts of swearing, which she liked, being somewhat foul-mouthed herself. Yet to respond with such rage to her hesitation over the job struck Bella as extreme. But then she saw it wasn't about her at all. He was staring at a message on his screen and started to read out loud.

As part of a global reorganization of Atlantic Energy, Stella Bradberry is to step up to the newly created role of Chief of Staff. She will report directly to Stephen Hinton and will play a key role in shaping the company's strategic direction.

In addition, she will retain her leadership of the Economics Department. Stella is an exceptional performer within the group, and I look forward to working with her more closely. I know she has broader skills that will benefit the group going forward.

James stopped reading and said: "Come on, Bella. Let's go out for a drink. And we can celebrate your new job."

"I don't know if I can," she said. "I'll have to call the child minder. And I haven't accepted it yet."

"And I'm going to tell you why you must."

Stella

"I've been thinking about this, and I've got the solution."

Stephen's voice was excited; he was talking so loudly that Stella had to hold her mobile away from her ear. He was in Norway, and she was in the changing rooms at House of Fraser by London Bridge. She was fighting to do up the zip of a pair of jeans that had a motif of diamonds on the back pockets.

"The answer is for you to take the new job—and to retain your existing one, too. Obviously we will need to get you more assistants. But you are a first-rate economist, and I want you to continue to have a department to manage. I have high expectations of you, Stella."

Stella, who had been looking over her shoulder in the mirror to see whether the jeans accentuated or disguised the sagging of her bottom, sat down heavily on a dainty little stool. As she listened to Stephen's words, she was suddenly clear in her mind: She did not want the job. She had too much work to do as it was; indeed, at that very moment she should not have sneaked off shopping but should have been finishing the monthly outlook.

"Well," she said slowly, "although I'm really flattered—"

"You deserve this, Stella. Well done. We'll get the announcement today."

"I'm not sure whether—"

"We'll discuss the details when I'm back," Stephen interrupted her. "I must go now, I'm getting a helicopter to take me out to one of our platforms to rally the troops. Complete waste of my time, don't know why I allowed myself to be talked into it. Catch up later."

And I don't know why I have just allowed myself to be talked into a job I don't want, thought Stella.

"How are you getting on in there?"

A young assistant was standing outside the curtain. Stella pulled back the curtain and asked her: "Do these jeans look ridiculous on me?"

"Oh *no*, not at all. They look *great* on you!" said the shop assistant.

"But don't they look as if I'm trying to be young? Surely diamonds are meant to grace the bottoms of twenty-year-olds and not forty-year-olds?"

"I've sold these jeans to customers much older than you. Most twenty-year-olds can't afford them."

Stella looked at the price tag, which said £169, and thought she was probably right. So she decided to buy the jeans, and as she peeled them off her, she thought that in the space of five minutes she had let her boss steamroller her into a job that was too big and the shop assistant steamroller her into a pair of jeans that were too small. This thought amused her, and she scooped up the jeans along with a wraparound dress and an oyster satin blouse and took them to the till. The dress was clinging jersey material and Stella had felt self-conscious in it, but she'd decided to buy it anyway. The blouse had tiny pearl buttons and was by far the most feminine item of clothing she had ever bought.

Feeling light-headed with her purchases, she got a cab back to the

office. On the way she called Charles, but he was not picking up, so she
sent him a text:

```
I'm taking the job.
```

He texted back:

```
Vg
```

Stella crept into her office, trying to hide the two large House of Fraser
bags she was carrying. She wasn't sure why she felt so guilty about going
shopping for an hour and a half in the middle of the afternoon, given what
long hours she worked and how she almost never skived, but she still did.
She was just tucking the bags behind the coat stand when Rhys came in.

"I've accepted the job," Stella said.

"Yes!"

He ran up and down on the spot in a parody of delight, and some of
his enthusiasm infected her. Maybe this would be the best of all worlds,
she thought. Maybe the thing that was wrong with her, the reason she
was behaving in such unpredictable ways, was that she was bored. A new
job might be just what she needed to be more herself again.

"Have you been buying yourself a present to celebrate?" he asked,
eyeing the bags. "What did you get?"

"Oh, nothing," said Stella.

"It doesn't look like nothing. Can I see? I love shopping."

"Well, I don't. I usually hate it," said Stella. "And no, you can't see."

But Rhys had got out of his chair and walked over to the bags. As he
did so, Beate walked past the glass door and looked in inquiringly.

"Leave my shopping alone," Stella said in a mock commanding voice.

Rhys laughed. "Shall we go out for a drink to celebrate?"

Stella pictured herself wearing the new dress and sitting on a stool
and having a glass of champagne with Rhys and was wondering whether
she could say yes when her phone went.

"Mum, where are you?" Clemmie was sounding aggrieved.

"I'm at work," said Stella.

"But you said you'd get home early to help me rehearse for *Twelfth Night*. Have you forgotten?"

"Of course I haven't," said Stella, who had, for the first time ever, forgotten a date with her daughter. "I had to finish something, but it's all done. I'll be home in twenty minutes, I'm leaving right now."

Bella

At Coq d'Argent, James and Bella sat facing each other by the window with a view over the gray slate roofs of the Bank of England. Between them was a bottle of champagne in a silver ice bucket.

James raised his glass. "To your brilliant career," he said.

Bella laughed. "It hasn't been very brilliant so far," she said.

"You puzzle me," he said. "I don't understand why you are where you are. You speak fluent Russian, you are so bright and enterprising. Why aren't you running the world?"

Bella took a large swallow of her drink, feeling the bubbles lift her up. "Do you really want to know?" she asked.

He said he did with such a show of sincerity that Bella started to tell her story. There were quite a few versions of this story, each one more or less true but designed for a different audience. There was the version she told herself at night, which was toughest on herself. There was the one she told her friends, in which the romantic and dangerous elements were played up. And then there was a flatter, somewhat bowdlerized version, one suitable for a boss.

She told him how her father, who ran his own business building upmarket Barratt homes, had set his heart on his clever daughter not only going to university—something he had never done—but going to Cambridge. But Bella had disappointed him by not getting the grades.

"Oh?" James looked surprised. With the confidence and lack of imagination of someone who had always got A's himself, he could not understand how others might not have managed it.

"I didn't work hard enough," she explained.

What she did not say was that by the time she was sixteen, she had stopped working altogether. Every lunchtime she had gone to the park behind school and smoked weed with Shorty, who was both the tallest boy in the school and the most dissolute. She just scraped passes at A level and was lucky to have got into Bangor to read Russian.

"Dad thought this was a total disgrace," said Bella.

"I assume he's got over it by now," said James.

"I don't know. I haven't had a proper conversation with him for five years."

"Blimey. Why not?"

And Bella explained that her mother had told him to pack his things when she found that his increasingly frequent trout fishing trips were actually excursions to a luxury new-build in High Wycombe, where he was shagging the accounts manager from his office. She didn't add that her mother had done a little digging and found that Suzy from Accounts was the latest in a succession that had included Chloe, who had headed the sales team, Joanne from Marketing, and—briefly—Janice, the receptionist at the show home.

James sat forward. "So you haven't forgiven him?"

Bella shrugged. "Well, I suppose I've forgiven him for shagging this other woman. But I haven't forgiven him for being a completely crap father."

In fact, he hadn't been quite as absent from her life as Bella liked to make out. She had barely seen him in recent years but had seen some of his money, which came into her bank account every month and helped her pay the mortgage.

"So did your mother throw him out at once?"

"Pretty much, I think. I was at college by then. They had a bit of counseling, but then Mum got a private detective and found he had been lying about lots of other things, too. So then she kicked him out, and since then she has put all the energy she used to put into looking after him, into squeezing every last penny out of him."

"Did you take your mother's side?"

"No, not really. She has issues of her own. She took it in her stride that I never finished my degree, but her main disappointment was that I didn't meet someone rich or titled. She used to go on and on about how the daughter of a friend of hers went to Bristol and at the freshers' fair picked up some chinless wonder called Sebastian who turned out to be the grandnephew of the Duke of Marlborough and they never looked back and they are getting married and blah blah blah."

James tipped some more champagne into her glass and more into his. "And so you didn't meet a Sebastian at Bangor?"

"No. I met Xan. The students in my year all seemed young and nerdy, and I thought I was too cool for them. Xan was a second-year student from Belfast. He was much more...intriguing...than the other guys, and he had this great gravelly voice. He and I used to drink, and though I used to get quite drunk, he would get quite out of control."

James kept her gaze, raising the glass to his lips and putting it down again. He seemed to be sucking the story out of her. Bella was telling him more than she had planned to but was enjoying her confession. She didn't want to stop.

"By the end of the first year, I was pregnant. At first I didn't realize, and I went off to Russia with the other students, and it was there that I found out. I flew home to have an abortion—but when I got back I found I couldn't do it. Even though I was only nineteen, I really wanted the baby. Xan said he did, too. I didn't go back to Russia and dropped out of college and moved in with him in his student room. He never went to lectures, and he spent the whole day smoking skunk with his mates. The place was filthy, and I couldn't deal with it. So I moved back home with Mum and had Millie on my own. I'm not complaining—I mean, sometimes it's hard, but we are very happy the two of us, and I can't really imagine it now any other way. Xan has been in my life and then out. He's still using, is a danger to himself and to Millie, and I've had to get a court order to stop him from seeing her."

James took another sip of champagne, swilling it around in his mouth before swallowing. "I'm sure I would have cracked and broken—you're clearly made out of strong stuff," he said.

Bella was starting to feel exotic and heroic, as if he, by some trick of the light, had made hers a story of moral victory rather than a humdrum tale of police stations and lawyers' bills (paid for by her father, as it happened).

"That's ridiculous," she said. "I'm sure you wouldn't have cracked. When you have children, you can't afford to crack."

As soon as Bella had said this, she wished she hadn't. She thought of James's wife, who did have children and had cracked. The same thought had evidently occurred to James, who got his BlackBerry out of his pocket and checked it anxiously.

"So," she said, changing the subject, "I suppose you were always successful, right from birth?"

"My story," he said, "is really rather boring. I went off to boarding school when I was eight, then Winchester, Cambridge to read law, decided I did not want to be a lawyer, and got a job at AE straight out of university. I married someone I met at university. We have two lovely boys. And that's it. My whole life."

As he said this, his face changed: He looked distant and distracted. Was it that he was reminded of the importance of his home? Bella wondered. Or was it that he was depressed by the predictability of his life?

She looked at her watch. "I should really go soon," she said.

"Stay," he said. He brushed her hand lightly, and his hand felt smooth and warm on the back of hers.

"I can't," she said. "I'm already plastered and already too late. I must go."

"And we haven't talked about the job," he said. "But we can do that tomorrow. Shall I get you a cab?"

"No," she said. "I'll get the tube."

"I'll come with you."

Together they went down the escalator at Bank station, and he waited with her on the northbound platform even though his own way home was south.

"High Barnet 2 mins," said the indicator.

"You don't have to wait," Bella said, wishing he would go.

"It's a pleasure," he said.

The train clanged onto the platform, and the doors opened.

"Thank you for the drink," she said. "See you tomorrow." She turned to him, and suddenly and most unexpectedly, he gave her a hug.

Bella got into the tube carriage and sat down. As the train pulled away, he was looking at her and smiling. Bella could still feel the pressure of his hands on her back.

Stella

It was Stella's first day on her new job, and she had decided that with this new beginning must come an ending. She was going to stop this thing— this flirtation—with Rhys. He was taking up too much space inside her head. When she was at home she saw him in her mind's eye, still sitting at her kitchen table where he had sat three weeks earlier. In the office she saw him leaning against the door, and when he wasn't standing there in the flesh (as he was for an inexplicably large fraction of the day), she made excuses for him to come and talk to her.

And now he not only e-mailed her during the day but had started doing so at the weekends, too. The last Saturday, after a party to celebrate her parents' fiftieth wedding anniversary supper, she had looked at her BlackBerry in the cab on the way home and there was a message, sent at 11:34, that said just one word:

Drunk.

"What are you laughing at?" Charles had asked.

"Nothing," Stella had said.

But it wasn't nothing; it had become something. Never mind the fact that the evening had been lovely—her entire family gathered together at the Orangery restaurant in Holland Park. Stella—as the richest member of the family—had insisted on paying for the whole event, and they had been grateful. And Charles had given a speech that had been generous and witty; and Stella's mother, who hardly ever showed any emotion, had laughed, and then, when Charles had said that his parents-in-law's marriage was a thing of beauty, she'd dabbed at her eyes with the stiff linen napkin.

But the significance of this big event had been eclipsed in Stella's mind by this one stupid word. She felt thrilled and agitated that he was thinking of her at nearly midnight on a Saturday night and that he'd needed the courage brought by alcohol to let it show.

And then that night she had had a strange dream in which she had been in the office and both Charles and her father had been there. Rhys had asked her to dance, and the two of them had done slow dancing around the photocopiers and paper-recyling bins while Charles and her father looked on and clapped in time with the music. She woke up the next morning still feeling his touch from her dream and knew that this flirtation was not something harmless that brightened up the working day.

It was an obsession, and it must stop.

I'm going to tell him nicely that things between us have got too close and that it's unprofessional, she thought as she put on her new, clinging dress. I'm doing something that is not only dangerous, it is pathetic and undignified. Emily is quite right. I'm a forty-four-year-old, premenopausal wife and mother getting excited about e-mails from a young, ambitious boy who is flirting with me because I'm his boss.

That morning, Rhys was sitting at his desk waiting for her, as he now was every morning. Stella walked straight past him into her room. He got up and followed her in.

"What's the matter?" he said.

"Nothing," she said, not looking at him. "It's just that I've got a very busy day, it's my first day in the new job."

Rhys ignored this. "I've got something for you. I made it for you last night."

He handed her a CD with a sheet of white paper covered in his writing, a neat, backward-sloping script. "I wanted to give you some songs I thought you might like. You could put it on your iPod now and listen on the flight."

"I don't have an iPod," Stella said, trying to ignore the surge of pleasure that was racing through her body.

He laughed. "Why doesn't that surprise me? Do you have a CD player, or is it steam wireless at your place?"

"It's kind of you to have done this, but I don't think I should accept it."

"Why not? It's just a CD. You'll probably think all the songs are total crap, but I like them."

"Rhys," she said, "it's not just about this CD. In fact, I really don't think we should e-mail each other anymore except when it is on strictly work matters."

"Fine," he said quickly.

And Stella, relieved and shocked that she was now saying what she had rehearsed, started to gabble. "I mean, obviously," she said, "I'm not suggesting that there has been anything between us. Of course there hasn't. But I just felt that in the last couple of months we have been getting into bad habits, spending too much time talking to each other, and it's getting in the way of work. I need to think of how things look to other people on the team—"

Rhys was turning to go, but Stella was still talking.

"—and obviously I have come to like you, Rhys, as a person as well as a colleague—"

Gavin Meredith, one of the statisticians from the production division, chose this moment to put his head around Stella's door. "Am I interrupting something?" he asked.

"No!" Stella almost shouted. "We've finished..."

Rhys left the room, and Stella, mouth a little dry, discussed the latest oil production data with Gavin. She was still holding the CD and the list of songs firmly in her hand. I've done it, she was thinking.

"I thought it might be helpful to give you a heads-up on the retardation in the futures market," Gavin was saying. "I got Sanjay to run some numbers, and it is the biggest it's ever been. I've done some printouts for you."

Stella felt an urgent need to get Gavin out of her office. "Thanks," she said. "I'm getting one of my trainees, Beate Schlegel, to do some work on the retardation—I'll pass the printouts on to her."

Gavin dispatched, Stella sat at her desk and stared at the graphs in front of her. In her head she could hear Rhys's voice saying, "Fine." How dare he say it was fine not to e-mail her anymore? Did it mean so little to him that it was really neither here nor there?

She took the CD and threw it into the bin, but it missed and lay on the floor. Cursing, she picked it up and purposefully put it inside. Then she reached into the bin and took it out again and put it in the bottom drawer of her desk.

She could not concentrate on the report she was meant to be reading. She thought of sending Rhys a message to say that she was sorry if she had been too severe. Would he see that as kind? Or as too obvious a climb down? As she was wondering this, she received a message from him.

Stella. I don't want to bug you or be a nuisance in any way, but that was a bit awkward and there are a couple of things I would like to say. Would you like a quick drink before you go tonight?

She e-mailed back:

No, sorry. I think it is probably better if I get home promptly.

And then one from him that simply said:

Ok.

She went back to her report, but now the same line was moving in front of her: "Brent crude 3 months trading 50 basis points higher..."

Should she go? No, of course not. But what if she just went quickly, just to tell him nicely that she had some feelings for him that were not entirely professional and that therefore it would be better if they did not see each other? This thought made her feel easier. Surely that would be fine? And kind. And if you thought about it, not unprofessional. She needed to have a proper conversation with him, and that would be best done, surely, off office premises, where they wouldn't be interrupted by Gavin or by anyone else.

It made a lot of sense. In fact, more than that, she owed it to him. Surely.

So she clicked on his last e-mail, hit reply, and wrote:

On second thoughts, could manage very quick drink at 6?

She texted the nanny to say that she was going to be an hour late and instructed her to get dinner going and check Finn's homework. And then she turned back to her e-mail. There was a reply from Rhys. It said simply:

x

She stared at the message. How could one little *x* mean so much? She kept clicking on it to have another look. He had never put a kiss on his messages to her before. But of course *x* meant nothing. It was what you did when you were twenty-seven.

Bella

The following morning, Bella woke with a bad head and a feeling of unease. She checked her mobile, but James had not replied to the text she had sent him the previous night. She looked again at what she had written:

```
thanks for the drink realy loved it, bella
xx
```

There were three things wrong with it. The message was babyish; she had spelled *really* wrong, and as for the two needy little kisses—no wonder he hadn't replied.

Bella got dressed quickly, tied her hair back in a ponytail, and applied no makeup. Happiness was so fragile, she thought. Yesterday, she had felt like Maria in *West Side Story*: "I feel pretty, / Oh, so pretty."

Today she was a drab young woman with no man in her life who had made a fool of herself with her boss.

When she climbed out into the drizzle at Moorgate, her phone was bleeping. There was a little unopened envelope with "James" written next to it. Her heart surged. She opened the message.

```
Can you check if Stella is coming to the
environmentalists' lunch today? James.
```

"Was the appraisal okay last night?" Anthea was asking, her voice heavy with concern that Bella knew she did not feel.

"Yes," said Bella.

"Well, I'm ever so glad you're taking it so well. Has anyone told you how much longer you have in ER, and where you'll go next?"

"I'm staying."

"Oh!" Anthea's face darkened.

"Not as a PA," Bella explained. "He wants me to do a different job. To be a researcher."

"Researcher?" Anthea repeated dumbly. "Well," she said. "Time will tell."

Time will tell what? Bella wondered. She thought about the phrase and how silly it was. Time didn't ever tell anything. Things sometimes happened if you waited long enough, but just as often, in her experience, they didn't.

She opened her e-mail and there was a message from the head of facilities, replying to the one she had sent him about the oil barrel. He informed her that it was not in accordance with health and safety regulations and that it would interfere with "the integrity of the reception space." Bella was sure the first point was not true. She had gone to the trouble of reading the company's eighty-page health and safety manual, which was full of stuff about not standing on chairs to change lightbulbs and instructing staff to hold the handrail as they walked up and down stairs, but nothing on obstacles in reception.

She sighed noisily, and Anthea looked up. "What's the matter?" she said sharply, as if feeling that now that Bella was being promoted, she had forfeited her right to complain.

"Nothing," said Bella. She got up and walked down the corridor to see Nathalie, Stella's PA. She could have sent her an e-mail more easily, but she felt the need to get away from Anthea's brooding presence.

Bella found Nathalie sitting outside Stella's office, leafing through *Grazia*. She liked this about Nathalie. She was perfectly efficient at getting things done but made no effort to look busy when she wasn't.

"James wants to know if Stella's coming to his lunch today," she said.

"It's in the diary," said Nathalie. "Congratulations, by the way. I hear you are a researcher."

"News travels fast," said Bella. "It's not even official yet."

"So what will you be doing?"

"I don't really know. I don't really think it means anything much, and they aren't paying me much more. It was just that James was told that he couldn't have two PAs, and so he's decided to keep me on but give me a fancy title."

"You have to watch it with him. He's a total lech."

"Is he," said Bella, disliking the edge in Nathalie's voice. "Has he tried it on with you?"

"Well, no," said Nathalie. "But he had that thing with your old boss, didn't he. And I think something's going on with him and Stella."

"*What?*" said Bella.

"Although Stella thinks she's being really discreet, there are things that I'm picking up on. She's distracted. She is looking prettier. At first I couldn't believe it because she's so sorted, and she's got such a great marriage and stuff. But now I'm certain. She's started wearing lipstick and nipping off to the ladies' to put on more mascara. And the other day I saw her wildly deleting messages and she looked up guiltily as I came in. And have you seen that foxy dress she's wearing today?"

"Well," said Bella, "I haven't noticed James behaving oddly at all."

"You wouldn't," Nathalie said authoritatively. "The men don't show so much."

"How come you are such an expert on all this?" Bella asked.

"I've worked in offices for a long time. I've seen a lot."

"Have you ever . . . ?"

Nathalie laughed. "Mind your own business!"

"Oh, go on."

"Well . . . not since I worked here. But when I was at CR Leisure, I shagged some guy after the office party in the shower rooms. I was drunk, so I can't really remember it, but I think it was the worst shag of my life."

They both laughed, causing Stella, who was walking past and into her office, to look at them sharply. They waited until she had gone in and closed the door.

"See what I mean?" said Nathalie.

"What?"

"Really stressy."

"That doesn't prove anything," said Bella. "Isn't this her first day in the new job? So she's allowed to be stressed. And if she was shagging James, wouldn't she be happy?"

"*Happy?* Have you seen his fat belly?"

Bella said nothing, and Nathalie asked: "So who do you fancy?"

"No one," said Bella.

"Well, obviously," said Nathalie. "None of them are fit. But if you had to...?"

Bella laughed awkwardly. To avoid replying to the question, she said: "How did you know about James and Julia?"

Nathalie gave her a pitying look. "There are no secrets in this place," she said.

Bella returned to her desk feeling troubled. She was sure Nathalie was wrong, but she needed to know. She went and stood at the door of James's office, and he waved her in.

"Stella is coming to the lunch," she said, studying his expression carefully.

"Oh," he said. His face did not move.

And then she said: "Facilities say the barrel is against health and safety rules, even though I don't think it is."

"Just tell them that the CEO wants it. That will shut them up. And Bella," he went on, still looking at her in the same flat way, "there's something else."

He started to rummage through the papers in his briefcase and produced a bag from HMV. He passed it to her as if giving her a sheaf of photocopying. "There you are," he said briskly.

Inside was a CD of Van Morrison's greatest hits.

"What's this for?" she said. It was a pretty stupid question. But the joy that was racing through her veins had befuddled her mind.

"For?" he echoed. "It's not for anything, except to listen to. I daresay you know the track called 'Brown Eyed Girl.' It's one I especially like. I know you think that I can't see what is under my nose. But it has not escaped my notice that you have brown eyes."

Part Two

ADDICTION

Stella

When Stella looked back, this was the moment when, if she had behaved differently, all that followed would not have followed, and life would have continued on its proper course. The turning point was that drink. Before the drink she could have stopped; afterward it was too late.

So why didn't she stop before, if she could have? Stella told herself that she *had* tried; in fact, she had only agreed to the drink as a way of stopping things. But she knew this wasn't true. As she went out to that drink, she had been lying to herself about her motives, about her thoughts, and mostly about her heart.

"Where shall we go?" Stella asked.

"Let's find somewhere quiet," he said.

They started walking, not down toward the champagne bars of the City but up north toward Old Street. They walked quickly, some distance apart.

"Thank you for doing this," he said.

"That's all right," she said.

And then they walked in silence.

"You know," he said, "this feels weird. When you are used to seeing someone in the office, and then you see them outside for a drink, it's all awkward and you don't have anything to say to each other."

Stella laughed. There was something sweet about the way Rhys said the first thing that came into his head. It reminded her of how Finn used to greet any pause in adult conversation by saying, "Embarrassing silence."

In fact, she had been feeling the same thing herself, but in her case it was more panic than awkwardness. Who is this man—this *boy*, she had been thinking, and what am I doing with him?

They came to a desolate pub, quite empty apart from a line of blinking slot machines sitting on a red-patterned carpet. The air smelled faintly of bleach.

"I think we're safe from AE people here," he said. "What would you like?"

She said she'd like a small glass of red wine and then, thinking that the wine would be horrible, said that she'd like a bottle of Beck's instead. But then she thought maybe she shouldn't have alcohol at all but fruit juice instead. Eventually she said: "What are you having?"

And he said that he was having a glass of red wine, and she said that in that case she would, too.

Stella looked at him from behind as he stood at the bar. His hair came down into a pale point above his collar. She wanted to touch it, just to see what it felt like. No, she told herself, she didn't want to touch it. She wanted to tell him firmly that they must stop all this. She was going to say that she liked him very much, thought him charming, and enjoyed his company, but that their relationship was becoming unprofessional and that she was going to suggest moving him to another department.

Rhys returned with two large glasses of wine. He raised his glass and chinked hers. "Cheers."

He looked at her, not smiling. She took a sip and winced as the acidic liquid hit the back of her throat.

"I want to tell you something," she said.

"But I want to tell you something first."

Stella nodded, glad to have a few more moments before giving her speech.

"I want to say that I've been a complete twat and a show-off. But something has happened to me in the last three months, and I don't care if I lose my job over it. I have thought about you all the time since that first day when you gave that presentation. You are amazing and beautiful and fascinating and witty, and I adore you. This is surreal, I can't believe I'm saying this. I'm not even drunk."

Stella's world tipped and swayed. She didn't look at him. She looked at the carpet, at the red petals of the rose, and noticed how the color darkened to magenta at the center.

"That's ridiculous," she said. "You can't fall for me. It's completely absurd. I'm married. I love my husband. I love my children. And they are waiting for me. And this is mad."

"I know it's mad," he said. "But that doesn't change it."

"You don't mean it, anyway," Stella went on. "You have a beautiful girlfriend. There are seventeen years' difference between us in age."

Rhys said he couldn't care less how old she was. That he didn't have a thing about middle-aged women; he had a thing about her.

Stella fixed her eyes on the wet circle her glass had made on the table. What she felt was not joy, but shock. A feeling of the purest terror, that life would never be the same again.

Rhys leaned toward her and put his hand on top of hers. She looked at their hands together. Hers looked dry and wrinkled. His hand was pale and soft, and the touch made her stomach go down like in a lift, a sensation so unfamiliar, so intoxicating. Slowly she pulled her hand away. "I have to go," she said, getting up and putting on her coat.

They went out into the street, stunned and silent. An empty cab wheeled past, and she stuck out her arm.

"Can I come with you some of the way?" he asked.

"No," she said.

"Can I hug you?"

"No," she said, but he opened his arms and she leaned toward him, and he held her for a few seconds until she pulled free and got into the cab and it drove away.

Bella

When Bella had booked the bus to take the External Relations team from the office to Theakstone Lodge, she had not thought she would be on it herself. PAs were excluded from team activities: Bonding was not considered part of their job.

Bella was mainly dreading the course. She didn't feel like a researcher and was fearful that she would do something that would expose her to the others as an impostor. She was also worried about leaving Millie, who had been almost as reluctant to stay with her grandmother as her grandmother had been to take her. But mostly she was worried about James. The previous morning, she had told him that she had been listening to the Van Morrison CD, and he had looked at her blankly, as if he had forgotten giving it to her. Since making her a researcher, he had given her almost no work to do, so much of her time she spent pretending to be busy and almost wishing she were still a PA.

The bus was filling up with colleagues, most of whom were wearing jeans and sweaters, making Bella feel stupid in her new black skirt and jacket. James was last onto the bus, and for a moment she thought he was advancing purposefully up the aisle to take a seat by her, but he sat in the row in front of her next to his number two in Investor Relations.

Bella passed the slow journey through South London looking out of the window and listening to James's conversation.

"The market has built-in expectations that we'll smooth the yield," James was saying.

What the hell does that mean? Bella wondered. When she was a PA, she didn't care if she didn't understand what was happening around her, but now her ignorance was making her anxious.

James's mobile was ringing.

"Hi, darling...Well, no, don't do that if you don't feel up to it...I'm on the bus, so I'll call you tonight."

Bella had come to recognize his different voices. He had his work voice, which was deep and no-nonsense. Then he had the voice that he had used to talk to her when they had had their drink, which, if not exactly soft, was lower. The voice he was using to talk to his wife, Bella thought, was his work voice, only slightly quieter. And then there was the voice he used for his sons, which was full of love.

At Theakstone Lodge, a tall young man in a zip-up cardigan was waiting to meet the coach.

"Hiya! Hiya!" he said as each person got out. "I'm Jay, and I'm your facilitator for the next twenty-four hours. I suggest you check in, go up to your rooms to freshen up, and come down for a meet-and-greet. See you in fifteen."

Bella had never been in a hotel on her own before. She put her overnight bag on the suitcase stand and admired her bed with its crisp white cover. She went into the bathroom and ran her hand over the smooth sweep of the basin, shaped like a large white fruit bowl, and then pinched the deep white towels. She looked at her reflection in the mirror and thought she looked too young and too grubby to be staying here. She brushed her hair, put on more mascara, and rang Millie, who was grumpy, as her grandmother had said she was too young to watch *Desperate Housewives*.

Downstairs, the full team of twenty-three External Relations managers sat in a large circle on gold chairs of the sort that people hire for weddings.

"Sorry," said Bella, sitting herself down on the last chair and putting a bag of objects underneath it.

"Now that we are all present and correct, I'd like to welcome you on behalf of Ideation! We're at the beginning of a twenty-four-hour journey that will unleash our creativity, reenergize us, and be a load of fun."

Bella looked at James, who was stony-faced.

"So," Jay went on, "let's dive straight into our first warm-up exercise. I asked each of you to bring something that says something about yourself. Something that is surprising, and that will give us a key to your unique spirit, your authenticity."

Slowly, they started to go around the circle. One man had brought his child's first tooth. Men can get away with slushy displays of parental love, Bella thought, but women cannot. Ben had brought the key to his motorbike, which was cheating, as everyone knew he rode it. Most of the other men brought something to do with sport. Four of them produced golf balls, leading to a lively discussion of handicaps, which Jay had to silence. There were only two other women in the group. One produced a book of travel writing about the places she hoped to visit when she had more time—a gratuitous reference to how hard she worked. The other brought a swimming hat and told the team the not especially interesting detail that she went swimming twice a week. Bella waited for her turn with growing dread. She realized that she had misunderstood the exercise: The aim wasn't to bring along something surprising, but to bring along something safe that didn't say anything about you at all. Bella looked at the three things in her lap.

"You seem to have a lot there," said Jay.

"Yes," she said, blushing scarlet. "I couldn't decide, so I brought three." She could feel James's eyes on her.

"If it takes three things to unlock the authenticity of you," Jay said, "then go right ahead!"

"Here is a saw," Bella said rapidly, holding up the item. "I brought it because I like doing DIY. And here is a book of Russian love poems, because they are beautiful. And here is a microphone, that belongs to my daughter. We like doing karaoke together."

There was a brief silence. James was looking straight at her and raised an eyebrow.

"That's great! Sensational! Thank you, Bella," said Jay. "And finally, what about our leader?"

James fished around in his pocket and produced a small wooden chest of drawers no more than two inches high. "I made this. I like to make miniatures."

Bella looked at him in amazement. This really was unexpected. The chest was perfect but was also perfectly useless. Bella watched him pull out the drawers, his fingers looking delicate and gentle as they pulled the tiny knobs.

Stella

Stella was standing in the check-in queue at Heathrow. She had had no sleep but didn't feel tired so much as displaced. It was as if she had undergone a change so drastic that she could not understand how the rest of the world could seem so much the same.

When she had got home from her drink with Rhys the previous evening, Charles and Finn had been on the sofa watching the closing minutes of Juventus versus Arsenal. She had kissed Charles briefly on the back of his head; she didn't want him to see her face. But he'd turned and looked at her in what seemed to her like an outlandishly, preposterously normal way.

"Sorry I'm so late," Stella had said. "There was something I had to finish."

Charles had grunted, leaning forward on the sofa, watching Juventus score in the ninety-first minute.

"No!" groaned Finn, bending his arms backward over his head in the new body language of disappointment.

Stella had looked at them on the sofa. That is my husband, and that is my son, she'd thought. While they were watching the match, I was holding hands with a colleague.

She'd stood in the doorway. She should be feeling guilt, but this feeling was different: more a sense of distance. Guilt meant feeling wretched, and she hadn't felt that. She had felt euphoric, as if she were floating. She was looking down on her life below, and it appeared to be carrying on precisely as normal.

Everyone was saying the sorts of things they always said. The only person who was not normal was Stella, but no one seemed interested in what might have happened to her or to notice any difference. Only Charles's mother, who had come over for dinner, had seemed moved by Stella's late arrival.

"My dear, you spend far too much time at work. What are you getting up to?"

Stella had said that there was a lot going on at work at the moment but that things would calm down soon.

The old lady had considered this for a moment, then looked at Stella anxiously again and said: "My dear, you spend far too much time at work. What are you getting up to?"

Once again, Stella had said there was a lot going on.

The question and answer were given another three or four times, and the meal had gone on in its normal way. Clemmie had been a little nicer than usual, cheered up by having got 99 percent on her physics exam; Finn had talked sweetly to his grandmother about the level he had reached on his violent computer game, which she'd listened to with the greatest tolerance and a minimum of understanding.

Stella had eaten, though she wasn't hungry. She must have talked, too, though she couldn't remember what she had said. The children went to bed, and Stella, feeling the need to make amends, had driven Charles's mother home and gone into her flat, sorted out her rubbish, hung out some washing, and talked to her for a bit. When she had got back, Charles was in bed asleep. Stella had looked at his body, once long and lean but now slack around the middle. She'd pushed away the image of Rhys, the smell of his coat.

She'd got into bed beside her husband and closed her eyes. There was no chance of sleep—indeed, she had not even wanted to sleep. She'd lain there playing the events of the evening over and over in her mind. At about three a.m., with the certainty that comes at that early hour, Stella had decided that Rhys would be regretting the drink. That he had not meant to say those things or not meant to hug her. She was certain there would be a text from him on her phone saying as much. She'd got out of bed, taken the phone from her jacket pocket, gone into the bathroom, and locked the door—something that she had never done in the house before. She'd turned it on, the second it took to come to life feeling an eternity. There'd been a new text message. It was from Rhys and had been sent at 2:38 a.m. It had said:

Xxxxx

The woman at the British Airways desk was asking Stella if she wanted an aisle seat or a window seat.

What makes you think I care which sort of seat I have? Stella wanted to say. I have had no sleep. I am hysterically happy and also deeply miserable. For what it's worth, I'm going to a meeting in Arizona for which I am quite unprepared. Where I sit on this airplane does not interest me.

"Window seat," she said.

She put her bag onto the conveyor belt, and the woman said: "Did you pack this bag yourself?"

"Yes," Stella said.

"Are there any sharp objects, liquids, inside?"

"No," said Stella.

While she gave the routine answers to the familiar questions, she was thinking: He is obsessed with me. I know this is laughable. But he says he is. Rhys, for God's sake. I can't stop thinking about a man called Rhys. Not even a man. A boy. A boy called Rhys. What a stupid name. What a stupid woman.

Stella settled back into her window seat, closed her eyes, and stopped trying to chase away the thoughts. She let herself relive the moment. The taxi was idling, its door open, and she was standing on the curb and his arms were clamped around her. And then earlier, he had looked at her over the little pub table and said she was amazing, beautiful, fascinating, and witty.

Each of these words gave her a jolt of pleasure. Stella was used to being admired and loved. But she was not used to being admired by someone like him. Nor was she used to being told she was either beautiful or—even less—sexy. She hugged these words to herself, but as she said them over, she started to doubt them.

He had said these things, certainly. But did he mean them? He might have thought he did at the time, but surely he didn't, not really. Could he desire her?

"Excuse me."

An immensely fat man was easing himself into the seat next to her. Even in the wide seats of club class, his flesh was pressing against the armrest that separated them. Stella moved away, shifting her papers.

His breathing was heavy, and he jabbed his fat fingers at his iPod for a bit, and Stella tried to concentrate on her briefing paper.

CROSS-PRICE ELASTICITY OF DEMAND ON RENEW-ABLES OF OIL PRICE FLUCTUATIONS

"That looks like fun!" he said.

Stella gave a thin smile. She read the first paragraph, then read it again.

The plane was starting to taxi down toward the runway. "All mobile phones and electronic devices must be turned off now, and kept off for the duration of the flight," the stewardess was saying.

Stella still had a signal. She sent a text saying:

```
Will be airborne in seconds. Think would
be better if we are not in touch for next
three days.
```

She sent it, turned off the gadget, and returned her seat to the upright position.

Bella

Bella had had one vodka and tonic before dinner, at least four glasses of wine at dinner, and then afterward in the bar had reverted to vodka and tonics. She was now on her third.

All evening, she had been aware of him. Aware of where he was standing and whom he was talking to. A couple of times he had smiled at her, and she had willed him to come and talk to her, but he hadn't. He had once looked at her pointedly, as if there were some shared joke between them, but had stayed put. Then, at about midnight, Bella had gone over and sat on the bar stool next to him.

"I'm wasted," she said. "And I'm still cringing about the poems. I mean, everyone else had normal things—did it look like I was trying to be too intellectual?"

"No, not at all," he said. "Why did you think that?"

"Dunno. I just…" She smiled at him stupidly.

"I think you'd find that many of us like poems and only regret that we don't have more time to study them."

He glanced at his watch, and then, in an attempt to prolong the conversation, Bella said: "So what kind of poems do you like, then?"

"Ah, well," he said. "I like lots of poems."

"Go on, then. Recite me something."

This seemed to throw him. And then he said: "'Is there anybody there?' said the Traveller, / Knocking on the moonlit door…'"

"I don't know," Bella said. "Is there?"

He laughed. "I can't remember how it goes after that. But it's been a long day, and I'd better turn in."

Without having any clear idea of what she was doing, Bella got up unsteadily, announced that she too needed to get to bed, and followed him to the tiny lift. Once inside, she leaned against him. "I'm trashed," she said.

"Bella, no, I don't think so," he said, but then undermined his protest by seizing her and kissing her with such urgency that even through her drunkenness Bella wondered if his desperation was greater than her own.

She was not sure precisely what had been the order of events after that. Had he led her to his room? Or had she simply followed him? She couldn't remember, and perhaps it didn't matter much.

Either way, she did go to his room and stood in the middle of the floor, wondering where to sit down. The chair had his suit carrier on it, so Bella lowered herself onto the edge of the bed and then, when he did not sit next to her, got up again unsteadily.

"Would you like a nightcap?" he asked, opening the minibar. He took out two small bottles of red wine and handed her one of them. "So sorry about just now."

Bella started to laugh.

"What's so funny?" he asked.

"Nothing. Everything. Whatever."

In fact, she was laughing because he had apologized as if he had just trodden on her foot rather than kissed her with more passion than any-one had kissed her for a very long time.

Then he said: "This is all a little…confusing."

Bella stopped laughing. She took a large swallow of wine and refused the packet of dry-roasted peanuts he was offering her. He moved his suitcase off the chair and gestured for her to sit down.

"Is it okay if I use your loo?"

In his bathroom, his things were arranged in a neat line on the glass shelf: silver razor, Gillette Fusion HydraGel, Pantene shampoo, and Sure Aerosol for men—Sensitive. Bella gripped the side of the basin and looked at her flushed reflection. She picked up his toothbrush, ran some water on it, and put it in her mouth.

When she returned to the room, she found he had taken off his jacket and was turning on and off the lights in the ceiling and the standard light in order to try to get the bedside lights on.

"Bella," he said, "I know this is irregular. But would you mind coming and lying with me? Just for a minute."

Bella moved onto the bed and closed her eyes. The room was shifting, and James was pressing himself against her. He released her bra with surprising dexterity.

Stella

Stella landed at JFK and turned on her BlackBerry. There were three texts from Rhys. The first, sent at 7:56, just seconds after she was airborne, said:

```
Dear S, just got your message. ok, I will
try to be silent for three days.

Rx
```

The second, sent at 9:34, said:

```
Scrub that. I don't like silent, I'm thinking
about you in midair. Nothing happening
except I'm staring at your empty chair. I
had a Danish for breakfast which I could not
finish. Xxx
```

The third, sent at 12:43:

```
I miss you. How long is this bloody flight?
It seems to have been going on for DAYS.
Will you call me when you land? xxxxx
```

Stella scrolled down through the messages, her cheek muscles contracting involuntarily into a smile, which she hid by putting her hand over her mouth.

"Good news?"

Her neighbor was eyeing her. Was it that obvious? Could he see right into her heart and see that it was leaping and twirling?

In the terminal building, Stella stood by baggage reclaim and typed in his number. He answered after one ring.

"Hello," she said.

"Hi," he said. "Where are you?"

His voice, far away in the Moorgate offices, sounded absurdly Welsh.

"I am waiting for my connecting flight to Arizona."

"Oh."

And they were both silent.

"Where are you?" she asked.

"I'm just walking away from my desk. Now I'm in the corridor by the recyling bins. If I suddenly start talking about OPEC production figures for March, you'll know why."

"I got all your messages. You weren't meant to be sending me any. We were meant to be silent for a bit."

"But you've just called me," he pointed out.

"So I did," she admitted, laughing.

"When are you getting back?"

"Thursday."

"I know, but what time is your flight?"

"It's the red-eye, so early. About six thirty, I think."

"I'll meet you."

"No, you can't do that. This is mad. Rhys, I do mean it. I must think."

"Okay," he said reluctantly. "So long as you reach the right conclusion."

"I have to go now, my baggage is here." She hung up.

Immediately the phone went again, and even though Stella hadn't spoken to him for about fifteen seconds, she was glad to do so again. Without looking at the phone, she took the call. "Hello again," she said, her voice soft, and laughing.

"Mum?"

It was Finn.

"Hello, darling," she said in a slightly different tone of voice. "How are you? I've just landed in New York."

He ignored this. "Mum, where are my shin guards?"

Hearing his gruff voice, she felt a simple love for her son. He was so guileless and so lazy; yet he expected love and in his short life so far had not been disappointed.

"I've got no idea. Probably where you left them."

"Cheers, Mum," he said, and hung up.

Bella

Bella had woken to find the bed empty next to her. Through the thin partition wall, she could hear the shower. On the floor, beside two empty bottles of wine, her clothes were strewn about—one shoe leading into the bathroom, the other poking out from under the curtain. His were folded neatly on the chair, and the little chest of drawers had been placed neatly by his bedside table.

Bella lay as still as she could. Her body felt poisoned by alcohol but renewed by what she queasily decided was the best sex she had ever had. Her mind was all at sea. She wasn't sure if the predominant feeling was dread at the stupidity of what she had just done or simple happiness. She wished he would come back to bed.

The shower stopped its racket, and after a brief silence, James emerged with the hotel's white towel wrapped tightly around his midriff and his white flesh hammered rose pink by the pressure of the water. He was not looking at her.

Bella studied his back with a queasy mixture of longing and profound embarrassment. Seeing someone almost naked whom you are used to seeing in a suit was quite surreal. He turned and she looked at the dark hairs that sprouted from around his nipples. This is my boss, she thought. I have done something quite mad. I desperately want to do it again.

"Hello," she said propping herself up on the pillows.

"Good morning," James replied in his brisk office voice.

Bella's happiness shrank, and her feeling of dread spread.

"I hope you're feeling up to this morning's session?" He gave an awkward laugh.

"I'll be fine," said Bella. Her tongue stuck to the top of her mouth, and her eyes were glued together with the previous night's mascara. She pulled the sheet up over her breasts with a sudden prudishness that struck her as belated given what had passed between them a couple of hours earlier.

"Do you want to go back to your room to sort yourself out before anyone else is up," he asked. It was more of a command than a question.

"Okay," she said. This was horrible, she thought. Why couldn't he kiss her or touch her or say something nice?

She put on her dirty, crumpled clothes and tiptoed along the corridor to her room with the floor lurching under her feet. There was a purpose to a hangover, she thought. It protected one from all thought except the simple practicalities of putting one foot in front of the other. The extent of the humiliation and misery that she was surely going to feel soon was, for the moment, in abeyance.

She reached into her pocket for the room key, but it wasn't there. She looked in her bag and then knelt on the carpet to rummage around, lifting out her purse, various bits of makeup, wrinkled-up receipts, and sweets wrappers. But she could not find it.

"Good morning! Is everything okay?"

Bella looked up to see Jay, who had just come out of his room in a brand-new white nylon tracksuit and seemed to be going for a run. "Yes, fine," she said. "I'm just looking for something."

"Catch you later," Jay said cheerfully.

Bella waited for him to go and then returned to James's room and knocked gently on the door. By now, he had got on his boxer shorts and black ankle socks and a crisply laundered shirt that he was buttoning somewhat laboriously. Bella looked down at his legs, which were white and rather slender. She badly wanted to put her aching head against his chest, and for him to put his arms around her and propel her back onto the bed, which, she noticed, he had smoothed out to make it look as if no one had been there at all.

"I think I left my room key in here," she said.

He frowned and picked up his papers and looked under them. No key. He bustled around the room, lifting things and putting them down again.

"Think back to last time you saw it," he said in the tone of voice that a weary father might use to instruct a child.

But in this case, she couldn't think back to last night. If she thought back, she remembered coming into the room and sitting on the bed and giggling wildly. She remembered lying fully dressed on the bed, and now she did remember James saying, "Bella, Bella, we must not do this," as he kissed her. The key might be in the bed, and she picked up the white duvet, averting her eyes from a series of pale stains on the sheet below. There was no key.

"Reception will have a spare," he said. "Let me know if you have any difficulty."

I *am* having difficulty, Bella thought. I'm having difficulty with this whole weird situation.

"See you later," she said.

At breakfast, Bella could feel the table swaying. Across the room she could see James calmly spreading jam onto his croissant, stirring his coffee carefully with a little silver spoon, and listening politely to Jay.

Bella had positioned herself next to Ben, who was eating his full English breakfast with relish. She tried not to look at the puddle of yellow oil that had formed around the button mushroom.

"What time did you throw in the towel last night?" he asked.

Towel? The word stuck in Bella's mind and with it the image of James emerging from the shower.

"What time did you go to bed?"

"Um, I'm not sure. I think I left just after you..." She looked at the bowl of fruit she had collected from the breakfast bar. She did not want to eat it.

Jay got up from his table and clapped his hands together. "Good morning! Hope everyone is feeling fresh and ready to roll. We're going to do a warm-up exercise to get our creative juices flowing before we move into the kitchen. I want each of you to laugh. That's it. Think of something funny and let it all come out!"

There was silence from the Atlantic Energy managers.

"Come on," he said. "Just start by going 'Ha-ha-ha,' and you will find that your body will connect with the humor and unleash your endorphins."

"Hahaha," they all started.

Ben was the first to go off into genuine delighted giggles, and after a surprisingly short time, the others started hawing and guffawing. Despite her hangover, and despite the fact that she had just committed career suicide, Bella started to laugh and laugh and did not know how to stop. And then she turned and saw James standing slightly apart from his two dozen hysterically laughing underlings. He looked like the saddest man she had ever seen.

Stella

Stella settled into her airplane seat and pulled the synthetic blanket over her.

The trip had not been a success. The research and technology for which they had such high hopes was being conducted in three sheds with corrugated iron roofs. None of the scientists could agree on when the fuel would be able to be produced in sufficient quantity to make it viable.

Stella was regretting her gung-ho enthusiasm to the board and was wondering how best to break the news to Stephen that the company was proposing to invest £500 million in slimy green stuff in a test tube that was probably worth nothing at all.

Still, she marveled at how very little she minded. Only a few weeks earlier, she would have viewed this as a calamity. Now, all she did was type a few briefing notes into her laptop, close it, and think of Rhys.

Stella was exhausted. The thought of Rhys was incompatible with sleep. His image threw her into a state of physical and emotional anxiety that made her rigid with wakefulness. In the last seventy-two hours she had had a total of seven hours sleep, and now she drank a large glass of red wine, took a temazepam, and fell into a drugged slumber from which the stewardess shook her awake four hours later.

Stella made her way groggily to the airplane toilet—sticky and evil smelling after so many hours of constant use—and saw in the mirror a thin, tired woman with red eyes and one swollen eyelid. The inside of her head felt hot and dry. She brushed her hair, which the static in the cabin had plastered to her scalp, and brushed her teeth. Thank God he isn't coming to meet me, she thought. I could not bear him to see me like this.

She went back to her seat and looked out on the baggage handlers driving their lorries in the gray London morning and the line of huge metal birds linked to the airport by their bendy umbilical cords. Stella usually liked coming back home and was always happy at the thought of seeing her family again. But this time she had just one thought: This is where Rhys is. She imagined him now in his bed, asleep. What did he wear in his bed? she wondered. Did he sleep on his back or on his side? What did he like for his breakfast? Did he snore? How could one desire someone so much and yet know so little about them?

The passport queue moved briskly, and she picked up her suitcase and hurried out to the taxis. She would go home, have a shower and change, and get into the office for her meeting at ten thirty.

She saw him first. Or rather, she saw his sign first. He was standing alongside the Kurdish taxi drivers and tour operators: a tall, fair man in a sea of dark ones holding up little signs. His sign was huge and held with two straight arms high above his head. GORGEOUS GREEN GODDESS, it said. It was written in fat felt pen on a large piece of cardboard.

His face was deadpan. He looked at her seriously. "Hello," he said.

"I told you not to come." But in her chest, her heart was thumping wildly. She wanted to shout for sheer joy.

"That isn't a particularly nice response. I got up at five to do this." He took her case and led her toward the taxi rank.

"God," she said. "The trip was a disaster. I really don't see this technology being ready for us to exploit within the next fifteen years, if that. The founder would not let me talk to the scientists directly, their own economist was ill, and so I was just given a sheaf of papers and shown a couple of outdoor algae ponds."

She was gabbling, her eyes fixed on the raincoated back of the man in front of them in the taxi queue. She was aware of Rhys standing beside her, looking intently at the side of her face, but she didn't trust herself to turn toward him.

He touched her cheek with the back of his hand.

"Don't," she said.

Eventually, they reached the front of the queue and climbed inside a waiting taxi.

"Stella…"

She let him pull her toward him so that her head was against his chest, and through his shirt, jacket, and overcoat she could feel the beat of his heart.

"Stella—"

He drew her face toward his and kissed her. The kiss was tentative at first, clumsy and halting. The voice inside Stella's head that had been saying no was silenced. She felt there was nothing else in the world at all—just the inside of the taxi and her and Rhys. She closed her eyes as he kissed her and then opened them to see his hair cut short by his ear and his birthmark, which struck her as being a thing of great beauty. She touched it gently.

"This is like the movies," he said.

Stella laughed.

"What's so funny?" he said.

"What is so funny," she said, "is that I'm happy and I'm going to let myself be happy just for these few minutes until I get out of the taxi and think about the rest of my life."

That wasn't exactly what had made her laugh. It was his saying something so sweet and innocent—and so wrong. This was not like any movie that she had ever seen: a young man in bad shoes in a clumsy and desperate embrace with a jet-lagged oil executive nearly two decades his senior.

He kissed her again, moving his leg round so that he knocked over her briefcase. Stella looked up and saw the driver's eyes briefly scan her through his rearview mirror. What did he think? she wondered. He looked away quickly, showing no particular interest. Evidently he had seen more surprising things in his time. The thought was vaguely comforting.

Rhys was touching her hair and looking at her as if he had never seen her before. She reached out and ran her hand over his face and lips and kissed him with a light-headed despair.

The traffic on the M4 was stationary, but the taxi lane was moving, and for once Stella regretted it. She thought of the scene in *Madame Bovary*, when the horse-drawn cab drove around and around Rouen with the curtains drawn so that Emma and the dashing young law student could make love in the back.

"Stella," he whispered into her ear. Her name sounded lovely on his lips. "Will you come back to my flat?"

"I can't. I'm scared."

"Don't be," he said, holding her face in his hands.

"But even if I wasn't scared, I still can't. I promised the children that I'd see them before they go to school and make them pancakes."

The cab pulled up in Camden High Street in front of an electrical shop.

"You must get out here," she said. "I'll see you later."

Rhys stood on the pavement and winked at her. He looked, she thought, like a truanting schoolboy.

Presently, the taxi pulled up outside 7 St. Mark's Square, and Stella, who until a few days ago had found her life within it happy and uncomplicated, climbed the York stone stairs, passed through the sentry of twin clipped bay trees, and went inside.

Bella

Bella was at her desk in the office, trying to draft a message. It had been twenty-eight hours since she had risen from his hotel bed, and during that time she had gone through a cycle of emotions. Embarrassment. Dread. Anger. Self-reproach. Longing. Humiliation. And then, as she sat at her desk pretending all was perfectly normal, anger again.

The team-building session in the kitchen had been farcical. She had been assigned the vegetable-chopping detail, and her unsteady hands would not chop the turnips and squash into sufficiently orderly cubes. She had cut her finger and watched the red blood stain the white turnip and thought she might be sick. An Elastoplast had been found, and she'd sat to one side, useless. James, meanwhile, had been making pastry, a job that he'd applied himself to with great solemnity. Mostly he'd had his back toward her, and at one point she'd caught his eye and he'd given a thin smile. But otherwise, nothing.

Now Bella was looking at a blank screen.

"Hi, James," she started to type.

This is a bit awkward, but I just wanted to say sorry about what happened. I was really drunk, and I know that isn't an excuse, but I wondered if we could put it behind us? From your silence in the last day and a half I get the idea that you regret what happened and that you are cross with me for my role in it. As I said, I am sorry.

Bella paused and then went on typing, faster now.

That's crap. I'm not sorry. And what I'd like to know is WHY are you so cross with me? It's all very well for you to shag your new researcher and then to pretend it never happened. But how the fuck do you think that leaves me feeling?

And another thing: how is it ok for you to be giving me Van bloody Morrison CDs and take me out for champagne and pretend to be so interested in my life one minute and then ignore me the next? I used to have a lot of respect for you, but I now have NONE. You are a creep and a weirdo with your silly little chests of drawers— and it was horrible shagging you—it's certainly not an experience I want to repeat so you need have no fear on that score…

"Bella."

James was looking down at her. Flustered, she clicked on the message to make it disappear.

"Have you got a minute?"

She got up and followed him into his office. He gestured to her to sit down but remained standing himself. Seeing him, Bella didn't feel cross anymore. He looked so awkward that she felt a desire to put her arms around him and kiss him. Instead she crossed her legs and waited expectantly.

"Two things, Bella," he said at last. "First, can you let me have all the slides for the investors' presentation? Please make sure they contain the most up-to-date oil production figures. Can you also check with Stella and see if we've got the latest forecasts? And one other thing."

Here it comes, thought Bella.

"I want to start a database on the website of all the good environmental things that we are doing globally. At the moment there are many initiatives being carried out at country level and departmental level, but I would like a one-stop shop where they can all be accessed. Can you bring all the files together, so I can give them to our Web designers?"

"Sure," she said.

And then he walked around to his desk, and she didn't exist anymore.

Bella went back to her desk and wanted to cry. She had been an idiot. He was an arsehole led by lust, and now he just thought that he could go on as before. Had he not enjoyed it?

Her screen had gone to sleep. She clicked on it to bring it back to life, and there in the middle it said: "Message sent to James Staunton."

Oh, my God, thought Bella. Jesus Christ.

Her heart started to beat wildly, and she could feel herself flushing a deep crimson. She had been so flustered that she must have pressed send instead of delete. She had never, ever meant him to see that message. It was just a way of getting it all out of her system. She looked at the message again. She had just told her boss that he was a creep and useless in bed. It didn't get much worse than that.

Stella

Stella walked into reception and there, just through the swing doors and in the middle of the marble atrium, was a large barrel sitting where there had been a bank of orchids in steel containers. It was mounted on a black granite plinth and seemed to her slightly vulgar and monumentally stupid. On it in red neon was the oil price—$150, +$4—and the share price—1120, up 59p.

She got out of the lift on the thirteenth floor and walked toward her desk.

"Good trip?" Nathalie asked.

"Tiring," said Stella.

Did she look odd to Nathalie? she was wondering. She felt as if her mouth must be looking funny, bearing the imprint of Rhys's lips. If she could still feel them there herself, surely there must be an outward sign? For the sake of saying something, Stella said: "Hideous thing in reception. Is it some dreadful scheme of James's? I thought he had better taste."

At this, Nathalie looked at her oddly and said: "No comment."

Oh God, thought Stella. She knows.

But then her PA continued in a more normal tone of voice: "Stephen wants to see you now—didn't say what, but it's important—he's got a window between eleven twenty and eleven thirty."

Stephen was on his mobile but beckoned her to come in. He was frowning and nodding into the phone.

"How was the trip?" he asked.

She made a face and tried to remember. So much had happened since she'd landed at Heathrow five hours earlier. "I think there are some fairly serious issues," she said slowly. "I fear we need to revisit the entire project. The technology is far less well established than we had been led to believe. They have done small controlled experiments, but there is no sign that it is going to work on a mass level. If you ask me to call it, I don't think it should be worth anything at all in our share price at the minute."

Stephen frowned. "Stella," he said, "I'm not asking you to do anything that you aren't comfortable with. But I think the Russian situation is slipping away from us. And so we need your project both to support the share price and to provide a competing, more upbeat narrative. Can I leave it with you?"

"Yes," said Stella. "Of course."

"I'd also like you to sit in on this morning's meeting of the divisional directors. Ask Jackie to give you the briefing papers."

As Stella got up to go, she said: "What the hell is that barrel doing downstairs?"

The CEO's face darkened. "What do you mean? It enables every visitor into this building to track the daily movements in Brent crude and in AE shares and buy into what we are trying to achieve..."

"Oh yes," Stella said hastily. "I quite agree. I just thought the barrel itself was a little, well, a little literal."

"Stella," he said, "I know that you share my passion for the arts. But this is an oil company. It's not an art installation."

Yes, I'm aware of that, Stella thought to herself. As it was, she smiled and got up to go.

Stella took her place around the table with the twelve top operations managers.

"Gentlemen," said Stephen. "And lady," with a pointed look at Stella. "Before we get cracking, just to say that I've asked Stella to join us at these meetings in her new capacity of chief of staff. I know she'll have a lot to contribute."

Wrong, thought Stella.

"Congratulations," said the head of Exploration and Production, leering at her. He took off his jacket, and Stella noticed that sweat had made the light blue of his shirt dark under his arms.

She tried to concentrate on the first item: an update on a program to raise safety standards at all refineries. The investment project, she heard, had run into difficulties and was now ahead of budget and behind deadline. But this made no sense to her. She could still feel the impression of Rhys's kiss, which instead of fading was, if anything, getting stronger. He had left a faint scent on her skin. She longed to leave the meeting and go out and see him at his desk. She thought of his body bent over his desk and of his little birthmark and of his hands with their bitten nails.

Had she ever felt like this for Charles? It was so long ago that she couldn't remember, but she thought not. She had been happy and excited and proud to have landed someone so handsome and clever and so eligible as her husband. But it hadn't been like this. She hadn't been possessed.

Stella's BlackBerry was flashing, and she held it in her lap, pretending to be studying the handout that the head of Downstream Oil had just passed around. The message was from Rhys.

```
Dearest S Can you come to my flat this
evening? I have been having some very
```

```
improper thoughts about you. PLEASE say yes.
Hurry up out of that meeting Rxx
```

A blush of pleasure spread over her face. The thought that Rhys was in the grip of a similar desire seemed miraculous. She hugged the thought to herself, oblivious to the meeting that was grinding on around her. She simply typed:

```
Yes.
```

There was no battle with her conscience. He had asked her to come, and she was going to. Never mind the jet lag. Never mind the fact that she was supposed to be going to a lecture on the economics of oil extraction from deep waters. Never mind the fact that she really should get home to see her children. This was bigger than all of it.

Seven Sisters was a part of London that Stella had often driven through on her way to see friends in Suffolk but had never visited before. Rhys had assured her the fastest way to get there was by tube and had drawn a map to guide her from the tube to his flat. He had gone straight home from work, while she had gone briefly to the lecture and had stood at the back of the hall with his map in her pocket and her heart in her mouth.

She emerged into the night air at Seven Sisters, went past a boarded-up kebab joint and a shop with rotting bananas in front of it. She almost ran, feeling outlandish in the cashmere coat she had bought at Bloomingdale's two days earlier.

Number 23 Wilton Rise was a three-story Edwardian house that had been subdivided into flats. A neglected front garden was given over to weeds and council recycling boxes filled with bottles.

Now that she was here, outside his front door, all the certainty that she had felt in the meeting had drained away and been replaced by fear. What am I doing? she kept asking herself.

The top bell had a plastic sign next to it that said: WILLIAMS—PRESS HARD. The sight of his writing made Stella feel a little calmer, and she pushed the buzzer. The door clicked open and she pushed her way into a dark hall that smelled of damp and frying. From upstairs, she heard his voice calling, "You've got to come all the way up to the top." Stella ran up the five flights of stairs, arriving short of breath at an open door at which Rhys was standing. I can't do this, she thought. She made no movement toward him, and he made none toward her.

He had changed out of his suit and was wearing baggy, low-slung jeans and a ribbed cardigan with a zip. Clemmie's boyfriends wore similar outfits. But the detail that moved her more was that his feet were bare. A long white toe stuck out from under the frayed denim. This was more intimate, more embarrassing, than if he had been naked. It said: I am at home here. This is where I belong.

And this, thought Stella, is where I don't belong. She looked down at her own shoes with their inch-and-a-half patent heels and at her black trousers with the neat crease along the front.

"What a delightful flat," she said.

"Don't," said Rhys. "It's crap. I've been to your place . . . you could fit the whole thing into your front room."

"Yes, but we bought it ages ago—we got onto the property ladder long before prices started to go up."

What was she doing? She had come to this godforsaken place to visit a man whom she had thought about obsessively for months, whom this morning she had kissed wildly and passionately in a taxi, and now here she was discussing the property ladder.

"Do you want a drink?" he asked. He went into his tiny strip kitchen and started opening cupboards.

The room smelled powerfully of Pledge and Jif. The sofas and the tables she recognized from the Ikea catalog, which she had thumbed through last year when they were fitting up their house in France. On the table was a stack of lad's magazines: *FHM*, *GQ*, and *Men's Health*.

She looked at them and laughed. "Do you read this stuff?" she asked him.

"Yes," he said.

"Why?"

"Because I'm a man, and because I'm twenty-seven. What do you read, *Saga*?"

Stella laughed and started to feel a little easier. He came back from the kitchen with two large glasses of red wine and a tube of sour cream Pringles. He picked up his glass, and Stella saw that his hands were shaking. He sat down, not next to her but on the armchair.

"Thank you for coming," he said.

"That's okay," she said. "This is nice wine."

He asked if she would like to listen to some music, and she said yes. He fiddled with his iPod, which started to play something quite unfamiliar.

She put a Pringles in her mouth but couldn't swallow it and took a gulp of the wine, which made her cough. Rhys came over to the sofa and patted her between the shoulders, and she closed her eyes. Slowly he moved his hands up from between her shoulders and started to rub her head. She leaned against him. She felt as she had at fourteen, when she had gone around to the house of a boy she had had a crush on. They had sat side by side on his bed and he had put on JJ Cale and had rolled a joint, and she had kissed him. The kiss had filled her with exultation of what was happening, but terror at what it would lead to.

"I can't have sex with you now," she said.

"I know," Rhys said. "It's okay."

"I'm scared."

But what she was mostly scared of now was not sex, though she was scared of that, too. She was scared about wanting him so much that she would never be able to go back to finding her old life enough and being happy in it. This fear sat there glinting like a knife, but for now there was so much happiness, too, that it coated it with a cladding of light polystyrene packaging and made her think that the knife was safe. No one was going to get cut.

Rhys kissed her again and pushed her down so that they were lying side by side on his cream leather sofa. She put her hand under his T-shirt and felt his back, his skin as soft as the skin of her children. She chased this comparison away. She lay in his arms kissing him, and the image of her children retreated, and she felt that her body fitted perfectly into the shape made by his. She closed her eyes and breathed in, and wanted to stay there, doing that, forever.

Stella looked at her watch. She had been there for fifty minutes already and had to begin the long trek back to Primrose Hill. "I have to go," she said.

"I'll take you to the tube."

Out in the street, he put his arm around her as they walked along, and Stella again had the weird sensation that he was her first boy-friend and she was doing this for the first time. No one will see us, she thought, not here. Their strides were different, his long and languid, hers short and brisk, but he adjusted his to make them fit hers, and they hobbled along.

At the Seven Sisters tube, he wrapped his arms tightly around her and kissed her again.

"I don't know what's happening to me," she said.

"You are wasting away because you've had nothing to eat." He produced a Twix from his pocket. "There you are," he said.

Stella got back to find Charles watching *Newsnight*.

"Did you have a nice evening?" he asked.

"Not especially. The speech was tedious, and then I got cornered by this guy who was a marine biologist and who had interesting things to say about the Russian whales, and so we went out for a drink, we went to Soho House, and I'm starving because all I've had is nuts—is there any dinner left?—and also did you know that Stephen is on my case about this green petrol thing?"

Stella knew that talking so much was unwise. She knew that you were meant to stick as close to the truth as possible. But she also knew that she must keep on talking to remind herself who she was and to root herself in her real life. And in any case, it didn't matter what she said to Charles, as he wasn't listening anyway.

She sat on the sofa, and the BBC's economics correspondent was standing in front of a moving chart that kept on changing color.

"I'm tired," said Stella.

"Night," he said absently.

Bella

Bella's first impulse had been to sign on to his e-mail account from her computer and delete the message. But as she was no longer his PA, a prompt had come up saying: "Access Denied."

She got up and went toward his office but found the door closed and James inside with a couple of visitors. Through the blinds she could see him talking calmly and wondered if this meant he hadn't seen it. But then he looked up, and upon seeing her hovering, he turned his head and looked the other way.

When the meeting was over and James had led the two men out of his office, Bella seized her chance, went to his computer, and looked at his inbox. Hers was sitting there close to the top in black, showing that he had opened it. She pressed delete, and as she did so Anthea came in.

"Can I help?" she asked officiously.

Bella said that she was just helping James with a computer problem. Anthea raised an overplucked eyebrow but was prevented from expressing a view on the matter by the arrival of James himself.

"Bella is fixing your computer," Anthea said in a voice tight with disbelief.

James looked at her coldly. "Thank you, how kind," he said.

"It seems to be working fine now," Bella said.

Back at her desk, she wrote another message:

Dear James

I did not mean to send you that e-mail, and I did not mean the things I said in it. I was angry and upset, but I now see that was ridiculous and unprofessional. Please forgive me.

Bella.

She sent it, though she knew it would do no good. She had been given one chance to make something of herself and she had blown it. Three days earlier, her future had looked brighter than at any point in the last eight years. She had been promoted out of the PA ghetto. She had a boss who rated her and was looking after her. But then she got drunk and made a fool of herself. She had done, as Karen had said so woundingly, that clichéd PA thing of shagging her boss. Maybe she would have got away with it, but now that he had seen the e-mail, he would no longer want her working for him. She would have to go back to being a PA for someone else.

Stella

In the morning meeting, Stella sat around the table with eleven people from her department so that they could tell the others what they were working on. Stella was good at keeping these meetings short and never let any of her team talk for more than a minute or so.

But today she could not focus on what any of them were saying. She had had so little sleep that she was hardly functioning. She had thought that the jet lag would have overcome the excitement and would have let her get some sleep, but she was wrong. Every time she had closed her eyes, Rhys had been there in the dark. Now here he was, sitting three spaces away from her. She could not see his face; all she could see were his arms on the table. He had taken off his jacket and had rolled up his sleeves to show his wrists. She looked at the hands and thought how yesterday they had touched her skin. She looked at the soft hair on his forearms and at his nails, which were bitten to the quick.

"What is the time frame on this project?" someone was asking her.

Without any idea which project was being referred to, Stella said, "We need to keep the momentum up," an answer that seemed to do the trick.

Afterward, the others left and Rhys loitered, taking an implausibly long time to collect his papers. Stella too seemed incapable of leaving the meeting room. The two of them stared at each other across the table.

Rhys said: "I have to kiss you."

"You are mad," she hissed.

"I know," he said. "But that doesn't change the situation. When can you come back to my flat?"

Stella longed to be in his flat right then. She wanted to be back on his sofa. More than that, she wanted to be in his bed. The doubts she had had the previous night had gone: When you felt something this strongly, she reasoned, it could not be wrong to do it.

"Tomorrow morning," she said. "I have nothing until an eleven a.m. meeting here. I'll invent a breakfast meeting and will try to get to you by seven thirty. Is that too early?"

Rhys looked at her and said: "Four in the morning would not be too early."

He sauntered back to his desk, and Stella watched him go, looking at the back of his jacket and at the firm backs of his legs and wondering how it was possible to be quite so undone.

She sent a message to Nathalie saying:

```
Fyi: Forgot to put in the diary—have got
breakfast meeting with some people from
Defra. Then will try to go to gym. Won't be
in til 11.
```

In twenty-two hours, she would be in Rhys's bed. She did not know how to make the hours pass until then.

She opened her laptop to look at the U.S. notes. She had been asked to make the petrol project look more positive than it was, but she had no stomach for it. Perhaps she could downplay some of the negative factors a little, but she was not going to lie about this. She was doing enough lying as it was.

Bella

All day Bella had waited for a reply, and at five o'clock, just as she was thinking about going home, a message arrived from him, sent from his personal e-mail account.

> Dear Bella
>
> I have, of course, read the e-mail that you did not mean to send. At first I was angry, as it seemed not just undeserved, but— forgive me—childish and somewhat petty.

Forgive you? thought Bella. Why should I do that? It's not petty to mind about being shagged and then cast aside.

> However, I have thought about it further, and I see that you are right to be angry with me. What I did was not merely unprofessional, it was irresponsible.
>
> Can I try to put events into a context that might make it a little easier for you to comprehend what must have seemed like puzzling behavior from me?

Whatever, she thought.

> From the first time you walked in my office, Bella, when I saw your Marmite eyes flash at me, I found you unbelievably alluring.

Marmite eyes. Bella liked that.

But when you started working for me, I came to admire other things about you too. Your humor. Your quick-wittedness. Your originality, and your own breed of intelligence—which leads you to insights that people with ten times more experience frequently miss.

A feeling of warmth spread through Bella's body.

And then, at Theakstone Lodge, we had both had too much to drink. One could say that was all it was, a drunken and undignified act. I am sorry if, judging from the remark in your e-mail, you did not enjoy it.

Oh, but I did, thought Bella.

However, from my point of view, that is not sufficient explanation. I am old enough not to leave behind every last vestige of sense just because I have had too many glasses of indifferent Chilean Merlot.

No; what happened between us was something that I had longed for.

Over the past weeks I have been thinking about you far more than I ought. That evening I had been deeply impressed by you, by your beauty and your vivacity. I was moved by the objects you showed the team. And I am sorry if you thought my chest of drawers ludicrous—I am aware that many people see them in this light. The alcohol simply served to silence the voices that counsel me against acting on my desires towards you. I think you may have gathered by now that my wife has not been well. She has for many years suffered from a depressive illness that at times is more severe than at others. The last few months have been hard for her.

I am keenly aware of my duties to her, and of my love for her.

Bella drew back from the screen as she read these words. What makes you think I want to know how much you love your wife? she thought.

She is doing a wonderful job in bringing up the boys, bravely dealing with her illness. She does not deserve to have as a reward a husband who cheats on her.

And then there are the boys. My sons matter to me more than anything else in the world, and I am not prepared to act in a way that could cause them harm. I simply cannot play Russian roulette with their happiness.

So to have an affair with anyone would be wrong. To do it at work would be even more wrong. I am powerfully aware that to involve myself with a direct report is extremely unprofessional, and dangerous to my career.

I really don't want to go on reading this, thought Bella. I have so much more to lose than you. I could get fired, lose my income, and have no way of supporting my daughter. Who also matters to me more than anything else in the world, only I don't feel the need to go on about it.

Fortunately, from the general tenor of your message, you seem to agree that what happened was an error. It is good that we can agree on that.

But I didn't mean that, Bella wanted to shout. It wasn't an error. It was lovely.

So where do we go from here? One option would be to get you moved to another department. If that is your wish, I will ensure that you get a position that will stretch you professionally in the way that you deserve.

However, it is my strong preference that you continue to work here in ER. Not only do I have every confidence that you will continue to do an outstanding job, I have a more selfish reason for wanting you to remain here. It is as simple as this, Bella. I enjoy working with you.

Last night, Hillary was watching a DVD of *My Fair Lady*. I wasn't paying attention, as I was much preoccupied by work and, if I'm honest, by thoughts of you. However, I did sit up and listen when Henry Higgins says, "I've grown accustomed to her face."

Please forgive the sentimentality, but the line struck a chord with me.

This was better, though Bella wasn't sure she saw herself as Eliza, any more than she saw him as Higgins. But then she read on to the end.

Perhaps you would let me know your views on this. I have no right to expect you to say yes, but if you do it will make me very happy indeed.

Finally, Bella, I wanted to say sorry. If this incident has resulted in pain or embarrassment, I sincerely apologize.

Kindest regards

James.

When she had got to the end, Bella went back to the start and read the message a second time and then a third. Each time it left her with a different feeling. On one it was the coldest, most alienating message one could ever receive. Full of pomposity and written as one might write a business memo. She could not imagine ever writing a message to someone whom she had had sex with and signing it "Kindest regards." On another reading, it was a hugely selfish message, all about his love for his family and his need to do the right thing, with not even the most glancing mention of her needs. Yet on a third reading, it seemed quite different.

This man wanted her, if not as a lover, then as someone to have close by. He had, he said, lost sleep over her. He could not offer her anything, but he did not want to give her up. It wasn't much of a deal, and the long-term prognosis was not good. It was something she knew that she ought to give up. But it was something that she couldn't.

He says I have Marmite eyes, Bella thought. He says he can't stop thinking about me. He has grown accustomed to my face. And I have grown accustomed to his.

After the third reading, Bella had talked herself round to a feeling of relief and optimism. She had not lost the job, and she hadn't altogether lost him, either. Clearly they could not repeat what had happened in the hotel, but there would still be a tension between them that would be exciting, but not dangerous. She would concentrate her energies on being professional and enjoying the job. She would understand that he genuinely liked her but would expect nothing further from him. That would be best for her—and for him. Everything, she thought, would work out fine.

Stella

For the sixth night in a row, Stella barely slept.

She lay in her bed tense and wakeful, with Charles slumbering beside her. At first she felt pure excitement—a drug so intense that it made sleep impossible. But around three a.m., the excitement started to change: Now it wasn't just joy and anticipation. It was doubt and fear, too. This was madness. It was too dangerous. And it was wrong. She was not an adulteress. It wasn't in her nature.

At three a.m., she got out of bed and sat in her nightdress on the stairs. I am going to send him a text saying I can't do this, she decided.

She got her mobile from her briefcase, but there was a text from him sent at two a.m.

```
Can't sleep. Why do I have to wait another 5
and a half hours?
```

With all her heart, she typed out a different message from the one she had planned to send:

```
And I can't either. Now it's only 4 and a
half xx
```

She got back to bed and closed her eyes and tried tensing and relaxing every muscle in her body. But it was a long and dull business, and halfway through the second leg she got bored and her mind found its way back to Rhys again. At five thirty she gave up on sleep, got up, and ran herself a bath. As she lay in the hot water, she looked at her body, not as something that she had lived in for forty-four years, but as something she hardly knew. A body of that age was an odd thing: Viewed in some lights and from some angles it was passable, in others it was not. Lying under the water, her stomach was flat and smooth, but as she bent to take out the plug, it hung down in a dangle of loose flesh. She dried herself and moisturized her skin, using the expensive body lotion that Charles's mother had given her for Christmas. Then she put on the black lace knickers that she had bought a few days earlier in New York. She looked at herself in the bathroom mirror. She had never owned such things before, and when she had tried them on in the shop—over her own pants, for hygiene's sake—she'd thought they might look sexy. Now, looking at her wired body in the early morning light, she thought the pants looked pathetic—desperate, almost. She took them off and put on plain white knickers instead that had gone a touch gray from too many washes. They were better: It was undignified to look as if she were trying.

At six forty-five she woke Finn, who was lying sprawled diagonally across his bed in sleep so deep, he appeared to be in a coma. She kissed his lank hair.

"Time to get up," she said.

In Clemmie's room she tiptoed over the clothes, bras, tights, and bags that were strewn all over the floor to the bed. Asleep, her daughter looked as she had looked when she was about four. Stella bent over and touched the scar on her eyebrow from when she had fallen off the slide in France.

"It's quarter to seven. Come on, darling, I've got to go now. See you tonight. Don't go back to sleep."

Clemmie opened her eyes and gazed at her mother groggily. "Okay," she said. "Bye."

"I love you," Stella said.

She didn't usually tell her children she loved them; she viewed it as slushy and self-evident. But at that moment, despite what she was about to do, she felt how strongly she did love the two of them and wanted to point it out.

Stella did not wake Charles but put on her coat and stepped out into the dark morning. She felt no guilt about what she was about to do. Her life felt quite simple. She was going to Seven Sisters, and she was going to see Rhys. On the tube, she could not read. She counted the stations from Euston, to King's Cross, Highbury and Islington, Finsbury Park, and then, at last, Seven Sisters.

Rhys opened the door and this time took her in his arms. They stayed like that, swaying, their bodies touching all the way down their length, in the open door with the smell of old frying coming from the flat below. Rhys's skin was slightly damp from the shower.

Still holding on to her tightly, he led her into the bedroom. "Come here," he said, sitting on the bed and pulling her down.

Stella suddenly found herself resisting, wishing that she were any-where else than in the bedroom of this young colleague. This time, her fear was purely physical. She had not had sex with any man other than her husband in nineteen years. No other man had seen her undress. To show her body now to a man seventeen years younger, a man whose girlfriends were young and beautiful, filled her with terror.

"I don't know if I can do this," she whispered into his ear. "I haven't bonked a man apart from Charles since I was twenty-five."

"*Bonked?* Is that what you call it?" he asked, laughing.

"Well, what do you call it?" she asked.

"Shagged. Fucked. I dunno. But whatever, I'm frightened, too," he said. "I've never done this when I was sober at seven forty-one in the morning."

Gently he took off her skirt, but he got the zipper jammed, so she had to do it. And then when he saw her white underpants, he laughed again. "You are beautiful," he said, "but your pants are awful."

And she laughed, too, and was no longer frightened, and she lay on this young man's Ikea bed, on his cheap poly-cotton duvet, and kissed him with an intensity so frightening and a happiness so sharp that she thought she might die.

Stella's phone was ringing. It was in her bag by Rhys's bed. She put out an arm and picked it up. It was Nathalie.

"Where are you? Your ten o'clock visitors are here. Are you at the gym?"

"No. Yes," said Stella. She instinctively pulled the duvet up over them, as if Nathalie could see her naked body locked against Rhys's. "In fact," she went on, "I haven't got to the gym yet, there's been a slight problem at home—" She looked at Rhys and pulled a face. He was planting kisses on her shoulder and up her neck.

"But I just called you at home," Nathalie said doubtfully.

"It's a problem with my mother...it's not serious...I'll be forty-five minutes."

"See you later," said Nathalie.

Stella hung up. "Shit, shit shit," she said.

"You are a crap liar," he said. "And you've gone bright red."

He tried to enfold her in his arms again, but she stood up. She hated being late, she hated missing appointments. Hurriedly she got dressed, while Rhys lay in bed looking at her.

"I would like to keep you forever," he said. "Like a ferret that I have in my pocket that I can get out and stroke."

"A ferret?" said Stella. "But they have horrible pointed noses. And don't you keep them up your trouser leg?"

"That would be fine, too," he said, laughing.

Afterward in the taxi, Stella buried her nose in her jacket, which smelled of him. She felt exhausted and ecstatic. I'm an adulteress, she thought. She whispered the word to herself, but it meant nothing. I don't care about anything except for this. I am free from care. This is why people make such a fuss about sex, she thought. There is the moment when all of life becomes one moment. When everything else disappears. She remembered reading somewhere that having sex with someone you love releases the same chemicals in the brain that are produced by heroin. How long, she thought, how long will it be before I get another fix?

Bella

Bella's desk had moved some thirty feet along the corridor as a symbol of her new, enhanced status. This meant she was out of Anthea's line of vision and so could type at her computer without being observed. But now that she was free from Anthea's banal observations, she found she missed them. She was quite isolated, her desk a little island in an open-plan sea, with no one to talk to without getting up and moving. Today, in particular, she wanted company.

All day she had been trying to reply to James's message, but all her words seemed wrong. In an hour and a half of drafting, she had come up with messages that were too needy, too angry, or just too intimate. So she settled for something brief:

Hi James—

thanks for your message, and sorry it's taken me so long to get
back. yes I would like to carry on as your researcher. Thanks for
apologizing, but I don't think you have much to apologize for. It is
me who should be sorry for sending that stupid message. And I
didn't mean what I said about either the chest of drawers or the
sex. I was trying to be hurtful because I was feeling bad.

Bella

But then she thought that she should not refer to what had passed
between them. And she did think the chest of drawers was weird. And
she also thought that he did have plenty to apologize for so didn't see
why she should let him off the hook. And maybe she shouldn't begin
"Hi," as he had started with "Dear."

So she tried yet again.

Dear James

Yes I would of course like to go on being your researcher. And
don't worry about the rest; it's all fine.

Bella.

This was better. Though she did want him to worry. And it wasn't
entirely fine. So she made a third attempt.

James—yes, I would like to go on being your researcher.

Bella.

But she couldn't really send that. It was too cold. It was the sort of
thing that James might send himself. No, she would wait until he had a
moment on his own and go and talk to him.

This was harder now, as she had to get up from her desk and walk twenty paces to where she could see into his office. From there she could also be seen by Anthea, who was watching her antlike to'ing and fro'ing with a suspicious interest. Each time Bella looked, his chair was empty. On the fourth visit he was back, and she knocked and was waved in.

"I've been trying to write you a message," she said, her voice sounding high and tight.

"Oh?" He smiled at her with a vague and slightly detached air.

"But it wasn't coming out right. All I wanted to say is that I have decided that I would like to stay as your researcher."

"Good," he said. "That's great." He nodded briefly and went back to his computer.

Bella turned to leave his office, feeling let down. After all that agonizing, after all that dissection of his message and crafting of hers, to be greeted with a brief smile and pat on the head was curiously deflating. If it was going to be like this, she'd rather go back to being a PA for someone else. All that stuff about longing for her and thinking about her and crap about *My Fair Lady* was drivel. He clearly didn't mean any of it.

Stella

"Sorry," said Stella to the Iranian economist, who had now been sitting outside her office for almost an hour. "I had a family emergency."

He nodded politely.

Stella gestured for him to sit down, and as she took her seat she noticed a faint but unmistakable smell of sex, of her and Rhys and of both of them together. She shifted her chair slightly farther away and carried on with the meeting.

Afterward and back at her desk, she signed on to her Hotmail account. There was a message from him, as she knew there would be.

Dearest dearest loveliest sexiest ferret

Hello. I miss you.

That was lovely, you are lovely…

Can I make an excuse to come and see you NOW NOW?

Rhys. xxx

(and a few more) xxxx

Stella smiled at her computer screen.

Dearest R

No, you can't. Not now. Get on with your work. SXX

She applied herself to some numbers. She might have had no sleep, but she was filled with a crazed energy and so did not sense that Rhys had got up, walked across the open-plan office floor, and come into her office and was standing by her desk.

"Hello," he said. He was standing too close to her.

"Hello," she said.

They stared at each other.

"I need to kiss you," he mouthed at her.

He had his back to the glass wall, but she was facing it, so if anyone looked in, they might see that her complexion was high and that she was staring at him with an intensity that did not belong to a manager talking to a trainee.

"Step back," she said. "You are too close."

He edged very slightly closer toward her. "Rhys," she hissed, "don't."

"I'm not going to leave this room," he said, "until you have agreed to meet me in the lift."

"That's mad," she said.

"No, it's not. The south side lifts. No one uses them. I'll go there now and you follow in five minutes. Get into the one closest to the swing doors, and I'll be in it." He turned around and walked out of the office.

Stella looked at his departing figure. Precisely four and a half minutes later, she got up from her desk, walked past Nathalie, past Beate, and past half a dozen other members of her team, through the swing doors to the bank of lifts. A man was standing there, whom Stella knew by sight but not by name. He had already pressed for the lift, and they waited in silence. The button pinged, heralding the arrival of a lift, but it was the one farthest from the swing doors. The man got in, but Stella held back. He looked at her quizzically, and Stella said that on second thought she wanted to go down, not up. The doors shut on his puzzled expression.

Stella called the lift again. This was utterly mad; she could not do this. Just as she was about to turn tail, the other lift pinged and the doors slid open and inside was Rhys, looking at his shoes, the very model of unconcern. She held back for a second, and he, sensing her hesitation, moved his hand a little toward her.

With no idea that her mind had willed it, she stepped into the lift and as the doors slid shut was in his arms. She inhaled his smell and pressed her mouth hard against his. She slid her fingers in between his shirt buttons and felt his skin, which was warm and smooth. As the lift began to slow, they sprang apart and each stood frozen against its opposite walls.

The doors opened at the ground floor and the group treasurer was standing there, clutching a cup of coffee he had got from the canteen.

"Hi," he said to Stella, stepping into the lift as the two of them got out.

"Hi, Evan," Stella replied, the desperate normality of her tone ringing false in her ears.

"Do you think he noticed anything?" Rhys asked.

"I don't know," she said. "And I don't care."

They pressed the button to go back up, and the other lift arrived, empty. When the door closed, he held her face between his hands. "Stella," he said, "this morning was the happiest I have ever been in my whole life. I love you."

Stella closed her eyes with joy. He loves me, she thought. When she opened them, she could see an endless line of the two of them locked together reflected in the lift's double mirrors. She, a tall, thin woman smiling inanely; he, a young man half an inch smaller, looking at her with earnest solemnity.

"We look a mad pair," she said as the lift arrived back at the thirteenth floor.

"I don't care," he said.

When Stella got back to her desk, her mother was calling on the mobile. This struck her as odd, as her mother never rang during working hours: She was of that generation that thought it was too expensive to ring before six p.m.

She answered. It wasn't her mother; it was her father.

"Forgive me for calling you when I know you are busy," he said.

Stella glanced at Rhys, who was standing in her office, pretending to ask for advice on a report he was writing.

"Hello, Dad," she said. "I'm not busy. It's nice to hear from you."

"I thought you ought to know," he went on, "that this morning your mother took a tumble down the stairs."

"Oh, my God," said Stella. "Is she okay?"

"Well, it was fortunate that it was a cold morning, so she had put on a thick dressing gown that may have lessened the bruising to her body."

"Bruising? How bad is she?"

"She's in the Radcliffe. The doctors are quite positive."

"She's in hospital? Why the hell didn't you call me this morning?"

"I didn't want to disturb you. She fell. You couldn't do anything about it. And as she was concussed I didn't want to alarm you until we knew what the doctors said."

"Well, I am alarmed. I'm coming now."

"I wish you wouldn't. There's nothing you can do."

"I'm coming now," Stella repeated.

She put down the phone and looked at Rhys. The spell of lust had quite gone. "My mother has fallen downstairs and is in hospital. I'm going to Oxford now," she said.

"I'll take you."

"No, I want to go on my own."

"Can I at least come with you to Paddington?"

Stella agreed absently and got into a taxi with him. That morning she had been naked in his bed, but now he seemed to her like someone she did not know at all. She could not escape the thought that this was her punishment. If she had not gone to his flat that morning, her mother would never have fallen. At the very minute that she was being transported under the gray-and-black duvet in Rhys's bedroom, her mother had been thudding down the oak stairs of their Oxford house. And—worst of all—she had told Nathalie that the reason she was late was that something had gone wrong with her parents.

Stella put her hands over her face, and Rhys put his arm around her. She shook him off. Nonsense, she told herself. Of course this wasn't her punishment. She had had sex with someone who happened not to be her husband, and at around the same time her mother had fallen. The two things were quite unrelated; they were morally and causally independent from each other. Her mother, a passionate atheist and logician, would have been even more horrified at her daughter's hokery-pokery reasoning than she would be about her adultery. Stella knew this was so, yet she still knew that, bogus logic or not, this was a sign and a warning. Her mother was unconscious, and it was her fault.

At Paddington, she told Rhys to go straight back to the office. She allowed herself to be kissed lightly on the cheek, and as she watched him go she made a deal with herself.

If my mother is all right, I will give up Rhys.

Bella

Bella was sitting at her desk, looking for images to jazz up a presentation that James was giving on AE's safety record, when the fire alarm sounded. Bella loved fire drills. They reminded her of school, and of the delight of missing lessons, and the double delight when you missed the end of the lesson and didn't get any homework.

But today even a fire alarm didn't cheer her up. Usually so good at making the best of things, she had been feeling miserable at work the last few days. Even though she was enjoying the work, James had continued to be, if not cold, cheerfully distant—which was possibly worse. She kept opening and rereading his long message to her, giving particular attention to the bit where he said she was in his thoughts all the time. But if that was so, why would he hardly look at her? Why did he leave no openings for them to chat as they used to? She knew that the present arrangement was in her long-term interest, that it would be mad to have an affair with him, even if he wanted such a thing, which he clearly didn't. She knew too that what mattered most of all at the moment was her job. She must keep it, and she must make the best of this chance. She might never get another.

Bella took her handbag and reached the stairs at precisely the same time as James, who was clutching a large green AE golfing umbrella. They walked past the lift, where Anthea was already stationed wearing the fluorescent jacket with FIRE WARDEN written on its back, which she always kept hanging neatly in the cupboard with her coat and kettle. She was sticking notices onto the lift doors telling people not to use them.

There was a crush of people snaking down the stairs, and Bella found herself pushed against James. Her shoulder touched his upper arm, giving her a thrilling jolt. "I remember one time," she said to him, "when we had a fire drill and the teacher forgot to bring out the register, and so we played hooky and spent the rest of the day in the park and I ended up snogging the head boy."

James gave an awkward laugh, and the people who were descending the stairs in front of them turned to see who had used the word *snog*.

The twenty-three hundred London employees of AE were spewing out of the building into the cold day, chatting in clusters and laughing. They looked to Bella like guests at an enormous drinks party, though without any drinks. In the crowd, she could see Rhys standing on his own, jabbing at his BlackBerry.

"I don't want to hang about here," said James. "Let's go and find some coffee."

There was a Pret A Manger on the corner of Moorgate, and they went inside. James queued for coffee and brought the cardboard cups to the table where she had stationed herself.

"Bella," he said, "I don't think I managed to say to you how very glad I am that you are staying in the department."

"I'm glad, too."

Then, after a brief pause during which he looked at her intently, he said: "Would you mind very much if I were to hold your hand under the table?"

Bella wanted to laugh with pleasure and relief. She quite liked the subjunctive; more than that, she liked the invitation. She reached under the table and found his fingers, which felt warm and dry and smooth.

To make contact, both of them had to lower their shoulders and sit in an uncomfortably lopsided way, drawing considerably more attention to themselves than had they held hands normally. She pointed this out to him, and he laughed and said: "Bella, there is no one like you."

"There is no one like you, either," she said. "You send me a ten-thousand-word treatise on why it was a big mistake to shag me and ten days later you're holding my hand under the table in Pret A Manger."

"Ah, yes," he said, smiling. "I do see a little inconsistency there. But on the other hand, or rather on this one"—giving the palm of hers a stroke with his thumb—"I am finding being in the office with you terribly difficult, and I'm trying so hard to be good, but I think a fire alarm means that ordinary rules are suspended, don't you?"

Bella nodded dumbly. She was so surprised at the turn of events, she did not know what to say. But mainly she felt steeped in unexpected happiness, and even though her shoulder was now aching from bending it toward the table, she did not want him to let go of her hand. The sensible edifice of argument that she had built over the last few days collapsed as easily as a house of cards.

"I am not terribly good at this sort of thing," he said. "But shall we go for a walk for a bit until it's time to go back?"

Neither of them had finished their coffee, and as it was raining outside, James opened his umbrella and pulled her close to him under it and led her briskly through the dismal streets tucked in behind the City Road. He didn't say where they were going, and she didn't ask.

After walking for quite a long time, they passed a desolate pub and beyond it a playground tucked in between two tower blocks. There was a bench with a slat missing, a vandalized slide, and a sand pit that had a large dog turd lying in the grubby sand.

James got out a large linen handkerchief and wiped the bench so that they had somewhere dry to sit. He took her in his arms and kissed her with a ferocity that quite surprised her.

"Bella," he whispered. "Beautiful Bella. I'm sorry to be so confused. You are in my mind all the time, but it's so complicated."

He kissed her again and then said: "Though at the moment it doesn't seem complicated at all." With one hand he held the umbrella over their heads. With the other he touched the skin on her back underneath her sweater.

Bella looked at his face made green by the light coming through the pea green AE golfing umbrella. He did not seem plain to her anymore. A face changes depending on how far away you are from it, and at a distance of barely a centimeter, he looked almost handsome. She closed her eyes and surrendered herself to this feeling of happiness, the feeling of his hands on her skin, banishing all idea of what she was doing or where it might lead.

A movement distracted Bella, and she looked away from James to see a small pair of Nike trainers and pink sweatpants with "Just Do It" written on the leg. James tilted the umbrella upward, and there was a fat black child of about five or six staring at them. She might well have been there for quite some time.

"You aren't allowed to do that," she said, her stare unbroken.

Bella was inclined to laugh. It struck her as delightful to be told off by such an unlikely authority figure. But James, evidently, did not think it funny; he seemed upset by the small girl. He stood up hastily, and the expression of intensity about him was all gone.

"She's right, of course," he said to Bella as they hurried out of the playground. "We aren't allowed to do that."

They walked back to the office in silence to find the drill long over and everyone else back at work.

Stella

On the train to Oxford, Stella stared out of the window and repeated to herself the deal that she had struck with herself.

If Mother is okay, she said to the smoking chimneys at Didcot, I am going to stop this with Rhys. If Mum is all right, she said as the train pulled into Oxford and she caught sight of honey stone spires, I'm giving up Rhys.

In the cab taking her up from the station to the hospital, she received a message from him that said:

```
Dearest Ferret

Have been turfed out of office due to fire
alarm, and am standing in rain outside. Am
thinking of you and your poor mum. Hope
she's ok. I'm not going to pester you, and
no need to reply to this, but I want you to
know I love you. Rxx
```

Stella read it quickly and deleted it.

Her mother was lying in a public ward at the John Radcliffe Hospital. She looked twenty years older than when Stella had seen her six weeks earlier at their golden wedding party. Her pelvis was broken, and she had a large dressing on the side of her head.

But she greeted Stella with a smile and gave her hand a surprisingly firm squeeze. "You are so silly," she said, "to disrupt your busy day for my stupid little tumble."

Stella returned her mother's squeeze and found that her eyes had filled with tears.

Her mother, seeing her only child weeping, said briskly: "Really, Stella, don't be so silly. I'm fine."

But Stella, having started to cry, found that she could not stop. She was crying out of relief that her mother was going to be okay, but also for how frail she looked in the yellow hospital gown with its bows up the back. She was crying out of exhaustion, but mostly, far more than the rest, she was crying because she was in love with someone whom she was giving up.

She blew her nose noisily. "Sorry, Mum. I'm so relieved that you're okay. Tell me exactly what happened."

"I'm a stupid old fool who tripped and fell—and that's all there is to say about it."

Stella's mother batted away further questions and instead inquired after her grandchildren. Then she asked: "How is Charles getting on with his documentary about the working classes?"

"He's been away filming a lot, and I think he has seen the first rushes and thinks they are promising. Everyone is very excited about it." She was improvising; she didn't know how it was going, as she hadn't asked for information recently and Charles hadn't volunteered any.

"That is wonderful," her mother said. "It really hasn't been good for him being so creatively unstimulated. He is capable of doing such wonderful work—the last program, *Devil Wife*—"

"*Wife from Hell*," Stella corrected her.

169

"It was awful for him to be involved with such a dreary program. This new one sounds like something he can put his intelligence into. He has such a talent for communicating social truths to a mass audience."

Stella listened to her mother praise her husband and entertained the old thought that her mother liked her son-in-law more than she liked her daughter. The thought was unfair: Stella's mother was loving in her own way and had always been supportive. Even though she had never really understood why Stella wanted to go into business (she viewed commerce as a curious thing for a person of intelligence to want to engage in), she nevertheless admired her daughter's success and was proud of her in her way.

But what her mother prized above all else was integrity, and whenever she read in the papers that the oil companies were behaving badly, she would ring Stella to remonstrate with her. The thing that she could not tolerate, either from organizations or from people, was lying or dissembling of any sort. When Stella as a teenager had stolen a bottle of her father's wine and got drunk and been sick, what got her into trouble at home was not the theft of the wine or the drunkenness—which her mother took in stride—but her attempt to cover it up.

But now Stella, sitting by her mother's bed and holding her hand, had something bigger that she was keeping from her. Stella imagined what her mother would say if she knew her daughter, who was now going through the motions of her hospital visit so amiably, had that very morning been in the bed of a young subordinate. If she knew how she was deceiving her husband and her children. If she knew that the good daughter she believed in and was proud of was really a sham.

I can't bear this, Stella thought. I am giving up Rhys. Not for some stupid superstitious bargain, but for my mother. I will give him up so I can be the daughter that she thinks she has.

Bella

Bella returned from the fire drill intoxicated. She definitely wanted this; she wanted him; she didn't care if it was unwise. She didn't care that he was her boss, or that he was married, or even that his wife was mentally ill. That was his responsibility.

As she sat at her desk, her phone went and Bella snatched it up, seeing his name on the display.

"Er, hello," he said, his voice low and hesitant.

"Hello," said Bella, feeling happy and tongue-tied and inclined to laugh.

He cleared his throat and paused and then said: "Look, I had an idea. And before you tell me that my idea is inconsistent with the e-mail I sent you, let me get in first and agree with you."

Bella laughed again.

"Tomorrow afternoon," he went on, speaking more confidently now, "I am supposed to be visiting some investors, but I thought I might cancel. I wondered if you might like to meet me somewhere private?..."

"Yes," she said, glancing around the office to see if anyone was taking an interest in the way she was blushing and whispering into the phone.

"I'll sort something out and text you details."

Within ten minutes, she received a text that said:

Great Eastern Hotel. Liverpool Street.
1:30 pm

She stared at this and felt such a pressing need to see him that she got up and walked past his office, but he wasn't there. Instead she bumped into Anthea, who looked at Bella's high color and shining eyes and asked if she was okay.

In a rush, Bella said she had a tooth that was playing up—a fiction that Anthea appeared to swallow, as she took it upon herself to describe the root canal she had had done, and how much it had cost, and the crown that went onto it, and then the root broke and so she was going to have an implant...

The next day, Bella got up early, had a shower, and put on a matching set of polka-dotted bra and pants that she had bought a couple of years before but had never worn, as the special occasion she was saving them for had never come. At breakfast with Millie, she chatted and laughed and didn't care that Millie had not practiced her recorder, and her daughter said almost plaintively: "Mum, why are you laughing? You never laugh."

Bella felt slighted by this and wondered if it was true.

In the office, Bella dispatched a full day's work in three hours, marveling at the elasticity of work. At exactly twelve forty-five, she got up from her desk, took her bag, and left the office without saying a word to anyone. She propelled herself through Finsbury Circus and down Broadgate to Liverpool Street. The City was full of workers going out to get a sandwich, people for whom it was another humdrum day.

A footman in a brown-and-gold uniform held open the door of the Great Eastern, and the Victorian red-brick exterior gave way to a sleek, modern interior. Bella stood in the vast shining reception space trying to look casual, as if waiting to have sex with her boss were the most natural thing in the world. There was no sign of James. She was sure that the woman at the desk was eyeing her with suspicion. She moved away and sat on a low suede sofa, seeing as she sat that her tights had a hole in them. What am I doing here? she thought. This is mad, she thought. For a minute she considered getting up and walking back past the footman, when there was James coming through the door, looking anxiously at his watch. He was lugging a suitcase, which, when he turned his back on her to sign the piece of paper that the woman at reception politely offered him, Bella could see had a label stuck to its side that said SALE, with "£69.99" crossed out and "£49.99" written in instead.

Bella watched him take the plastic room key and decline the offer of a porter to carry his case. He walked over to the lift, and she went and stood by him, on the other side of a spherical orange tree that was growing from a silver pot. They got into the lift with a pair of German tourists, and she looked at him with a feeling close to dread. What was she doing with her boss in a hotel in the middle of the afternoon? If she had been able to leave at that point, she might have; instead they got out together at the fourth floor. He led her down miles of corridor painted dark purple and opened the door onto a sunny room with white bedcovers and red cushions. And only then and only after he had carefully hung a sign on the outside of the door saying DO NOT DISTURB, did he kiss her. He let out a small groan.

"You have no idea," he said, "how much I have been longing to do this."

She laughed and felt flooded with happiness. She kissed him and touched his hair and ears and cheeks. As she moved backward toward the bed, she tripped over the case. "What's that for?" she asked, laughing.

He said he didn't feel able to arrive at a hotel with no luggage and so had gone to M&S to buy one, which was why he'd been late. Then he had worried about the case being empty and so had bought some things to put in it. Bella laughed delightedly. A man who bought an empty suitcase in order to commit adultery clearly did not do this all the time.

She bent down and unzipped the case. Inside was a sack of potatoes, a bag of apples, two sandwiches, and a bottle of wine.

"I thought you might be hungry," he said.

"Raw potatoes are my favorite," Bella replied. "You're so funny—and so respectable."

"Bella," he said, "come here."

She lay in the luxurious bubbles of the hotel bath while James bustled around, patting himself dry after his shower and checking his Black-Berry.

"What time do you need to be home?" he asked. His voice was now flat and businesslike, quite different from the way he had whispered into her ear just half an hour earlier.

"I'm fine," she said. "I don't need to get to the child minder's till six. So I've got another twenty minutes."

She got out of the bath and came toward him, wrapped in the thick white towel. He made no move to kiss her and instead said: "Here's money for a taxi." He held out a twenty-pound note.

Bella recoiled as if she had been hit. "I don't want your money. I'm not a hooker."

"Listen," he said, softening slightly, "that was lovely. Thank you. Thank you for everything."

But he wasn't looking at her, and since when did one say "thank you" for sex? It was something that two people did because they both wanted to. Bella went down in the lift and walked back through the lobby, past the orange trees and the smirking receptionist, and got onto the tube feeling, after such intense joy, quite empty and spent.

Stella

"Beate has performed pretty much in line with my expectations," Stella was saying to Russell.

She had called a meeting in her office to discuss the performance of the trainees, and Russell was sitting with a checklist on a clipboard, putting ticks in boxes.

"She scores highly on finishing and initiative," she went on. "However, she has difficulty interacting with others, and I have found her to be short on emotional intelligence. Clearly it is not my call on where to post them next, but I think she might benefit from a spell in HR. There is a lot that you could teach her, Russell."

Russell nodded sagely. "And Rhys Williams?"

"He's matured a good deal in the past few months," she said. "But as he is not an economist, I really don't see there is much point in keeping him in the department. He now needs to be given a chance to show what he can do. I would suggest an off-site posting. Something in Alaska...?"

*   *   *

Later, at her desk, Stella was fighting to keep her resolve. It was right to give up Rhys, she kept telling herself. It was right for her mother. It was right for Charles and the children. It was also right for her work. It was even, she reasoned, right for Rhys. He would get a good new assignment.

For her, it was going to be hard, she thought, but the hardest bit had already been done. She had spoken to Russell, and they had agreed that Rhys would have only a couple more days working for her, and then she would not see him for months, after which the two of them could just be friends.

This line of thought, which seemed so very sensible—responsible and coolheaded—to Stella at the time, later struck her as laughably delusional. She had not just done the hard bit, she had done the easy bit. Taking a decision to stop and talk to HR was a cinch. Actually stopping was another matter altogether.

Three hours later, Stella had stopped telling herself that she had done the right thing and was sitting at her desk feeling despairing. She looked up to find Beate hovering outside her door, blinking at her angrily through her jazzy glasses.

"Have you got a minute?" she asked.

Stella nodded but didn't ask her to sit down.

"I have just been told I am to be posted to Human Resources," she said. "Were you aware of this?"

Stella nodded uncertainly. "I knew it was a possibility," she said.

"I have done exceptional work in this department. I have been in the top decile of all measurements of leadership performance, and so to put me into HR is illogical. The only possible reason for it is that this is gender-based stereotyping."

"Listen," Stella said soothingly, "you are on a three-year training program. You will stay in HR for a short stint, probably only six months, and then move on to something else. For what it's worth, I feel that although your grasp of forecasting is strong, you could benefit from assistance with the softer side."

Over Beate's shoulder, Stella could see Rhys approaching. He was looking straight at her, his eyes wide open and accusing, his shoulders slightly hunched, his face dark. Stella frowned slightly, a silent warning to him to look more professional. This signal had no effect on him, but it made Beate turn around.

Rhys went on staring at Stella, who found her spirits strangely lifted by the blackness of his expression. He would not look like that unless he really minded.

"Are you staying in Economics?" she asked him.

"No," he said. "They are sending me to Alaska to manage a community project there."

Stella smiled tightly and looked at her watch. "I have a meeting now with the CEO," she said.

She gathered her papers and walked along the corridor, leaving Beate and Rhys looking after her. As she sat down with Stephen to discuss a possible joint venture in Canada, she stole a look at her BlackBerry.

```
????????? I DON'T FUCKING BELIEVE THIS
```

She messaged back:

```
Sorry. I can explain. Let's have tea later x
```

They sat in Moorgate Starbucks, which seemed to Stella even dirtier than usual. Her mug of Earl Grey tea was weak and tepid.

"It's hard to explain," Stella was saying. "But when Mum fell yesterday, I made a deal with myself that if she was okay, I'd let you go."

"*Let me go?*" He looked at her with fury. "And why?" he went on. "Because your mother is okay, so you thought it would be a nice idea to destroy my life as a result? That makes a lot of sense!"

"Don't be so hysterical. I'm not destroying your life."

"Don't be so fucking cold."

"I'm not cold. I'm just trying really hard to do what is right. And this is dreadful for me."

"Oh fine, well, that's all right, then. I don't suppose you have any interest in whether it might be dreadful for me?" He got up, leaving his tea undrunk, and walked out.

Stella took her bag and followed him into the street. She caught his sleeve and pulled at it. "Rhys," she said, "this is tearing me in two. I can't cope with it. Of course I don't want you to go to Alaska, but you can't stay here, either. I can't do this. I love you—I really love you. But it's all impossible."

Stella had not planned to tell him that she loved him, not then and not ever. But Rhys, on hearing the words, put his arms around her. They were standing in the middle of Moorgate. It was five in the afternoon and broad daylight.

The two of them staggered into a side street and into a doorway. It was the back of a restaurant, and out of the air vent hot, greasy air was pouring. Stella stood in the hot, stinking air and let herself be kissed. She kissed him back, giddy with relief.

And three-quarters of an hour later she walked back into the building, slightly disheveled, with the lightest heart in the world. The oil barrel blinked at her. "Brent crude: $120.56, down $20.80," it said.

All night, Stella had been worrying about how best to accomplish her mission. James was the answer, she had decided. It was going to be difficult, but she would try her best.

In the end, it wasn't difficult at all. She had barely sat down on James's sofa before he had started to complain about head count and how the collapse in the oil price had greatly increased his impossible workload. And so Stella had been able to say casually: "Why don't you take one of my trainees? Rhys Williams has just done a stint with me, and he's a bit older than the others, and I think you could train him up to be quite useful. I found him a bit prickly at first, but have been increasingly impressed. I think Russell may have other plans for him, but if I were you, I'd get in first and grab him."

James had grumbled a bit at this and said that his shortfall was much more serious than anything a trainee could sort out, but then he'd shouted through to his PA to get Russell on the line.

"Strike while the iron is hot," he'd said.

Charles was sitting on the sofa reading the *New Statesman* and didn't look up when Stella came in. She walked over and sat beside him, put her head on his shoulder, and kissed him on the cheek, feeling the peculiarity of her situation. She wasn't pretending to be pleased to see him: She was pleased. The storm that was raging through her life at work had not hardened her heart at home. It was quite wrong to think, she reasoned, that Charles and Rhys were rivals for her love. The happier she was with Rhys, the more she had left for Charles.

The odd thing was, she told herself, that an affair with Rhys was making her a better wife, a better mother, and a better daughter.

She punched her mother's number into the phone. "Hello, Mum," she said.

"I can't talk to you now, darling. A frightfully nice young man is just completing the paperwork, and then I can go home."

Her mother was going to be okay. Everything was going to be okay.

Bella

Bella had felt dejected the previous evening. She had sat on the sofa with Millie and let her watch *EastEnders*, followed by *Hollyoaks*, in which a young woman was being pursued by a man twenty years older.

"That's disgusting," Millie had volunteered.

Bella had laughed uneasily and stroked her daughter's fair hair.

There had been no word from James. For those four hours in the hotel room, she had felt beautiful and desirable. She had also felt something that she could not remember ever feeling before—a sense of being in a little bubble with him in which the rest of her life didn't exist. Inside the bubble she wasn't his most junior researcher; she felt that the power balance between them was reversed—that he wanted and needed her more than she wanted and needed him. It was a thrilling position to be in.

But now the bubble had burst, and she was back in her life and desperate for something—anything—from him. It was not so much that she no longer felt he needed her: She felt that she didn't exist.

She placed her mobile on the arm of the sofa and kept looking at it instead of at the television, willing a message to arrive. At about nine thirty, she could bear it no longer and sent him a text that said:

`Hello.`

And at nine fifty-six he replied:

`Hello.`

It wasn't what she had wanted, but it was better than nothing.

The next morning when she got to work, James was in his office with the door closed, talking to Stella. As Bella walked past, he caught her eye and gave a complicit smile. Her distress the previous night was absurd, she decided: He was there and looking at her.

After a while, Stella left and James came out of his office. "Have you got a minute?"

Bella went into his office.

"There are three things I'd like to say to you," he said. "First, I would like to kiss you, though I fear that would be ill advised."

Through the slatted blinds they had a view of a dozen desks, most of which were occupied by people getting on with their work.

"Second, your text nearly caused a major incident at home. I had taken the precaution of saving your name under 'Bill,' but when it bleeped last night my younger son was fiddling with it, and wanted

Lucy Kellaway

to know who Bill was and why I had a text from him that just said hello."

"God," said Bella, "sorry. It was just that I was worried not to have heard from you…"

"It's fine," he said. "Though better not to text me at home in future."

Bella agreed to this, and he went on.

"The third thing is that we are going to have a new member of the team—a trainee who has been working for Stella. I think his name is Bryn, and she speaks very highly of him."

"He's called Rhys."

"Oh, do you know him?" he asked.

"Yes, he's nice, I think."

James frowned. "I made the error of asking her if he was good-looking, as I was concerned that you might fall for him. She gave me the strangest look and said, 'Oh no,' terribly emphatically. It was all rather awkward, and now she doubtless thinks I'm gay."

Bella laughed at this, amused at the way that straight men of his age clung to a stupid, schoolboyish fascination with homosexuality. "I hate to break it to you," she said, "but he is good-looking. Sort of."

"Damn," said James. "I had planned to put him in the empty desk next to yours. I thought you could look after him—you'd better not get too friendly."

Bella was delighted by his jealousy, though she knew there was little chance of getting too friendly with Rhys. Since their lunch in Roast she had barely seen him, and when she had he had behaved oddly. Sometimes he greeted her with great cheer, at other times he was morose and moody. Still, it would be nice having him sitting there, so long as he wasn't going to be too clever and show her up.

Given that Rhys had been with the company for only six months, he seemed to Bella to have amassed a lot of stuff. He had several different gym kits that he stowed under his desk and a towel that didn't look especially clean, which he draped over the coat stand next to Bella's jacket. He had a set of headphones and numerous chargers for various bits of electronic kit.

His screen saver was a picture of Girls Aloud clad in hot pants, aiming their bottoms at the camera and then looking around over their shoulders to pout.

"I can't believe you like Girls Aloud," Bella said. "My daughter loves them, but she's seven."

"They're crap," he said.

"They why have them as your screen saver?"

"Dunno. I just think they're funny. It's so un-AE, and I also think Kimberley is quite cute in those hot pants."

Bella laughed and thought what fun it was going to be sitting with him.

"What are you doing for lunch?" he asked.

Just as Bella was about to say that she had no plans, his mobile went and he answered, turning his back on her and whispering into the phone. Bella decided that he must be talking to his girlfriend, though why he was doing it in quite such a gauche manner, she had no idea.

He talked for a bit more in the same stilted way, and then, just before he hung up, he said what sounded like "Woof."

"Sorry," he said to Bella, "something's come up—we can't have lunch, but can we do it later in the week?"

Bella went down to the canteen on her own. She took her tray to where a group of PAs were sitting discussing how much they liked the credit crunch, as the prices in the shops had come down. Nathalie was proudly telling everyone how she'd haggled at Dorothy Perkins and persuaded the shop assistant to knock 10 percent off a pair of gloves.

As they were talking, Bella looked up to see Rhys saunter into the canteen, take two sandwiches and two bottles of water, pay for them, and disappear. This struck her as odd. Wasn't he meant to be having lunch with his girlfriend?

Stella

Rhys had been gone for precisely one morning, but Stella was already missing him. Every time she looked up from her work, she no longer saw his back and the mess of his things, only an empty desk, with its chair pushed in neatly. That day, she was supposed to be having lunch with an economist from Harvard whom she found pompous and patronizing. He had proposed lunch some six months earlier, and Stella had chosen the furthest of the dates offered in the hope that somehow it would never arrive.

Then, just as she was about to leave to meet him at the Avenue in St. James's, she had a call from his PA. He was coming in from the airport and his flight had been delayed due to fog and he wasn't going to make it.

"Oh dear," said Stella, passing off her delight as disappointment. "I'm so sorry that his day has been disrupted." She put down the phone without making any attempt to find a new date and dialed Rhys's number. Rhys answered, sounding peculiar and stiff.

"Are you overheard?" she said.

"Yes," he said.

"Listen. Something fantastic has happened," she said. "My lunch has been canceled. What are you doing right now?"

"I've just fixed up something, but I can cancel it."

"Shall we go to your flat?"

"There's no time," he said. "I have a meeting at two forty-five, and I have to get back by then."

Stella felt a prickle of irritation. But then he said: "Roof?"

And she said: "See you by the fire doors in ten minutes."

Rhys was waiting for her by the half flight of stairs leading up from the fifteenth floor. They pushed through the fire door that said ZONE C—EMERGENCY EXIT ONLY and climbed the fire stairs to the top and stepped out onto a flat roof covered in pebbles in which a few buddleias had seeded themselves.

There was a low parapet around the edge that Stella made a move to sit upon, but Rhys pulled her back, saying that he was afraid of heights. He steered them toward the sloping edge by the side of the building, and they squatted down together.

"It's cold," she said.

He took off his coat and placed it over both of them. He gave her a sandwich—roast beef and horseradish on white bread, exactly what she would never have chosen herself—and started eating his own.

Stella leaned against him under his coat and felt entirely happy. She was doing something that was dangerous physically, emotionally, and professionally, yet she felt quite safe. She was ruling over London, and Rhys had his arms around her.

"Can I ask you something?" he said.

"Yes," she said.

"Why do you like me?"

Stella laughed. "I have no idea," she said.

Bella

Bella had been back from her lunch for nearly three-quarters of an hour when her mobile phone went. It was Rhys.

"Hi, can you do me an enormous favor?" he asked.

"It depends," said Bella. "But yes, probably."

"I've done something a bit stupid. I'm stuck up on the roof. I went up there to look at the view, the door has closed behind me, and I can't get back in. Can you come and let me down?"

Bella said fine, though she wondered what he was up to. She couldn't make him out at all. He had said he was going out to lunch with someone—but then he had bought sandwiches in the canteen, and then he was locked on the roof. She hadn't even known that you could get onto the roof, but he explained where the door was and she pressed it open to find Rhys looking red-faced and breathless on the other side.

"What on earth were you doing up there?" Bella asked as they walked down the stairs.

He shrugged. "There's an amazing view."

Just as they were about to go through the swing doors back toward their desks, Rhys said: "Damn, I've left something up there. I'll be back in a sec."

Bella sat at her desk, thinking about what an odd person he was. The wild impulsiveness that made him do things like going through fire doors onto the roof had seemed bold and attractive when she'd first met him. But now it just seemed stupid. Why couldn't he spend his lunchtimes going to the canteen like everyone else?

When he returned, Bella asked: "I thought you were having lunch with Rosa?"

"Oh no," he said lightly. "We split up."

"What did you leave up there?" Bella persisted.

Rhys was prevented from answering by the approach of James. He walked straight up to him and said he would like him to prepare a paper on consumer attitudes to a windfall profits tax on oil companies.

Watching James give orders to Rhys and watching Rhys nod respectfully gave Bella a thrill. She alone knew what James was like when he wasn't like this. The previous lunchtime, they had gone back to the Great Eastern, and as Bella had sat in the bath afterward, James had held up his hands as if holding a camera and pretended to take pictures of her.

"Click," he had said. "I'll want to keep these when I'm old to look back on to remember what has been one of the happiest days of my life."

"But you *are* old," Bella had pointed out, the brusqueness of her reply hiding her pleasure.

Now he turned to her and was looking at her levelly. "As you know, I am visiting New York next week for a meeting with analysts. I think it would be helpful if you came along—it would give you a greater feeling for how the investment community rates us."

Helpful. Bella loved his use of the word. It would be helpful. Very.

* * *

This time, persuading her mother to look after Millie was easier. She had now decided that her daughter's new job was a good thing and that if Bella was earning more, she was more likely to find a decent boyfriend. She had also noticed how pretty Bella was looking and thought this would probably lead to her finding a man; it did not occur to her that it was the result of her having found one already. If she had known the truth about this particular man, her response would have been quite different—as the victim of adultery, she felt that any woman who ever had sex with a married man was a vixen, a temptress, the very devil.

Anthea had booked the flights: three business-class tickets for James, Bella, and Philip Miller, the finance director. But James, on seeing the schedule, had said calmly that it would suit him better to fly out from Gatwick rather than Heathrow, and it would be a good idea if Bella was on the same flight, as he'd be able to brief her on the trip. Anthea looked as if she were about to say something, but apparently she had second thoughts and did as she was told.

Bella was about to go home when Anthea came by her desk.

"You and I need to have a chat," she said.

"Sorry," said Bella, "I have a lot of stuff to finish off before the trip."

"I think it would be better if we had a chat anyway."

Bella stopped reading the paper that explained the complicated link between movements in the oil price and company profitability and followed Anthea into her old office. She sat at her old desk, picked up a stapler, and started to fiddle with it.

"People say a lot of things about me," Anthea said. "But one thing that they don't say is that I'm blind. They don't say I'm disloyal, either. And so, because I'm not blind"—she jabbed at her eyes as if to prove it—"I've been able to see what's happening between you and James. I realized that something was going on from the beginning. I saw how you egged him on. I saw how you tried to get his attention—showing off with the Russian translations and that business over taking those tickets to his house."

Bella considered pointing out that she had not studied Russian in order to bag James. And that doing the wife a favor was not usually a prelude to shagging the husband. But she didn't say anything.

"Every time you go out together, I see. The fire alarm was ridiculous. Do you think people didn't notice?"

"It's not what you think," Bella said feebly.

"I'm a very broad-minded person, and I don't gossip."

Bella let both these assertions pass.

"However, I've always believed that anything like this in the office is not only wrong, it is unprofessional, and it reflects badly on the entire organization."

"Have you said anything to James?"

"No, I haven't, and I'm not going to. I know that James has strayed"— she clicked her tongue and wiggled two fingers on each side to indicate a pair of quotation marks—"at least once before and that it never lasts with him. He is a normal man with normal"—she paused—"urges." She inclined her head knowingly. "So if a young, attractive woman comes and sits on his desk and bats her eyelashes at him, then he responds."

"I have never done that," Bella protested.

"But even though you are at fault in this, it's you I'm worried about. You and I have always had a very good working relationship— haven't we?"

"Oh yes," Bella said weakly.

"You do know that you have everything to lose, don't you? When he tires of you, you'll be out."

The lecture was brought to a halt by the arrival of James himself, who put his head around the door, ignored Bella, and said to Anthea: "Can you book a car to take us straight from JFK to our first appointment. I think time may be tight?"

She smiled at him. "I've done that already."

"You're a star," he said.

Bella watched Anthea pull the straight face that she pulled when really pleased. The thought occurred to her: Did Anthea have feelings for him, too?

Stella

"Why are you going to the doctor?" Clemmie was asking.

"Because I need a breast checkup," said Stella.

"Have you got a lump?" she asked, alarmed.

"No, but I haven't had it done for ages, so I thought I'd better."

Clemmie accepted this, as there was no particular reason why she shouldn't. "Hope you're okay," she said.

"Thanks, darling. I'm sure I'll be fine."

She wasn't going to the doctor for a breast examination. She was going because when she had had sex with Charles the previous night, she had noticed a strong, unpleasant smell of fish that was still there in the morning. While the children were eating their cereal, she looked it up on the Internet and diagnosed herself as having bacterial vaginosis, a condition that required treatment with antibiotics.

In the waiting room, she texted Rhys.

```
At doctors. Have repulsive complaint that is
all your fault. Stink like fish shop. Sx
```

He e-mailed back:

```
!!??xX
```

Which Stella did not think was sufficiently sympathetic.

The doctor on emergency duty that morning looked ludicrously young, though he was probably a year or two older than Rhys. Stella recognized him as the one she had seen two months earlier when she had taken Finn to be seen because he had pulled a muscle in his calf playing football.

"So," he said brightly, "what can I do for you?"

She rattled off her symptoms quickly, as if trying to distance herself from them. "I have vaginal itching, a foul-smelling discharge, and have noticed an unpleasant smell—rather like fish—on intercourse."

He cleared his throat and shifted a little. "I am sorry to have to ask you this," he said. "But it will help me get the right treatment for you. Have you had more than one sexual partner in the last week?"

It was a long time since Stella had known such embarrassment. She remembered going to the doctor during her first year at university with cystitis and being asked if she was sexually active. Not understanding the question, she had replied, "It depends what you call active," and the doctor had then solemnly explained that he was asking her if she was a virgin.

Stella fixed her eyes on the machine for taking blood pressure. "Yes," she said.

"Typically," the young doctor said, "the vagina contains a balance of healthy bacteria, known as lactobacilli, and dangerous bacteria, known as anaerobes. The acidic environment of the vagina aids in keeping this bacterial balance in check. Sometimes, however, the environment in the vagina is disrupted, and as a result, the number of anaerobes begins to increase."

Stella listened to these medical words with relief. They were something to hide her shame behind.

"Lie down, please, and take off your trousers and your underpants. I need to do a swab." He pressed the button on his intercom and said into it: "I need a nurse in room three for an internal exam."

A young woman knocked on the door and came in. Stella knew that the nurse was meant to be there to protect her honor: Male doctors were no longer allowed to do internal examinations without a female chaperone. Yet the audience made Stella feel even more wretched than she was feeling already. She took off her clothes and lay on the high, hard bed so that the doctor could collect samples from inside her and pop them into test tubes. She looked at her pale legs bent at the knee and felt revolted not just by her body, but by her whole being.

"You can get dressed now."

He gave her a prescription and told her that she must finish the course.

Out in the street, unable to find a taxi and late for her meeting, Stella felt rising panic. She hated the person she was becoming and wished that things could be simple. Boredom, which she used to dread, she now longed for. She thought of Clemmie this morning, she thought of how easy it had been to lie to her trusting daughter. She thought of the doctor and of the pretty nurse as witness to her shame. But then she thought of Rhys, and thought of being without Rhys, and that thought filled her with an even greater panic.

In the cab she dialed his number; his phone rang twice and then went through to voice mail. Wonderful, thought Stella. I have had to lie to my children, bear some disgusting infection, be late for work, and he can't even pick up his bloody phone.

But when she got into the office, she found a Post-it note stuck to her screen. It said:

In my veins there is a wish,
And a memory of fish

Stella smiled. What was the indignity of having to spread one's legs to a young doctor when one was in love with someone who knew just the right lines from Auden? She tore a page out of her pad and completed the quote:

Here am I, here are you:
But what does it mean? What are we going to do?

She put it in an internal post envelope, wrote his name on the front, and dropped it into her out-box.

Bella

Bella sat on the train to Gatwick, worrying about her clothes. She had gone shopping at the weekend and bought a cheap pin-striped suit from Zara that was tight and full of Lycra. When she had tried it on the previous night, she had thought she looked all wrong for a business meeting, and the suit didn't go with her shoes, which were too clumpy. This worry was crowding out bigger worries: What should she do about Anthea? Was she going to tell? She badly wanted to tell James that they had been found out but feared that he might panic and call it off.

But mostly she was worried about James himself, that he was the worst choice of man she had made yet. He was married, he was her boss, apparently he "strayed" all the time, and she was almost certainly going to get horribly hurt and then fired. She had turned this over and over in her mind in bed the night before and hit upon a strategy. If he was using her, she would use him, too. She would use him to show her New York, to have a lovely time. If he wanted her for sex, she would want him for sex, too. She would keep everything light. She would be in the moment.

James accepted two glasses of champagne from the stewardess and raised one to her.

"Here's to you," he said, taking a tiny sip. "You look radiant."

"I am," she said, taking a gulp. "So much so that I feel like getting plastered."

"I don't normally drink on transatlantic flights," he said. "It's so dehydrating."

Bella felt a tiny prick of disappointment. Even when he was being reckless, he was sensible.

"But then," he went on, "I don't normally do this. In fact, I have never done anything like this in my life before."

"Never?" she asked. "Swear?"

"Swear," he said, taking her hand and squeezing it.

The doubt that she had banished returned, larger than before. "Can I ask you something?" she asked.

"You can," he said.

"Do you promise you won't be cross?"

"No," he said. "I don't promise that. But I can say that given everything I know about you, I cannot imagine a circumstance in which you might make me cross..."

"Okay. I want to ask you about Julia."

"Julia?"

"Yes, Julia."

"What about her?"

"You tell me."

James withdrew his hand from hers. "What do you know?"

"That's not the point, and it isn't what I asked."

James paused and recrossed his legs the other way. "Okay," he said. "We had a brief"—he paused, as if searching for just the right word—"liaison. It was a mistake, and although I take full responsibility for what I did, I really wasn't in my right mind. It's not something that I am proud of. I don't think either of us came out of it in a good light."

"But you did well out of it?"

"What do you mean by that?"

"Well, she left AE because of you, and you took on her job. She lost everything—you gained everything."

"Bella," he said firmly, "with all due respect, you don't know what you are talking about."

"I do. I know exactly what I'm talking about. I was her PA. And because both of you are IT-challenged, you have no idea about security and I saw all the messages."

"You did *what?*" He looked at Bella in the most horrible way. "They were private. That was a breach of trust."

"All I did was read some e-mails—it's my job to read e-mails. As for you: First you shag a colleague, then you dump her. You show no remorse—instead you take her job. Then you shag your new PA. And you think you are a decent man because you have told this PA that you love your wife. You aren't decent—you're a hypocrite. And then you have the nerve to say that this is a first for you."

Bella sat back in the chair. She was shaking. What on earth was she doing? Why had she taken the happiness she had felt ten minutes ago and torn it into tiny pieces? Why was she already breaking her own rule that she was going to take it easy and enjoy the pleasure he was offering for now? She could not bear listening to him lie. She couldn't bear not knowing the truth.

"Bella," James said. "Bella. Let me speak." He tried to take her hand again, but she snatched it away. "With Julia I was at a low point. Things at home were difficult: Hillary was distant partly as a result of the medication she was taking, and Julia made a huge play for me. And I was weak and went along with it—it was mainly a physical thing..."

Bella winced.

"But then Hilly had a relapse and went back in the Priory, and I felt so awful I broke it off with Julia. I didn't tell her about Hilly, as I didn't really think it was her business. I'm not proud of what I did. But I tried to end it decently; it was a shame that she didn't really feel like being professional about it herself."

"Decently," Bella said scornfully.

"I had never done anything like that before, and vowed I would not again. But then along came you, Bella; and this is something different. I think about you all the time. Do you know that? You are brave and lovely, and I can't believe that you have fallen into my lap. And right now I feel a sort of happiness that I don't deserve, that I never thought I would feel again in my life—"

"But what about your wife?" said Bella, slightly mollified. "She isn't well yet. And doesn't that count as far as you're concerned?"

"Yes, it does count," he said. "It counts more than anything. I am carrying the guilt of that. I feel terrible about it, but that's my responsibility, not yours. But will you do me a favor? Can you not mention it for the next three days?"

The taxi pulled up at the Ritz-Carlton Hotel on Central Park South. James gave $60 to the surly driver and got their bags out of the boot, Bella's cheap black wheelie case looking quite wrong against James's Mulberry suit carrier.

Bella had last been to New York in her gap year, when she had traveled around on a Greyhound bus and had slept on the floor of a friend of her sister's in Queens and had a windswept picture taken at the top of the World Trade Center. In the nine years since then, the world had changed and so had she.

A porter took their cases and showed them to their rooms. Bella's had a view over Central Park, and down below there were horses waiting to show tourists around. A white orchid stood in the window. The room contained two double beds, which she thought a terrible waste. She hung up her suit on the padded hanger in the wardrobe and renewed her deal with herself. She was not going to make any more scenes. She was not going to worry about the future. She was going to enjoy herself.

The phone in her room went, and she picked it up.

"Who's that?" said an Englishwoman's voice.

"It's Bella Chambers."

"Oh. Where is my husband?"

"Hello, Hillary," Bella said stiffly. "This isn't his room. The switchboard must have made a mistake."

"Okay," she said sharply, and hung up.

Bella felt a mild dislike for this woman, which she knew was not fair. She felt a stronger dislike for herself, which she thought wasn't really fair, either. It was up to James to feel bad, not her.

That evening, there was a private dinner for investors at the Four Seasons. The table was set for twelve—six investors, three investment bankers, James, Philip, and Bella. Apart from Bella there was only one woman, an exceedingly thin blonde of about forty in a navy suit and flat pumps. Bella, who was in killer heels and a tight black dress, felt absurd, as if she had come to the wrong place.

Fortunately, nobody was interested in talking to her, and as there was just one conversation around the table, it was easy for Bella to remain silent. She tried to compose her face to look as if she had plenty of wise and important things to say if she chose to say them, only as it happened she didn't. The effort got harder as the evening wore on, as Bella, unlike everyone else around the table, was drinking every last drop of the five different wines that the waiters were assiduously pouring into large crystal goblets.

At the end of the meal, the conversation fragmented and Bella found herself staring at the silver clip in front of her that held the menu. "Nasturtium, heirloom tomatoes, and mustard flowers," she read out loud. And then, to no one in particular, she said: "If the tomatoes are heirlooms, wouldn't they be off by now?"

There was a brief silence around the table that James broke by giving an awkward laugh.

"Sorry," she said later in the hotel bedroom, as James peeled the dress off her.

"It doesn't matter," he said. "You're so funny."

He insisted on kissing her all over her body until she no longer felt like a gawky, tarty ignoramus, but imagined herself the most desirable woman on Manhattan.

Shortly before three a.m., James drifted off to sleep and Bella, too wired to contemplate sleep, felt a sudden urge to talk to Millie. For the last twelve hours she had not thought of her daughter once, and now she worried that the intensity of her private, separate happiness might have caused something bad to happen to her.

She tiptoed into the bathroom and dialed the number. Her mother answered and said: "Why aren't you in bed? What time is it there?"

"It's three a.m., but I'm jet-lagged. Is Millie okay?"

"Yes, of course she's okay. Do you want to talk to her?"

And then to Millie, Bella said: "I'm going to bring you to New York one day, and we can go on a horse ride in Central Park and eat hot dogs…"

Millie seemed unmoved by this but told her mother that she had not been allowed Coco Pops for breakfast.

As she said good-bye there was a rumble of thunder, and James woke and called out to her to come back to bed. Bella slipped under the white duvet, and he clung to her. He was sweating and his eyes were closed.

There was another crack of thunder overhead. He groaned and buried his face into her neck.

"What's the matter?" she whispered.

"I can't bear storms," he said, his voice muffled as his mouth was pressed to her.

Bella had hated feeling responsible for Xan, but to find herself comforting the man who had just hosted a dinner at one of the most prestigious restaurants in New York gave her the deepest joy. She closed her eyes and pressed her body against his.

"I'll look after you," she whispered.

At six a.m., James reached for the remote control and turned on CNN.

"London stock market opens 460 points down," it said on the ticker at the bottom of the screen.

"Shit," said James.

The cowering man of the night before had gone, and he was his efficient work self, sitting naked on the edge of his bed, staring at his BlackBerry.

On the television, the anchor was saying: "And over to our London business commentator, Nancy Silverman."

Bella watched an American woman with a helmet of platinum hair standing in front of the Bank of England and saying that Gordon Brown's rescue plan had failed to reassure the markets.

"Don't you think," Bella said to James, "that it's funny the way that people talk of the markets as if they were a person who needs calming?"

James looked at her as if he had no idea what she was saying. "Shh," he said sharply, and bent his body toward the television screen.

"One of the heaviest losers is the oil giant AE," the woman was saying. "Its common stock fell by £3.56 this morning on news that the Russian government is nationalizing its stake in its Siberian oil field."

"Shit," said James again. "Shit, shit, shit."

Stella

Stella was staring at her screen. The markets were diving, and the AE share price was in free fall. She couldn't help feeling that this unraveling of the financial system, though shocking, felt right. Until then there had been two worlds, the private world she shared with Rhys—which was dangerous and out of control—and the public, professional world—in which things were safe and orderly. But now both worlds were being torn apart: There was general mayhem.

Stella had got into the office early, having canceled a planned visit to Rhys's flat. She had called him the night before from home, crouching in the bathroom and talking in a whisper, to say that as the markets were so volatile, she could not risk skiving and neither should he. He had said fine, in a tone of voice that meant the reverse, and hung up.

The next morning, he came and stood in her office. "What upsets me," he said, "isn't the fact that you did not come round this morning. It's that we'll never have any normal time together, to do the things that normal couples do—we can't even go to the movies, let alone walk on a beach, or even hold hands in public, or even talk on the fucking telephone."

The idea that he thought they were a couple gave her a thrill. She had wondered what was the right word to describe the two of them; language didn't stretch to their situation. They weren't a couple. She wasn't his girlfriend. And not his mistress. Possibly she was his lover, though that word sounded too grown up. But whatever they were or weren't, he wanted to walk on a beach with her, and that fact made her feel quite light-headed.

As a result of the market turmoil, Stella's three o'clock meeting had been canceled, and she found she had two and a half blank hours in her diary. She called Rhys.

"Will you come to the movies with me?"

"When?"

"Now."

"Are you asking me out?"

Stella laughed. "I am."

Kissing Rhys in the taxi, Stella no longer felt any embarrassment about the driver; he could think what he liked. Instead she was transported by the audacity of their skiving; bunking off in the middle of the afternoon to hold hands in the darkness of the Renoir Cinema while the markets were imploding felt even more forbidden than going to Rhys's flat for sex.

Of the three screens, one was showing a film that had already started, another an obscure French comedy about an Algerian documentary maker, and the third a revival of *Brokeback Mountain*, which they had both seen already but decided to see again. They got their tickets and went into the semidarkness of the cinema, which was quite empty apart from two women, each sitting on her own.

Rhys bought a bag of popcorn and steered Stella toward the back row—which was no longer up against a wall, as it had been the last time she went to the cinema to kiss a boy—which, she thought to herself, was probably before Rhys was even born. Now it had a corridor behind it, and the seats were too wide to allow much intimacy. When Rhys put his arm around her, Stella had to lean her entire body toward him, giving herself a crick in the neck.

The first time she had seen *Brokeback Mountain* was with Charles. She had thought it overrated, but he had been impressed by the cinematography, about which he had given her a lecture on the way home.

This time she saw a different film. The two young cowboys were her and Rhys, locked in a mutual and passionate love that was impossible and was destroying the rest of their lives.

Her eyes filled with tears, and Rhys, who had been watching the side of her face more assiduously than he had been watching the film, put out his hand and brushed a tear away with his finger and then put the finger in his mouth.

"Don't be sad," he whispered. "Be happy. I adore you."

Stella moved as close to him as the generous arm of the cinema seats would permit and wanted to stay in the darkness forever.

As they emerged into the daylight, Stella saw from her BlackBerry that the stock markets had lost another 4 percent of their value, that the oil price was down another $15, and that $4 billion had been wiped from the company's market value. There were six missed calls from James's assistant in New York. Stella's happiness, which had been so intense a few minutes earlier, was now gone. She must not let her job unravel along with everything else.

Bella

James, Bella, and Philip were on the fifty-fourth floor of the offices of FirstAmerica Bank. The presentation to investors was due to start in ten minutes, and James was pacing up and down, talking on the phone to Stephen, who had been tracked down in Moscow.

"I've no idea where the leak came from," James was saying. "But there will clearly be questions about it, and so we are going to need to say something…I would like to give them something else to think about that they can make into a positive story…Well, yes, but Stella's slides are not exactly upbeat…"

James hung up and said to Bella, "Can you get Stella on the phone for me urgently?"

Bella called her, but there was no reply. She e-mailed her and then sent a text but got nothing back. Then she called Nathalie.

"Where is she?" she asked.

"I have no idea," Nathalie said grumpily. "I've been trying to get hold of her myself."

Bella thought this odd. Why, she thought, on a day when the markets were in meltdown, would she turn off her BlackBerry?

When Stella did call back some three hours later, James was busy talking to analysts and had told Bella to instruct Stella to send some more optimistic slides for the afternoon's presentations. Bella wasn't looking forward to telling someone senior to do something that she didn't want to do and wasn't at all sure that she would be able to hold her ground.

Yet far from being prickly, Stella was charm itself. She apologized for having been hard to track down, and when told that she needed to rewrite her conclusions about sustainable petrol and about the medium-term prospects in the oil market, she simply said: "I'm just returning to the office now from a meeting, but I'll do it as soon as I'm back. Tell James he'll have it in half an hour." And then, as if talking to an equal, she asked, "What's the mood like there?"

"Everyone is so shell-shocked, I don't know if they'll give a stuff about our long-term projections," Bella said. "I think they are worried about the next five minutes."

Within half an hour, Stella's new slides—which now claimed that petrol made from algae could transform the company within five years and also showed how the company was strongly profitable at almost any oil price—arrived and were added to the presentations.

James greeted their arrival with a smile. He was standing in front of a screen in a long meeting room, being introduced by one of the bankers who had attended the dinner the night before.

"In the last few hours we have witnessed a perfect storm," the banker was saying. "We have seen the tectonic plates of the global markets shift, and we are moving into unchartered territory. But it is my pleasure to introduce James Staunton of Atlantic Energy to update you on the seismic shifts within the oil industry..."

Bella listened to this talk of extreme weather conditions and marveled at the smooth appearance of the speaker. His hair looked as if it had been painted on, his suit was immaculate, and his teeth were unnaturally white. There was a gleam in his eye, though whether this was excitement or fear, she did not know.

James, by contrast, was looking disheveled. His shirt was crumpled, his tie knot wasn't quite straight, and his hair looked wild. But there was a straightness to how he talked that Bella admired.

"We are entering a new future," he said. "We don't know what it is going to be like. I'm not going to lie to you to pretend I know what will happen. I don't."

As he said this, he caught Bella's eye, as if speaking straight to her.

No, she thought, neither do I.

Stella

Stella rewrote her forecasts as quickly as she could, not merely because there was an urgent need for them, but because she found doing it so distasteful that she wanted it over quickly.

This was the first time in her working life that she had produced figures she believed to be wrong. Often in the past she had put a spin on the facts, but this time she was implying that something was exciting and viable when it wasn't.

She finished the work, sent it, and tried not to think about it. She wasn't deceiving investors—that was too strong a word. She was misleading them. None of the facts she had used was wrong exactly; she had simply been selective in the facts that she had chosen. She told herself that she had been given no choice in the matter. Stephen and James, both of whom were mainly decent and trustworthy, had told her to do this, so if she hadn't, they would have written the forecasts themselves, probably even less cautiously than her revised effort. And in any case, she reasoned, this was what it was like being senior in a company. You had to do distasteful things sometimes. So long as you stayed on the right side of a line. Stella knew that what she had just done was borderline, but that she would go no further.

She couldn't avoid making a comparison with the daily deception in her private life. She wasn't merely misleading Charles. She was lying to him. She was lying to her children. She was also lying to herself—by telling herself that she was managing and that the strength of her feeling made it all right.

But then she reasoned that even though she was indeed deceiving Charles and the children, they were not going to find out. They wouldn't get hurt; she would make sure of it. Stella was pretty sure that she would be hurt, and hurt horribly, but she didn't want to think about that now.

It was odd, she thought, that in all this moral decay the only person in her life whom she was not deceiving was Rhys. And because her relationship with him was the only one with any honesty in it, it was this relationship—which was so very wrong—that was the only one that felt right.

When she had sat with Rhys that afternoon in the cinema, she had felt in a state of grace toward him. There had been no lies. There had just been her and him and his hand on her wet cheek. But outside, everything was complicated and awry.

Nathalie had put her head around the door and asked: "Where were you this afternoon? Lots of people were trying to get hold of you."

And Stella had said: "Didn't I tell you? I was at a conference at the International Energy Agency. I thought I'd put it in the diary?"

Nathalie had said: "Oh, right."

But her tone of voice left Stella feeling uneasy. She was going to have to be more careful. She was a cat with nine lives, and this was one life lost. She had eight more left, and she was going to stop this before she got down to the last one.

Bella

On Bella's last night in New York, she and Philip and James had dinner together, and the two men talked to each other about the market meltdown and then about golf, and Bella felt as if she might as well not have been there at all. She drank too much wine and ate all of her vast T-bone steak and had a large, babyish ice-cream sundae for pudding and so was feeling quite sick by the time they got to the hotel room. They got undressed in silence, and James said that he was so tired after the previous thirty-six hours that he had to sleep. Bella was left lying in the dark on the smooth white sheets, feeling hollow and lonely and wishing that she had never come to New York.

But then at about five, James woke and made love to her with passion and said these had been two of the most memorable nights of his life. And then he said, as they lay side by side, "I'm frightened."

And Bella replied: "But the storm passed last night."

"I'm frightened of another storm. It's not just the markets, though it's partly that. I'm frightened of what is happening between us."

The immigration queue was slow, and they stood in it in silence. There was no trace of the intimacy of the night before. It was as if James were already mentally back at home with his family and Bella was in the way. James announced that he was going to get a taxi from the airport but he could drop her off anywhere on the way. Bella said no, it'd be quicker to get the train from Victoria. He nodded agreement and gave her a quick kiss on the cheek.

"I'll see you tomorrow. Hope you get back safely."

Bella had just missed a train and sat on the platform, too tired to want to think about what had happened to her. All she wanted was to see Millie again. But when she arrived at her mother's, Millie barely said hello, and when Bella asked, "Did you miss me?" her daughter shrugged.

Stella

Stella and Rhys were lying in his bed. It had taken them forty minutes to get to his flat in a cab; they had spent forty-five in bed and in another five they would have to get up and go back to the office. She was lying on his chest, silent. It was not a silence of contentment, more one that comes when the words are too heavy to utter.

"What's the matter?" he said.

"Nothing."

"Tell me."

"No, no," she said, "really, it's nothing."

But he persisted, and eventually she said: "This is going to be over soon, you will find a proper girlfriend, and I can't bear that thought at all."

"I think that is quite unlikely on recent form. You keep trying to dump me, but I refuse to be dumped."

He laughed, but instead of feeling cheered, Stella was made anxious by his good spirits. Rhys could only be feeling happy, Stella thought, if he didn't notice how bad things were, or if he did notice and didn't care. Both were equally depressing.

"Can we have lunch tomorrow?" she asked.

"That would be lovely," he said, "but it'll have to be quick, as James will be back from New York, and I'm behind with the presentation I'm working on."

"What?" said Stella, her melancholy turning into anger. "What do you mean you're behind?" She sat up in bed, not bothering to pull up the covers, and stared at Rhys.

He looked puzzled. "It's not a big deal. I'm just saying I'm a bit behind with my work, and it bothers me."

"Oh, great," said Stella, moving farther away from him across the bed. "Do you have any *idea* how 'behind' I am with my work? I have infinitely more work than you—not to mention two children and a husband and a mother-in-law and two houses and two huge jobs. I am bending over backwards to make time for you, meaning that everything else gets shortchanged, and I don't say one word about it, and you start moaning because you are a bit behind with one simple presentation."

The words poured out of her in a fluent, angry torrent. Rhys shifted his body so that it was no longer touching hers. "Thanks for reminding me how fucking successful you are," he said coldly. "You know what? My job matters to me. I might not be at your elevated level, but I've come a long way, and I did that by trying. Not by having contacts."

Stella got herself out of bed and cast about for her tights, so hastily and happily discarded less than an hour earlier. As she pulled them on, her toenail caught the nylon and made a hole.

She was angry with him; but more than that, she was angry with herself—or with the person she was becoming. Never before in her life had she been needy; to be needy toward a young man who evidently didn't give a shit about her was pathetic.

She put on her coat, got her bag, and closed the door of his flat without saying a word. She ran down the dirty staircase and out onto the street. Just as she turned the corner from his street into Seven Sisters Road, she heard her name and turned to see Rhys running toward her in his socks, holding his tie and shoes in his hand.

"I'm sorry," he said.

"So am I," she said.

And in relief, she kissed him long and hard in the middle of the street.

Bella

The first day back from New York, James had been busy, and Bella had only glimpsed him once, from behind. She had even less idea of what he was thinking than usual, and as the day went on she became increasingly anxious. She kept checking her phone to see if he had sent her a message, but there was none.

Bella was meant to be writing up a report on investor feedback from the New York trip, but instead she stared blankly at her screen. Why had he not sent her anything?

Into her phone she typed: "Where are you? X"

And as she sent it, one from him arrived, crossing hers. It said: "Plse come up to the boardroom asap."

What was this? thought Bella. The message was more imperious than intimate. She wondered if they had been discovered, if Anthea had said something, and if he had chosen the theatrical surroundings of the boardroom to call it off.

She went up to the thirteenth floor and stepped out of the lift onto a pale velvet carpet. The quiet seemed ominous to her, and she opened the heavy door into the boardroom. The room was almost entirely filled by a vast elliptical table, dark and gleaming, around which all eighteen members of the AE board could sit comfortably.

Bella had been in this room only once before, and that was when she had had to take something up to Julia, who was giving a presentation. But now, empty of people, it seemed even more intimidating than when full.

James was standing facing her, with his back to the picture windows and the extravagant view over the City, looking at her with a fevered intensity. "My visitors have gone," he said, "and I have this room booked for another fifteen minutes."

He took the trolley on which the remainder of the visitors' biscuits were sitting and began to wheel it outside. "We don't want to be disturbed by catering," he said.

He returned to the room, closed the door, and then put a chair against it.

"What are you doing?" Bella asked.

He held out his open arms to her.

"We can't," she said. "Not here."

"We can," he said. "No one will come. Promise. I thought about you all last night when I got home, and all through a tedious meeting with environmentalists just now. Please."

She remembered that he had said something to her, when they were lying in bed in the hotel, about having sex on the boardroom table. But Bella had thought he was joking. She couldn't imagine how anyone would prefer a hard, unyielding surface to a soft, comfortable bed. And this sort of risk struck her as insane; she would have expected him, of all people, to deplore such madness.

Yet as James put his arms around her, Bella felt his need for her and again felt the unfamiliar shifting of power between them.

"Please," he begged.

Bella stepped out of her pants and tights and hoisted herself onto the table, lifting her skirt and feeling so foolish that she started to laugh. It reminded her more than anything of her first ever sexual experience, when her nine-year-old friend Jenny had instructed her to pull down her pants while she inspected the various different holes.

"Shh," said James.

The table was slippery under her back and hard under her head. The edge of it was cutting into her thighs most uncomfortably. James let out a groan of pleasure: It was all over quickly.

"Thank you, beautiful Bella," he said, and kissed her forehead and her neck. "I adore you."

Bella lifted herself up and got off the table, leaving a wet smear behind on its shiny surface.

The expression of religious rapture left James's face, and he stared at the mark, horrified. "Oh God," he said. "Where can I find something to clean that up?"

James left the room, and Bella was getting back into her tights when he returned with a plastic bottle of bleach.

"You can't put that on the table," she said. "It's not meant for wood." But James had already poured the viscous liquid onto the table.

Instantly, the French polish crackled and bubbled.

"Fucking hell!" he shouted, scrubbing at it furiously and making the patch worse. "Shit!" he shouted. "Shit, shit!"

Bella, who had been just about keeping a giggling fit at bay, now started to laugh.

"Be quiet," James hissed at her as he spread the corrosive bleach farther out on the table. "It's not funny."

Stella

Stella had moved to the room two down from the CEO's corner office. He had wanted her to be next door to him, but this would have involved moving the finance director, which could not be countenanced. Stella was now in the office next to James and had eighteen more ceiling tiles than he had—a fact that he pointed out with a brave pretense at humor—along with two sofas and a splendid view down toward Canary Wharf. But for all this splendor, she liked her new office less than the old one. It felt too big for her, too imposing.

The new arrangement was making the logistics of her affair even more difficult. Early mornings were now impossible, as Stephen got into work at seven a.m. most days, and now that her office was next to his, Stella no longer felt able to roll up at nine.

Evenings were no good, either, as Stella really did need to be home. She had made an uneasy deal with herself: As long as her affair with Rhys was conducted in office hours and took no time away from Charles or Clem or Finn, she could go on with it. As Seven Sisters was so far away, they had started to go to a hotel close to the office. This was not only faster, it was also safer. It was getting increasingly difficult to explain long absences during the day to Nathalie, but going to the hotel for an hour was relatively easy: Stella simply said she was off to the gym. Nathalie even commented on how much weight Stella had lost through all her exercising, not understanding that love, guilt, insomnia, and stress reduced her boss's weight more effectively than any amount of work on the cross-trainer had ever done.

Yet Stella disliked the hotel for being so impersonal. Some of her happiest moments had been watching Rhys in his black toweling dressing gown getting mugs out of cupboards in his tiny kitchen and making her a cup of tea, and then she could trick her mind into thinking he was really hers. The flat also freed them of an awkward skirmish over money. The hotel was £260 for a night, a sum that Stella could pay with ease and Rhys with considerable difficulty. However, he disliked being paid for, both as a matter of pride and because it reminded him of the difference in their circumstances.

So they had reached the uneasy compromise that Rhys would make the booking, and Stella would give him the cash, and he would go to the desk and pay at the end. Rhys was a born negotiator and had brazenly negotiated day rates—something that Stella would have been far too embarrassed to do—and then when they turned out to be such regular customers, he had negotiated another discount for loyalty. But even with the deductions, they were paying £130 for what was often less than an hour.

"That was five pounds a minute," Stella said that afternoon, when they went to the hotel for just half an hour. She had meant this as an idle observation, but Rhys flew into a rage.

"How dare you try to measure my contribution to your life in terms of money," he shouted. "I've put my whole life on hold for you. You just want young cock."

The obscenity of the phrase sat between them.

"I was joking," he said into the silence. But it didn't feel like a joke, and neither of them was laughing.

Stella put on her clothes, threw some notes on the bed, and walked out of the hotel, leaving Rhys with one sock on, casting around for the other one.

Bella

Bella and James had got into a routine of sorts. Whenever he could clear a few hours, he would send her a message and they would meet at a soulless hotel by Old Street roundabout.

He said it was more convenient than the Great Eastern, but Bella suspected that it was more because it was cheaper and more anonymous. James had explained to the manager that he needed somewhere to do some work during the day where he would not be disturbed.

Bella had stopped finding his coyness sweet and found it irritating. If some hotel receptionist knew he was shagging his young researcher, so what? Half the City was probably doing it, too.

The arrangement was that he would go to the hotel, check in, text her the room number, and she would wait five minutes and go straight to the room. The pattern was always the same. While they were together in their bubble, they were perfectly happy. But as they were about to leave to go back to the office, James became wooden and Bella increasingly miserable.

"Why are you always like this afterwards?" she asked him one afternoon as he was getting dressed in his usual businesslike fashion.

"Like what?" he asked.

"You're cold and unreachable."

"I'm sorry," he said. "I can't help it. I have to prepare myself to go back to my normal life, and to do that I have to shut all feeling down. It is the only way I can cope."

This answer mollified Bella a little. She was cheered by the idea that he had to shut all feeling down in order to go home.

On that particular afternoon, when she knocked at room 304, James was already in his underpants and holding out a Mappin and Webb carrier bag. "I've got something for you," he said.

Since the Van Morrison CD he had bought her nothing, a fact that Bella sometimes remarked to herself when she was in the mood for collecting grievances. She wasn't in the least materialistic, but she was romantic. She needed signs that he minded about her, and presents did that.

Inside the bag was a black velvet box tied up with a pink velvet ribbon. Bella carefully undid the ribbon and opened the box. Lying on a padded bed of satin was a string of pinkish pearls with a gold clasp.

"Are these for me?" she said.

"Who did you think they were for?"

Bella picked them up. Her mother had a string of pearls a bit like these that she had inherited from her great-aunt. She never wore them on the grounds that they were too conservative. Bella stared at the pearls in horror.

"Don't you like them?" he asked.

"I love them," she said.

He took the necklace and fastened it around her neck. "Bella," he said, "you look quite beautiful."

Bella would have liked to feel gratitude that he had chosen something for her and had spent a lot of money on her. Instead she felt resentful that he didn't know her better and frustrated at the waste. And cross with herself at having an even more unworthy thought: Could she exchange them for money instead?

He kissed her with such tenderness that Bella softened a little. She must stop being so spoiled: It was really rather nice to be given pearls in the middle of a Tuesday afternoon. She bent down to take off her shoes, and as she did so she saw inside his briefcase. There was another identical gift bag that he was taking home. The second string of pearls must be for his wife.

Stella

Back in the office, Stella went into the ladies' to put on makeup and to try to hide her distress. Looking at herself in the mirror, she saw that she was not wearing her earrings—she must have left them at the hotel. They were particularly precious to her: dangling drops of Venetian glass that Clemmie had given her for her last birthday.

She called the hotel and was put through to housekeeping. "When did you vacate the room?" the man on the other end asked.

Stella told him, and then he asked: "And how many nights did you stay?"

"I didn't stay for a night," Stella said. "I just needed an hour's rest during the day."

There was a slight snigger on the other end of the phone, but Stella, fresh from having been told she was after young cock, found that this additional humiliation did not move her at all.

At home that evening, she resolved to be more present with her family. Rhys had texted her midafternoon to say sorry and that he loved her, and she had said sorry in turn. She was relieved to have made up with him but felt exhausted at the emotional swings. She also despaired at the new pattern: that every time they had sex, they ended up arguing. She did not understand how she could want to hurt so badly someone whom she thought she loved. Perhaps it was that they had so little time together that each second had to be intense. And if it could not be intense in a good way, the coin flipped, and it was intense in a nasty way.

Stella decided to spend the evening sewing name tapes into Finn's new rugby kit, a task that she would normally have given to the nanny but that she was undertaking herself as a sort of pointless penance. Even though Finn could not have cared less about who sewed the tapes into his uniform, or even if it had tapes at all, the mindless stitching made Stella feel a little less horrible about herself.

While she sewed, Finn started scrolling through the songs on her brand-new iPod, peering at the names through his new Harry Potter glasses. "Wicked, Mum. Why have you got 50 Cent on your iPod?"

Stella looked at her son warily. "Oh," she said, her voice betraying how flustered she was feeling, "I heard it on the radio and bought it on iTunes."

"You couldn't have done," he said calmly. "When you download it the cover graphics come up. This one has been imported from a copied CD."

"Well, I don't understand these things," said Stella. "Some of the things on my iPod I've bought, and others I haven't. I don't know which song that is. I don't like it anyway."

This last bit was true, at least. She didn't like 50 Cent, but she did like some of the other music Rhys had introduced her to. Her favorite was Coldplay's "The Scientist," which she had played again and again.

Each time she and Rhys had a row she listened to the words, feeling that Chris Martin was singing them just for her.

Finn put down the iPod, having lost interest in where his mother had got her songs from. He picked up his PSP instead, and Stella went on stitching, resolving to be more careful.

Later that evening, as Stella and the children were sitting down to dinner, her mobile went. It was in her bag on the floor, and Clemmie bent down and answered it. Stella felt no anxiety about this, as Rhys never called her in the evenings.

"Yes," she could hear her daughter saying. "No, I'm her daughter... Oh, okay... Yeah, fine, I'll tell her." She put down the phone. "That was someone from housekeeping at the City Novotel," she said. "They've got your green earrings."

Stella stayed in hotels all the time, and to leave something in a hotel was not in itself suspicious. And "City" didn't reveal that the city was London. "What a relief," she said. "I was so upset to have lost them."

"But Mum," said Clemmie, "you were wearing them this morning."

"No, I wasn't," Stella said evenly. "I didn't put on any this morning." And she pointed toward her earringless lobes. "Now can you clear the table?"

Clemmie looked puzzled but took it no further.

Stella's heart was beating furiously, and she felt sick at herself. What thickening of the arteries had happened to make her able to lie so barefacedly to her daughter? In the space of thirty minutes she had lost two more lives. But, thought Stella, she still had six left.

Stella had lain awake the previous night, trying to make sense of the day and of the disaster that had nearly struck. The problem, she thought, was that she and Rhys didn't have enough time together. She would not have left the earrings behind if they hadn't been so rushed, and if they hadn't been so rushed, they would not have had such a horrible scene.

The answer, she decided, was to get him back working for her again, and then she would be able to control his workload as well as her own. Now that she was chief of staff, she was expected to have an executive assistant, and she thought that she could give the job to Rhys.

She did, of course, realize that to promote him was unprofessional, possibly corrupt, and dangerous to both of them. But she squashed that thought by reasoning that it would allow them to be together all the time. His current stint with James would come to an end soon, and after that he would be sent to Alaska. Doing this would keep him by her side. And in any case, she reasoned, Rhys was talented and she was sure he would do the job at least as well as anyone else.

Stella got into work early the next day to execute this plan, and as she arrived, the cleaner was just leaving.

"Hello," said Stella. "How are you? How is your family?"

Bonita shrugged and said her family was well but that she wasn't going to be working at AE any longer.

"Oh dear," said Stella. "Why?"

"They say I put bleach on the boardroom table, but I didn't do it. I didn't even come to work that day."

"But that's ridiculous," said Stella. "Haven't you told them that it wasn't you?"

Bonita gave her an almost pitying look. "Of course. But they didn't listen."

Stella watched her gather her things and go. She thought the cleaner was facing unemployment with considerably more equanimity than Stella was dealing with her own, self-imposed problems.

She turned on her computer and drafted an e-mail to Russell saying that she wished to start at once interviewing for an executive assistant. Then she e-mailed Rhys telling him what she was planning.

He e-mailed back:

don't I have a say in this?

Stella frowned at the screen and typed out a reply:

Of course you have a say in it. I thought you would be pleased—
it's a massive promotion.

Rhys: So I'm sleeping my way to the top?

Stella: No, you aren't. You deserve this. You're a genius.

Stella sighed, closed down her Hotmail, and asked Nathalie to find
out who in the company was responsible for their cleaning contract;
then she drafted a second e-mail:

Dear Shane

I understand we have just fired a cleaner for allegedly using the
wrong cleaning product on the boardroom table. She says that
she was not even working on the day when the damage was
done. Did we investigate this at the time? Can you please let me
know precisely what happened?

Stella

Within five minutes, she had a reply. Last time she had complained to
the facilities manager, it had taken five days for him to reply. This, Stella
was realizing, was one of the advantages of being chief of staff rather
than chief economist.

Hi Stella,

Thank you for your message. As a result of the incident, which
will incidentally cost us in excess of £5000 to repair, we have
put the cleaning company on probation. The decision to fire an
individual was taken by the management of KleenTeam, not by AE
personnel.

Shane Edwards

Facilities Manager

"Thank you for your reply," wrote Stella, who, having got the bit between her teeth, was enjoying this correspondence.

I am surprised that you think we can hide behind decisions taken by companies to which we outsource. All companies that work with us as partners must be able to prove to us that they treat their staff decently. Can I leave it with you to find out what happened in this particular case?

Thank you,

Stella

Later that day, she got the following reply:

I have touched base with Kevin Patchett of KleenTeam. He informs me that no decision had been taken to fire Bonita Carlos and that she remains on the payroll. I hope this answers your question.

Rgds, Shane.

So they were all covering their backs. Stella considered pointing out that they were liars but didn't feel the need to score any points with Shane, so she let it go. The cleaner, it seemed, would get her job back. It was her good deed for the day. There hadn't been many of those recently, she thought.

Bella

Bella and James were lying in their hotel bed one afternoon, and Bella asked: "What were you like when you were a little boy?"

James hesitated and then said: "I think I was a very careful child."

"Now why doesn't that surprise me," she said.

He then told her that he couldn't really remember his childhood at all.

"Is that because it was such a long time ago?" asked Bella.

James laughed. "No," he said. "I just can't remember it."

He told her how he had only one childhood memory: being taken to Kensington Gardens by his nanny and losing a toy soldier that he had been given for Christmas.

"So then what happened?" Bella asked.

"Nothing," he said. "We went back to look for it and didn't find it, and I was really upset."

"Well, if that was the most upsetting thing in your childhood, it doesn't sound very bad."

"It was traumatic, actually. But why do you want to know about my childhood?"

"Because I want to know everything about you."

This wasn't true. She wanted to know nothing at all about the biggest slice of his life—the Wimbledon slice—and her interest in his childhood was an attempt to stake out a claim on his life from before he got married.

"You know everything there is to know about me," he said. "In fact, I think you know me better than anyone in the world."

"That's a lie," she said.

"I am lying to everyone else," he said. "But I'm not lying to you."

From the beginning, James had made it clear that Bella must not contact him at weekends, though sometimes he would break his own rule and send her little messages saying:

```
Good night.
```

Or:

```
Good morning
```

Or:

```
I'm out shopping
```

She longed for these messages, as she decided to invest in them all the emotion that they did not betray. She took them as a sign that he was thinking about her and wished he were with her.

The Saturday following the day he had told her about the soldier, there had been no such messages. Bella had checked her phone every five minutes throughout the day, feeling increasingly angry. If he was closer to her than to anyone in the world, how could he spend two days a week pretending that she did not exist? After she put Millie to bed on Saturday night, she drank two glasses of wine and sent him a text saying:

```
Please call.
```

And then she waited for her mobile to ring, but it didn't. At lunch-time on Sunday, she got a text that read:

```
Sorry, didn't see text until now. Hope all
well?
```

Bella stared at it in disbelief. Hope all well? *Hope all well?* She texted back:

```
No, all not fucking well. All totally shit.
```

She waited ten minutes, and when no reply came, she texted again, saying:

```
forget it
```

And then on Monday he asked what on earth the matter had been, and she said she had felt miserable and missed him, and he replied that he had missed her, too, obviously. He always did, he said.

Briefly, she felt better. But then he said: "Bella, you mustn't text me at home. Last time my son saw it, but this time it was my wife. She's not one to snoop, she trusts me as a point of principle. But she saw your last message and gave me a curious look. I suddenly had a feeling of total panic. That all of this was unraveling, and that I would lose everything."

Bella looked at her boss coldly. "I'm sorry for causing you any embarrassment."

He missed the sarcasm and said: "Well, no harm done. Let's put it behind us."

Stella

Stella had hoped that she would be able to conduct the interviews for her executive assistant on her own, but Russell had insisted on sitting in on them. They saw half a dozen candidates during the morning, the strongest of which was Beate. She had made a PowerPoint presentation of her achievements and had thought carefully about what the job would consist of and what she would bring to it. The performance was as impressive as it was alienating.

Rhys's interview was much more shambolic. He had given the job little thought and was more or less reading from the prompt sheet that Stella had prepared for him the night before. Afterward Russell said: "There was no contest. Beate has grown so much during her spell in HR."

"Yes," replied Stella. "But I have worked with both of them for months, and he is the talented one. He has rough edges, for sure. But we can deal with those."

Russell raised his eyebrows in surprise.

"I appreciate your feeling on this," Stella went on. "But in the end I need to trust my own instinct. And that tells me that Rhys is the one to go for."

On his first day as her executive assistant, Rhys got up from his desk and came into her room at least every fifteen minutes throughout the day. And when he wasn't standing in her office, she could see him sitting bent over his desk. It felt like the happy times when he had just joined her department as a trainee and was trying to get her attention. Stella now looked back on that period—which was just nine months ago but felt like another age—with regret and nostalgia. It was before the guilt and self-hatred had set in, but when his admiration was so obvious that it made her feel admirable.

But within two weeks, she was beginning to wonder whether the new arrangement had been a mistake. Spending more time together did not reduce the tension between them; it increased it.

Stella now was obsessed with the idea that his interest in her was cooling. And being able to see him all day was more torment than reassurance. She felt he was coming into her office less often, and when he did he stayed only briefly. She watched how well he was getting on with the others and started to feel lonely. Every time she heard him laugh, she was aware of his separateness. Every time she looked up and he wasn't there, she wondered where he was.

"I'm going to cancel the dinner I'm meant to be going to tonight," she said. "I've got my appraisal with Stephen at six, but I can come to you after that?"

"Oh God, I'm sorry," he said. "I'm having dinner with Rosa. I can't cancel, as I canceled last time."

At first Stella hadn't minded that he still saw Rosa from time to time. He had split up with her the week after he had come to dinner but had said they were still friends. Stella now found that she minded very much indeed. It wasn't really that she thought they had got back together, but that she minded everything that distracted his attention from her. This minding was mad and ugly, she knew, but she did not know how to stop it.

"Fine," Stella said coldly. "Now where are the briefing notes for my four o'clock meeting?"

Stella's annual appraisal was usually a farce.

The CEO would solemnly tell her that she was a high achiever, but Stella, instead of feeling cheered by this, was usually left feeling demoralized. Perhaps it was because she was annoyed that every year they had to fill out the "areas for improvement" box, and every year this said that she needed to forge closer links with the international subsidiaries, which meant more travel. As if she weren't traveling enough as it was. Or perhaps it was hard to sit and listen to someone praise you in this stupid, stilted way without feeling that the whole thing was a charade, and one in which your actual efforts were irrelevant.

This year, for the first time, Stella was nervous. She knew she had made little of the new job, which seemed to involve nothing more than attending a few more meetings with Stephen and being copied on a few more e-mails. She clearly hadn't really grasped it—or "stepped up to the plate," as Stephen liked to call it—at all.

Moreover, the time she had put into the job in the last six months had gone down by half and her concentration by much more than that. No one had said anything, but she knew she was slacking, and so, presumably, did they.

Stephen was not smiling. "I don't want to be disturbed," he said to his PA. "I need a full hour with Stella."

Her heart sank at this. He pointed to his armchair in a gesture to sit and made a big thing of closing the door.

"Stella, what can I say?" He paused, and Stella braced herself for the blow.

"Class act. Total class act. You do not cease to amaze me. You have taken on this new job, and have surpassed my expectations. And more than that, you have continued to excel in your old role as head of Economics."

Stella looked at him warily and waited for the "but."

"We have this stupid form that we have to fill in," he went on, "and so I suppose we'd better go through the motions. But a couple of words first. You have proved that you can step out of your ivory tower in Economics and into the real world. Your revised forecasts for the investor briefing were compelling. Thank you. We have a very powerful tale to tell and you have told it.

"I am going to tell you something that I would ask you to keep under your hat until we announce it next week. I have thought long and hard about this, and I know it will ruffle some feathers. But as you know"—here he gave an indulgent little laugh—"that is not something that I'm ever too scared of doing."

He paused for effect and then went on: "I have decided to put you on the board."

Stella gave a spluttering noise, which Stephen took to be a sound of joy.

"Yes," he said. "It is unexpected in the sense that neither chief of staff nor chief economist is typically a board position. But you have shown the ability. You deserve this in your own right. But I should also say something else: I don't think we are diverse enough as a board. And I'm not merely talking about gender. I'm talking about outlook.

"You, Stella, are so rare. You are fiercely honest and independent."

I'm not, thought Stella.

"You take risks," he said.

More than you know, she thought.

"But above all," he went on, "you are a loyal and supportive colleague. I know that I can trust you implicitly. I'm not saying that I don't trust the other members of the team. But I sometimes feel that they have agendas. You will always stand up to me and say the truth. That is what we want on this board."

Stella smiled and nodded. Here was this wonderful thing fallen into her lap, and she was quite unmoved. Never had she put so little into her work, and never had the rewards been so great. Was there no relationship between effort and reward, or was there a time lag operating so that she was still coasting on past performance? But mostly she just thought: I don't want to be on the board. I don't deserve it, and I can't cope with it.

"Thank you," she said. She could think of nothing else to say.

Stella called Rhys. He picked up at once, but from the noise in the background she could tell he was already in a bar.

"I've something to tell you. You mustn't tell anyone, as it hasn't been announced yet. I'm joining the board."

"That's great," he said.

Stella felt this wasn't quite the response she was after. "You don't sound very pleased," she said.

"I am," he said flatly. "It's just that I can't really talk right now.

"So do I get a rise," he went on, "now that I am executive assistant to a main board director?"

Stella felt a chill. Was this a joke? She certainly hoped so.

At dinner that night when Stella announced to the family that she was going on the board, Charles laughed. This was not the response she was looking for either.

"Incredible, Stella. So it paid off?"

"What paid off?" she asked.

"You've been going in early so much and working late and have been so preoccupied."

"Have I?" Stella had thought he hadn't noticed or cared particularly.

"Now you've made it, can you slack off a bit?"

"No," she said. "I don't think it works like that. I think it may get even worse from here."

Finn was briefly diverted from his computer game. "If you are getting more money, then I don't see why I can't have a plasma screen in my bedroom."

Charles's mother, who had come round again for dinner, beamed at Stella. "Hallelujah! Stella's bored. Well, it's not before time, if you ask me."

"No, Granny," said Clemmie, "Mum's *on* the board."

Bella

Bella wanted James to spend a night with her at her flat. She had wanted this for a long time: If only she could get him onto her territory, their affair would feel more real and she would be increasing her foothold in his life. But each time she asked, he said that although he would like that, it was complicated.

"It's not complicated," Bella protested one day. "It's simple. You want to, but you are guilty and frightened of being found out. Complicated, no. Compromising, yes."

She expected this to make him angry. But instead he laughed. "You are a genius," he said.

"So are you going to come?"

He hesitated, then said: "I can't. Sorry."

After the "hope all well?" incident, Bella had said that she wasn't sure she could carry on like this; their affair was making her too unhappy. She hadn't meant it as a threat, but he had suddenly announced that he could come and spend a night at her flat the following week. He had been due to go to Aberdeen on a two-day visit to inspect the work on one of the refurbished oil platforms in the North Sea but decided that he could get there and back in a day if he made an early start, which would free him to stay the night with Bella.

In preparation for his visit, Bella spent the weekend cleaning. She cleaned the cupboard under the stairs and vacuumed behind the sofa— even though she didn't really imagine him shifting the furniture around to see how many crisps bags and one-penny coins were underneath it, knowing that everything was clean made her feel more confident.

At lunchtime on the day, she went to the M&S in Moorgate and wandered up and down the aisles with an empty wire basket. Should she get the Lamb Hot Pot with Rosemary Potatoes, which was £6.99, or the Salmon with Dill Sauce, which was on special offer at £5.50, but then she'd also have to buy the new potatoes and they were £1.99? Or maybe it would be better to buy two steaks instead?

She picked up a packet of Thai chicken crisps but then took them out again and replaced them with Greek olives stuffed with anchovies, which she didn't particularly like but thought would look more sophisticated. The trouble was that she had no idea what he liked and suspected that he really didn't like anything much from M&S. Eventually she chose the salmon and a bottle of wine that was more expensive than she could afford and two bunches of freesia.

All afternoon, she was in a state of anxiety. She had wanted this for so long, but now that it was happening she was afraid. She could not imagine him sitting at her little table, let alone washing in her bathroom or sleeping in her bed.

Even less could she imagine him with her daughter. Often Millie asked her if she had a boyfriend, and when Bella said no, Millie always asked why not. Bella usually said that it was because she didn't meet anyone she liked and anyway she didn't need anyone, as she had Millie, to which her daughter always replied: "I don't want you to have a boyfriend." But then more recently she had started saying that she wouldn't mind if Bella had a rich boyfriend so that she could have lots of nice things. At least James looked rich. Unfortunately, he also looked married.

Bella had fixed a playdate for her daughter that day and persuaded the mother to drop her off just before bedtime, so that Millie and James would hardly see each other.

James had insisted that they not leave the office at the same time but meet by his dark green BMW in the underground car park. Bella got there first and stood by its side, trying to look inconspicuous as George Matthews, her old boss, walked past her on the way to his car.

"What are you doing here?" he asked.

"I'm being given a lift home with my shopping," she said.

He seemed quite satisfied by this entirely implausible explanation, which Bella decided was because she was so far beneath his radar of interest that she could have been standing there stark naked and he would not have registered anything amiss.

As soon as James came down and they got into the car together, Bella stopped feeling anxious. She put her shopping in the back and sat on the gray leather seat beside him as he skillfully maneuvered the car out of its tight space. The simple business of sitting next to him in his car as they crawled up Goswell Road was thrilling to her. She didn't want excitement from him—she wanted normality. She leaned over and put her head on his shoulder, and he absently kissed her hair.

She turned the key in the front door, which opened onto a small, grubby hallway strewn with pizza flyers, and climbed the stairs. Opening the door to her own flat, she saw it through his eyes. It didn't look clean and loved, as it had when she'd left for work that morning; it looked tawdry, with its grubby beige carpet and magnolia walls with circular scars where Blu-Tack had been. She hung his coat on the rail that was coming slightly out of the wall and thought how outlandish it looked there.

"Your flat is lovely," he said, not looking at it but taking her in his arms.

She led him into the cramped kitchenette, poured him some wine, and peeled the plastic wrapper off the fish. "I hope you like salmon," she said.

"I love salmon," he replied.

Bella thought about doing this every day, of making a meal for him, of learning to cook and having him sit at the table and watch her while she did it.

The doorbell went, and Millie marched into the room. She looked warily at James. "Who are you?" she asked.

"I'm a friend of your mum's—we work together," he said in the same soft voice that he used when he spoke to his own sons on the phone.

"Are you her boyfriend?" Millie demanded, looking at him unblinkingly.

"Well . . . ," he said. "I'm a man, so I can't be her boyfriend."

Millie was unmoved by this semantic dodge and protested noisily about being put to bed. In the end, Bella had to carry her daughter to her room and bribe her to stay there by promising that she would take her ice-skating at the Sobell Centre at the weekend. Millie whined in a voice loud enough to have been heard by James next door, and when Bella eventually pried the girl's arms away from her neck and returned to the kitchen, she feared his disapproval.

Instead he said: "She is sweet and beautiful, just like you."

The meal that she had thought so hard about didn't get eaten at all in the end. They went to bed instead and had sex quickly and then again more slowly. And then they got into her small bath with the black mold that Bella had failed to clean off the grout and the noisy air extractor. He passed no comment on the state of the bathroom, but soaped her back and looked at her with what she took to be real love.

At around two a.m., Millie woke and went into her mother's bedroom. Bella was lying with James on top of her and did not hear the door open. Millie stood at the open door, observing the scene.

"Fuck off!" she shouted, holding up her middle finger. "Go home! I hate you."

Bella wriggled out from underneath him, and Millie glowered at her mother's naked body. "I'm going to take you back to bed," Bella said, putting on her dressing gown and taking her daughter in her arms.

She carried her into her bed and got in beside her, stroking her hair until she went to sleep.

When she returned, James mumbled: "I'm sorry." And then he drifted off to sleep.

Bella didn't sleep. She lay awake, feeling the unfairness of everything: that her happiness should come at the cost of her daughter's, and that James, for all his noisy guilt about his family, should be sleeping easily in his lover's bed while his sons in their comfortable beds in Wimbledon slept easily in theirs.

Stella

The board appointment brought on the most violent argument yet between Stella and Rhys. The pattern was familiar to both of them: her established success versus his ambition. Her settled family versus his desire for a proper girlfriend. Her desire to have him properly and his desire to have her, and yet the certainty of that never coming to pass.

The difference this time was that the argument did not blow over quickly, as their earlier arguments always had. Stella could not say sorry. Every time she considered apologizing, she would think: He is using me for advancement. But then, as Friday came and the thought of a whole weekend of estrangement loomed, Stella waited until everyone else had gone home and went over to his desk. She smiled at him.

"I'm sorry," she said.

But he didn't say sorry back. "This is fucking killing me," he said. "I don't think I can go on doing this."

"Come," she said, and led him into her office.

"I don't think I can go on like this, not having you."

"But you do have me," she said.

"That wasn't what I meant. I don't want to fuck you occasionally in a hotel room. I want you properly. Come to my flat."

"I can't," she said. "I'd love to, but I can't."

"You see?" he said, standing up so violently that he overturned the chair. "It's hopeless."

"We can have a quick drink," she said.

"I don't want a quick drink. I want you. Please," he said.

"Where?" she asked.

"Here. We can do it here."

"No," she said. "You are out of your mind."

He flicked the switch that brought down the blinds between Stella's office and the corridor. "They've all gone home," he said.

Stella put her arms around Rhys. Over his shoulder, she looked at the neighboring office with its brightly lit windows and people working inside. "They can see in," she said.

"So what," he said. "They don't know who we are, and couldn't care less. We've taken bigger risks than this." He had his hands on her hips and was kissing her.

"We can't turn the light off. They come back on every time you move. There's a sensor in the corner."

Rhys said, "Give me a hand," and he hauled Stella's desk chair onto the table and climbed onto it, wobbling wildly. "Find the Sellotape," he said. "And a thick envelope."

He stretched up and taped the envelope over the sensor, and within a few minutes, during which time they stood a few feet apart looking at each other bleakly, the room was dark. A thin light came in from the blinds and from the lighted offices opposite.

Stella locked the door. "I don't know if I want to do this," she said weakly.

"Come on," said Rhys. "We've gone to all that trouble."

So Stella took off her dress and lay on the floor of her office still in her pop socks and her bra.

"Stella," he said, "I love you. If I could have two years with you, I would happily die."

Stella found this both exhilarating and frightening. No one had ever felt like this about her before. "Why two years? What's so special about that?"

"It's long enough to be worth dying for afterwards," he said.

The carpet was rough under her back, but she didn't care. Her mind went completely blank. Everything else was chased away.

It was at about this moment that the door clicked. Someone was trying to come in. They froze.

From her vantage point on the floor, Stella could see a pair of black shoes and a pair of dark trousers in cheap material pausing on the threshold of her office. It was almost certainly a security guard who must have had his own key. He took one step forward, but as the light did not come on, he did not venture into the office and in the darkness did not notice two half-naked bodies in frozen embrace on the floor behind the desk. He went out and locked the door again.

Afterward, Stella started to laugh. The risk and the relief together had made her light-headed. Rhys laughed, too, and briefly they were united. So this is what happens, she thought. To maintain the thrill and to glue us together each time we fall apart, we need to go on taking bigger and bigger risks. She thought back to four months earlier when she had kissed him in the lift and how that seemed to be the most daring thing imaginable.

"We'll get found out. It's too dangerous," she said as she struggled into her dress.

"We'll be okay," he said.

"You'll be okay. It won't matter for you."

"What?" he said, suddenly angry. "I stand to lose my job, and my reputation, but I suppose that doesn't count. And in the end it is all about you and your perfect life."

"Let's not have this conversation again," said Stella. She put her arms around him. "Rhys, all I meant was that I am doing something mad, and increasingly madder. But I can't stop, and I don't want to stop. I am doing it because I adore you." She kissed his eyes and his forehead and ran her hands over his face as if committing its contours to memory. Then she put on her coat and got her briefcase, and the night security guard said good night to her just as he always did.

Life number six was gone.

At home that night, Stella took off her dress for the second time in three hours. Charles was lying in bed reading, but as his wife got undressed he glanced up at her.

"What's that red mark down your back?" he asked.

"It's a rash," she said. "It hurts, I don't know what it is—probably just stress." The idea that stress had given her a vivid, smarting carpet burn on her back was so implausible that Stella wished the words back in her mouth.

"Hmm," he said. "It looks nasty. You should get it looked at."

He spoke with the bored concern that husband and wife have for each other's minor ailments after twenty years together, but Stella felt that this was another life slipping away. She had only four left.

"Come here," he said.

Stella moved across the bed toward her husband. He ran his hands over the burn on her back, and she winced.

"What's happening to you, Stel? You are getting so thin," he said.

"It's this job," said Stella. "It's all too much."

"Don't worry," he said. "You'll cope. You always do."

Her husband's gentle concern was too much for Stella. She curled herself up against him and started to sob.

"What is it?" he asked.

"I'm just exhausted," she said between sobs. But what she was thinking was: Save me, Charles. Please save me.

Bella

"You've lost weight, you cow."

Karen kissed her friend on both cheeks, and together they went into the Moorgate branch of Pret A Manger.

"It's love," Bella said. "It's the most effective diet in the world."

"Hmm," Karen said flatly. "I've put on nearly a stone since the summer." She took a Diet Coke from the fridge and fruit salad and took them to the till.

Bella looked at her friend with affection. She had indeed gained weight, and the striped dress she was wearing was pulling at the buttons down the front.

"Are you still seeing that guy?" Bella asked as they settled themselves at their table.

"Which guy?" asked Karen.

"The one you told me about—the music producer."

"No, I dumped him, but mainly to get in first, as I suspected he was about to dump me. So how come you are looking so happy? I thought you said this guy was an autistic, hypocritical cretin and you wished you'd never met him? Weren't those your words?"

"Yes," said Bella, laughing sheepishly. "But that was last month, and it's got better since then. He came to stay at my flat a few days ago, and since then things have felt different. There was a terrible scene when Millie walked in and found us in bed together—"

"Jesus, that sounds heavy."

"It was, but in some weird way it's brought us closer, if that makes sense?" Bella knew it didn't make sense, but in her current optimistic mood she didn't care. "When things are good between us, they are very, very good. It's like we're in this bubble—the rest of the world doesn't exist."

Karen sighed. "Lucky you," she said. "So is this the real thing? Is he going to leave his wife so you can live happily ever after?"

"I don't know," said Bella. "I haven't ever asked. I try not to put pressure on him. I think he's got to work it out himself. A few weeks ago I would have said definitely not, but I have a feeling that things are beginning to shift. I want him to be mine more than anything else in the world. But at the same time I don't want to break up his marriage."

Karen nodded and said, "But I don't think you should feel badly about it. It's not you breaking up a marriage, is it? If he cheats on his wife, that's his fault."

She then said: "Did you hear about Ruthie Woodall?"

Ruthie had been in their class at school and much disliked by both of them, as she was too pretty and a show-off and always had the lead part in the school plays.

"She's just finished shooting a movie with Ricky Gervais. There was a nauseating piece about her in G2, saying that she's the new comic talent of the moment."

Bella stuck her fingers into her mouth and made sick noises, and Karen laughed. Then, out of the corner of her eye, Bella saw James walk past the window, enter the sandwich bar, and walk up to the chilled cabinets. He did not seem to have seen her. All at once she saw him as Karen would—a fattish, baldish businessman—and her first feeling was shame. Love is not blind, she thought.

But then, as she watched him fish in his pocket for coins to pay for the large sandwich, packet of crisps, and slab of chocolate cake that he had chosen, she felt a flood of tenderness for him. He's not good-looking, she thought, but I don't care. He is a lock to which only I know the combination code, and I'm not going to share it with anyone.

"What are you looking at?" asked Karen.

"Nothing," said Bella.

Stella

"I took the kids to see *War Horse* at the National last night," Emily was saying. "I adore Michael Morpurgo, but the play was even better than the book. The horses were quite amazing...I cried in the end when the horse dies."

Stella looked with envy at her friend. She couldn't remember the last time she'd taken her children to the theater or to anything at all. And the thought of crying over wooden horses from a children's book struck her as belonging to an age of innocence that she could not imagine ever returning to.

"Maybe I should try to get some tickets," she said doubtfully.

And then Emily said: "How are things with you? Are you still snowed under with work?"

"I don't know," said Stella. "Things are crap—"

Her voice cracked, and Emily, much surprised at this turn of events, put out a hand. And Stella, who had not planned to tell her friend, who had confided in no one about her affair with Rhys, started to tell her the whole story.

"I'm hopelessly stuck. I keep trying to stop, but I can't. But then I can't go on. Last night, I couldn't sleep and I woke at four a.m. and looked at my messages. There was a message from him, and I realized I was hoping that he would be calling it off. That he would have the strength that I lack to get us both out of this hell. But instead his text was a poem about separation—something to do with a thread and a needle. It made me cry. I cried because it was so sweet, and because I'm completely helpless. If he wants me, I'm there. I am barely holding on. I spend all my time with him or thinking about him. I am a ghost in the rest of my life. I give nothing to my work, and instead of being found out, they keep promoting me. I give nothing to Charles or to the children. Charles has noticed that I'm sometimes a bit stressed and tearful, and he's trying to be sweet, but he has no idea what is going on."

"Don't be silly, Stella. You give your kids so much and you've worked so hard in the past I'm sure you can coast for a bit."

Stella did not find these words consoling. Emily was trying to be sympathetic but did not sound as if she meant it.

"I worry that I'm about to do something really extreme. I can't live at this level of madness, it's too painful. And I keep on nearly getting found out. I thought at the beginning that I had nine lives, but I've used up most of them, and still can't stop. The weirdest thing is that the only person who knows something is badly wrong is Charles's nutty mother, who has Alzheimer's. She says over and over again: 'When are you giving up that job?' Yesterday, I so desperately wanted to confide in someone, I told her. As I was driving her home, I said: 'I am having an affair with someone who is young and who I adore, and who has spoiled my life.' And she looked at me and said, 'Well! Fancy that!'"

"God," said Emily. "Wasn't that mad?"

"Of course it was mad," said Stella, "though she never remembers anything for more than three seconds. It wasn't as mad as the rest of it. Do you know what this feels like? It feels like I'm in a car driving down the motorway the wrong way, and I'm wearing a blindfold. Rhys is with me in the passenger seat and we are both screaming. I know we're going to crash. But that adds to the pleasure. Do you know what I mean?"

"No," said her friend. "Frankly I don't. Stella, I'm really worried about you. You absolutely have to stop this now."

"I know that," Stella said angrily. "I've just told you that. But I'm trying to explain to you why I can't."

"I don't understand," said Emily. "I've never known you to say you can't do something before. Stel, this isn't you."

"Well, if you haven't felt this, you can't possibly understand. Experiences this intense cut across reason. They are their own reason."

"Possibly," said Emily. "But do you want to know what I think?"

Stella nodded, even though she wasn't sure that she did.

"I think this is about control for you. You have never been out of control in your life. You are both thrilled by it and scared shitless. It's not a good look."

"You know what?" said Stella. "I'm really fed up with being called a control freak. Charles calls me a control freak, and so do the kids. If I didn't control things, I wouldn't get things done. If everyone was passive, the world would be in chaos. I'm not a control freak. I am a conscientious and hardworking woman, and yes, I do take the fucking initiative."

But afterward, running through the conversation again, she decided that Emily was right. The problem was that she could not control Rhys. She would lose him eventually. And there was absolutely nothing she could do to control that.

Part Three

WITHDRAWAL

Stella

"Stella, have you got five?"

Russell was hovering at the door of her office in a most annoying fashion.

"No," said Stella, "I haven't. I've got a meeting with Stephen and our lawyers." She gathered some papers from her desk and walked past him.

"It's quite important," he said.

"Ask Nathalie to find five minutes in my calendar this afternoon."

Stella went to the meeting and didn't give the matter another thought. But when she returned, he was sitting in her office waiting for her.

"Is this a good time?"

"Fine," she said wearily.

"Stella," he said, "this is a little sensitive."

She inclined her head.

"But basically, in a nutshell, I've received a complaint from a member of your department about your... your behavior."

Stella said nothing, and he continued. "Obviously we take our whistle-blower rules seriously, so I cannot reveal the identity of the person who has raised the matter. However, I do happen to think that the complaint is a little—how shall I put it—far-fetched. But, for my sins, obviously as HR director I need to ensure that we go through the motions, to make sure we are ticking all the boxes, if you will. Basically, in a nutshell, the issue concerns yourself and your executive assistant, Rhys Williams. One member of your staff has alleged favoritism and has even stated—forgive me, Stella, this is not easy—that there might be an unprofessional relationship between the two of you of a sexual nature, and that this is clouding your judgment."

Stella felt as if she were shrinking. It was the most peculiar sensation—as if she were removing herself from here and going somewhere else where this was not happening. She focused her eyes on Russell's soft yellow cashmere sweater and said, "I don't know what you expect me to say. I absolutely refuse to deny something that would be so outlandish."

He waited, as if expecting more, so she went on: "There have never been any complaints by people in my department before. Rhys, as we have discussed, is a talented and unusual man. I promoted him for his leadership potential, and would stand by that. I do, it is true, spend a great deal of time with him, but that is because he is my assistant. It would be strange if I didn't. So I really cannot imagine where any of this is coming from—"

Russell smiled and shut his notebook. "Thank you, Stella," he said. "Sorry to trouble you with something so sordid. Not to say . . . improbable. But you must understand that I was only doing my job."

"Of course I understand. And I was only doing mine. So is it closed?" As soon as she had asked the question, she regretted it.

But Russell was too embarrassed or too frightened of her to notice how guilty it sounded. "Yes," he said. "It's closed."

And that, thought Stella, was life number six. She had only three left.

Bella

At ten o'clock in the evening, Bella got a text from James. It said just one word:

Disaster.

She texted back:

What. ???

But she received no reply. When she got into work, she went straight to James's office without stopping to take off her coat. Anthea witnessed this in knowing silence. James was sitting at his desk, looking at her evenly. His face, thought Bella, bore no expression at all.

"This arrived in the post yesterday," he said.

He got an envelope out of his briefcase and put it on the coffee table. Bella took it and opened it. It said ISLINGTON COUNCIL on the top and was a fine for driving his car in a bus lane.

"So," she said.

"Look at the date. Look at the time. Location. Look at the bloody picture."

The date was five days earlier, the time seven thirty in the evening, the location Holloway Road. The attached picture was blurry, but it showed James's murky silhouette at the wheel, with Bella's smaller one leaning toward him.

"Hilly opened it and worked out that I was meant to be in Aberdeen that night."

"What did you say?" Bella asked. Going through her head was the idea: This was it. This was the crisis that she had been waiting for. Hillary would chuck him out, and he would be hers. She knew she shouldn't be feeling so exultant. She should perhaps feel terrible about the misery of his depressed wife opening this awful envelope, but she didn't.

"I said that I had had to pick someone up on the way to the airport, and she seemed to believe me. It was a really bad moment, though." He was looking at her accusingly.

"It's not my fault," said Bella, seeing that this was not going to end in the way she'd planned at all.

"No," he said doubtfully. "But if something happened, if I was thrown out and living in a bedsit and not allowed to see my boys..."

Bella wanted to say: Well, perhaps you should have thought of that before you shagged me. But she didn't say that. Instead she gave a forced smile and said: "I'm glad you got away with it."

She turned on her heel and went back to her desk, and as she left she heard him picking up the phone. I bet he's calling home, she thought. And sure enough, she could hear him saying: "Hello, darling. Just wondered how you were. Do you want to go out to dinner tonight?"

You are a creep and an idiot, thought Bella. Your wife will smell a rat the size of the *Titanic* if you suddenly start being nice.

Stella

Stella had decided again to end it. This time, it wasn't because of guilt or because she was frightened of discovery. Losing so many lives already, instead of making her fearful, had started to make her complacent. If she had narrowly avoided discovery in the past, she would go on narrowly avoiding it in the future.

She didn't want to get out to save her marriage. Her marriage, she thought, was the same as it had been for ages. It wasn't ideal, but it was fine. She cared for Charles just as much as she had a year ago.

No, she was getting out to save herself. The pain of going on had got too intense. She needed to escape from the hateful person she had become. In hating herself, she had even come to hate Rhys, in a way she was sure he did not deserve. In the early days, Rhys had made Stella feel funny and engaging and reckless and young and invincible. Which was partly, she thought, why she had started to love him. But the person she now was when she was with him was very different: mad and needy and dishonest. She did not want to be this person anymore. She wanted to find her old self again, but she worried that it was too late. Perhaps her old self was dead. And sometimes she wondered if she loved Rhys at all or whether this was a compulsion that had very little to do with him. Nietzsche had it right. Ultimately, one loves one's desires and not that which is desired. The thought gave her some hope: If it wasn't really Rhys himself that she loved, maybe she would be able to do without him.

She had made up her mind: She would have the conversation with him the next day. She had thought about it carefully and decided best to have it in the office, which would keep it brief, and it would lessen the risk of relapse. Kissing him in her office in the middle of the day was not an option.

The following morning, she sent Rhys an e-mail that said:

Have you got a minute?

Her courage almost failed her when he came into the room and smiled at her and said she looked nice in her dress. She got up and closed the door and sat down, fixing her eyes on the air vent set in the wall above the door.

"Rhys," she said, "there's no good way of saying this. I can't do this anymore. If we go on, I think I will go insane."

He nodded dumbly. And then he asked: "When did you decide?"

"Last night," she said. "I lay in bed and was so miserable I cried and cried and could not stop. Charles came in and asked me what was wrong, and he was trying hard to be sweet, and I so needed comfort, but I couldn't tell him what the matter was."

"I don't want to know how sweet Charles was," he said coldly.

"I'm sorry," Stella said. "I'm not trying to make you feel wretched. I'm just trying to explain. I am beset by fear of losing you, so much so that I can't enjoy being with you at all. I feel we have reached a point where it is all pain. I can't remember the last time that we were simply happy together. Can you?" she asked.

He said nothing.

"You have to look at the trend. There are some up and down cyclical movements around the trend, but the trend is down. It's not going to get any better."

She had meant this mention of economics to sound ironic. It just sounded cold. Rhys said nothing. "Are you okay?" she asked, meaning the question to spark grief, which she could then respond to and forgive, just as she had done so often before.

Instead he looked straight at her and said: "Take a guess."

He stood up and walked out of her office.

Twenty of them filed into the boardroom on the thirteenth floor: the usual eighteen, the company secretary, and Stella.

The chairman, Sir John Englefield, took off his watch and laid it officiously on the table. "Good morning," he began. "Before we get into the formal business of the meeting, I would like to welcome Stella Bradberry, whom all of you know. In line with our articles of association, we need to take a vote on her appointment to the board. Can I assume that we have consensus on this?"

Stella looked down at her blotter, to the side of which was a patch slightly lighter than the rest of the table, a blemish that had been almost invisibly repaired and polished. She fixed her eyes on it and tried to focus her mind. This was a board meeting. She must hold it together.

"Thank you," she said.

"We've got a busy meeting today," Sir John went on. "Obviously we are going to need some time to discuss the situation in Russia, and the new business climate created by the fall in the oil price, but first we have a presentation on our new IT system. Over to you, Kevin."

Stella watched the director of global IT go through a presentation about platforms and add-ons, slide after slide.

Why didn't Rhys message her? Why had he said nothing to her at all for twenty-four hours, save the minimum demanded for work? Why didn't he fight to keep her? Was she really worth so little to him? She got out her BlackBerry and sent him a text.

```
I'm in the board meeting. I love you. I
didn't mean it. Sorry.
```

She looked at what she had written. It was weak. He would despise her. She should wait and see if she felt better in a couple of days. But she would not feel better in a couple of days, she was sure. She looked at the message again. It was true, and what was true could not be wrong.

She pressed send, and the minute it was gone her spirits lifted. She had learned something. Her affair with Rhys could not be declared over by an act of her will. She loved him, and that was stronger than everything.

"Before we get on to today's agenda, I think it would be helpful if we took AOB first," the chairman was saying.

He went around the table asking board members if they had any other business. Most appeared not to have. One non-executive director said that he would not be available for the meeting scheduled for April two years hence and proposed moving it two days forward. The other board members started jabbing at their BlackBerrys to see if they were available on that distant day.

"Stella," the company secretary was asking, "which of those dates works for you?"

"They both do," she said. In two years, thought Stella, my car will have crashed along the motorway, so what difference could it make to me whether the April board meeting is on the twenty-first or the twenty-third?

The next item was to approve the results statement to be released to the stock exchange the next morning. James had drafted this announcement and had come into the boardroom to present it.

He looked at Stella but then looked down at the point on the table where the French polish was uneven. "I would like to draw your attention to the revisions made to the statement following the conference call with the drafting committee," he said. "We have inserted the sentence 'We anticipate current market volatility to persist with consequent effect on short-term profits from E and P activities.'"

The non-exec who was sitting next to Stella looked up from his Black-Berry, on which she could see he was writing a message beginning, "My darling Tim." "I'm a bit uncomfortable about us saying 'short-term,' as it implies that we are not predicting volatility for the medium term," he said.

James looked exasperated. "With respect, I don't believe it says any such thing."

The debate to'ed and fro'ed, with those favoring "short-term" and "medium-term" lining up against each other.

"Why not say 'in the future'?" said Stella. This was her first suggestion as a director, and it seemed reasonable, if a little basic.

No one took any notice. The chairman said: "I propose taking out 'short-term' and substituting 'going forward.'"

Everyone agreed this was an excellent idea, and the words were inserted.

Stella's BlackBerry flashed. Her heart stopped—and then started again when she saw it was a message from the Office for National Statistics with some inflation numbers she had asked for.

Twelve more messages landed; each time she felt a lift of the spirits and then a fall when the sender was not Rhys. The thirteenth message had his name next to it. Stella opened it. She didn't need to read it. She understood what it said simply by seeing the shape of the words and absence of kisses. The words made no difference. They said:

```
Of course it's tempting. I love you. But I
can't go through that again.
```

During the following three hours of the board meeting, Stella made no further suggestions. When the meeting was over, Stephen said to her: "So what did you think?"

"It was long," said Stella, and then, pulling herself together, said: "I thought it was fascinating to get so many different minds engaged simultaneously on these issues. Though I was quite surprised that some of the non-execs weren't always up to speed."

Stephen nodded approvingly. "I knew I could trust you to cut straight to the chase," he said.

On her way back to her office, Stella had to walk past Rhys, who was staring intently at his screen. She should have gone straight past him but found herself stopping at his desk. "Hello," she said.

"Hello," he replied.

Then she said, "The board meeting is over."

"Yes, I gathered. How did it go?"

He asked the question so correctly, so politely, that Stella almost wished he had said "I hate you" instead. His professional coolness implied that he was coping, whereas she was not.

"Thank you, it was fine."

She propelled herself into her office and sat at her desk, her heart thudding in distress. She bowed her head in an attempt to hide the tears from Nathalie, who was eyeing her curiously. She got up and walked briskly to the toilet and shut herself into the cubicle marked DISABLED. She leaned against the closed door, put her hands over her face, and was so fraught with emotion that her legs would not hold her up. She put down the seat of the loo and collapsed onto it, her body convulsed with silent tears. In her mind there was only one thought: Don't make a noise. The sobs racked her body so that she released a shuddering sigh and had to flush the toilet several times to cover the noise. She could hear others coming and going, signs of normal office life that to Stella came from a world in which she no longer belonged.

After a while the sobs started to subside, and she tried to breathe in and out without her breath catching. She wet some toilet paper and pressed that into her swollen eyes. The water ran down and made a dark patch on her shirt. She waited until she could hear nothing from the surrounding cubicles and then opened the door.

She looked, if anything, worse than she had expected. Old and crumpled, and the new suit for the board meeting looked ridiculous, as if made for someone else: someone who was a proper professional business-woman, someone who did what she said, someone who did not fall in love with young subordinates and did not weep over them in the loo.

Stella thought of the card game Funny Folk—she had loved it as a child—where you matched heads against bodies. She looked as if some-one had taken the body of a smart executive and matched it with the head of a madwoman.

She put on a little eye shadow to try to hide the red around her eyes but succeeded only in accentuating it. She smeared some pink lipstick on her mouth and practiced smiling at herself in the mirror. Just as she was baring her teeth uncertainly at her image, the door opened and Nathalie came in.

"Oh, there you are. I've been looking for you," she said. And then, with concern: "Are you okay?"

Of all the questions in the world that Stella did not want to be asked, this was top of her list. Obviously, she thought, I'm not okay.

"Yes," she said. "I'm fine."

Bella

"Two things, Bella," James was saying. "I understand that the *Telegraph* wants to interview Stella about her board position and write a piece on work/life balance."

He smiled a little stiffly. It was nearly a week since he had told her about the bus lane ticket, but since then they had been back in each other's arms in the hotel more passionately and more desperately than before.

While they had been in the hotel, Bella had felt triumphant. Disaster had struck, but instead of running away he was still with her, courting further disaster. It proved, she reasoned, that this was what he valued in his life more than anything. But as soon as they left the hotel, he was aloof and confused.

"Can you check that she's okay with that," he went on, "and also get her to call me? I want to go through the points that she needs to stress. We need to get a win for AE out of this as well as a win for Stella herself."

"Sure," Bella said bleakly.

"And can you do me some briefing notes on what you think are some of our greatest diversity successes? I'm sure Russell will be more than happy to give you the data, but perhaps you can cut through the HR crap and present some concrete facts in normal language?"

Bella sat at her computer, trying to marshal some diversity facts for Stella's interview. She must not think about James. She must try to hold it together. The numbers in themselves were rotten. Forty percent of graduate trainees were women at entry level, but two ranks up, at associate level, it was only 17 percent, and by the level of general manager, it had fallen to just 6 percent.

However, Bella had been asked to present the numbers positively and so found that ten years earlier, only 5 percent of general managers were women. What percentage increase was that? She took her calculator out of her drawer but couldn't remember which way round to put the numbers.

So she got up and walked down the corridor to find Rhys at his new desk. She sat on the edge of it. "I know this is an embarrassing question...," she began.

Rhys's face tightened apprehensively.

"...but what is six expressed as a percentage of five?"

"Really," he said. "I've no idea."

"Are you telling me," said Bella, "that you work as assistant to the head of Economics and you can't do a simple sum?" She laughed to show that she was teasing him, but Rhys did not think it funny.

"Of course I can sodding do it. I'm just not in the mood."

So Bella went off and asked Anthea, who said at once: "It's an increase of twenty percent."

At lunch that day in the canteen, Bella was joined first by Ben and then by Beate. Now that she was no longer a PA, the fast-track employees were much more likely to sit with her.

"Beate," said Bella, "I'm doing a briefing note on diversity, and wondered if you think women are discriminated against here?"

"You only need to look around you," said Beate. "Where are the successful women?"

"Well," said Bella, "there's Stella."

"Yes, but what is she doing to help other women? She is our Margaret Thatcher. She has climbed up and pulled the ladder up behind her."

Bella thought this a little unfair but did not say so.

*　　*　　*

Later that afternoon, she took her work into James's office. The visit was unnecessary, but the sight of him bent over his desk made her want to go in and touch him. She needed him to smile at her to show some sign of warmth. Nothing else mattered to her.

"I've done the thing for Stella," she said, hovering at his door.

"Thank you," he said, barely looking up. "There was something else I wanted to walk by you. I don't know if you know, but every year I throw a big Christmas party in my house for the team, and also for a few friends in other departments. There was some uncertainty this year about whether we would hold it, as Hilly's been so unwell. But she's—touch wood—a bit better, and so we're going ahead. I've told her that she doesn't have to do anything apart from being there to welcome everyone, and that you and Anthea will sort everything out. You don't mind, do you?"

Bella stared at him in horror. As he spoke, James wasn't even looking at her but was scrolling idly through his e-mails. "As a matter of fact," she said, "I do mind. I don't give a flying fuck whether your party goes ahead or not. There is no way on earth that I'm going to make lovely chitchat to your wife about canapés and then shag her husband behind her back."

James looked panic-stricken and gestured at her to keep her voice down.

"I will not be quiet," she hissed. "And I don't give a shit who hears. I've put up with this for long enough. You even had the *nerve* to say to me that if you ever got found out, you would blame me. I don't know why I didn't dump you then. I suppose it was because I thought you'd fire me. That's just the sort of shitty thing you'd do."

Bella turned and ran out of his office, and as she did so Anthea stared and got up and came after her.

"Are you okay?"

"What does it look like?" she spat at her, and went down in the lift and ran out of the building and stood shaking with tears outside.

The brief feeling of release and power in saying—shouting—what she thought was quickly overtaken by dread. Why had she done that?

What had possessed her? She might have lost the job and might have lost him, too. She stood outside, struggling to calm her breathing, and her phone rang.

"I think you'd better come back in," he said. "It's all right, I've explained you're under a lot of stress at the moment."

"Well, that's all right, then," she said bitterly.

She went back up in the lift and sat at her desk and started to type up the notes for the interview. She did not look up at James once. At one point, he walked past her desk and tried to catch her eye, but she stared resolutely at her screen. Later, just before she was about to go home, she received an e-mail from him. She opened it with trepidation.

> Dear Bella, I'm very sorry if I unintentionally upset you. That was
> not the idea at all. I'm sure that Anthea will be perfectly capable of
> organizing the party. Can we just put the whole thing behind us?
>
> J

She read it and pressed delete. He did not begin to understand how difficult this was for her. Or if he did, he didn't care. And there was that same phrase—put the whole thing behind us—that he had used to Julia.

At five thirty on the dot, Bella got up and walked out without saying good-bye to anyone. She walked down Moor Lane briskly, anger making her numb. As she reached Moorgate tube, she heard her name. She turned and saw James, breathless and jacketless, running toward her. It had started to rain, and the drops were making dark blue splatters on his light blue shirt.

"Bella," he said, "don't do this. Please."

"Do what?"

"Shout at me in the office, dump me, make a scene, refuse to talk to me or answer my messages. Why the hell do you think I'm risking my marriage and my career? It's because I'm attached to you. That should go without saying."

"It does not go without saying," Bella said. "It needs saying all the time. It needs shouting from the rooftops. I don't want these dregs of 'attachment' anymore. Fuck off, James. Just do me one favor. Let me stay until I find a new job."

She got out her Oyster card and went through the barriers, leaving him standing there, staring after her.

The first thing Bella did when she got home that night was to check her messages. It was the second thing and the third thing, too. She shouted at Millie for not eating her baked beans and made her cry. Then she cried herself. This silenced Millie, who put her thin arms around her mother.

"Don't cry, Mum," she said.

To be comforted by her daughter, as if she were the helpless child, was too much. Bella fought to control herself.

"I'm fine, darling," she said, giving a wide and entirely unconvincing smile. "Let's do something fun. Let's bake some fairy cakes. We can put pink icing on them." Even as she said this, she knew that there was no icing sugar in the cupboard and that at eight o'clock at night she didn't feel like taking Millie down to Morrisons to get some.

"It's okay, Mum," she said. "Let's just watch *Desperate Housewives*."

So they put in the DVD and Bella watched the inhabitants of Wisteria Lane being a lot less desperate than she was feeling.

Stella

Stella was late coming into the office, as she had an appointment with Finn's housemaster. Her son had been selling firecrackers to his classmates, and the school was threatening to suspend him.

"As I am sure you are aware," the long-faced schoolmaster said to Stella, "Finn has broken two school rules. Boys are not allowed to trade on the school premises, neither are they allowed dangerous items."

"Oh dear," she said feebly.

In fact, she thought he had done well to spot an arbitrage opportunity: He had bought the firecrackers with his pocket money in bulk and was now selling them individually. Finn had at least shown some initiative. Maybe he would grow up to be a trader. She remembered Rhys telling her that he had sold sweets at school, then she tried to suppress the thought. She must stop thinking of him.

"I thought it would be helpful to have this conversation, as it is important that school and family are singing from the same hymn sheet when it comes to enforcement of rules," he went on.

Stella endured the rest of the telling off, nodding and agreeing at the right points, but it took longer than she had thought, and by the time the taxi pulled up outside the office, the *Telegraph* journalist had already been waiting in her office for twenty minutes. She started guiltily when Stella came in; she had evidently been looking at her desk, on which there were three signs of Rhys: a Twix bar, a picture of a ferret that he had downloaded from the Internet and made into a card, and a yellow Post-it note on which was written the Auden quote about fish.

"Hi!" she said as if greeting an old friend. "I'm Zoe Stevens."

She was not what Stella had been expecting. She looked about twenty and was wearing a shocking-pink coat.

"How do you feel to be the first female executive on the board of a major oil company?"

I feel, thought Stella, as if something big is sitting on my chest and I can't breathe. I keep getting these surges of panic. I feel okay for about twenty minutes, and then a wave of despair breaks over me.

She gathered herself together and said: "It's a bit scary to be labeled as the first woman to do this, it's like being the first man on the moon. That was a small step for man and a big step for mankind. This is a small step for woman and a big step for womankind."

What the hell was she saying? That her appointment to the board was significant? The journalist was scribbling furiously.

"That didn't come out right," Stella said. "I don't mean that this is a big deal at all. I don't think that it matters terribly whether the people on the board are male or female, so long as they are doing a good job." She tried to push out of her mind her own inglorious performance at the first meeting.

"So does that mean that companies should be gender-blind?"

"No, not at all," said Stella, and launched smoothly into the diversity speech that James's researcher had prepared for her. As she talked, she felt calmer and better. This is what work is for, she thought. It isn't to earn money. It is to give you a life raft when you are drowning.

"That's very interesting," said the journalist, who was looking bored and had stopped taking notes. "But what I'd really like to do in this interview is get across the full Stella Bradberry, what you have achieved at AE, how you juggle home and family, and how you keep up an active social life."

Oh God, thought Stella, but she smiled politely.

"So: Let's go back to your school days at Oxford High."

"I was at Headington," said Stella.

"Yes, of course, Headington. I think you were at school with the prime minister's wife? What was she like back then?"

"Well," said Stella, "she is a friend, but I don't think this interview is about that. I thought we were meant to be talking about how AE fosters women."

"Yes," she said. "But our readers see you as a role model. They'll want to read about how you juggle your life."

Stella privately noted the irony of this but said nothing.

"They'll want to know: You are married to a well-known documentary maker and have two daughters. How do you manage it all?"

"I've got a son and a daughter," Stella corrected her wearily, "and I juggle it all with difficulty, like every other working mother. I don't believe in having it all. If I am in one place, I'm not in another. But for me the thing that makes me privileged is choice. I'm not the heroic working mother. I have money for nannies and a cleaning lady, and a very nice husband at home who does the cooking. The women I really admire are the ones who are trying to bring up their kids on their own and doing cleaning jobs at night to make ends meet."

The journalist wrote some of this down and then said: "What would you say were your key skills as a manager? Do you think women are better at managing than men?"

"Well," said Stella, "I'm not sure. Sometimes I think we are better at motivating people, because we have practiced on our children."

"Do you think you've been a good mother, then?"

"I'd rather not talk about the family, if you don't mind." Upside down, Stella could see that she had scribbled something on her pad that she couldn't quite read.

"Do you feel a special interest in promoting women?"

"I do when I see that a woman is falling behind through a lack of confidence. I see that all the time."

"But," the journalist said, "I understand that you have just promoted a young man to be your executive assistant?"

"Well, yes," said Stella. "There is no conflict between trying to help women and giving senior jobs to men. I'm not in favor of positive discrimination. I believe in giving the job to the right person. And in this case the man—Rhys Williams—was incredibly talented."

"Can I ask you something else?" said the journalist as she was gathering her things and had turned off the tape recorder.

"What is that fragment of a poem on your desk?"

Bella

The first Saturday in December each year, Atlantic Energy threw a party for the children of employees.

Last year, when oil prices were over $100 per barrel, the party had been in the Science Museum and Millie had been beside herself with excitement to be given a Sylvanian cottage by Father Christmas (the fat and not terribly cheerful marketing director, who had subsequently been transferred to Nigeria). This year, in recognition of hard times, the party was to be held in the office canteen, and a memo had gone round saying that there would be no gifts. This had produced such a storm of self-righteous indignation on the intranet site that there had been backpedaling. There would be gifts, but the value would be limited to £5 per child.

Bella had not asked James if he was going, but then she had not asked him about anything, as the two of them had spoken little in the past week. He had been traveling a good deal and when in the office had reverted to his old behavior. He did not look at her, and he communicated with her only as much as professionalism demanded. Bella was trying to get through the bleak days in the same spirit. She had built a wall of books and files on her desk and moved her computer so that she did not have a view of his office. This was not entirely successful as a strategy, as it meant she kept getting up and peering around the tower of books because she wanted—needed—to know whether he was in his office and what he was doing.

She had written herself a list of rules to get her through the day:

1. Work HARD!!
2. Don't walk past his office. Take long way to coffee machine.
3. Smile.
4. Look busy.
5. Fix lunches with people.
6. Dress up. .

She had included number six on the principle that if she looked fine, she'd start to feel fine. It wasn't working so far, as she was feeling awful. Too awful to follow any of the rules, in fact.

Probably, she calculated, James would not go to the party, as hardly any of the senior people turned up. If he did go, she would keep out of his way.

Millie, at eight, was old enough to know that a party in a staff canteen—even when decked out with tinsel and strobe lights—marked a falling off in standards. In sullen silence, she ate the burger and lukewarm chips served on a flimsy cardboard tray. She cheered up slightly when the disco started and stood up to dance, leaving Bella alone at the table with a paper cup of mulled wine and a cold mince pie. She was soon joined by her old boss in Chemicals, his wife, and their exceptionally plain daughter.

They shouted inanities at each other over the music until Bella realized she had lost sight of Millie. She was just wondering whether to go and find her when she saw James coming toward her. Her heart leapt and then leapt again to see that he was holding Millie by the arm. He's found Millie and is using her as a way of talking to me, Bella thought.

But then James looked up and Bella saw from the expression on his face that things were not that way; not at all.

Stella

Stella dreaded the children's party, which was invariably tawdry and noisy. Attendance was not compulsory, but she felt obliged to go, as people noticed if their seniors didn't turn up.

She had told Finn that as penance for his school disgrace he must go with her, and as they arrived at the office at three thirty on Saturday afternoon, he seemed to be in almost as low spirits as she was. Stella looked around for anyone she knew and wondered at the fact that despite having worked at the company for over twenty years, she had never seen most of these people before or didn't recognize them in their weekend clothes. She had a brief conversation with the group treasurer and his wife, who had twin six-year-old daughters. The sight of him made Stella think of the day she and Rhys had kissed in the lift and he had been waiting with his cardboard cup of coffee as they had got out. She thought about the elation she had felt that day. And then she wondered: Could this man have been the whistle-blower? But if so, he was doing a good job of hiding it, with a spectacularly dull discourse on the pros and cons of the two girls being in the same class at school.

From the other side of the room, Stella saw James standing with his sons, the eldest of whom was about the same age as Finn. Her son was wearing a hoodie with trousers slung so low that most of his skinny twelve-year-old behind was on display; James's boy, meanwhile, was wearing a neat checked shirt tucked into his trousers. He and his younger brother were standing awkwardly at their father's side.

Stella went up and kissed James. She usually didn't kiss colleagues, but she felt comforted to see him. He was looking quite wretched, too, she thought.

"Enjoyable party," he said grimly.

"Is Hilly here?" she asked.

"No," he said. "I'm giving her an afternoon off so that she can do some Christmas shopping. She's been under a lot of pressure and needs a break."

Stella nodded understandingly, though she wondered why a woman who had nothing to do but shop all day would need a break to do more shopping at the weekend.

A girl of six or seven who had been swaying her hips on the dance floor with a fierce determination stopped swaying and approached them. She was wearing a shaggy sheepskin jacket and platform boots, giving her a Lolita-ish air that Stella thought slightly grotesque. She marched up to James and stared at him with inexplicable hostility.

"Where's my mum?" she demanded.

"Hello, Millie," he said. "I haven't seen your mummy. Sorry. This," he said, turning to Stella, "is Millie, the daughter of my researcher Bella Chambers."

"Cool jacket," said Stella, "and you're a great dancer." Other people's children did not really interest her, and no matter how hard she tried to be nice, it never came out sounding right.

Millie blanked her, stared at James, and said loudly enough to be heard over Wham!'s "Last Christmas": "You left your dirty socks at my house."

James closed his eyes for rather longer than it takes to blink, took Millie by the arm, and said: "I'll help you find your mother."

James's older son looked on with mild surprise.

IN OFFICE HOURS

Bella

On the Monday after the party, James called Bella into his office. He closed the door, and they sat facing each other on the red leather sofas.

"I have been thinking about this all weekend," he said. "Of course I'm not blaming Millie for what happened. But it was most unfortunate."

What was most unfortunate, thought Bella, was that I ever met you.

"I don't know what my sons made of it. Probably nothing. They are both innocent for their age."

As opposed to Millie, Bella thought, who is anything but.

"Unfortunately, Stella overheard her remark and could see its import. This puts me in a difficult situation. In my experience once one person knows about it, the truth is out."

"Anthea has known for months," Bella said quietly.

"*What?*" he said. "She can't know. We were so careful, and I never used my public e-mail to you."

"She does know. She worked it out for herself ages ago. She confronted me with it before we went to New York."

"Why," he said, "why didn't you tell me?"

"Because I thought you would react exactly as you are reacting now."

James put his head in his hands. "This is so difficult," he said. "It is going to look so bad for me. I promoted you, remember."

"Are you saying," Bella asked bitterly, "that you promoted me because you wanted to shag me?"

"No, I'm not. You deserved it. But it is my reputation that will suffer most."

Bella felt that he said this with very little conviction. "That's crap," she said. "You will now be shown to be a serial shagger, which will make you an object of envy. I will simply look pathetic. And then, I imagine I'll get fired. I can't imagine why I expected a man who is terrified by a rumble of thunder to have any strength of character at all."

He put up his hand to make her stop, but she took no notice. "That's enough," he said.

255

At that point, Anthea put her head around the door. "Sorry to interrupt," she said brightly, "but your visitors are here."

"Thank you," James said stiffly.

Bella sat at her computer, feeling sick.

She could not leave things like that. It was not that she was afraid of
the sack that would now most definitely follow. It was that if this really
was the end, she needed to make it a nicer one.

> Sorry. I was upset because I hoped you'd say that you didn't mind
> who knew. I wanted you to say that you were proud of being
> associated with me, and the thing that made you miserable is that
> you can't bear losing me. Instead you just banged on about your
> precious reputation.
>
> As for me, I don't give a shit about my reputation. I care about
> Millie. I care about losing you. That's it. What Anthea or Stella or
> Nathalie is saying about me doesn't bother me at all.
>
> Bella

This time Bella did not have to wait long for a reply.

> Dear Bella
>
> I want you to know that of course I care about losing you, too.
> Of course you matter to me enormously. Of course under other
> circumstances I would be proud to be with you. However, this
> is very difficult. I don't just have myself to think about. I have my
> family and my job. I can't make them disappear.
>
> I feel terribly unhappy about the situation, too. But I simply don't
> know what to do.
>
> James.

Stella

When her affair with Rhys had just started, Stella had dreaded the weekends. They were two long days of estrangement during which she sleepwalked through domestic tasks, waiting to come back to life on Monday.

Now the weekends were a relief. They were flat and colorless, but at least there was a kind of peace in knowing that she would not see Rhys for two days. It was not a cessation of pain, exactly, more a break from the source of it. Now it was Monday to Friday that Stella found unbearable. The simple sight of him sitting at his desk, jacket off and sleeves rolled up so that she could see the hairs on his arms, was excruciating to her. Talking to him was painful. So was not talking to him.

His presence drained all interest from everything around him, leaving her agitated, excited, miserable, shot through—still—with tiny pricks of hope if he looked her way and smiled. Sometimes Stella fancied he looked miserable: sullen and introverted. When he was like that, she could cope with the day. If, on the other hand, she heard his laugh from across the room, she felt an electric shock, a stab of pain that went on hurting long after the laughter had stopped.

At one point, she even tried listening to her iPod as she sat at her desk to block out any chance of hearing him. But that was useless, as most of the songs on it he had given her. And music had a way of attacking one's heart. When at lunchtime she had walked into Pret A Manger and was queuing to buy a sandwich, "The Scientist" by Coldplay was playing, which she thought of as their song: "Come up to meet you, tell you I'm sorry / You don't know how lovely you are..." She had had to put down the sandwich and walk out of the shop.

In short, Stella was barely coping. She was behind at work, inattentive in meetings, forgetful, and bad-tempered. She knew she was in danger of screwing up something important at work, but the thought didn't bother her unduly. Without Rhys, nothing mattered.

She clicked off the paper she was meant to be reading about possible participation in a Saudi gas project, opened her Hotmail, and started to write down the message that she had been composing in her head for the last two weeks:

My darling Rhys,

We have exchanged so many words. We've said things we didn't mean. We've said good-bye and not meant it. We have said good-bye and tried to mean it. Words don't have any value between us anymore. But pain works in a way that words do not. To be apart from you means a level of pain that I can't bear. I can see you now as I type this. Your head is bent over your keyboard. What are you doing, my darling? I want to touch your funny face. I want to kiss you and to be kissed back. But more than that, what I want is to have you back in my life. I know this is unfair on you and I understand that you want to get on with your life. You say that I have nothing to offer you, as I'm already taken. But what you don't understand is that I can offer you my heart for now, and hope you might find it enough to go on with, just for a while.

When I broke it off two weeks ago, I thought we could go back to how things were 9 months ago when you used to pop in and see me all the time. But that was fantasy: we can't go back. Too much has happened between us, and in any case I'm a different person now. The person who I am includes you. As Frank Sinatra put it—I've got you under my skin. And so trying to cut you out means making deep surgical incisions, and I feel as if I am bleeding to death. Please come with a bandage.

Your very own Stella

She looked through it. It wasn't dignified. She had never sent a less dignified message in her life. But what use was dignity when the pain was so bad? She pressed send, and across the room, Stella could see Rhys take the mouse in his hand and click on his e-mail. She could see the back of his head. She saw him glance at the message and then switch to another screen. Someone came over to his desk. He was talking to him calmly. But when he had gone he went back to his e-mail and typed something quickly. Stella could see the plain blue screen that says "Message Sent." In the gap of a few seconds that it took for his words to travel from his computer, Stella felt her future happiness in the balance. She opened the message.

I need to think. Rx.

Her first sensation was relief. Last time he had said no. Now he said he needed to think, which must mean he was going to say yes. But as the day progressed, she felt more and more uncertain. What was there to think about? He was in pain, too; she knew it from the stoop of his back. And here was a way of making it stop. How much more thought was needed for that? She waited for a message, and there was none. And then at five minutes to four, it came.

Dear Stella

I have thought about it. I can't do it. We would be in the same place a year from now, and my life is draining away. I love you. But to go on would kill both of us. Sorry. And you are not my own Stella, and you never were.

Rhys.

Stella looked at the message. She could feel her body recoiling from the screen. She shut it down and then opened it up again. No, no. It couldn't be.

Nathalie put her head around the door. "Your visitors have arrived in reception," she said. "I'll go and get them."

"Give me a minute," said Stella.

*   *   *

At home that evening, Stella had—for the first time—surrendered her whole self to misery. She had gone straight into bed, claiming that she felt too sick for supper and had a thumping headache. Clemmie, having never seen her mother ill before and worried by the way she seemed unable to speak, got into bed next to her. Finn brought her a cup of hot chocolate.

Stella allowed her hair to be stroked by her fourteen-year-old daughter and watched the steam rise from the cup by her bed. Her children loved her and needed her and trusted her, and she had betrayed them. The thought distressed her doubly. She knew exactly how deeply in the wrong she was—but she could not feel it.

She sent the children downstairs to watch TV and said that she needed to rest. This, at least, was not a lie. She drank half a bottle of Night Nurse and hoped that sleep would come.

I am in an intensive care ward, she thought as she lay in the dark. There has been a crash on the motorway, and I am wounded, but I will live. Rhys is in the men's ward nearby, and he is wounded, too, though I don't know how badly. I hope he is okay. No, I hope he is suffering at least as badly as I am. There would be comfort in that. But he can't be suffering as much as me, or else he would not have sent that message. She started to cry again.

There had been no lives lost, she tried to tell herself. The crash had not resulted in a pileup, maiming her children. In fact, they had not been in the accident at all.

Stella must have slept, as she was woken by Charles getting into bed by her side. She opened her eyes and saw the clock said two a.m.

"Are you okay?" he asked, kissing her shoulder absently.

"I'm fine," she whispered into her pillow.

The following morning as she got dressed, she repeated a mantra to herself: This pain is a punishment. I was wrong, and now I am paying for it. I will march through my days, and one day I will feel better.

She went on muttering this to herself as she went to the tube. Her phone bleeped with a text message. That won't be Rhys, she said to herself. Don't hope. Hope is your enemy. It is over, he won't be texting you. As she repeated this to herself, she was simultaneously reaching for her phone. It was him.

```
We need to talk?x
```

Stella's heart skipped. Her solemn pledge to dedicate her life from now on to being a good mother, a good wife, and a good person vanished in a second.

```
Yes, of course. Am on my way in. Starbucks
in 35 minutes?xx
```

Rhys was sitting at a grubby table at the back of the murky brown interior when Stella arrived. "Let me get you something," he said.

She watched his familiar hands counting out his change and bringing the drink and setting it down.

"I'm sorry about yesterday. I was so upset," she started to say.

"Yes," he said. "I felt really dreadful, too."

Stella smiled at him in relief, but he did not smile back.

"I just need to get out for a bit and want to go and spend some time away. I might even go back home."

"Yes, that's fine," said Stella. "A good idea to think it over…"

"No, Stella," he said. "I don't need to think it over. I am not changing my mind, but I just need to get out for a bit."

"Are you sure?" Stella looked at him, feeling panic rising in her throat.

He nodded.

And then she suddenly said, "You can't go on working for me."

His face hardened. "What?"

"You can't go on as my EA."

"That's fucking great. So the new deal is that if I'm not shagging you anymore, you fire me?"

"No, it isn't. But we can't work together anymore."

"Are you telling me to resign?"

"No, but—"

"I don't believe this. You can be a hard bitch."

"Shh," she said. "Not so loud."

Over by the counter, one of the marketing associates was paying for a coffee and looked up at them curiously.

"I think you'll find that you have done very well out of this," Stella said. "If you hadn't met me, you would have done a brief assignment with James, who by the way doesn't rate you, and now you'd be toiling away in Alaska."

"Great," he said, eyes bulging with fury. "So you throw it in my face that you have promoted me more than I deserved. So all that stuff about me being brilliant was just a trap?"

"And so is that what it comes down to in the end? It's just your career? I couldn't give a shit about whether I promoted you more or less than you deserved. I said you were brilliant because you are. But so what? That is career stuff, and it doesn't interest me in the slightest. What interests me is love. And I thought we had that. But now I sit here and watch you calmly tearing it into little pieces while you flap about your job." Stella was not crying. She was looking at him with a fury so intense that it was exhilarating.

"It's all very well you saying that," he said. "You have totally made it. You are the first fucking woman on the fucking board. You have nowhere further to go in your own career, and so you simply fuck up the careers of others."

Stella stood up in the middle of this and, with as much self-possession as she could manage, picked up her cardboard cup of coffee and walked out onto the street, almost colliding with Beate, who was on her way to get her morning cappuccino.

Bella

Bella had decided not to go to James's party. She was not obliged to go, as it was outside work time. Pretending to be professional between nine and six was so hard that she didn't want to have to go on doing it in the evening as well. Neither did she want to have to see his beautiful family house again, or his weirdo wife, or the children with their expensive little shirts that she had once seen him buying online from the Harrods website.

That morning, James had said to her as he'd walked past her desk: "I do hope you are going to come tonight."

And Bella, not looking at him, had said she would try, but it depended on babysitters. In the middle of the afternoon, her phone went and it was Rhys, whom she hadn't seen for a couple of days.

"Where are you?" she asked.

"I'm at home. I've been in Wales for a few days at my mum's, and am suicidal with boredom. I'm not sure whether to go to the party tonight, but I thought if you were going, I might be persuadable. Shall we go and get hammered first? I'm feeling like total shit."

"I'm not feeling that great either. Getting hammered sounds like a good idea," Bella said doubtfully.

So Rhys arranged to meet her at the pub, and then Bella said: "How do you feel about your fame and stardom?"

"What?"

"You are mentioned in the *Telegraph*. It says you are brilliant."

"*Really?* I haven't seen the papers." There was a note of pleasure in his voice.

"It was a big interview with Stella, and she went on and on about how brilliant you were."

"Oh," he said, sounding much less pleased. "What did she say?"

"I can't remember exactly. It was a weird interview. I'd briefed her on the diversity agenda—which was what the interview was meant to be about. But she went banging on about some W. H. Auden poem. James is furious, as he says she came over as a total flake and there wasn't a win for AE at all."

Rhys went quiet after this, so Bella said: "See you tonight."

Stella

The article in the *Telegraph* came out on the day of James's party. There was a picture of Stella on the masthead of the business section, underneath which it said: NEW FACE OF SUPERWOMAN.

And inside was a picture of her taken from below, looking not merely tired and haggard, but quite mad. Underneath, the caption said: "Stella Bradberry: 'Young people stimulate me.'"

In another mood, this unintended irony would have made her laugh. As it was, she looked at the picture and wanted to cry.

"Stella Bradberry is running late," the piece began.

She bustles into her office, looking distracted, apologizes for keeping me waiting, and says that she has a lot on. This is no exaggeration. She has just joined the board of the second largest oil company in the UK, and is one of the sharpest economists in the country. She is the trusted lieutenant of CEO Stephen Hinton and is playing a key role in restructuring the £14bn company. She is said to be the most influential woman in British business, and is on first-name terms with all the Middle East oil ministers. When Bill Gates is in town, it is Stella Bradberry he sees.

That is total bollocks, thought Stella. I have met Gates once, and that was with Stephen. And the idea that I have cozy chats with Gulf state oil ministers is hilarious.

But there is a softer side to Bradberry. On her desk there is a little Post-it sticker quoting the W. H. Auden poem "In my veins there is a wish, And a memory of fish," and on her iPod she has Keane and Snow Patrol rather than Bach and Beatles.

How dare she look at my iPod, Stella thought. And how dare she write all this drivel.

Despite being a woman and paying lip service to the diversity agenda, some might say that Bradberry has pulled the ladder up after her. Her team is entirely male, and earlier this year she raised eyebrows in the company by giving the job of her executive assistant to a young man who had only been with the company for a few months.

When challenged on this, Bradberry looked slightly flustered.

"Some of these young people joining AE are exceptionally talented," she said. "And Rhys Williams is one of them."

Stella could not bear to read on.

Bella

Bella and Rhys arrived when the party was in full swing. They had had three drinks each in the pub and got lost on the way from Wimbledon tube station.

The alcohol had improved Bella's mood somewhat, but Rhys's exceedingly low spirits—which had at first cheered her, as it was comforting to find that someone was in an even worse state than she was—were starting to get her down. Bella had asked what was the matter, and he had said everything was total shit and that he hated his life.

"Everything can't be total shit," said Bella. "Your job is fantastic. And you were in the newspapers this morning as a genius."

"Don't go on about that," he snapped.

Really, Bella thought, you are such a baby.

The door was opened by a man in a bow tie, and inside Bella could see James's younger son in a light blue dressing gown handing around crisps and the older boy, clad similarly, only in a darker shade of blue, distributing olives.

"Cute," said Rhys. "It's like *The Sound of Music*. Do you think they are going to start singing, 'So long, farewell, auf Wiedersehen, goodbye'?"

Bella laughed, accepting a crisp from the child and a glass of champagne from a waiter.

James was standing with his back to the fireplace of the handsome sitting room, with a circle of guests forming around him. He was evidently about to give a speech.

"Stay with me," she said to Rhys. "This whole party freaks me out."

"Me, too," he said.

James banged his silver fountain pen against his glass, and the party fell silent. "This is not a speech," he said.

"Shame!" cried a disembodied voice that Bella thought was probably Ben's.

"But I just wanted to say what is normally called 'a few words.'"

There was a rumble of laughter, though it did not strike Bella as funny.

"It's been a really tough year," he went on, "but I'm proud of the work we've done. There have been some scary moments"—he paused, and there was another murmur of laughter—"but I think we've come through them stronger as a company and stronger as a team."

"Blah, blah," Rhys hissed at Bella.

She smirked, and at that very moment James's eyes found her face in the crowd. Bella felt duplicitous. His speech might be banal, but he said it with such power that it all sounded real. I would follow you, Bella thought drunkenly, to the ends of the earth.

And then he said: "And finally, Hillary—where are you? I want to thank you for this lovely party. And thank you for putting up with me." He smiled at his wife.

Bella pulled on Rhys's sleeve. "Get me another drink. I'm going to get completely rat-arsed," she said. How could he, she was thinking. Hillary hasn't lifted a fucking finger for the party. Anthea did most of it.

"Let's go and talk to Stella," said Bella. She pulled Rhys over, but he resisted.

Bella had started to say to Stella how much she had enjoyed the interview in the papers when James's wife came to join them.

She nodded at Bella and kissed Stella on both cheeks, and the two older women started to talk about their children's schools. Bella looked at Hillary up close. Her face had lines on it that were partly filled with skillfully applied foundation. Her dress was low-cut, and Bella thought her cleavage looked a bit crepey. When she got to that age, she would cover up a bit more. And then Bella noticed that round the neck of her boss's wife was the same pearl necklace that was sitting on Bella's chest of drawers at home. But while Bella's was a single string, Hillary had three strings held with a diamond clasp.

The withdrawn manner Hillary had had when Bella had come round with the tickets had quite gone. Instead, she was talking loudly to Stella and looking at her with a mad intensity. "James minds so much about Harry getting into Winchester," she was saying.

Bella glanced around the room to see where Rhys had got to. She was starting to feel drunk, not in a cheerful way, but in a queasy, morose way. She did not want to listen to this conversation but did not know how to escape it, either.

"I think boarding school does so much damage," Hillary was saying. "In fact, you only need to look at James himself. I often think his emotional development has been stunted by being sent away to boarding school at eight. Though sometimes I think he was just born autistic."

For a moment Bella felt an odd sort of camaraderie with his wife, who appeared to be even more drunk than she was herself.

"What do you think, Bella?" Hillary asked. "You probably see more of him than I do myself."

I can't cope with this, Bella thought.

"What would you say it was?" James's wife went on. "Stunted emotional development through boarding school, or was he just born with this extreme male gene?"

"Um," said Bella. "Well, I don't really know, as obviously I don't see the same side of him as you."

Hillary took a large swallow of champagne, as did Bella.

"But," Bella went on hurriedly, "boarding school is weird. I can't imagine sending my daughter to one."

At that moment, Stephen broke into the circle and put his hand on Hillary's arm. "I have to go," he said. "But thank you. It was a great party."

Hillary looked at the CEO blankly, as if she had no idea who he was. Bella took advantage of the interruption and slipped away to find Rhys. But instead of finding him, she walked straight into James.

"Hello," he said. His voice was hard and angry. "I saw you turn up with Rhys."

"Yes," she said simply.

"Isn't that a bit tactless?" he said.

"What?" she said. "Tactless? And isn't inviting your former mistress to your house so that you can praise your wife to the skies and parade her in the necklace three times the size of the one you gave your mistress—isn't that a bit tactless?"

"We can't have this conversation here," he said, taking hold of her arm as if she were a hooligan. "Let's go into the garden."

Stella

"Here comes the most influential woman in the oil market," said James as Stella stepped out of the cab after an interminable journey to Wimbledon. "Welcome."

Hillary was standing behind him in the hallway looking absent, as if there were something that she had lost. She had put on weight since last year, and Stella, who was now unable to prevent herself from doing an age audit of every woman in her forties, decided that she was aging badly. She must be forty-one but looked closer to fifty.

"Hello, Stella, you look so thin…have you stopped eating?" Hillary asked.

Stella smiled and kissed her, assured her that she ate plenty, and told Hillary that she was looking marvelous. She pushed past her into the room, which contained all the most senior people at AE. In another mood, she might have been scornful of such naked ambition displayed in a guest list; but today she was indifferent to it. The only guest in the world she cared about appeared not to be there.

"Ah, Stella," said Sir John Englefield, approaching and giving her a peck on the cheek. "Fascinating profile this morning in the *Telegraph*. But I didn't know you had an interest in poetry."

Stella smiled at the chairman and gave a humorless laugh. "Idiot journalists trying to find color," she said. "It was just something of my daughter's..."

Over his shoulder she was scanning new arrivals for Rhys, but every time the door opened, it was someone else. The relief she thought she would feel did not come. Instead she felt despair that he was not there. She had not seen him for five long days, and the absence was bearing down on her. It did not, as the poem had said, go through her like thread through a needle. It stifled her like a blanket. Just a sight of him would allow her to breathe again and make her feel better.

The door opened again, this time revealing Bella, who was looking flushed and pretty. At first Stella did not see Rhys, who was standing behind Bella. Then she saw him whisper something to her, and Bella turned, looking at him and laughing. No, thought Stella.

Rhys's eyes were fixed on Bella, and he did not raise them to look into the room beyond. He took two glasses of champagne and gave one to Bella.

Stella accepted a miniature salmon flan from a woman with a tray, not because she wanted it, but to give her something to do. It stuck to the roof of her mouth, and she took a gulp of champagne to wash it down.

"No," she said out loud.

"Don't you think so?" Sir John looked at her in surprise. He had been talking about skiing in Gstaad at Christmas.

Stella was saved from having to explain herself by the sound of metal being tapped on a crystal glass. James, it seemed, was preparing to give a speech.

Stella looked at him carefully and thought he seemed entirely in control. Perhaps he had not seen Bella arrive with Rhys. Or perhaps Stella had misheard the child at the party. Perhaps she had got the wrong end of the stick. If James had been having an affair with Bella, surely he would not have asked her to his house? Or perhaps it was just a brief and sordid thing that was embarrassing to both and didn't count.

James was thanking Hillary and giving a Christmas toast just as Bella approached from one side, pulling Rhys by the sleeve. The possessiveness of the gesture made Stella feel sick. You do not tug the sleeve of a colleague unless you have had sex with him. This principle, which Stella's fevered mind had invented on the spot, struck her as irrefutably true.

Rhys met Stella's eye before turning his back to get another drink. He did not smile or acknowledge her at all.

Bella was trying to talk to her about the *Telegraph* interview and, like a true strumpet, was looking at her with such innocence that it was repulsive to see. Stella wanted to get away, but Hillary joined them, making escape impossible.

"Is Finn sitting common entrance this year?" she asked.

"Yes, but he's not working very hard," Stella said doubtfully.

Hillary started to say how their older boy was down for Winchester and the headmaster of the prep school had said that he would pass the exams easily. The trouble was that she wasn't sure it was right for him, but James had his heart set on it. Stella thought about Finn and about how he was likely to fail his exams and about Charles, who, far from being difficult about his son's schooling, seemed impervious to the fact that he was being schooled at all.

And then Bella butted into the conversation and started talking about her own feelings about educating her daughter. She's self-centered as well as a tart, Stella thought.

She made her excuses, thanked Hillary for the party, and went to get her coat. But as she did so, she walked straight into Rhys, who was swaying drunkenly.

"It's good to see you," he said.

Stella stared at him incredulously. "Are you trying to hurt me?" she said.

"I don't know why you are so angry," he said. "All I ever did was love you."

Stella gave a bitter laugh. And then started to cry. "I have to get out," she said, opening the back door, which led onto a cast-iron balcony. Rhys did not follow.

Down in the garden below, they heard a man's voice saying: "These past two weeks have been exceptionally difficult for me."

Then there was a pause, while someone—a woman—said something that Stella could not hear.

"That's not fair. I'm not good at this—just because I don't show it doesn't mean I don't feel it. I have missed you in a way that has taken me by surprise. I was quite unprepared for just how awful I have felt."

And then there was silence in the garden.

Bella

Bella sat at her desk the day after the party with a savage hangover and a deep, if somewhat confused, feeling that things were, if not exactly good, at least much better than they had been. For the first time in weeks, she had come into the office feeling some of the old excitement. She had been a little disappointed that James had not sent her a text that morning but still felt sure enough that his clumsy speech in the garden had been genuine. He had said he wanted her and that being without her had made him "too damned miserable." Surely he wasn't going to change his mind again so soon.

Just as she was settling down to do some work, her phone rang. "James Home," it said on the display. Bella thought this strange, as she had seen his briefcase in his office, which suggested that he was in.

"Hello," she said softly.

But the voice wasn't James's. It was Hillary's.

"Thank you for the party last night," Bella said in a brisker tone of voice. "It was a really great do. So much nicer than the Christmas parties that we have in the office. I had a really good time, but I must have had a lot of champagne because I'm paying for it this morning." The words were tumbling out, but even to Bella's ears they sounded tinny and wrong.

There was a pause, and then Hillary said: "Do you feel pleased with yourself?" Her voice was thick and slow.

"Sorry?"

"Do you feel pleased with yourself?" Hillary repeated.

"Um, I'm not sure what you mean," said Bella. She was panicking but hoping that if she went on saying nothing, the bullet that was aimed at her would somehow miss.

"You do know what I mean. You know exactly what I mean."

"I'm afraid I don't."

"Well, I'll have to tell you, then. You have been fucking my husband. It was you in the car with him. It was you who was with him at the Great Eastern Hotel. You were fucking him in New York. It is you who is stored in his mobile under the name Bill. And it was you who came to my house last night, stood around in your nasty tarty dress, and then snogged him in *my* garden."

"No," said Bella. "No, I don't feel pleased with myself."

Hillary ignored this. "I'm never wrong about people. When you delivered the tickets to me in the summer, I knew you were trouble. And what did you think you were doing? Looking at the competition to see how old I was? Do you think it's clever to tempt these men with their midlife crises? Do you think it's clever to talk so politely to their wives on the phone while shagging their husbands behind their backs? Of course I blame him, too, for being weak, but you are vicious. You have ruined the life of a woman you hardly know." Hillary was sobbing into the phone.

"I'm sorry," Bella said feebly.

There was a click and Hillary was gone. Bella hung up and went into the loo, where she knelt down in the cubicle and was violently sick.

Stella

Stella was in Stephen's office when he got the call. His PA took it and buzzed through.

"Sorry to interrupt, but it's James Staunton's wife. She says it is urgent."

Stephen picked up the phone. "Hello, Hillary," he said smoothly. "Marvelous party last night. Thank you so much..."

Stella watched his face fall from smarmy impatience to alarm.

"Oh, dear," he said. He stood up and turned around so that he was staring out of the window and Stella could see only his back. "Oh dear, I see... Um, no. I don't condone it. Obviously not. Would you like me to talk to him?... Please, Hillary. Look, I'm terribly sorry. This is an awkward situation... Please don't cry. Hillary... are you there?... Hillary?" He closed his eyes, sighed, and put down the phone.

"What was that?" asked Stella, knowing perfectly well what that was.

"I shouldn't tell you, though I expect you may have *surmised*." He said the last word with an arch pomposity, as if to distance himself from the sordid nature of the facts.

"Something to do with James?"

"The stupid idiot has had an affair with someone on his team. That was his wife weeping and gnashing her teeth."

"Oh, dear," said Stella. "But why did she tell you?"

"I don't really think she knew what she was doing. She was babbling incoherently. She apparently saw her husband locked in an amorous embrace with this young woman last night in the garden, which cannot have been a particularly pleasing sight. I suppose she phoned me because in the heat of the moment she had forgotten that revenge is a dish best served cold, and all that."

He paused and went on. "Funny, I thought it was a perfectly good do last night. Everyone rather well behaved for a Christmas bash. But then one never knows what is going on under the surface. Still waters, one could say."

Stella ignored this philosophizing and said: "Does she expect you to sack him? Surely she wouldn't want that?"

"No, I think she expects me to sack the girl and read him the riot act. Though I don't think she had thought any of it through. She was just having a hormonal moment." And then, as if suddenly realizing that he was addressing a woman, he said: "No offense to present company."

Despite everything, Stella wanted to laugh. "No offense" was what Finn said to her before he told her that she looked old or that her cooking was worse than the nanny's.

"Tell me, Stella, what am I supposed to do about this? We are all adults. I don't expect anyone to be an angel. God knows I'm not one myself." He looked at Stella in an unpleasantly suggestive way. "But I really would expect people to have the good sense—the taste—not to conduct affairs with subordinates whom they then promote."

Stella swallowed.

"Does everyone know about this affair? Did you know?"

"Well, I had my suspicions," said Stella.

"Why didn't you tell me?"

"Because—," Stella started to say, but Stephen interrupted.

"I know why. Because it wasn't your business."

Stella nodded uncertainly.

"Look, Stella. You are a morally upright person—and I'm sure you find it terribly hard to imagine how people get themselves into messes like these. But they do. This sort of thing looks so sleazy if it gets out. I think we need to have a policy to cover this. I think I'll talk to Russell about it."

"Do you really think it's a good idea to involve HR?" Stella asked cautiously, thinking of her recent conversation with Russell.

"You're right," said Stephen, nodding. "We don't need the dead hand of HR on this. Can you draft something yourself and then liaise with Russell? And in the meantime, I'm going to have a word with James. Really, this wasn't in my job description. CEO of global oil company— task 1: Tell your senior executives to keep their bloody trousers on."

Bella

James called her in. He was looking odd. Not distraught, just stiff. There was a dead look in his eye.

"You should know this," he said. He was speaking slowly and precisely. "Last night Hillary saw us in the garden."

"She called me," said Bella. She was still shaking and finding it hard to speak.

James didn't seem to have heard her but went on in the same monotone: "She has responded with anger and hostility, which is perhaps not surprising. I have assured her that you will be transferred immediately to another role."

Bella stared at him in horror. This was the man she loved. Who had told her in the garden, fifteen hours earlier, that he adored her and that he could not bear to be apart from her. She could understand that he was in shock. But what she could not understand was why he was looking at her as if she had a nasty contagious disease and needed to be kept away from him for fear he might catch it. He could not even, she thought bitterly, spare one thought for her, or how she might feel, or what it was like to have his wife shouting wildly down the phone. Her suffering in this just didn't register.

"We are going to have to find you another job. I will make sure it is a good one. In fact, I might ask Stella if she'd take you."

"I'm not a bundle," said Bella.

He looked at her, and for just a moment she thought his mask was going to slip and that he was going to weep. "No," he said. "You are not a bundle, Bella. I am aware of that."

And then, after a brief silence, he said: "I loved you, you know."

Loved. One letter, one minute change in tense, was the most painful thing of all.

Stella

Stella would have liked to have had a conversation with James about it. One in which she would have said: I think I may know some of what you are feeling. It's total hell. I don't blame you—I pity you and feel sorry that it's all such a terrible mess.

But she didn't do that. Not because she thought James would tell—he might now be a serial adulterer, but was not a gossip. But because she dreaded his response. It was normal—or what passed for normal—for a man to have an affair with his much younger PA. But for a woman to do the same would seem perverted. Yet so desperate was she to tell someone who might understand that she was feeling so very bad, she might have risked his amusement—or even his disgust. What stopped her was the look on his face as she went into his office.

He looked entirely blank. There was no sign of distress or even embarrassment. She had heard his words in the garden the night before, and though they had been delivered in a slightly stilted way, she believed them to be genuine. Surely he was suffering at some level; but if he was insisting on wearing a mask like this, then so must she.

"Stella," he said, "this is somewhat sensitive, but I would like to ask you a favor."

Stella nodded.

"Bella Chambers, who I believe briefed you for your recent interview, needs to move on from my team for personal reasons. I don't really want to go into details, but I do not wish her to return to the secretarial pool and be punished for what was not her fault. I wondered if there were any openings on your team…?"

Stella thought of the intense dislike she had felt for Bella at the party the night before, and even though it turned out that her jealousy was probably unfounded, it still left a bad taste. She did not want this pretty girl sitting near Rhys, even if Rhys himself might shortly be moving.

"I'm sorry," she said. "I have a PA and an EA, and that seems enough."

"Stella," he said, "please. Is there not some research project? She is very bright and willing…"

This last word, with its unintended innuendo, hung between them for a second. And then he said in a slightly different tone: "It said in the

Telegraph yesterday that you were keener on promoting young men? This might set the record straight?"

Stella looked at him closely. What was he saying? Did he know? "That's bollocks," she said. "But yes, if it helps you and helps her, I'll take her."

"Thank you, Stella," he said.

Bella

Bella knocked on Stella's door and was beckoned inside.

Stella was at her desk, calmly typing at her keyboard. Her life seemed so settled, Bella thought, so grand and so happy. Presumably, Stella knew all the sordid details and was judging harshly this stupid PA who slept with her boss and then needed rescuing. It was all so humiliating.

And then Bella thought of the previous evening, and Stella witnessing her talking to Hillary. What a low opinion of her she must have.

This was particularly painful—Bella admired Stella and wanted to be liked by her. When she had presented the diversity numbers to her, Stella had been so clever at sorting out the waffle. She was informal, but she was also scary. Perhaps it was because she set such high standards herself that she couldn't understand how other people made a hash of their lives.

"I understand," Stella was saying, "that you have come to the end of your research stint in External Relations and are interested in Economics. James says that you are a brilliant linguist, that you pick things up very quickly, and that you have huge promise. He said that you deserve to be on the management fast track."

Bella gave a strained smile. The idea that he thought her worthy of the fast-track program would have given her such pleasure a few months ago. Now, she neither believed it nor cared.

"I have been looking at your latest work and development plan," Stella went on, "and I think you have a lot of skills that we could use. I don't have a job for you to be slotted into at once, so for now I will ask you to help out Nathalie, and to work on projects for me and for members of the department. The job is ill defined at the moment, but if you are willing, we will be able to find things for you to do."

"Thank you," said Bella. "I really appreciate this."

Stella smiled. "It's utterly self-interested," she said. "I need good people. The only spare desk is with Nathalie, but you won't be doing PA duties, as Nathalie has that more than covered, as you can imagine. I hope that is okay?"

"Thank you," said Bella again. Her eyes were filling with tears, and her voice was shaky. She thought she might cry. Why was it that when people were nice to you at work they made you cry, but when they were horrid you kept your dignity?

"Are you okay?" Stella asked.

Bella fought to get control of herself. "I have been humiliated today, and made to feel like a worthless piece of scum. It's just a shock when someone starts to be kind, especially someone like you. I doubt if you have ever done a stupid thing in your whole life."

"Oh, I have," Stella said suddenly.

Bella thought she looked a bit odd. Could it be that she was so moved by Bella's plight that she was inclined to cry, too? Such softness was quite unexpected.

But just as Bella was thinking that, Stella stood up and said briskly: "Nathalie will sort out your desk and so on."

Bella was putting her things in a crate to move from her old desk in ER. She had had to stop in the middle of it and go to the loo to weep. The distress she felt came in waves. She would feel almost normal for a bit, and then she would feel as if she'd been struck down by guilt and anger mixed in with grief. As she put her last pens into the box, Rhys came by.

"I suppose you've heard," she said.

He nodded.

"Does everyone know?"

He nodded again.

"What are they saying?"

He shrugged and said: "Nothing much."

"I don't believe that," said Bella. "I suppose they are saying a great deal. Every time I go into a room people shut up at the sight of me. If I wasn't so miserable, I'd really mind. I suppose they're saying I'm an idiot."

Rhys didn't comment on this.

"Do you think I'm an idiot?" she asked. She picked up a picture that Millie had done when she was six of the two of them holding hands and put it in a crate.

"Yes," he said, "obviously you are. But then we are all idiots."

"You're not," she said. "You are in other ways, but you'd never be so stupid as to have an affair with someone who is not only taken, but who is also your boss. Things don't get more stupid than that."

"No," said Rhys, "they don't."

He said this with a surprising amount of feeling. Why was he rubbing it in? she wondered.

"So why do it?" he asked.

Bella looked up and could see James sitting at his computer, eyes fixed on his screen. "I can't talk to you here. Will you come down to the canteen with me and get a cup of tea?"

And so they walked to the lift together, Bella feeling not just the eyes of Anthea upon them, but the eyes of the entire team.

"Do you really want to know why?" she said as they sat down in the canteen with cups of tea that she didn't feel like drinking. "It's because I was tired of dating stupid boys who either looked down on me or couldn't cope with Millie. Or who drank eight pints of lager and threw up. James isn't like that. I admired him. And he admired me, or so I thought."

"Really," said Rhys. "I thought he was a bit of a pillock. Seemed to have something wedged up his arse."

Bella smiled. She was so angry with James that the idea that others despised him made her feel better. "Yes," she said. "I don't know what I thought I was doing. Maybe it was just proximity. Or maybe work is so boring that doing something forbidden is exciting. But it's not as if I set out to do it. In fact, I set out not to. But he was nice to me, and I was flattered, and I thought, Why not?"

Bella knew that this wasn't true. But she wasn't going to tell Rhys how much she had loved James and how even now, even in the middle of it all, she still hoped—and sometimes even expected—that he would come back to her. Neither was she going to tell another version of events that sometimes she thought was the true one: that she had fallen for him, and made a play for him, and forced him to ignore his guilt. She had played on his weakness, just as Hillary had said.

"You're right," Bella went on. "I was an idiot. And—guess what—it's always the woman who pays the price. No one has suggested that James be moved somewhere else. I'm being packed up and sent to a different job, and expected to be grateful for not being fired."

"That's an incredibly sexist view."

"It might be sexist, but it's also true. How many men do you know who have suffered from the bust-up of office affairs?"

"Well, I haven't counted. But you are wrong anyway. The reason that you've been dumped on isn't because you are female, it's because you are below James in the food chain."

"Well, yeah, but that's always how it's going to be, isn't it? How many women date their male PAs?"

"Point taken," Rhys said doubtfully.

Stella

On the last day before the Christmas break, Stella went back to the doctor. This time she insisted on an appointment with her own GP, a woman in her mid-fifties who had seen Stella through two pregnancies but not much since. She sat in the waiting room and picked up a copy of the *Financial Times* and stared at the front page. G8 MINISTERS SEEK TO REASSURE MARKETS, it said. She tried to read the story but could not take it in. After a while her name was called, and she went into the doctor's treatment room.

"What can I do for you?" the doctor asked, looking at Stella over the top of her reading glasses.

"I have been having difficulty sleeping," she said. "And I'm also a bit anxious. Not all the time—I'm fine for a bit, and then a wave of panic hits me. I keep bursting into tears."

As if to prove the point, she started to cry. The doctor handed her a paper tissue. "I'm sorry," said Stella.

"Has something happened?" the doctor asked.

"No, not really. I've just got a lot on at the moment. I've been promoted into a new job, and it's Christmas, and my mother-in-law hasn't been well...," said Stella.

The doctor was looking at Stella's notes on the screen and had doubtless seen the record of her last, humiliating visit there three months ago.

"There was something else that has been a bit..." Stella hesitated while she thought of the right word. "Destabilizing. I've been having an affair with someone at work. But now it's over."

The doctor nodded. "I see," she said.

Stella found it was not a relief getting the truth out into the open. The admission sounded so banal, so humdrum, and so entirely of her own making.

"It's all a mess," Stella said. "I never meant to do this. But it has hijacked my life and..." She started to sob again. "Sometimes I think I'm going mad," she said.

The doctor handed her a form on a clip pad and told her to fill it in. There were twenty questions to which she had to check Strongly Agree, Agree, Not Sure, Disagree, or Strongly Disagree. Stella dabbed at her eyes with the hankie and looked at the first sentence:

I take less pleasure in things than I used to.

Stella ticked Strongly Agree. What a stupid question.

I have difficulty sleeping. She ticked Strongly Agree again.

I often feel blue for no reason. Actually she felt more than blue, she felt black, but she had every reason to do so.

And on she went through the questionnaire until she came to:

I feel suicidal.

She did not feel suicidal, although if she had to fill in many more moronic forms like this one, she might be shunted in that direction.

Stella handed the completed questionnaire back to the doctor, who on looking at the answers proceeded to tell her exactly what Stella had said at the outset: that she was suffering from anxiety and depression and insomnia. She gave her beta blockers and antidepressants and warned her that she must not drink any alcohol.

"Are you still in touch with this man?" she asked.

Stella nodded. "I have to be. He works for me."

"Ah. I see. And what about your marriage?"

"My marriage is fine."

The doctor, who showed no sign of having heard, said: "It often helps to go see a Relate counselor. If you look up 'Relate' on the Internet, you'll be able to find the name of someone convenient. They are usually good."

"But," protested Stella, "I don't want to see a Relate counselor. I love my husband. This is something quite separate."

She said that if Stella didn't want couples therapy, she recommended that she go for some cognitive behavior therapy and gave her the name of a psychiatrist in Harley Street. She said the pills would start to work in a fortnight and that the therapy would take longer.

Stella made the driver wait outside a chemist's while she got the drugs and a bottle of water. She took a beta blocker and the first antidepressant and felt stronger as she swallowed them. She was sorting herself out, she said to herself. She was not going to go under.

By midmorning, the pills were making Stella feel dizzy. She could not concentrate on the latest set of management accounts, which showed that the company was going to miss its December forecast by a wide margin.

Instead she decided to go out and have a walk. Once outside, she drifted past the shops and upon seeing Reiss decided on a whim to buy a Christmas present for Rhys. Nothing big, just a token to show him that she did not feel bitter or angry. She would make a joke of the name: for Rhys from Reiss.

In the front of the shop were piles of cashmere sweaters. She liked the idea of him wearing something she had given him and started to finger the colors. Bright colors did not look good on him, she thought. Gray might be better.

"Can I help you with sizing?" said a shop assistant.

"It's for my..." Stella paused, knowing it was ridiculous to feel so embarrassed in front of an assistant whom she would never see again and who could not have cared less. "It's for a friend," she said. "He's about the same size as you." She took the medium sweater to the till.

When she got back to the office, there was an envelope on her desk with "Stella" written on it in his writing. She snatched it and tore it open, then stared at the picture of St. Paul's Cathedral under snow. Inside it said: "To Stella and family. Happy Christmas. Best, Rhys."

Stella looked at this in dismay. Which was worse, she wondered, the "Stella and family" or the "best"? She thought of the jumper, chosen with such care. She could not give it to him now. Instead she sent a message saying:

Thank you for the thoughtful card.

It was cold, but that was what she meant it to be.

Bella

On the morning of her last day at work before Christmas, Stella called Bella into her office.

"I hope you won't mind if I set you an unusual task. I've been asked by the CEO to draw up a 'love contract policy'—a code of conduct for relationships between colleagues. Would it seem like some sort of terrible aversion therapy if I asked you to do some legwork and find out what other companies do?"

Bella found she did not mind. It was a relief to have her situation alluded to. There could not be a single person in the company who did not know, but still no one had said anything. It was even more of a relief to be given something to do. She had spent the past week at her desk pretending to be busy and walking up to the vending machines far more often than her desire for a Diet Coke merited, in the hope of catching a glimpse of James.

"Well, at least it's something that I know about," she said, "which makes a difference from writing reports on relative share price performance."

Stella looked at her and laughed with what struck Bella as real sympathy. And then she said, quite out of the blue: "How are you getting on with your Christmas shopping?"

Bella said that it was nearly all done, though she kept on buying more things for Millie. She wanted Christmas to be really good for her this year.

Stella got a Reiss bag from behind her desk and held it out to her. "Perhaps you have someone you could give this to? It's a jumper I bought for Charles, but it isn't the right size and I can't find the receipt, so it'd be a relief if you took it."

Bella looked inside at the pale gray cashmere jumper. She didn't have anyone to give it to but thought she might wear it herself. The softness of the wool looked comforting.

"I can't accept this," she said. "There must be someone who'd like it in your family."

"Just take it," Stella said almost sharply. "You'd be doing me a favor."

Bella took the bag back to her desk, and into Google she typed "love contract" and read:

Love contracts relieve the company of any liability during the time period of the office romance prior to the signing of the contract. If a manager chooses to date the reporting employee, they are advised to notify Human Resources. In these instances, the manager will be the employee who needs to change jobs in the company, assuming a position is available.

She scrolled down through the policies disbelievingly. The love contracts were silent on love itself, silent on the emotional price that there was to pay. And that the price was in this particular case both monumental and being paid entirely by her. She had lost him, and she missed him. She would never get him back, and this thought was too hard to bear.

Bella picked up the Christmas card she had bought for him a week earlier but hadn't resolved whether to send or not. After much deliberation, she had written inside: "Dear James, I hope you have a lovely Christmas, and that everything is ok for you at home. Love, Bella x."

But she didn't hope that he had a lovely Christmas, and she didn't hope that things were okay for him. She ripped the card in two and put it in the bin.

As she did so, her phone buzzed. "James," it said. With her heart in her mouth, Bella opened the message.

Hello.

It wasn't a passionate declaration of love. But it was a cracking of his will. She hugged herself. This one humdrum word had transported her from despair to optimism. She regretted having torn up the card.

"Hello," she texted back.

After the briefest of pauses came another message:

What are you doing this afternoon?

She replied:

```
Working.
```

Then there was nothing for a while, during which time Bella started to regret the brusqueness of her reply. After about ten minutes, another text came:

```
Great Eastern—right now?
```

This was what she wanted more than anything, but not like this. She wanted him to say that his relationship with her was precious, too precious to give up. She needed him to say sorry and to make amends. She could not accept such a graceless invitation.

```
No. Fraid I'm busy.
```

She sat back and waited for another attempt to persuade her, but none came. Bella started to panic—she had longed for this and it had come, but she had spoiled it. She started to draft another, kinder message when her phone bleeped again.

```
Please
```

And without thinking at all, she just messaged:

```
Yes
```

She got her bag and said to Nathalie, "Millie is ill. I've got to get her from school."

A few months ago, she would not have considered using her daughter like this, but in her present mood Bella didn't care. Neither did she care whether Nathalie believed her. None of it mattered. She ran through the streets and pushed through the revolving doors without waiting for the man to spin them for her.

*   *   *

James was waiting by the lift, obscured by an extravagant display of gold and silver branches.

"Thank you," he said, holding her fiercely to him. "Thank you." And then he whispered, "Happy Christmas, darling."

Bella closed her eyes and smiled into the tweed of his jacket. She had gone from perfect misery to perfect happiness in just one hour. He had never called her darling before. Which must mean he was not going to give her up.

That afternoon in the hotel room, surrounded by matching oak furniture and trouser press, kettle and minibar, Bella had the most intense sex of her life. For those minutes, she felt that this man was hers and hers alone. He was hers in a way that was deeper than discovery and shame, deeper than the pain of his wife's discovery and the uncomprehending fury of his children.

"Do you think," she said, "that this room has ever seen such happiness?"

James said nothing. He had moved away from her, but this time it wasn't to lie in his own silo of guilt; he was getting something out of his briefcase.

"This is your Christmas present." Out of his bag he brought another box from Mappin and Webb. Bella opened it. Inside were the earrings to go with the necklace.

"They are lovely," said Bella. She wondered if a larger pair were in his briefcase waiting to be given to Hillary but pushed the thought away.

"I've got something for you, too," she said. "I'm sorry I didn't have time to wrap it." She produced the Reiss bag and gave it to him.

"Happy Christmas," she said. "I love you."

Stella

Stella's Christmas was bleak. The sleeping pills were helping her sleep, but the antidepressants made her feel so giddy and so fuzzy in the head that she stopped taking them.

On Christmas Eve, she took the children ice-skating at Somerset House and put on skates herself and made her way stiffly and slowly around the rink. For one brief moment, she thought she saw Rhys gliding around on the ice. But it turned out to be an impostor—someone who did not have his clear blue eyes and his crooked smile, someone else altogether.

She had had no contact with him at all for six days, except for one text on Christmas Day. At midnight, when everyone else had gone to bed, Stella, exhausted and broken from the effort of trying to look happy for so many hours at a stretch, sent him a text saying:

Happy Christmas x.

He replied within minutes with the same message, only without the x. Apart from this one lapse—which made her feel considerably worse—she tried to immerse herself in her family. She showered them with Christmas presents and treats, but the harder she tried, the worse she felt, because there was no escaping the size of her failure. There was a crater of unhappiness separating her from her family, one that she could not imagine ever being filled in.

New Year's Day was the bleakest and the coldest. The children were bored and fighting, and Stella took refuge in her study to do some work. But she could not concentrate on any of the e-mails that had arrived over Christmas and instead typed a message to Rhys just telling him what she had been doing, knowing that she would never send it. She even typed "broken heart" into Google and clicked on the first site that came up offering advice:

Get plenty of rest. Have lovely, scented baths. Tempt yourself with healthy, delicious foods. Maybe buy some luxury, fleecy pajamas and a furry hot-water bottle cover. This is a time when you need to indulge and comfort yourself.

Stella shut down the computer in disgust. She had gone somewhere so cold that even the most sweetly scented hot bath or warmest pajamas would make no difference.

Bella

The Christmas break was interminable. James was at his house in Wiltshire and had told her that it would be difficult to e-mail but that he hoped she would understand.

She didn't understand. He wasn't umbilically attached to his family; she knew he checked his BlackBerry endlessly for work messages when he was at home and so to send her the odd message could not have been that hard.

At the end of Christmas Day, when Bella climbed into her old childhood bed at her mother's house with a heavy stomach and heavier heart, his name appeared on her phone.

```
Happy Christmas. Things a bit calmer here.
Usual orgy of consumption. Hope you've had a
lovely day.

James.
```

Bella read this with rage and then disbelief. Was that the best he could do? It was worse than no message at all. She typed back:

```
No, I didn't have a lovely day. I had a shit
Christmas. Huge row with mum. Xan turned up
at her place on Christmas evening off his
head, and mum let him in, as she has never
really understood the drugs thing.

But the killer is this. Your chilly, distant
```

```
messages from your happy family Christmas. I
don't exist to you as a person. You are only
interested in your work. And I am checking
out of this whole thing.
```

She waited an hour and a half for his reply. It said:

```
That's not fair. This is a tricky situation.
If I didn't care for you I would have been
out of this long, long ago. I think we both
need to think about it. Let's have lunch
Tuesday. J
```

Stella

Stella got into the office first and walked past Rhys's empty desk. He had tidied it before the holidays, but even looking at the piles of paper that he must have touched made Stella feel agitated.

All through the holiday she had longed to see him again, but now that he was about to walk in any minute, she felt unequal to seeing him.

Nathalie had gone through most of the messages that had arrived during the holiday and had moved into a folder marked "URGENT" the forty or fifty messages that required Stella's urgent attention. Stella looked at them and felt no urgency at all. She opened the first one.

Dear Stella

I just wanted to touch base with you to check that you are coming to the Business Woman of the Year dinner on Thursday at the Dorchester. Obviously there is a lot of media interest in this, and so I'm sure that you will understand that we never announce the winner beforehand. But can I put it like this? It's rather important that you come. Can you let me know asap? You won't be disappointed.

All best,

Chloe Woodstock

Stella looked at this with a feeling of dread. She did not want to be Business Woman of the Year. She did not deserve it, she did not value it. She didn't want any more attention. She wanted to crawl under a stone and wait until she started to feel better.

At exactly nine a.m., Rhys appeared wearing a new coat that he must have bought in the sales. Even the idea that he had been out shopping without telling her and had bought this coat was painful, a sign of his ordinary life going on while hers had stopped dead. She waited for him to come and say hello, which he didn't. An hour and a half later, when he came into her office to discuss the day's work, she asked, "Did you have a pleasant Christmas?"

"Yes, very nice. You? Was yours good?"

"Oh yes," she said. "It was very nice."

They were standing in her office some distance apart. This was even worse than Stella had feared it would be.

"Rhys," she said briskly, "I think I've won this businesswoman award. Can you please write me a five-minute acceptance speech?"

"Yes," he said. "Of course." And then, as she had turned her back and was headed for her desk, he called out as an afterthought:

"Congratulations."

Bella

On Tuesday, James was already at his desk when Bella got in. He had had his hair cut, and she could see the pink of his neck. He smiled at her as she walked past his office. It was all going to be okay. He had sent her an e-mail overnight with a picture of him taken over Christmas slumped on a sofa with his belly looking particularly round, his cheeks red and hair unkempt. His message said:

Thought this might amuse you. I can't understand how you can like someone who looks like this? I am looking forward to our lunch. I have booked a table for 1 pm at St John

Jx

She had studied the picture and thought it looked sweet.

It's a mystery why I like you, but I do. b xxx

Bella got to the restaurant first and was shown to a table beside two florid-faced men. James arrived a couple of minutes later, hurried up to her table, and bent to kiss her. Bella looked down at the menu, which had all sorts of horrible things on it that she would not dream of eating, like brains and pig's trotters. She ordered mackerel and red cabbage, not because she liked it, but because she had read something in a magazine over Christmas about mackerel being good for the brain.

"Bella," he said, "you have lovely eyes. I suppose people have often told you that?"

"Yes," she said, "they have."

"Bella," he said, "there is something I want to tell you. Something I think we need to discuss."

"Yes," agreed Bella. She was thinking: He is going to tell me that he is leaving his wife.

The waiter brought a basket of bread and made a great thing of changing Bella's knife for a fish knife. While he was doing this, James said nothing. When the waiter was gone, he took a breath and said: "I have thought about this over Christmas, and I have come to a final decision."

She waited expectantly. He seemed to be having difficulty saying the words, which wasn't surprising given everything. He opened his mouth a couple of times, said nothing, and closed it again. Then, gathering courage, he said: "We cannot go on."

Bella felt as if there were a stone in her chest. It was making breathing hard and uncomfortable. She didn't say anything, but she nodded and kept nodding, and the stone was feeling larger and heavier.

"You see," he said, "I thought about it. I got away with it last time. Hillary is terribly upset and wary, and a lot of damage has been done. She hasn't forgiven me—not yet—but she has given me another chance. But if I went on, I would get chucked out. I keep thinking about living in a bedsit and never being able to see my children. If that happened to me, I couldn't forgive myself. You aren't risking Millie, she's yours."

Bella went on nodding, quite silent. Don't cry, don't cry, don't cry, she was thinking. She looked at what was on her plate. The bronze skin of the mackerel looked sinister, its flesh a pale gray. She put a bit on her fork and lifted it to her mouth. But her mouth was so dry, she could not swallow.

"It's not a decision I've reached easily," he was saying. She stared at him.

"I've been turning it over and over all through Christmas. And do you know what really made the difference for me?"

No, she thought, she didn't know what made the difference, and she didn't want to know, either.

"It was thinking about who I turn to in a crisis. And that person, whatever her shortcomings, is Hillary. You know, Bella, you said a really perceptive thing once..."

More than once, thought Bella. She had stopped nodding and was now staring at him in horror. The stone had grown and now occupied her whole chest and the top of her stomach. She stared at the red cabbage. It didn't look like food to her. Strips of pinky red, crinkly stuff. It would make a nice pattern for a cushion. Cushion, cushion, she thought, trying to block out his words. She tore the bread in half but did not put it in her mouth. Please, she thought, let me be anywhere else. Anywhere else than sitting here listening to this man talk.

"You said," he went on, "that my whole life is with Hillary. Well, it is."

This really can't get any worse, she thought.

He gave a rueful smile and reached under the table. His fingers brushed her leg. Bella pulled her chair sharply back. "Sorry," he said, "I was reaching for your hand."

Hand, leg, what's the difference, Bella thought. You will never touch me again.

"Bella," he said, "there is a lot I want to say. But now isn't the time and place."

Damn right, she thought. She nodded slowly.

"Please say something. This is hard for me, too," he said.

At this, her eyes filled with tears. He looked at her and said, "Bella, you'll be okay."

How dare you, she thought. How dare you speculate on whether I will be okay. "Of course I'll be okay," she said flatly.

"You've got so many friends, and you've got your family and Millie."

"Thank you," she said. "I know what I've got."

"Bella, you aren't making this easy for me."

"I'd like to go back to the office now," she said.

She looked at her plate and the hardly touched food. The red cabbage had made a watery pool of slightly purple blood, and it had stained the gray flesh of the mackerel. "Carnage," she said.

"What did you say?"

"Nothing."

James asked for the bill.

"Was everything all right?" the waiter asked anxiously, looking at Bella's plate. She nodded again.

No, she wanted to sob. No, not all right. So, so not all right. He doesn't want me. He doesn't love me.

James put his card into the machine that the waiter handed him, efficiently added a tip—always exactly 10 percent, which Bella thought mean. Outside, he hailed a cab and held open the door for her to get in.

No way, she thought. "I'd prefer to walk," she said.

He got into the taxi. Through the back window, she saw his head. He turned and waved at her, half smiling.

Bella gave a cough and wheeze. She wanted to sit on the pavement and howl. Instead she started to run. He never loved me, she chanted to herself. He doesn't want me. It is over. It is over. End. End.

Two blocks away from the office, she stopped. She looked into the window of Robert Dyas. Handheld vacuums were on special for £8.99. She turned toward the office but saw Stella coming out toward her. I can't do this, she thought. I can't face anyone yet.

She ducked into the shop. A shop assistant eyed her expectantly. Bella picked up the vacuum and took it to the till. The assistant smiled at her nicely and said: "It's cold out."

The kindness of strangers, she thought.

Back in the office, Bella looked at herself in the lift mirrors. Terrible, she thought. She got to her desk hoping to see a message on the keyboard saying: "I'm sorry, I didn't mean it." She looked at her e-mail, knowing that there would be nothing from him. But there it was: a message.

Dear Bella. Sorry if I seemed distant. This is hard for me, and I don't think I explained myself terribly well. I think I am suffering a little from shock myself. I feel I owe you a more considered message which I will send in due course when I return to normal.

James

She read it and tried to find something in it to hold on to. He was telling her he felt terrible, too. And then she read it again. He was telling her that he expected to feel "normal" very soon. She didn't expect to feel normal ever again.

She sat at the desk and looked at the screen. Please send me a message saying that it has been a huge mistake, she pleaded. You can't leave me. You said you loved me. You said I made you happy. You said I was bellissima.

And as she chanted this to herself, rocking at her keyboard, another message arrived. Bella gave a little sob of relief and opened it, registering that the subject line—"Briefcase"—wasn't quite right.

She read:

Bella. Sorry about this. But I was a little distracted earlier on, and I fear I may have left my briefcase either in the cab or in the restaurant. Did you see if I had it when we left?

James.

Bella read the message and knew that this was the very end.

Stella

Stella went into the ladies' toilets to put on her Etro dress. It was many months since she had worn it—the last time was for her parents' golden wedding, long ago when she was a nice, happy woman leading a busy but straightforward life.

Putting it on now, she saw that it hung loose on her; her shoulder blades stuck out at the back, her collarbones at the front. She wrapped a shimmering shawl around her, applied three colors of eye makeup in an attempt to create a smoky effect, but put on too much purple and ended up looking as if someone had hit her. The door opened and James's secretary came in.

"Ooh," she said. "You look lovely. Going out anywhere special?"

"It's an awards dinner," said Stella.

"Have you won anything?"

"Yes," said Stella, "I fear I have."

"Congratulations! Very well deserved, I'm sure."

A minibus had been booked to take a group of them to the Dorchester: Stella, Russell, Rhys, Beate, and five assorted AE women whom Russell must have rounded up to create the false impression that AE valued diversity. Stephen was arriving separately in his own chauffeur-driven car, and Charles, who had surprised Stella by insisting that he wanted to come—indeed, that he would not miss it for the world—was going to get there under his own steam.

The oil barrel blinked at them reproachfully as they passed through reception: "$42.45," it said.

On the bus, Rhys was holding forth and saying that the last time he had gone somewhere in black tie, someone had mistaken him for a waiter and asked him for a double gin and tonic. Only Russell was laughing, and his laughter was spasmodic. He didn't look like a waiter. He looked dashing, she thought. He had put on weight over Christmas, which Stella thought suited him. Some people put on weight when they are unhappy—but was Rhys unhappy? she wondered. In the last couple of days, he had stopped talking to her in a guarded, stilted way and had even smiled at her a couple of times.

But instead of reassuring her, this was making Stella feel worse, as it suggested that his pain had subsided, allowing him to behave toward her in a normal, friendly fashion.

The ballroom of the hotel was overlit and overfilled with thirty-eight large round tables for which each company had paid the organizers a large amount of money. The AE table was toward the front, and Stella slipped away from the others to inspect the seating plan. As she feared, she was sitting with Rhys on one side and Stephen on the other. She could not bear the thought of being in such proximity to him when they were so estranged, so she swapped his name over with Charles. Charles would protect her. But where was he?

When the starters arrived, he had still not appeared. So Russell, who was sitting by Rhys, looked at the empty chair and said: "Stella, we can't have you sitting next to Banquo's ghost." He got up and took Charles's place.

Stephen started to tell Stella about his latest trip to the United States, from which he had returned the previous morning. He was glee-fully spelling out how some of the U.S. oil companies were less well placed to deal with low oil prices than AE, a fact that he seemed to take as a personal endorsement. Stella fixed her eyes on him and tried not to look at Rhys, who was on the other side of the table and was laughing excessively loudly and calling for more wine.

Just as the starter was being cleared away, Charles burst through the double doors and swayed toward their table. Evidently he had been drinking, too. He bent over Stella and gave her a kiss.

"Sorry I'm late," he said. "Events—"

Russell got up to move, but Charles pushed him back down again. "I'll sit over there," he said.

So Stella watched in slow motion as her drunken husband went over to sit next to her drunken ex-lover. "Hello again," she heard Charles say as he shook Rhys's hand.

Stella couldn't hear what they were saying, but Rhys seemed to be telling a joke and Charles was laughing his social laugh. Rhys was not laughing normally, either. He was looking dangerous.

There was a banging sound, and the master of ceremonies got to his feet to introduce a female comic from Glasgow, who made a succession of bawdy jokes about drunken men in Scotland. Whoever had booked her had not done their homework properly. Then Dame Marjorie Scardino took the floor and told the audience how very much pleasure it gave her to present the award.

"This year," she said, "the entrants were even more dazzling than ever. But the winner is someone who has achieved outstanding success across the broadest field. She has vision. She does things her own way but is true to the company and true to herself."

At this, Stella glanced briefly at Rhys. He was staring at his raspberry confit.

"Ladies and gentlemen, the winner of this year's Veuve Clicquot Business Woman of the Year awards is..."

There was a long pause and a roll of drums meant to whip up the anticipation of the audience, though most of them were far too drunk to be paying any attention at all.

"Stella Bradberry."

The lights flashed and Tina Turner's "Simply the Best" blared out of the public address system.

Stella took the speech from Rhys, made her way through the tables picked out by a spotlight, and climbed the stairs onto the stage. She looked at the paper she was holding. On the front there was a Post-it note.

I'm sorry, ferret. I adore you. I can't live without you. You are beautiful tonight. xxx

Stella took this in, and a blush spread across her face. She folded the speech and came out from behind the podium.

"Thank you," she said. "Thank you for those words. And thank you for this award—" Her voice broke, and her eyes filled with tears. "I can't give a speech, but what I have to say is really simple. This is one of the happiest days of my life. I did not think this would happen to me today, and I will try to deserve it. From the bottom of my heart, thank you for choosing me."

Back at the table, Russell was beside himself. "Fantastic," he said. "Fantastic Oscar moment, Stella. You really gave it some emotion—this is going to be really controversial, but it shows that women in business can really be themselves. They can let it all out!"

Stella was too happy to contradict him. She despised people who cried at awards, and she hated the idea that people would think her such a pathetic softie. But today they could think what they liked. She had her prize, and the prize was Rhys.

She went around the table to kiss Charles, who whispered: "What was all that about, Stel?" She kissed Stephen and even gave Beate a kiss before giving Rhys a kiss that in public was all decorum but in private came with the delivery of her whole diseased heart.

Bella

For three days, she had been putting off making the call.

The woman who took her call at the outplacement agency was nice, though not terribly encouraging. She seemed surprised that Bella wanted to leave a research job at Atlantic Energy and warned her that in the current climate it would be hard to find a similar posting.

Bella told her that she didn't mind taking a cut in salary, and she didn't mind being a PA again; she just wanted to move quickly. The woman said that she would see what she could do.

Bella put down the phone and felt relieved. She didn't want to stay at AE; she could not bear the daily dose of unhappiness. But neither did she want to leave. It would be too final. And if no job could be found, then she would stay.

But within an hour the phone had gone again, and the woman said that there was a job as an assistant going at an advertising agency in Soho. It was more junior than the one she now had and the pay was worse, but there was scope for advancement. They would like to see her that very day.

So at lunchtime she went to Charlotte Street and was interviewed by a woman in the highest stilettos she had ever seen. Bella had had no time to feel nervous, but neither had she had any time to psych herself into the right mood to be an advertising researcher, even if she knew what that mood was. The interviewer asked her a few questions about herself but then gave up and they had a nice chat about who should have won *Britain's Got Talent*. It was not the sort of chat you would ever have with someone you were even slightly interested in hiring.

There was no way that she had got the job.

Stella

The theme of the World Economic Forum in Davos that year was "Shaping the Post-Crisis World." The title seemed particularly apt to Stella. She and Rhys—who at Stella's insistence was coming, too—would be reshaping their own world after the crisis it had survived.

Getting Rhys onto the list of AE people attending the conference had not been easy. As part of the company's draconian cost-cutting measures, the finance director had decreed that only six people could go to Davos, compared with thirty the previous year. However, Stella had insisted that she needed support, and as she was so favored by Stephen, the finance director did not dare query it.

The previous year, Stella had flown out with Stephen in the AE private plane, but at the last minute James had intervened to say that the company could not afford any more bad press. Other companies had announced that their CEOs were arriving by commercial flight, and so must Stephen.

Stella sat on the early morning flight to Zurich with Stephen on one side of her and Rhys on the other. As she briefed Stephen on what he was to say at the session he was chairing, Rhys pressed his thigh against hers so that she could feel its warmth spreading through her body.

At Zurich Airport they bumped into the senior partner of Allen & Overy, and Stephen, much to Stella's delight, accepted his offer of a lift, leaving her to make the three-hour journey to Davos alone in a taxi with Rhys.

As they drove through the snowy landscape, she lay against him, and he told her about his Christmas with his mother and how every night as he went to lie in his bedroom, he had wished she were there. He told her that all his aunts had asked him if he was getting married or if he had met anyone, and he had said no, there was no one. The anguish that Stella had felt over the last two months had quite gone. The pain of heartache was like the pain of childbirth, she thought. Once it had stopped, you couldn't remember what it felt like.

The taxi dropped them at the Arabella Sheraton, where Stella was booked. Nathalie had reserved a room for Rhys in a B&B in Klosters, which was a bus ride away, but Stella had assured him that there was no need for him to go there at all. They would simply pay for the room; no one would care if he slept there or not.

Stella had stayed at the same hotel several times before and had thought it blandly luxurious and borderline vulgar with its pastel colors and knotted-wood furniture. But this year she saw it through Rhys's eyes, and it seemed to her a haven, their own private home. Rhys gave a delighted whoop when they were left alone by the porter in Stella's room—and then insisted on them both going back out into the corridor so that he could carry her over the threshold.

"You are mine," he said. "Mine for two and a half days."

Stella laughed delightedly and thought how relative time was. If you were used to measuring out your time together in minutes, two and a half days seemed like a lifetime together.

They got into bed and he made love to her slowly and gently, and Stella, freed from the thought that time was about to take her back to her real life, abandoned herself to this joyous other life completely.

Then afterward, instead of having to rush back to the office, they got dressed together, and Stella put on Rhys's jumper under her coat, feeling as she had done at university when she wore her first proper boyfriend's rugby shirt to a tutorial. Together they left the hotel and went down the snowy hill to pick up their passes for the conference. On the way, they bumped into a distinguished Indian economist with whom Stella had shared a platform at Davos twelve months earlier.

"It's been quite a year," he said.

"Yes," she said, and thought: More than you can ever know.

Once they had got their passes, Rhys suggested that they go tobogganing. Stella, who was meant to be attending a session on the revival of Keynesianism, gladly agreed. They went up in the lift, and suspended above the snow in a dangling chair, he kissed her, and she laughed and thought that she could not remember ever being so happy.

As they waited for their toboggans at the top of the hill, Stella noticed a group of respectful Americans surrounding an elderly man who was holding forth on Gaza.

"Who was that?" Rhys shouted at Stella as they whizzed down the hill.

"George Soros," she shouted back.

And they both started to laugh again.

That evening, Stephen and Stella had both been invited to a cocktail party hosted by the Russian government at the Belvedere. She put on the dress that she had bought six months earlier at a time when she was trying to make Rhys admire her. Looking at her in it now, he told her that she was beautiful, and when she looked at herself in the mirror, she believed him. Rhys had not been invited to the party, but Stella had told the man at the door that he was her assistant and she needed him to be there. She said it with such authority that he shrugged and let them both through.

Once inside, Stella was absorbed into the crowd. Bill Gates caught her eye and nodded faintly. Nigel Lawson came over and kissed her on the cheek. Stella basked in the attention of these men, knowing that the only man whose attention she truly cared about was standing a few yards away.

Though where was he, exactly? She looked about and then caught a glimpse of him by the bar on his own. She made her way across the room toward him.

"Are you okay?" she said.

He shrugged. "It's not my thing. I'm going back to our hotel."

"I'll come with you," said Stella. She found she had no further desire for the party. She wanted to be alone with him in the hotel room.

As they walked between the two grand hotels in the snow, he caught her and kissed her. Stella shook him off, as it was too dangerous.

Up in the room, he ordered a bottle of champagne and lobster. Stella wanted neither but didn't protest. She wanted their first whole night together to be blissful; he must have whatever he wanted.

The next day they had breakfast in bed, and at eleven Stella got up in order to attend the plenary session at which Stephen was sharing a platform with the Russian oil minister.

Despite the intense dislike between the two men, and despite the fact that AE had almost given up in its battle to retain its stake in the Siberian oil field, Stephen was graceful and eloquent. The "spirit of Davos" was meant to forbid any harsh words, and he spoke of the need for transparency and the importance of Russia being open.

Afterward, Stella scooped up a couple of cakes and took them upstairs to where Rhys was still lying in bed. She felt a flicker of annoyance that he had not got up or shaved or picked up any of their clothes from the floor. Instead he was staring at the ceiling with his iPod on. But he called her to bed, and she let her irritation be stroked away. All afternoon they lay in bed and made love over and over again, and just as it was getting dark, Rhys announced that he wanted to go out into the snow.

They got dressed and went outside. It was bitterly cold, but there was no wind. They walked for a bit, and then Rhys said: "Let's stop here."

They lay down together, making deep impressions in the soft snow, and Stella clung to him and closed her eyes. At this time the next day she would be back home, and the thought filled her with terror. She had never thought of leaving Charles; she could not do that. But at that moment she wanted something worse: She wanted Charles to die, peacefully and painlessly, leaving her to be with Rhys.

The mood did not last. They returned to the hotel, cold and with melting snow in the seams of their clothes, and Stella anxious not to be late for the formal dinner that she had signed up for.

"Don't go to it," Rhys said.

"I have to," Stella said. "There will be an empty place if I don't."

And they had a row, during which Stella's phone went. It was Charles.

"Please don't answer it," said Rhys. "Just for once. Can't you turn it off and just be with me for another few hours? I'll turn mine off, too."

So Stella turned off her phone and turned up late for a dinner at which she was seated between the CEO of Boeing and a French member of the European Parliament. She discussed aviation fuel for a bit and then claimed a migraine and headed back to her room. As soon as she got there, she was aware that the mood had deteriorated in the hour and a half that she had been gone.

Rhys had been drinking his way through the minibar and was lying naked in bed, watching rugby on the TV. She told him about the Boeing guy and how the Frenchman had bad breath and kept patting her knee.

Rhys didn't laugh, and Stella got undressed and got into bed next to him. He made love to her but this time seemed more desperate than loving. He seized her upper arms and held them so tight that she cried out. They lay there in the dark, with the television still playing sport on mute, but Rhys was no longer watching.

"I don't know if, when I look back on this in years' time, I'll wish I had held on to you," he said.

"What do you mean?" said Stella. "I thought that you had decided you were holding on to me?"

"I can't have you, so how can I hold on to you?"

"But I am yours. In my heart I belong to you."

"Don't let's have this conversation again," he said. "You aren't mine, so I don't know why you bother to pretend that you are."

He told her how he had tried for five weeks and four days to tell himself that it was over and better over, but that he could not do it. But now, now that he was with her again, he couldn't even feel happiness; all he felt was anguish at the thought of it ending. He felt when he was with her an even greater sense of loss than when he was without her, and the feeling was so tinged with panic and jealousy that he could not cope at all.

Rhys buried his head in the pillow and started to cry. Stella held him and breathed in his misery like a scent. Love, she thought, has made a monster of me. I want this boy to suffer. If he suffers, he is mine. And if he is being weak and weeping, then I can be strong. I can stroke his hair and kiss his wet cheeks and say, There, there, I'm here. I'm here.

The hotel phone started to ring, probably a query about breakfast in the morning. Stella leaned over and unplugged it. The ringing stopped his tears. And for a while they lay there, still. Stella wanted to make love to him again, but he said he must sleep. He closed his eyes and was asleep with what Stella regarded as indecent haste. Her earlier security started to slip. If he was that upset, how could he turn it all off and go to sleep? And how could he look so peaceful in his own somnolent world?

Stella, awake and now desolate, gazed at him and started to shed tears of her own. She knew then that he was right and that this was impossible. What had been between them was destroyed and could not be mended. This was the end. She knew it this time. There had been so many false ends, but when you meet the real one, you know it.

Stella got out of bed. She was being picked up at five a.m. to be taken to the airport; Rhys was booked on a later flight. She could not bear to be in bed with him, and even though it was only three a.m., she got up and had a shower. Then she turned on her phone.

There were twenty-two missed calls and twelve texts, the first seven of them from Clemmie. The first said:

```
Shit maths exam. Call me
```

This was followed by similar texts in a rising tone of anxiety, until the last one said:

```
I don't believe this. I've just screwed up
my mocks and you can't even be arsed to
return my texts.
```

The next was from Charles, and it said:

```
Disaster. BBC said no to documentary. Head
of programming wants to run some tedious
crap on recession instead
```

And then Charles again:

```
What's happening? Why is your phone off?
```

The next three messages were from James:

```
Stella, we must talk
```

And:

```
Stella can you please call me
```

And finally:

```
Stella—this is urgent. I need a statement
from you. I have phoned your family and
they can't raise you either. Call me
urgently as soon as you get this.
```

She could not ring any of them. They would all be asleep in their beds at home. She looked at Rhys on the bed, asleep.

She lay down on the bed on top of the covers fully dressed and stared at the ceiling until it was five a.m. and her car was downstairs. She got up, picked up her suitcase, and closed the door behind her.

Bella

Bella was sitting at her desk, scrolling through job advertisements online, when Ben came bustling over in huge excitement.

"I've just had the *News of the World* on the line. They claim to have evidence that Stella is having an affair with—you are not going to believe this—with Rhys Williams."

"That's bollocks," said Bella.

"That's what I thought. Only it's not. They claim to have pictures of the two of them together at Davos. They are going to do an exposé on the scandalous secret of Business Woman of the Year. God, I *love* days like this."

"So what did you say?"

"I behaved as if I had a pole up my arse and said it wasn't our policy to comment on personal matters. But really, it's just too good to be true.

Mrs. Goody Two-shoes has been shagging the rough junior from the council estate. And then—you just couldn't make it up—she promotes him to be her assistant *and* spends company money on champagne in room service."

"I still don't believe it," said Bella. "I know Rhys really well, and I would have known if there was anything like this going on."

"Well, it's true whether you believe it or not. I've just told James"—as he said his name, Ben gave Bella a meaningful look, which she ignored—"who has gone mental. Says he is going to deal with it himself."

"Oh, my God," said Bella. "Poor Rhys."

"*Poor Rhys?* Have you gone soft? He's done very nicely out of this little number, thank you very much, promoted way above his merits. Though if he thought he could get away with it without being caught, he was a total idiot. I'm also surprised at his taste—I wouldn't fancy shagging someone that scrawny."

Bella didn't want to listen anymore, so she told Ben that she had work to do, though her work—writing up the love contract—now seemed even more laughable than it had before. She felt cross with Rhys for lying to her and hurt that he hadn't trusted her. But more than that, she wondered why he would go for Stella Bradberry. She was clever and admirable, but not really good-looking. And why would Stella have gone for Rhys? That was even harder to fathom. Bella had quite fancied him at first but then felt he was too young even for her. Yet even though he was a baby, Bella didn't think he deserved the storm that would surely now engulf him, and she decided to warn him.

Hi Rhys, not sure how to put this, but *News of the World* is planning to write a story about you and Stella having an affair. Don't know if it's true or not, but thought you should know. Do call me if you want to

Bella

She stayed at her desk and waited for a reply, but none came. Bella thought this odd, as he was usually glued to his BlackBerry.

Stella

From Zurich Airport, Stella called home. Clemmie had forgotten her rage of the day before but didn't want to talk, as she was in a hurry to get to school. Charles's voice sounded low and defeated, and he asked her why she hadn't taken his calls the previous night. She said that she had lost her mobile but now had it back, and he seemed inclined to accept the story. Then she called James, but he was in a meeting.

These three duty calls accomplished, she wondered whether to call Rhys, who would be just getting up to get his later flight.

As she had lain silently on the bed, she had resolved that there would be no further conversation between them at all of an intimate nature. It was too painful. But now she couldn't bear the thought of him moving around the room on his own. She wanted to hear his voice.

He answered on the fourth ring, his voice sounding thick.

"Hello," she said.

"Hello," he replied.

And then there was a long silence.

"What are you doing?" he asked.

"I'm waiting to get on the plane."

"Oh."

And then there was another long silence.

Stella could not bring herself to say good-bye. Instead she said: "Sorry."

And he said: "Yes."

She then hung up. She didn't cry; she had no more tears left.

Stella got into the office just after lunchtime to find James talking anxiously to Nathalie outside her office.

"Oh, there you are," he said. "I need to talk to you." He followed her inside and closed the door.

"What is it?" she asked.

"Stella, this is very awkward. I'm not sure how to broach it, so I'm just going to ask you straight. Are you having an affair with Rhys Williams?"

Stella looked at him levelly. "No," she said.

"This is important, Stella. Are you sure about that?"

"Yes, James, I am."

"Well," he said, "that's good. Because some arsehole at the *News of the World* is proposing to write a story saying that you are having an affair with him. They wouldn't care except that you are Business Woman of the Year, and we are really unpopular with the share price collapse and now this. Thank God you aren't. And I'm really sorry to have had to put you on the spot."

"That's okay," she said.

"I'll tell them that our lawyers will get them for libel if they print one word."

At first Stella felt nothing. Such is the power of shock that she was quite numb. But then a wave of sickness swept over her. She sat at her desk, but her hands were shaking so much, she could not type properly. Neither could she read the screen. Sitting there was a message from Rhys:

Bella says that we've been rumbled by the *News of the World*. I can't deal with this at all. That's what my mother reads.

R

And so that was it. In the end, what mattered to him was not losing her forever, it was what his mother might think. Stella looked at the chilly *R* and let out a low moan.

Nathalie put her head around the door. "Do you want me to get you a coffee?" she said.

"No, thank you, Nathalie, I don't." She said it more harshly than she meant; she was not strong enough to be able to tolerate any sympathy.

"But could you tell Bella I want to see her now?"

Bella

Bella's mobile was ringing. It was the woman from the agency.

"They are offering you the job," the woman was saying. "They thought you were sensational—a total natural—but the only problem is that they need you to start at once."

"Wonderful," Bella said flatly. "I'll ask my boss if I need to submit my notice. There isn't much to do here, so it might be okay. I'll get back to you."

As she put down the phone she felt no relief, no sense of triumph. She was leaving so as to avoid ever seeing James again, but the thought that she might not actually see him again now made her feel she faced a life sentence of bleakness.

Nathalie emerged from Stella's room. "She wants to see you now," she said.

Bella went and knocked at the door.

"Sit down, please," said Stella.

She was looking white and shrunken. Bella thought she looked ten years older than when she had left for Davos just a few days earlier.

"I understand you told Rhys that the news was out that he and I have been having an affair."

Bella inclined her head uncertainly.

"I don't know where these stories come from. But they aren't true. And what is more—and this is the bit that really shocks me—they are not for you to spread. I'm particularly distressed at this, given the kindness I have shown you in taking you onto my team when things were difficult for you." Stella was spitting out the words and staring at Bella with a mad gleam in her eye.

"I'm sorry," Bella said. "But I haven't been spreading stories. I just heard it from Ben, who took the call from the journalist. And I texted Rhys with it, as it concerns him. I thought he ought to know."

Stella stopped glaring at Bella and sat down heavily. "What are people saying about me? Do they believe these...stories?" she asked in a low, defeated tone of voice.

"I don't know," said Bella. "I haven't talked to anyone. I suppose some people are delighted because it's top gossip."

Stella laughed bitterly. "It might be top gossip, but it isn't true."

"But if it isn't true," said Bella, "they can't print it, and all this will go away."

Stella groaned. "Lying to you isn't making me feel better. I have lied so much for the last nine months, I have really lost my sense of what is true and what isn't. Lies seem more real to me than the truth."

Bella didn't know what to say to this, so she nodded quietly.

"Yes, I have been having an affair with Rhys. But it's over now." Stella paused and then said: "It's hell. It's complete hell." She put one hand over her face and with the other started wildly twiddling with her hair—a gesture that did not belong to the Business Woman of the Year.

"Yes," Bella said. "It is complete and utter hell. I know."

Bella had intended this to be sympathetic, but Stella bit back: "How dare you say you know? You don't know what this is like. No one knows. When you had the affair, and it came out, no one cared."

"That's a bit extreme," Bella said. "I cared, for one."

"Yes, obviously," said Stella. "Sorry, that didn't sound right. But I am a target. I have lost my reputation here. I have probably lost my job. I may have lost my marriage and my children, too."

Stella had sunk into a chair and put her head in her hands. "And I've lost him," she said in a low voice, almost to herself.

Bella went over to the older woman and touched her arm. She was genuinely distressed at Stella's misery, but it also made her feel better about her own. She was no longer the most wretched creature in the company, at the bottom of the moral hierarchy; she was able to offer comfort to someone in an even greater mess. "You did help me," she said, "and I would like to do the same for you, now, if there is anything you can think of that I could do...?"

"Thank you, Bella," said Stella. "But you can't. I might have asked you to speak up in my defense, but there is nothing to say in my defense. Not one single thing. I deserve whatever comes my way."

Stella

For the next few days, Stella held her breath. At work and at home she went through the motions of ordinary life, going to meetings and having breakfast with the children. This was the calm; the storm would surely follow.

Each time she spoke to someone at work, she wondered: Do they know? And what do they think of me? The only person in the office whom she could talk to without this sense of impending doom was Bella, but Bella had found another job and had asked to leave at once. Stella felt that she wanted—even needed—the younger woman to stay, but she said it was fine, Bella should go as soon as she wanted to. Since their discussion, no further reference had been made to Rhys, or to love—or to disgrace. But Bella had looked at her with an expression that was not full of loathing. She'd even brought her finished work on the love contract to show Stella, and the two of them had gone through it and laughed bleakly.

At home, things were still more difficult. Stella looked at her children with dread. Will they still love me when they know? The answer to this question, which she had so studiously avoided asking herself, was surely no. And what about Charles? Would he still want to live with someone who had so deceived him?

Yet with each day that passed and with each normal meeting that she went to and with each normal conversation she had with the children, Stella became less anxious. On day five, when nothing happened, she started to wonder whether maybe, just maybe, she might get away with it after all.

Bella

Stella had made no fuss about Bella going and had said she could leave at the end of that week. Bella had decided against having a leaving party, partly because she couldn't face it and partly because she couldn't afford it. If you were senior, the company paid for a party; if you were not, you paid for your own drinks. But on the day itself, she decided that she must do something to mark her departure, if for no other reason than to alert James to the fact that she was leaving. She didn't want to do him the favor of telling him herself; let him find out impersonally, she thought.

She typed a message and sent it to everyone in her department.

Hi

I'm leaving AE today after five long and happy years. It has been a great time and I'll miss all of you. Please come and have a piece of cake at my desk at 4:30 today.

Bella.

She had set aside the afternoon for putting her things into bags, but as she didn't have much, the job was done in less than twenty minutes. She thought of that day, almost exactly a year earlier, when she had done the same for Julia. It felt like a lifetime ago; Bella was filled with nostalgia for that time before she had started to work for James and before she had messed up her life for a second time.

At four twenty-five, Anthea came bustling over and Bella offered her a slice of cake. "I shouldn't really," she said, accepting a slice. "I've got my sister-in-law coming over and I'm doing the Jamie Oliver pasties. But I'll have a sliver, just to wish you well. I've got you these." She fished a card out of her bag and handed over a plastic bag containing a potted hyacinth from Marks & Spencer.

This act of kindness made Bella want to cry. "Thank you," she said.

"I really hope that it works out for you at the new place," she said. "I know you have been having a tough time recently, and I'm sorry."

Bella nodded. Her eyes had filled with tears.

Seeing this, Anthea went on: "There is nothing that escapes me about himself. I know him inside out and back to front. I'd say he really misses you. But what will be, will be." Anthea put her arms around Bella and hugged her. "Let me know how you get on," she said.

"Of course I will," said Bella, though she knew she wouldn't.

Ben had drifted over to join them. He helped himself to a large slab of cake and looked at Bella mournfully. "Now that we don't work together anymore, will you go out with me?"

Bella smiled and shook her head absently, looking over Ben's shoulder to see if James had decided to come for cake. She didn't want him there, but the thought that she might go without him even saying good-bye was making her feel giddy with misery.

Nathalie joined the party as it was breaking up and accepted a last piece of cake. "I'm sorry I'm so late," she said. "The shit has really hit the fan with Stella. She has been in with Stephen and James all this time. I think they are drafting a statement, so I feel I needed to stay around."

"Oh, dear," said Bella.

But really she was thinking, That's why James isn't here. It's not because he's a coward and not because he doesn't want to say good-bye. But because he can't. And that was good, because she wasn't sure that she could bear to say good-bye, either.

And just as she was gathering together her coat and her bag of belongings, she saw the little map that he had drawn for her showing how to get to the Great Eastern Hotel. Bella took it, screwed it up into a little ball, and threw it at the bin. It missed and lay on the floor beside it.

As she went to the lift, she walked into him.

"You are going," James said.

"Yes," she replied.

"Well," he said, and hesitated.

Well what? thought Bella. Well, you've broken another woman's heart and ruined her career? Well, this is another jolly mess? Well, I can't stand to see you go? Well, I'll miss you?

But James didn't say any of these things.

"Well," he said again. He was looking blank and frozen. "I suppose this is good-bye."

"I suppose it is," said Bella, and got into the lift, keeping in the sobs that she knew were coming until the doors had closed safely behind her.

Stella

Almost exactly a week after her return from Davos, Nathalie put her head around the door of Stella's office and said:

"James is on the phone. He wants to talk to you."

Stella picked up the phone.

"Stella," he said, "this is really ugly. I gave them your denial, and they tell me that they have CCTV pictures of the two of you. Something on the roof? That they have expenses from the hotel in Davos. And now they've got your denial, they are running with it as a lie-and-cheat story rather than just a cheat story. Can you come to my office now? I've got Stephen here with me, and Mark Weisman, our libel lawyer."

Stella walked down the corridor and into his office straight past Anthea, who was holding the door open but not meeting her eye.

The three men fell silent at the sight of Stella.

"Thank you for joining us," James said stiffly. He waited for her to sit down and then went on, "We were just wondering who leaked the story to them."

Stella said she didn't know. Now that the very worst had happened, she no longer cared. It could have been Nathalie. It could have been James himself. The more she thought about it, the more possibilities there seemed to be.

"Russell informs me that there was a whistle-blower incident a few weeks ago, brought by Beate Schlegel. We are assuming that she was the source. Does that sound plausible to you?"

Stella nodded dumbly. "Yes, Beate. Quite probably," she said quietly, fixing her eyes on a miniature chest of drawers that was standing inexplicably in the middle of the coffee table.

The lawyer explained that the newspaper could get around the privacy laws by claiming that the story was in the public interest. This might be possible if it could prove that Stella had broken guidelines on expenses and spent shareholders' money on Rhys Williams. It appeared that they had evidence of this.

Stella wanted to protest that her room service bill from Davos, even with the champagne and the lobster that Rhys had ordered—and then not consumed—was still less than the sorts of expenses that either James or Stephen routinely submitted, but what was the point?

"From what I understand of it, Stella," Stephen was saying, "it isn't the fact that you had an inappropriate relationship with the young man, or that you promoted him. It isn't even the fact that you got him into the room at Davos or all the stuff you ordered on room service. It isn't the CCTV footage of the pair of you on the roof, which, by the way, is against our health and safety regulations. It's the fact that you lied about it."

"I did not lie. James asked me if I was having an affair with Rhys, and I said no. I said no because it was over."

He looked at her with some irritation. "We could go on splitting hairs indefinitely, but all of us are busy, so let's not. The point is that we issued a categorical denial to the *News of the World*, and they have come back with evidence."

Stella took this in and then said with a calmness that surprised even her: "I lied to protect the company and to protect my family."

"I might have thought," said Stephen, "that if you were really interested in protecting either Atlantic Energy or your own family, you might have thought twice about doing this in the first place."

There was an unpleasant silence, and then Stephen went on: "I don't understand it, Stella. Why? Why you of all people, and why him?"

James was nodding sagely, and Stella looked at him with contempt and bitterness. If he fucked his secretary, that was fine for everyone and life moved on. But for her, this was a national event. She was a liar and a fraud and an outcast, a disgrace.

"Do you want to know why?" she said. "Do you want to know why I risked everything? Why I risked my job and my family?"

Stephen inclined his head. It seemed that he did want to know.

"At first I thought it was boredom. I was bored with success and bored with safety. This job encourages the taking of risks. We all get a buzz out of it. You do, and so do I. This was the ultimate risk. We all work so bloody hard that our emotional life is here as well as everything else. I also did it because I am middle-aged and don't want my youth to go."

"Really, Stella," said Stephen, "that's ridic—"

"Can I finish?" she asked. "You have asked why I did it, and even though it is none of your business, I'm telling you."

James and Stephen exchanged glances.

"I did it because I loved him. And I still do, and that is not something I am ashamed of. I am ashamed of the consequences. I am deeply ashamed of the embarrassment that this has brought my family and the company. I am ashamed of much of my behavior. But I'm not ashamed of loving him."

James was staring at her, his lips pursed, face devoid of any expression. Stephen groaned and put his head in his hands.

"I trusted you," he said. "I championed you. I don't even recognize you at the moment. This is going to look absolutely awful. They are already having a go at us on greed, and then incompetence for ballsing up the Russian license, and now, sleaze and corruption. We need you to stand up and make a statement. Apologize in public, and explain that he deserved the promotion and that you are paying back the room service bill."

"You can have the money back. It wasn't very much." She opened her purse and put £200 on the table. "But I'm not going to say anything to the *News of the World* or to anyone. I'm not making any public statements. The only statements I'm going to make are to my family."

"In that case, Stella," said Stephen, "I'm very sorry, but I'm going to have to ask you to resign with immediate effect."

"Okay," she said. "I resign with immediate effect."

"Stella," Stephen said, the anger in his voice infected now with a more conciliatory tone, "I am going to give you twenty-four hours to reconsider."

"I don't need it," she said. "I'm going now."

She went back to her desk. Nathalie was standing outside her office, looking baleful. "I'm sorry," she said.

Stella nodded and walked past her into her office and started to sort her things. Nathalie didn't offer to help. Was this out of embarrassment, Stella wondered, or was it because when someone is cut loose in disgrace, there is no point in human kindness?

She didn't feel at all tearful. She felt nothing at all. She stood in her office and wondered what to take. The laptop and the BlackBerry belonged to the company. In her drawer, she had a pair of tights and a pair of reading glasses that she now needed. There were some photos of the children. There was a picture of Rhys smiling at her that she had taken on her mobile and printed out. There was another of them together on a platform in the North Sea. She was looking radiantly happy, and he was looking off in the other direction. And there was the Post-it note and a Twix bar. She kept the pictures and the Post-it note and put the Twix into the bin. She picked up her mobile and dialed home. It rang for a long time, and then Charles picked up.

"Darling," she said, "it's me."

"It's the last couple of minutes of the test match, can it wait?"

"Yes," she said. "Yes, it can wait. It can wait forever. All the damage is already done."

Bella

Bella was rather regretting having agreed to the lunch. She had had a client meeting that morning that had dragged on, so by the time she got down to reception, he had been waiting for ten minutes. He had a bit more gray hair and had lost some weight. He looked older, she thought.

"Bella," he said, turning to her. "How simply lovely to see you. You look wonderful."

"Thank you," she said. "Sorry I'm late."

He looked at her, and there it still was, that funny thing between them, not quite dead after all.

"Is Pret A Manger okay for you?" she asked.

He said it was, and as they walked there, Bella started talking, too fast, telling him about why she was late and about how she liked Charlotte Street as an area and how she had never really liked Moorgate much.

They queued for their sandwiches and sat at a little round table of exactly the kind that they had sat at on the day of the fire alarm when he had held her hand. Bella wondered if he was remembering that day, too.

James asked about her job and listened as she described the agency and laughed when she imitated the head of Creative. He told her how happy he was for her and how he had known from the first what a star she would be.

"And what about you?" Bella asked.

"Well," he said, "professionally life has been good to me. I don't know if you saw, but I'm now on the AE board...?"

Bella hadn't seen that. She didn't read the business pages of the news-paper anymore. "Congratulations," she said.

There was a pause, and he asked if she still saw anyone from AE, and she said the only person she saw was Rhys.

"And what's he up to?" James asked.

"He's doing really well. Things were difficult for him—I think he was quite unhappy in Alaska. But then he joined a start-up company that does music streaming, and I saw in the papers that they are now a rival to iTunes. Last time I heard from him, he went on and on about how great the job was until I got tired of listening."

James laughed and asked what music streaming was, and Bella said that it would have all his favorite Van Morrison tracks on it and he could listen for nothing. Then she asked: "Do you ever see Stella?"

"No," he said. "She dropped below the radar as soon as she left. I felt that she had turned the page completely, and didn't want to be reminded of what had happened. Though I do hear about her. She has started her own consultancy business and is on the boards of various companies and even advising the government on its policy on renewables."

"So she shrugged off the scandal, too."

"Yes, in professional terms," he said. "And it wasn't that bad, really. One small story in the *News of the World*, followed up with a paragraph in a couple of the dailies, but that was it. No one cared much. But in emo-tional terms, who knows?" And then he said, as if imparting a truth that he had stumbled on by himself, "These things can do a lot of damage."

"Yes," said Bella.

There was a pause, during which he looked at her intently.

"Bella," he said, "I want to tell you something. I have given the matter a great deal of thought, and I have decided that it is best to come straight out with it, and tell you the truth with no embellishment."

Bella nodded apprehensively.

"You are the only person in my life I have ever really loved."

Bella raised an eyebrow.

"And I never said thank you for that. In fact, the truth was even bigger. You showed me how to love, but the sad thing was I was only just getting the hang of it when you left, and so I could never show you that I was learning. Things between us were so fraught. But since then there hasn't been an hour that has gone by without me thinking of you."

No, she thought. Please, not now. I don't want to hear this now. It is too late. It is too confusing.

"All that time I was worrying about saving my marriage for the boys' sake and worrying about my career. But it didn't work. Hillary has not been able—or willing—to forgive me. We have had a year of bitterness and mutual resentment. And last week she said that she wants me to leave."

"I'm sorry," said Bella.

"Don't be," he said. "I'm not sorry. I'm only sorry that I didn't have the courage to pursue things with you."

Oh God, thought Bella. A year earlier she would have given everything to hear this, but now she was embarrassed. She didn't want this man here at all.

"Bella," he said, "I know I was a shit and an idiot. You wanted love and I couldn't give it to you. I see all that now."

"No," she said, "no. You mustn't...And I don't hold any of it against you. It doesn't matter now—"

"No," he said, quite misunderstanding her and reaching for her hand. "It doesn't matter, I'm here and I can make it better."

"No...," she started to say. She should have gone on: No, you can't because I don't want this anymore. I have recently met someone, and though I don't know if it will work out, I want to give it a chance. He doesn't have a wife and sons, and he seems to like me in a normal, uncomplicated way.

But she could not say that yet. James was a man who still believed that he could get what he wanted, that things would work out his way, and she didn't have the strength, at that minute, to oppose him.

"Bella," he said, "I have a question to ask of you, as I think I mentioned in my e-mail. And I'm going to ask it now."

He paused and then said: "I want you to marry me."

"That's not a question," she said. "It's a statement."

He laughed and looked at her in a way that almost made her wobble.

"You win," he said. "Here is the question: Bella, will you marry me?"

Stella

Stella could not decide what to wear. In the last year, she had acquired an expensive new work wardrobe chosen by a personal shopper at Selfridges whom she had visited one bleak day nine months earlier in the vague hope that new clothes would mark a new start.

She put on a Paul Smith suit with a long pink jacket and looked at herself in the mirror. When she had chosen it she had thought of it as her I Will Survive suit, but she wasn't sure such an aggressive color would be right for this lunch. Neither was she sure if she wanted to show Rhys a version of her that had changed a great deal or one that hadn't changed at all.

She took off the suit and put on a black sweater. It was the same jumper that she had worn the day she'd had the drink with him in the dismal pub. The jumper that was the first item of her clothing to bear his scent. She still wore it often, even though the personal shopper had warned her to avoid black, as it accentuated how pale and thin her skin was becoming.

She took off the jumper and put on a gray jacket, black trousers, and flat shoes. She wasn't trying to make any statement at all, she decided.

Rhys was already there when she arrived, sitting at a table at the front of the restaurant and reading the *Evening Standard*. He was wearing jeans and a T-shirt; presumably, his new job did not call for suits. If anything, she thought, he looked even younger than the last time she had seen him.

He smiled and waved when he saw her.

"Hello," he said.

She bent to kiss him but was aiming for the wrong cheek, and they met in the middle. They both laughed awkwardly. She wondered if he remembered that first, equally clumsy kiss after dinner at her house, before it had all begun.

"You look great," she said.

But she didn't really mean it. What she meant was: Where are you? Here was this person whose face had worn a groove in her mind, and here was the real thing a year on, the same yet hopelessly different. The image in her mind and the real thing would not merge.

"So do you," he said.

"I spend more money on clothes now," she said. "I am fighting the ravages of age."

"Crap," he said. "You still look twenty-five."

She laughed at this lie, but it pleased her nevertheless.

They ordered some food, and Stella said that she would have a large glass of white wine. Rhys ordered water.

She asked him about his new job, and he said how much he was enjoying it and that he owned 5 percent of the company, and it was likely that in the next year they would either float it or it would be taken over—in which case he would make a lot of money.

"And what about you, Stella? What are you up to? I know some of it, I've read about you in the papers. I'm not surprised. You are brilliant, you always were."

Stella smiled and told him a little about her work, about the bits that she liked and the bits she didn't. As she spoke, her spirits were sinking. This was awful. He was friendly, but not intimate.

There was then a pause in the conversation.

"I heard that you are still with Charles," he said.

"Yes," Stella said. "I am."

Rhys nodded. He is disappointed, Stella thought with a sudden lifting of her spirits. He wants me to have split up with Charles so that he can claim me.

But then he said: "That's good. I'm glad. How are the kids?"

"Um," said Stella, "they are fine. Finn has got into Westminster upper school and is in the football team. Clemmie is likely to do well in her GCSEs and has decided she wants to be a doctor."

"Great," he said. And then, in a slightly softer voice: "It's good to see you, Stella."

Suddenly, Stella changed tack. She didn't want to tell him that all was well and that her children were fine. She didn't want this wall of polite civility between them. She wanted to tell him how it was.

"Actually," she said, "it's been a year from hell. I very nearly had a breakdown, but I'm—as you see—now okay. Charles and I are damaged but march along broken. I think he forgives me for my affair with you. It was the public humiliation that he couldn't bear. The stories in the papers, and the fact that young researchers at the BBC knew what his wife had done. And I suppose that was painful to me. I wanted him to mind more about the thing itself than the perception. I don't think I care at all anymore about how strangers perceive me. I don't expect people to understand, but being so on one's own has been terribly lonely."

Rhys nodded and said quietly: "I know."

"But time does make things better," Stella went on. "Work heals, too, and the plodding through family life helps. So mostly I'm okay now, I think."

"After you left I went to Alaska for a bit. I suppose you know that."

Stella inclined her head.

"I wanted to die. I was miserable in an intense way and kept on ringing home. My mother was appalled, and all my friends laughed at me. The only person who was really kind to me was Bella. She didn't mind me telling her how miserable I was, as she was feeling like shit, too. Even in Alaska I was too close to you—I had to get away even from the fucking AE logo, and that was why I quit. I felt better when I started this job, but I didn't stop loving you, Stella, or thinking about you. I never regretted what happened between us."

"No," said Stella. "I never regretted it. Not for one single moment."

"That's crap," said Rhys. "What about that time when you shouted at me that I was a cancer in your life and if you had one wish, it would be that we had never met?"

"Okay," Stella said, laughing. "That was then. And if we are playing that game, you endlessly told me how I had put your life on hold and what a catastrophe that was. But never mind all that. I don't wish I had never met you."

He shifted in his seat. "Stella," he said, "I told you I had something to tell you and something to ask of you. You have already given me the thing I was going to ask. It was forgiveness. You tell me that you didn't regret it. I wanted to see that you were not bitter after all the damage that has been done to you."

Stella smiled at him, her heart lurching with happiness and quite blind—willfully blind—to what was to come.

"And what I wanted to tell you is that three months ago I met someone. She is my age. She is not married. She is beautiful, and she is funny. She reminds me a bit of you."

Stella could hear the sounds in the restaurant. Her stomach contracted; she felt as if she were in a lift that was going down too fast. She must get away from here and away from him. She must run away. She must get back to somewhere warm and safe and peaceful.

"Stella," he said, "I wanted you to be the first to know: I am getting married."

Bella

Bella was back in the office, replaying what had happened in her mind and trying to make sense of it. When she had told James that no, she could not marry him, he had got up, carefully put his sandwich wrapper in the bin, and said good-bye to her with stiff civility. He had got into a cab, glanced back at her, and given a half smile. The look on his face had almost made her melt, and for a wild moment she had thought of getting into another cab to follow his.

But the thought did not last. Instead she had been filled with a sadness so thick that she could barely move. She had dragged her body back into the office and was now sitting at her desk, staring blankly at the work she was meant to be doing—a pitch for a new client. Instead, she started composing a message in her head. By the end of the day, she knew exactly what she wanted to say. She opened a new e-mail and began:

Dear James

Thank you for lunch. It was lovely to see you again. And thank you for asking me to marry you. No one has ever asked me to do that before.

I hope it won't make it harder for you if I say that if you had asked me that a year ago, I would certainly have said yes.

But if we had got married, I think we both know that it wouldn't have worked out. You are a decent man. And you do love your wife and your sons. If you hadn't, you would not have broken up with me. And if you had stayed with me, you wouldn't have forgiven yourself.

You have given me a lot. You gave me the confidence that I needed to get this job, and you were the first person at work to believe in me, and for that I will always be incredibly grateful to you.

If I gave you something good—as you so sweetly said—then I'm really happy. I know I used to have a go at you about not loving me and tease you about being autistic, but I take it all back. It doesn't matter now anyway. I will remember you with real affection, and I hope you will me, too.

Lots of love, Bella x

PS. I still think Van Morrison is crap

PPS. Sorry if you think the tone of the PS too glib, but I thought you'd like to know!

PPPS. I do really hope you will be happy, James. I did love you, you know.

Bella read it over and cried as she did so. Her mobile bleeped—it was her new boyfriend texting her to say that he was in reception. She pulled herself together and sent him a text saying, "Sorry, just coming."

She looked at the message one last time and took out the last line—not because it wasn't true, but because there was no point in saying that anymore.

She pressed send.

Stella

In the taxi on the way back from lunch, Stella noticed a funny thing. The sobs that were convulsing her body were producing no tears. The vision in her mind of Rhys with a young woman he loved and was going to marry was agonizing. Yet because it was a certainty it held steady in her mind, and even though it was as bad as bad could be, the steadiness made it more bearable. There was no room for the painful ebb and flow of hope and despair, no further scope for punishing herself with vain hopes of reconciliation. There had been so many ends, but this was the final one.

Back at her desk, she pushed to one side the pile of papers she was meant to be reading. She got up and closed the door to her office and sat at the computer.

"Dearest Rhys," she wrote. And then deleted it.

Dear Rhys,

She looked at this and changed her mind again.

"Dearest Rhys—" He was her dearest for one last time.

At the side of her screen, a little Microsoft prompt appeared: "It looks like you're writing a letter. Would you like help?"

Despite herself, Stella almost laughed. She thought, No. For the first time in ages I don't need help. I know exactly what I want to say.

First, I'm sorry to have made such a fool of myself just now.

IN OFFICE HOURS

I was shocked at your news. I hadn't been expecting it, and so I behaved like an idiot. To walk out of the restaurant like that was pathetic and undignified, and I'm ashamed of myself. Sorry.

Instead of having a fit, I should have tried to talk to you properly, one last time. There were lots of things that I wanted to say—I have been running a one-sided conversation with you in my head for a whole year—sometimes been angry, sometimes vengeful, often loving, sometimes just miserable. That conversation must end now, but rather than put it all in the bin—you know how I hate wasted effort—I hope you don't mind if I put a little bit of it on paper.

As I type these words I'm not crying, as I thought I would be. Instead I'm filled with a kind of euphoria that has taken me quite by surprise. It is as if by telling me that you are getting married (god, I hope she is good enough for you), you have seized a giant pair of scissors and cut loose the threads that still attached us. And now I'm free to find my life again.

Through knowing you I have learned some important things about life that—though obvious in a way—had not really occurred to me before. Happiness is not forever, and neither is despair. And although despair lasts the longer of the two—and my god, we had much more misery than joy out of knowing each other—it doesn't make the happiness worth nothing.

You taught me other things, too, about love—and about obsession. And above all, you taught me who the Arctic Monkeys are. And that Coldplay is good and Keane is bad. But more than any of that, you taught me that I can't always have what I want. We used to say that we were similar. We were both determined to get what we wanted at work, and determined that everyone should love us.

When I pleaded with you to come back and you said no, I went into a panic that was part the simple shock of losing you, but it was also the very first time that I had set my sights on something that I could not have. It threw me into a panic so intense, I thought I would die.

But I didn't die. And every day I did what I was supposed to do, and eventually the pain stopped. Or at least it didn't stop, but it had reached a manageable throb that I was so used to, I almost stopped noticing it.

But every time my mind returned to you, the pain started up again. Now, I think and hope it will stop altogether.

At a low point I did have a one-night stand with some man I met at a conference, but he made me miss you even more. Right now I hope that I am through with this sort of love, though I suppose you never know.

You have found love, and I hope you are happy. I hope you have picked the right girl. Your record as a picker is truly awful: but she can't be less suitable than a married middle-aged ferret with two children.

I am going home now. Charles has made a special supper, as it is his mother's 85th birthday. She is nuttier than ever, but still with us.

And I don't want to be late.

Good luck, dearest Rhys. I wish you well from the bottom of my heart

Stella xx

Stella read it through, took out the bit about the one-night stand, as the desire to wound him—which in the last year was so strong—had now gone. She took the kisses off, too, as they looked babyish and sad. She read it through again, and pressed send.